ROSEMARY

Winner of the 2002 Romantic Novelists' Association New Writer's Award

Rosemary thinks life couldn't get any worse when her mother dies in a tragic accident. Left penniless and alone, betrayed by the one man she thinks she can trust, her whole world changes when she finds she's adopted. Beth has spent a lifetime regretting giving up her only daughter. Surrounded by the riches of the Rushton family, she's determined that one day she'll find the child she lost and reunite her with her true family. When that vital first connection is made, neither of their lives will ever be the same again...

ROSEMARY

ROSEMARY

by

Margaret Kaine

Magna Large Print Books
Long Preston, North Yorkshire,
BD23 4ND, England.

British Library Cataloguing in Publication Data.

Kaine, Margaret
Rosemary.

A catalogue record of this book is
available from the British Library

ISBN   0-7505-2226-7

First published in Great Britain in 2003 by Poolbeg Press Ltd.

Cover illustration © Gordon Crabb by arrangement with
Alison Eldred

Published in Large Print 2004 by arrangement with
Hodder & Stoughton Ltd.

Magna Large Print is an imprint of Library Magna Books Ltd.

Printed and bound in Great Britain by
T.J. (International) Ltd., Cornwall, PL28 8RW

*For Phoebe and Luke
who have brought me such joy*

ACKNOWLEDGEMENTS

To my husband for his unfailing support, and my daughter Jo, for her valuable input.

My brother, Graham Inskip, for sharing his knowledge of the pottery industry, and also my gratitude to Gaye Shortland for her editing skills.

To all members, past and present, of the Wednesday morning Writers' Workshop in Wellington Street, Leicester, for their encouragement and constructive criticism.

'The cruellest lies are often told in silence.'

RL STEVENSON

1

The dark brown stain of the teapot's contents trickled obscenely down the kitchen wallpaper. Brenda Latham was hysterical, out of control, her features contorted as she grabbed whatever was nearest to her and threw it at the door. Rosemary, who had only just missed being hit as the china teapot hurtled past her, stared in horror at her mother.

'Hey ... watch what you're doing, for heaven's sake!'

Dodging her mother's flailing arms, she rescued the rest of the tea set which sat temptingly on the kitchen table.

'What good is breaking things going to do?' she yelled. 'You heard what he said, he's gone. This isn't going to bring him back!'

Her young eyes brimming with tears, she stood glaring at her mother. Their eyes locked in a battle of wills and then Brenda crumpled, collapsing on to a kitchen chair as she gave way to her pent-up feelings. As her mother sobbed, Rosemary's shoulders slumped in despair.

Shakily, she filled the kettle and switched it on. There had been rows before, terrible rows, with tension in the house and strained relationships for days, but her dad had never before threatened to leave.

'Is there another woman?' Her voice cracked on

the sentence, and she kept her back to Brenda as she waited tensely for an answer.

'What do you know about such things at your age?' Her mother's voice, though muffled with tears, was sharp, causing Rosemary to swing round in irritation.

'You might not allow any newspapers in the house, but I do live in this world, you know.'

Noisily blowing her nose, Brenda got up and restlessly paced the kitchen. She glared at the slim, fourteen-year-old girl, whose lightly freckled face beneath untidy dark hair was wet with tears.

'I don't want to talk about it,' she muttered. She wiped her swollen eyes on a damp handkerchief, and going over to the sink began to splash her face with cold water.

Mutinous, Rosemary made the tea, putting a generous two spoons of sugar in each cup.

'When will you stop treating me like a child?'

'Some things aren't for young ears,' Brenda snapped.

'Mum – it's 1970 for heaven's sake! Not that you'd ever know the permissive society existed, living in this house.'

'Don't be cheeky! You young people nowadays know too much, too soon.'

'Maybe, but it's better than growing up in ignorance like your generation did!' Rosemary flung at her.

Brenda sat again at the kitchen table, cradling the warm cup in her hands. She didn't need an argument with her teenage daughter. She was emotionally drained, exhausted by the violent scene with Keith. It was unfortunate that Rose-

16

mary had been in the house; the walls were so thin, she must have heard every word. Wearily, she pushed back her greying brown hair from her forehead, surprised to find it damp with perspiration.

'Don't you get upset. It's our problem, not yours.'

'It's a bit late for that,' Rosemary said with bitterness.

All of her young life, for as long as she could remember, she'd been conscious of friction between her parents. Most of the time it had been barely concealed, their hostility revealing itself in subtle innuendos and barbed comments. Did they think a child was deaf to such things? At least when she was younger, they'd restricted themselves to glowering silences. Now, their emotions erupted at the slightest provocation.

So, her dad had got himself another woman! Her lip curled in contempt, as she wondered what on earth she could be like. Not that she cared that much. Her father had never shown much interest in her. She often wondered if he resented her very presence.

Rosemary looked at her mother, who was sitting slumped at the kitchen table, one hand scrabbling in her handbag for a pack of cigarettes. They both smoked incessantly, her mum and her dad. The house stank permanently of nicotine.

'Mum,' she said, frowning, 'you don't think he'll really leave?'

Brenda looked up at her as she inhaled, and then gave a ragged sigh. 'That's what he says.'

'But if he does, what will happen to us? I mean,

17

how will we manage?'

Keith Latham had always been in work, but his heavy smoking and drinking ate a large hole in his wages. He'd once had a well-paid job as a sales representative, but that had been when Rosemary was a baby. She'd only ever known him to drift from one job to another. His latest was barman at the Dog and Gun, a popular pub frequented by day trippers on their way to the coast twenty miles away at Westbourne.

'God knows!' Brenda stared blankly at her.

'Couldn't you ask Father Kavanagh to talk to him?'

'Hah!' she sniffed. 'Fat lot of good that'd be – he doesn't even go to Mass half the time. Anyway, he thinks Father Kavanagh's an old woman.'

Rosemary bit her lip. 'You could get a job, I suppose. And I could, as soon as I leave school. I don't have to stay on for my exams.'

'You'll do no such thing!' Brenda bristled. 'Not when you're top of your class. And why should I go out to work? It was agreed, when we had you, that I'd stay at home and be a full-time mother.' She looked at her daughter, her expression hard. 'If he wants to go and live with his floosie, let him. We'll soon see how he likes keeping two homes going.'

She stood up and began to brush the cigarette ash from her jumper, her thin face pale and tense. 'Come on, let's clear this lot up, then you can go and fetch some fish and chips. Just the two of us, mind! If he comes back, he can bloody well get his own!'

But Keith Latham didn't come back, and later

18

that night Rosemary lay in her narrow, single bed and stared dismally at the grey cracks in the plastered ceiling. Like the rest of the house, her cheaply furnished room was in need of redecoration, but her dad was a man full of promises and not much action. It worried her sometimes that she felt so little for him. Often, cringing at his coarse humour, she would sit and stare at him, wondering how they could be so different.

She didn't take after her mum either, but at least she could relate to her. The small, bay-windowed semi tucked away at the end of a tiny cul-de-sac was Brenda's whole world. Rosemary remembered her saying once that a lousy husband was better than no husband at all. Despite her forced bravado, Keith's desertion would hit her hard.

Rosemary turned over, pummelling the pillow into shape, her shoulders hunching miserably under the bedclothes. One thing was for sure, life was never going to be the same again.

Keith Latham came home to collect his belongings in stealth three days later, using his knowledge of his wife's daily routine to let himself into the house while it was empty. By the time she returned from shopping, every trace of his presence had been eradicated. Wardrobes, drawers and bathroom cabinet all displayed their emptiness as though to mock her. For the first time Brenda faced up to the humiliating reality that Keith wasn't coming back. After twenty years of marriage, twenty years of what she saw as service, he'd rejected her. She'd be a laughing-stock, an object for sniggers and curiosity. The woman whose husband had run off with a bar-maid... Slow, hopeless tears of self-pity began to course down her cheeks. She stumbled down the stairs and, going into the chilly lounge, switched on the electric fire and huddled into an armchair.

She was still sitting there chain-smoking, her angular face strained, when she heard Rosemary's schoolbag fall with a clatter on the tiled floor of the hall.

The girl halted at the door as she saw her mother's stricken expression. 'What's happened? Has he been back?'

Brenda jerked her head. 'Have a look upstairs.'

Rosemary ran quickly up to the bedroom, and Brenda heard the rattle of drawers opening and closing, and her footsteps crossing the ceiling. It was eerie, but it seemed to her that the house already felt different, empty somehow.

Rosemary came slowly down to the living-room and, angrily pushing aside Brenda's careful display of scatter cushions, slumped on to the black vinyl settee. 'That's it then. I don't suppose he left a note or a message for me?'

Brenda shook her head.

'Do you know where he's gone?'

'Same place as he's been all week, I expect. With her!'

Rosemary looked down at the floor, her feet scuffing the beige shagpile carpet which was her mother's pride and joy. She'd wondered why her dad had given in and allowed Brenda to buy it on hire-purchase last Christmas. Guilty conscience, that's what it had been.

'You don't seem very angry,' she said.

'I've gone past anger,' Brenda said wearily.

Rosemary glanced up at her mother. She was well aware that Brenda was not the most practical of people. 'Did he leave you any money?'

Brenda looked at her vaguely. 'I didn't see any.'

'No, I didn't mean that. Have you got any money? You know, in the Post Office or something.'

'I've got this week's housekeeping, but your dad handled all the money, you know he did. Oh, and I've got thirty pounds in a Christmas Club.'

Rosemary let out a sigh of exasperation. They were doing Emily Pankhurst and the suffragette movement at school. Fifty years on, and here was her own mother as dependent upon her husband as though the equality of women had never been thought of.

'What about the mortgage? Is it in his name?'

'Of course.' Brenda looked at her in surprise. The questions that girl asked! But then she'd always had an old head on young shoulders. Sometimes she wondered which of them was the adult.

'Well, he's got to provide a home for me, at least until I leave school.'

Brenda stared at her. 'How do you know all this?'

'One of the girls at school was talking about it. Her parents have just got divorced.'

'I don't know what the world's coming to! You never heard of people getting divorced when I was a girl.'

'Well, they did. What about that Mrs Simpson? You know, the one the King abdicated for? She

21

was divorced.'

'Oh, I don't mean the upper classes, they've always had the morals of tomcats,' Brenda sniffed. 'I mean ordinary folk like us. People might have separated, but divorce – and I don't mean just among Catholics either – that really was something to be ashamed of.'

Rosemary hesitated and then said, 'What would you do if Dad wanted a divorce?'

'He could whistle for it,' Brenda said icily. 'Besides, the Church doesn't allow it.'

It doesn't allow adultery either, Rosemary thought, but that hadn't stopped him. She got up. 'I'm starving, and I bet you didn't have any lunch – you look dreadful. I'll get us some beans on toast. And, Mum...' She paused as her vivid blue eyes looked down into disillusioned brown ones. Theirs had never been a demonstrative relationship, but now Rosemary bent and awkwardly kissed her mother's cheek. 'You've still got me, you know.'

Brenda's eyes filled with tears, as she clutched at her daughter's hand. 'I know, love, and I thank God for it every day of my life.'

With a lump in her throat, Rosemary went into the kitchen and pulled the cord to the wall-mounted electric fire. She shivered – you could feel the winter chill already although it was only early October. Switching on the grill, she looked around the square kitchen, at the brown Marley tiled floor and cream and beige units, grimacing at their shabbiness. The house had been new when Keith and Brenda bought it in 1958, but whereas other houses in the road boasted improvements such as coach-lamps, storm porches, window shutters and leaded windows, the Lathams' house stood bare, the paint on the window frames and front door blistered and flaking. A sparse patch of grass which masqueraded as a lawn was reluctantly mowed by Keith during the summer, but as he never trimmed the edges, the garden always looked unkempt. In a narrow border at the side of the short slabbed drive, a few bedraggled Michaelmas daisies sprawled among the weeds.

The appearance of her home reflected the life within, Rosemary thought – dreary and depressing. As she took a sliced loaf from the chipped enamel bread-bin, she lifted her head and pondered. Perhaps she could buy some daffodil bulbs from the market – that would brighten the front up in the spring.

It was a beginning anyway, for unless she was very much mistaken, she'd be the one making the decisions from now on.

2

'I still think you should have gone to school,' Brenda protested, as she pulled out the twin-tub from beneath the work surface and positioned it before the sink. Straightening the hose, she screwed it on to the hot-water tap and began to fill the washing machine.

Rosemary bent to sort the laundry into piles,

then leaned against the draining-board. 'We've only got PE and Domestic Science this morning. I might go in this afternoon – it depends on how you are.'

'I'm perfectly all right, I've told you.'

Rosemary looked at her mother's haggard face with scepticism. It was five days now since her dad had cleared out his belongings, and she had tried going to school, but it was hopeless. Her ability to concentrate had deserted her. All she did was to sit in class, her stomach churning with anxiety, yet pride prevented her from confiding in her friends. Yesterday, when she'd arrived home to find Brenda lying on the settee, her face once again blotched with tears, she'd decided to take today off and try to rouse her from her misery.

'Well, you're not doing his flaming washing!' Rosemary extracted a couple of shirts, picked up some underpants and socks with distaste and flung them into a corner.

Brenda turned to reply, but the sound of a key, turning in the lock of the front door, caused mother and daughter to exchange looks of alarm and apprehension.

'It's him!' Brenda hissed. Hurriedly, she turned off the hot-water tap, and wiped her hands on a tea towel.

'I don't know how he dares to show his face!' Rosemary said bitterly. She didn't want to face him, this man who'd rejected her with never a word of explanation. It was as though she didn't exist, his only daughter who'd shared his life for fourteen years. It had surprised her just how much that had hurt.

Brenda took a deep breath and was about to move toward the kitchen door when suddenly it opened.

Keith Latham stood in the doorway, his gaze sweeping the kitchen, with its disorder around the sink, and piles of dirty clothes on the floor.

He glanced at Rosemary. 'What's she doing here?' he demanded, his pale blue eyes swivelling to meet Brenda's defensive brown ones.

Rosemary stared numbly at her father, wondering what any woman could see in him. In his early forties, Keith Latham's never handsome features were florid and coarsened by heavy drinking and smoking. Of medium height, with mousy thinning hair and a pronounced paunch, he was hardly God's gift to women. His mistress had probably come to her senses and thrown him out! Was that why he'd come? Was he hoping to just move back in as though nothing had happened?

Brenda stammered as she answered, 'She – she stayed at home today to keep me company.'

'Well, she can bugger off back to school. I want to talk to you.'

'But...' Rosemary began to protest, but Keith ignored her. Going into the hall, he retrieved a newspaper from the pocket of his damp raincoat hanging on the balustrade.

'Brenda,' he held the newspaper like a talisman, his arm raised. 'I told you, I want to talk to you. If you want the girl to stay...'

'No!' The whiplash of Brenda's tone caused Rosemary to look at her with alarm.

'I don't mind, Mum, I'll stay...' She took a step forward protectively, but found herself hustled out of the way as Brenda grabbed her arm.

'No, your dad's right, you should be at school. Go and get your uniform on. Go on,' she insisted. 'You don't need to worry about me. Married people have things to talk about in private.'

Rosemary stared at her in bewilderment. From the downcast, listless woman of a few moments ago, her mother was transformed. Now her eyes were glinting, the pupils dilated. Her sharp features, while deathly pale, were taut and wary. Rosemary could almost smell the fear on her and she glanced sharply from one to the other.

'Are you sure?'

'Do this for me, love. Please!' Brenda's eyes pleaded with her, and with reluctance Rosemary went up to her bedroom. Her mind racing, she hurriedly changed into her maroon and grey uniform, and picked up her schoolbag. What was going on? Why were they trying to get rid of her? She ran back down the stairs and paused apprehensively at the door of the lounge.

Keith sat on the edge of an armchair in the process of lighting a cigarette, while Brenda sat upright on the settee, her hands clenched on her lap. It was obvious they were waiting for her to leave.

'I'll say goodbye then.' Worried, she tried to catch Brenda's eye.

'Goodbye,' Keith said curtly.

Rosemary shot a baleful glance at him. She hated her dad for what he'd done – it was

26

disgusting, a man of his age.

'Mum?'

'Off you go, I'll see you later.' Brenda managed a travesty of a smile in an attempt to reassure her, but evaded her eyes.

Loth to leave, Rosemary let herself out of the front door, dawdling down the short drive. Then, heart pounding, she turned and hurried down the side path to the back of the house. Quietly, she pulled down the handle of the door. It was locked. The venetian blinds were closed at the small back window and, pressing her ear against the glass, she bit her lip in frustration. Keith had thought of everything.

Reluctantly, she walked along the cul-de-sac to the main road. She looked back at the semi-detached house, with its face blank and secretive behind the net curtains, trying in vain to imagine the scene inside. For a few moments she hovered on the kerb, then dodging the traffic crossed the road, beginning to rack her brain to invent a plausible excuse for her late arrival at school.

Keith waited until he heard the front door close and then with deliberation stubbed out his cigarette and picking up the newspaper from the floor at the side of his chair, placed it, still folded, across his knees.

Brenda kept her eyes on his, her neck and shoulders tensing.

Eventually, into the strained silence, he said, 'Don't you want to know why I've come round?'

Brenda's mouth twisted. 'I knew you'd have to come back sooner or later. You can't just walk out on all your responsibilities. What about the house and the bills and things, not to mention Rosemary? I haven't got any money of my own, as you very well know.' Her voice thickened with shame at both his rejection and her need to beg.

'Ah, yes. Rosemary.' Keith leaned back in his chair and, stretching out his legs, crossed them comfortably at the ankles. Brenda suddenly noticed that he was wearing new and expensive cavalry twill trousers. Her lips tightened. Baggy grey flannels had been considered good enough for her.

With watchful eyes she waited.

'I want a divorce.'

Brenda froze. She stared at him in shocked disbelief as the blunt words hung heavily in the air. Then, slowly, anger began to rise in her – she could feel its heat surging upward until it suffused her neck and face.

Keith casually lit another cigarette. He was perfectly calm.

'But we're Catholics!' she protested.

'So what? People lapse, you know.'

'I haven't.'

'What difference does that make? I'm the one who wants a divorce,' he countered.

'You're forgetting something. I'm not the one who committed adultery. You can't divorce me, and I'm certainly not going to divorce you. I married you, Keith Latham, 'til death do us part and that's how it's going to stay. So you can go back to your–' she searched for a suitable epithet, 'your trollop, and tell her I said so.'

Keith remained silent, his relaxed attitude

simply infuriating her further.

'How can you do this to me, after all these years? I've kept a clean house for you, there's always been a hot meal waiting on the table when you come in.' Her voice spiralled upward, 'I've done your washing, your ironing, even bloody well cut your hair! What more do you want?' Her voice broke as tears of desperation streamed down her face.

Keith's eyes regarded her coldly.

'Do you really want to know, Brenda? It's not what you've done, it's what you haven't done, or rather what you seem incapable of doing. A man wants more than a housekeeper, he wants a woman, a real woman, one who'll keep his bed warm at night with a bit of warm flesh to cuddle up to, aye and have a bit of fun. But you,' his eyes flickered with contempt at his wife's angular body, 'oh, no, we had to have twin beds – more hygienic, you said.'

'Is that what all this is about – sex?' Brenda spat.

'Lack of it, you mean. I'm surprised you can bring yourself to say the word, you've certainly never been keen on the act!'

Brenda averted her eyes, and challenged, 'What about Rosemary? How can you abandon your own daughter?'

'Rosemary.' Keith took a last drag on his cigarette. 'Yes. Let's talk about Rosemary.'

He took the newspaper and slowly unfolded it. Brenda's stomach lurched, her hands suddenly clammy. Her eyes darted nervously to the front page, trying to read the date.

He glanced up. 'Oh, it's a recent one, yesterday's in fact. Strange what you read in the newspapers, isn't it? Not that I'd know, seeing you suddenly cancelled all our papers last year. What was it you said? That with Rosemary at an impressionable age you didn't want her reading all the smutty articles. Let's save the money, you said, put it toward renting a colour television, and fool that I was, I went along with you.'

Brenda moistened her lips. 'I still don't see...'

'Oh, but I think you do, Brenda.' Keith opened up the paper and slowly turned the pages.

'Page thirty-seven, I think. Ah, here it is. I'll read it to you. Are you listening?

"SHERWIN, Rosemary. Would anyone knowing the whereabouts of Rosemary Sherwin, born on 3rd August 1956 at Westbourne, Hants, please contact..."'

He went on to detail a postal box number, and the address of the newspaper, while Brenda scarcely heard him, her mind frantically trying to absorb the implications of Keith's new-found knowledge.

'You knew, didn't you?' he accused.

She nodded. 'I saw it one day, just after Rosemary's thirteenth birthday. It was a terrible shock.'

'You didn't contact them?'

'No!' Her voice was sharp, and she glared at him, her brown eyes glinting in anger. 'Rosemary's mine,' she spat. 'She's my daughter!'

Keith slowly shook his head. 'That says it all.

30

"Rosemary's mine, she's my daughter", and that's how it's always been, hasn't it, right from when you first had the crackbrained notion? Before we moved here, you were cavorting around with a cushion stuck up your coat, pretending to be pregnant, and you kept it up until we got her. It's a good job we moved from one town to another, or it would have been the longest pregnancy on record.'

Flushing, Brenda said, 'I didn't want anyone to know she was adopted.'

He uncrossed his ankles and, carefully hitching up his trousers to keep their sharp crease in place, leaned forward.

'I know, and I humoured you, although you were lucky the adoption people didn't find out. Do you want to know why I agreed to have her in the first place?' he said. 'Because I thought it would soften you up a bit. It just shows how wrong a person can be. God, I'll never forget that first three months after we got her. It was "Change your shoes before you come in, Keith. Don't drink beer in the house, Keith." You were plumping the bloody cushions up even while I was sitting in the chair.'

'I had to keep the place spotless until after the random check. If the health visitor had given us a bad report, we could have lost her.'

'Pity we didn't,' he muttered.

'Keith!' Appalled, Brenda stared in horror at her husband.

'Well, I've never liked the girl, never felt comfortable with her somehow. And you certainly never had any time for me after you'd got her. It's

31

unhealthy, your obsession with that kid. Anyway, I didn't come round here to go over old ground. Look, Brenda, I've told you, I want a divorce.'

'And I'm telling you, over my dead body!'

'Oh, I don't think it'll come to that.' Keith took a pen from his inside jacket pocket and with a flourish drew a large ring around the newspaper notice.

'You wouldn't!' Brenda's eyes were frightened, and she felt the blood drain from her face. 'They couldn't take her away from me anyway – we adopted her all legal and everything.'

'Maybe not, but Rosemary would find out, wouldn't she? How do you know her natural mother wouldn't tell her? Once she found out where she lived, she could wait for her after school or something. Then there'd be solicitors involved. How would it look if I was living over the brush with someone? Still, if you want to take the risk...' He began to move out of the chair.

'No!' Brenda, who'd been sitting like a mesmerised rabbit, jumped up from the settee. 'Wait, wait a bit.' She cast about in her mind for a delaying tactic, and gabbled, 'Look, I'll make us a pot of tea, it won't take a minute.'

She escaped to the kitchen and while her shaking hands automatically filled the kettle, spooned tea in the pot, poured milk into cups, she fought panic. At all costs, her relationship with Rosemary must be safeguarded. It was true what Keith said. From the day she'd brought her home, the girl had been her consuming passion, her whole life. Nothing and no-one must ever be allowed to come between them. She straightened

32

her back, her decision made. If granting Keith a divorce was the price she had to pay to conceal the truth, then so be it.

Pouring out the tea, she put the cups on to a tray and carried it into the lounge.

'All right,' she said flatly. 'What do I have to do?'

Keith settled back in the armchair with satisfaction.

'That's my girl, I knew you'd see it my way. Right, I'll tell you something now, Brenda. The only reason I didn't leave you before was because of the money. Me and Shirl have had a thing going for years.'

She glared at him. 'You bloody hypocrite! And there's you off to Mass every Sunday. The Church won't recognise the divorce, you know.'

'Who cares? Legally, me and Shirl can get married, that's all that bothers me.'

'Her, you mean,' Brenda muttered. Curious, she asked, 'So, what's different now?'

'I came up, didn't I?' he grinned. 'A couple of weeks ago. I got second divi on Littlewoods.' As Brenda's eyes widened, he said quickly, 'Don't get your hopes up – it wasn't a fortune, but it was enough to make a difference. Now these are my terms. I'll pay the mortgage off and make the house over to you. Then I'll pay maintenance for you and the girl, but only 'til she's fifteen, mind. No nonsense about her staying on to take her exams.'

'But her teachers say she has university potential,' Brenda protested.

'Hard luck, that's all I can afford. Shirl and me

33

are emigrating, going to Australia. That's the package, Brenda, take it or leave it. You're still young enough to get a job. Rosemary can stand on her own feet. I've done as much for her as I intend to.'

He swallowed his tea and got up.

'Hold on a minute, Keith.' Brenda glanced in fear at the newspaper. 'How do I know you won't go back on your word?'

'I'm not a complete bastard, you know. Anyway, I'll leave you to think it over. Oh,' he paused in the doorway, 'make sure Rosemary isn't here next time. I don't really want to see her again.'

3

Rank body odour pervaded the entrance hall. The man, his threadbare suit scarcely concealing the dingy striped pyjamas he wore underneath, stood uncertainly in the doorway of Staniforth Public Health Department.

Rosemary schooled her expression into one of welcome and tried not to breathe in as she leaned forward and called through the reception hatch, 'Can I help you?'

The middle-aged man shuffled forward, his feet pathetically bare of socks in a pair of ill-fitting shoes.

'I've come about the Convalescent Home.' He peered at her with red-rimmed and bloodshot eyes.

'Have you got a medical certificate?'

Searching in a torn pocket he produced a crumpled piece of paper and held it out with a shaking hand.

Rosemary scrutinised it. As she'd expected, the diagnosis was 'general debility'. Glancing up, she gave a warm smile and said gently, 'I'll just let Miss Grocock know you're here. Would you like to take a seat?'

She indicated the row of shabby, wooden chairs opposite, but he stared at her blankly.

'Would you like to sit down and wait?' she repeated, raising her voice.

Comprehension dawning, he obeyed and went to sit, slumping in an attitude of weary defeat.

Rosemary turned to the internal telephone and dialled 12. 'Someone for Convalescent Homes, Miss Grocock.' She lowered her voice. 'I think he's another one from the hostel.'

'Oh God, and I've just finished my lunch!'

Rosemary's lips twitched as she replaced the receiver. Old Grocock might joke, but she was wonderful with the applicants. Some were post-operative cases, but many were victims of abject poverty or overwork. The ones from the hostel were the worst. 'General debility' said it all – even washing was too much of an effort, and she felt nausea rising at the stench of him, relieved as the plump, motherly woman descended the stairs and escorted him into a side office.

Twirling round on her typist's chair, Rosemary picked up a can of lavender air-freshener and went out into the entrance hall, only to turn and squirt the scented vapour directly into the face of the Medical Officer of Health, entering through the heavy double doors.

'Oops, sorry!' Her face coloured.

He smiled. 'That's okay. It's better than fly-spray.'

She grinned as she watched him ascend the staircase, admiring his pin-striped suit complete with red carnation in the buttonhole. She couldn't imagine him shacking up with a barmaid called Shirl and clearing off to Australia!

She'd been grateful to get a job as an office junior at the Health Department when she'd had to leave school. The alternative had been either to work in Woolworth's or at the biscuit factory. The irony was that the government had raised the school-leaving age the year after.

I was born too soon, she thought glumly.

Her promotion to receptionist had the added perk of day-release each Tuesday morning to attend the College of Commerce to learn short-hand and typing. The only condition had been that she must also attend an evening class once a week, with a warning that this compliance would be strictly monitored. She'd never missed a single lesson. Qualifications meant increments on the salary scale, and if working in an office was to be her fate, then she intended to climb to the top.

'Haven't you got any work to do?' The Home Help supervisor stood glaring at her.

At the acid tone, Rosemary jumped guiltily. 'Sorry, Miss Pritchard.' She took from her outstretched hand a pile of outgoing mail and began to put the envelopes through the franking machine. Aware of the other woman's impatient scrutiny, she fumbled a little, breathing a sigh of relief as the grey-haired erect figure turned and left with a sniff of disdain. Frustrated old bag! It was funny really, how all the top posts in this place were occupied by old spinsters!

She glanced hopefully up at the clock.

'Ah, clock-watching again – you'll cop it!' Lisa, the new office junior, perched on Rosemary's desk and began to munch an apple.

Rosemary grinned. She glanced down at Lisa's purple platform shoes. 'How you manage to walk in those things beats me.'

'S'easy. You just take small steps.' With her cute blonde bob, limpid blue eyes heavily outlined in black kohl, and chirpy humour, Lisa had livened up the department no end. 'Coming down the Palais tonight?' She arched one finely plucked eyebrow.

'No, I can't. I've already made arrangements,' Rosemary evaded.

'You always say that.'

Aware of the other girl's curiosity, Rosemary turned away, taking from her drawer a stiff brush and a small bottle of methylated spirits.

'Ugh, I hate the smell of that stuff,' Lisa complained. 'I thought the rule was to clean typewriters first thing Monday mornings?'

'It is, but I'll be in late on Monday.'

'Oh, why?'

'A medical appointment,' Rosemary said curtly. That was the trouble with Lisa, she was so open she expected everyone else to be the same. To what degree her own reticence was due to Brenda's warnings since childhood 'not to tell everyone your business', Rosemary wasn't sure. She only knew that when personal questions were asked, she had an automatic evasive reaction.

An hour later on her journey home, she sat on the front seat on the top deck of the bus, gazing blindly out of the misted window. Friday night, pay-day, and what special treat did it hold for her? A fish and chip supper and keeping her mum company while they watched the telly. If she tried to escape upstairs to play her David Bowie album, Brenda sulked. Just the two of them in a fug of cigarette smoke. It incensed her how money always had to be found to buy Brenda's fags.

I'm the one who does all the budgeting, she thought bitterly, but there's never any to spare for me. Seventeen and a half and she'd never even been to a proper disco, not that she'd got anything decent to wear anyway. There was never any money left over to spend on the latest fashions. She'd love some hot pants, but a cheap chain belt off the market was the most she could hope for. Otherwise, she had to wear 'sensible' clothes which could double up for work.

'I'm in here,' Brenda called ten minutes later, as Rosemary let herself in through the front door. 'Kettle's on.'

Rosemary searched in the biscuit tin only to find it empty except for a broken digestive. 'How've you been?' she asked, her mouth full of biscuit crumbs.

Brenda stubbed out her cigarette. 'Not too bad. And you needn't look at me like that, I'm trying to cut down. You don't understand, you've never smoked.' She broke into a bout of coughing.

'It's a good job. If I let my wages go up in smoke as well, we'd really be in trouble,' Rosemary snapped, then felt contrite as she noticed Brenda's pale face and shadowed eyes. 'What's the matter, Mum?'

Brenda slumped down at the kitchen table. 'Mr Walker's been round. They've taken someone else on permanently at the launderette. He said he was sorry, but I've just lost too much time.'

Rosemary's heart sank – she'd seen this coming. Now there would only be her meagre wage coming in. She sat opposite her mother and covered her hand with her own in a rare gesture of affection. 'Look, you're seeing a consultant on Monday morning. He'll sort you out – they'll take x-rays and everything.'

'Perhaps I should have been the one to go to Australia with all that sunshine. It was the stress, you know, the shock of it all. That's caused all this – I've never been right since.'

Rosemary raised her eyes to heaven in exasperation. She'd never understood why her mother had suddenly capitulated and agreed to a divorce. Her own protestations at having to leave school early had been swept aside. Hurt and bewildered at the time, even now the memory of Brenda's implacable coldness when she'd tried to dissuade her brought with it a feeling of rebellious anger.

As for her dad, some father he was, she thought bitterly. He never came to say goodbye before he emigrated, and now they didn't even know his address. It was obvious that as far as Keith Latham was concerned, she and her mother were history.

She looked at Brenda's strained expression and a feeling of desolation swept over her. She didn't know how they were going to manage. Hopefully, her mum's health would improve, but for a woman of nearly fifty, who'd lost her last job through poor attendance, another employer wouldn't be easy to find.

As though Brenda could read her thoughts, she suddenly said, 'You get a big rise when you're eighteen, don't you?'

'So?' Rosemary said miserably.

'Well, that should help. After all, we've no mortgage to pay like most folks.'

No, but we've got debts and I know who we can thank for that, Rosemary thought with bitterness. He might have conceded the house, but he didn't make any effort to leave it in good repair. Years of neglect had resulted in them having to have the front windows replaced last year, and if they didn't have the wet rot in the others seen to soon, they'd be past repair. They'd had to pay on an easy payment scheme, which of course meant high interest charges. Poverty's a vicious circle, she realised with sudden insight, even having to buy from Mum's catalogue on credit costs more than shopping around for bargains in the High Street. Brenda was hopeless about money – she seemed to think the bills paid themselves.

Suddenly, to her dismay, she felt tears of self-pity pricking at her eyelids. She was young, she wanted to be able to enjoy herself, to go out dancing, have money to spend on make-up and the latest records. She longed to be light-hearted, fun-loving, like Lisa and the others. She was sick of being sensible and practical, taking care of the household expenses. She felt so restless and impatient lately. There were stirrings inside her, a need for excitement. Rosemary only knew that there was another world out there, a world beyond the shabby semi-detached in a run-down suburb of a provincial town.

'I saw Mrs Lewis down at the shop,' Brenda interrupted her musings. 'You'll never guess what she told me.'

'What?' Rosemary asked absently.

'Their Sheila's having to get married!'

'Sheila Lewis?' Rosemary's voice rose in surprise. She'd been in her year at school, but in a lower form. Still, at least Sheila must have had a boyfriend, which was more than she'd ever had.

Brenda's eyes glinted with self-satisfaction. If Mrs Lewis had stopped Sheila from gallivanting, it wouldn't have happened. Perhaps there were some advantages in being poor after all.

She cast a sideways glance at Rosemary, basking in the glow of pride that the sight of her daughter always provided. She was such an unusual girl, not pretty in a chocolate-box sort of way, but arresting, yes that was it, Rosemary was arresting. The light dusting of freckles on her creamy complexion suited her. With her dark lustrous hair and deep blue eyes, she had grown into a very attractive girl.

But Brenda wasn't blind – she knew Rosemary was beginning to feel caged. Her constant fear was that some predatory male would intrude on their cosy life together. She'd been fortunate so far, but she knew it couldn't last. Her daughter was rapidly maturing, her body that of a young woman, curvaceous and full of promise. She sat savouring her handiwork, for that was how she thought of her, greedily drinking in her every expression, as Rosemary began to empty her handbag of old bus tickets and the week's trivia.

This lovely girl was hers, hers alone. She was the one responsible for her development, and the intensity of her obsessive love burned silently and steadily within her. But she was going to have to be careful, for Rosemary had an independent streak and a good head on her shoulders. The emotional dependence upon her daughter which she had deliberately inculcated since the divorce had kept Rosemary home at nights so far, but she could sense that she was beginning to chafe at the restrictions.

Rosemary clicked her bag shut and looked at her mother. 'You know, Mum, I've been thinking. We aren't the first people Dad's discarded like unwanted old shoes. What about his parents? All you've ever told me was that they fell out years ago. People think it's weird that I've never met them.'

'You know as much as me,' Brenda told her. 'When I first went down to London and met your dad, he told me he'd left home after a massive row, and so far as I know he's never contacted them since. It was a pity 'cos he was the only child.'

'So they don't know anything about either of us.' It was a statement full of pathos, and Rosemary's lips twisted.

42

'No, I don't even know whether they're still alive. That was one of the main things we had in common, being on our own so to speak. He hadn't got anyone, and well,' her voice fell, 'you know about me.'

'Yes.' As always, Rosemary's heart filled with compassion at the thought of Brenda's lonely and deprived childhood in an orphanage in the Midlands. When she felt suffocated by her narrow life and resentful of her mother's increasing dependence on her, she had only to remind herself of how little love there had been in Brenda's life.

It was understandable, after all, that she would be possessive, although it drove Rosemary mad at times. She reflected wistfully on how different her childhood would have been if she'd had not only a brother or sister but grandparents, or perhaps an aunt or uncle and cousins. She couldn't remember anyone even visiting the house. Brenda took pride in 'keeping herself to herself,' and had never been interested in making friends. Keith had prided himself on being a 'man's man' and had always been an absent figure in the evenings, and at weekends, preferring to play darts and drink at the local pubs.

Rosemary, discouraged from bringing friends home, had found her solace in reading, the written word opening up a world she could only dream of. Oh, she knew how narrow her life was, how lacking in experience of people and situations!

'Penny for them?' Brenda looked at her curiously, but Rosemary's face closed and,

43

shrugging, she got up.

'The usual is it – fish, chips and mushy peas?' she asked, though how her mother could eat the disgusting green mess was beyond her. Why couldn't they try a Chinese takeaway for a change? But she might as well suggest flying to the moon. Oh, why did life in this house have to be so boring!

'Yes, the money's on the sideboard. I'll cut the bread and butter and get the tea ready. We don't want to miss the start of *Coronation Street*.' Brenda bustled to set the kitchen table, and Rosemary picked up a shopping bag and let herself out into the rainy night.

She trudged the half mile to the chip shop, hunching her shoulders against the damp wind. A car drove by, its wheels too close to the pavement, splashing her legs with muddy droplets as she saw the lights of the shop window and smelt the pungent odour of frying. She glanced up at the sign, The Wise Plaice, and sighed before opening the door and stepping into the warmth. Some day...

4

The waiting-room seemed daunting, the rows of chairs in the Out-Patient Clinic crammed with people waiting to see the hospital consultant.

Rosemary hustled Brenda forward as she spotted a couple of vacant chairs in the middle row, and they squeezed into the narrow seats.

'Whew, what a queue,' Brenda grumbled, fishing in her bag for her cigarette packet.

Rosemary nudged her in exasperation, indicating the 'No Smoking' sign. 'Well, we're in plenty of time for our appointment,' she said.

'And what time might that be?' enquired a stout woman whose shoulder was pressing against her own.

Rosemary turned to look at her. 'Ten o'clock.'

The woman snorted, her round, flushed face creasing in derision. 'Think you're alone, do yer? I can bet you every one of these here,' she indicated with a fat forefinger the other people waiting, 'every one of 'em has ten o'clock printed on their appointment card!'

'But...' Rosemary frowned.

'Saves the consultant being kept waiting, don't it? Can't have his time wasted. Bloody God Almighty, he is. I should settle yourself down for a long wait, love. Two hours I was last time I come!' She pushed her perspiring face closer. 'You have told 'em at the desk you're here?'

Rosemary nodded.

Brenda, who was sitting primly, both gloved hands folded neatly on her lap, began to fidget. 'I can't sit here for two hours without a smoke,' she muttered. 'I'm gasping for one now.'

'Want a fag, do yer?' The woman leaned forward, her ample bosoms pressing against Rosemary's arm, as she attempted to peer short-sightedly into Brenda's face. 'Yer'll have to go outside and have a quick one. I should go now, just in case there's a miracle and you're called on

45

time,' she urged.

Brenda withdrew, looking at her with distaste, wrinkling her nose at the liberal scent of cheap talcum powder. 'Oh, right.'

With an apologetic glance at Rosemary, she stood up and hurried toward the exit, while Rosemary placed her bag conspicuously on the empty chair and eased her body away from the weight pressing against her.

'Mrs Latham?'

Startled by the sudden call, Rosemary jumped up and went to the desk. 'My mother's just slipped out for a moment.'

The receptionist handed her an envelope saying, 'That's all right, love. Can you ask her to go along to X-Ray, wait for the plates and then bring them back and take them with her when she sees Mr Merton.'

Rosemary nodded and clutching the envelope hurried outside.

Brenda was leaning against a wall, inhaling deeply.

'Put that out, Mum, you've got to go and have an x-ray.' Rosemary waited impatiently as Brenda took another puff and then ground the stub into the tarmac.

'Are you sure these x-rays aren't harmful?' Brenda asked as she followed Rosemary back into the hospital.

'What? That's only if you have lots of them. Look, it says X-Ray to the left.'

The waiting-room was simply part of a corridor with chairs pushed against one wall, and they made their way to the end.

A young man with his arm in a sling grinned at Rosemary as she almost stumbled over a walking-stick, before sitting next to him.

'Gosh, don't they get busy in these places?'

'Sure do.'

Rosemary glanced at him. His face was pale and slightly drawn – the pain she supposed, looking with sympathy at his arm.

'What have you done, broken it?' she asked.

'Not sure until the x-ray, but I think so. I fell off my bike when it hit a stone in the road. It was my own fault, I was looking at a pretty girl at the time!'

He smiled, and Rosemary was suddenly aware that beneath his pallor, he was extremely attractive.

'What about you?'

'Oh, I'm here with my mother, she's having a chest x-ray. You'll find it difficult to manage, what with it being your right arm,' she said, trying to imagine what it would be like to lose the use of hers.

'Tell me about it. I don't know how I'll go on,' he said, his forehead creasing. 'Especially as I live on my own.'

Rosemary looked at him in surprise. He couldn't be much older than herself, perhaps twenty-one.

'You don't live with your parents, then?' she asked tentatively.

'Haven't got any. I was brought up in a children's home. The problem is, you're turfed out to fend for yourself when you reach sixteen. Not that I'm complaining, mind,' he added hurriedly.

'I've managed okay so far, but when something like this happens... I'd really like to find some good digs. I've been looking around for a while but...' he broke off as a radiographer appeared.

'Tony Bartram?'

'Right! Cheerio, good luck to your mum.'

Thoughtfully, Rosemary watched him follow the white-coated radiographer. A germ of an idea began to take root. Well, why not? Even if he wasn't interested, then perhaps they could find someone else.

'Mum...'

'Oh, you've remembered I'm here!' Brenda snapped.

Rosemary rolled her eyes. God, her mother really got on her nerves at times. 'What do you think? I've just had an idea how we can solve our financial problems!'

Brenda looked at her warily. 'Go on, then.'

'Well, it was something he just said, about looking for some good digs. That's what we could do – take in a lodger. I mean it wouldn't mean that much extra work. I could help out with ironing and things. You never know, he might do the garden ... what do you think?'

Brenda stared at her. 'You mean take some complete stranger into our home, someone you've only met for five minutes? Have you taken leave of your senses?'

'Oh, he'd have to provide references,' Rosemary insisted. 'What I want to know is, do you agree in principle? Personally, I think it's a brainwave!'

Brenda considered. 'How much could we charge?'

'I'm not sure, but I could find out from the housing department when I go in to work. They'd be bound to know the going rate. Look, make your mind up. It doesn't have to be him, but I could catch him on his way out and see if he's interested.'

Brenda pursed her lips as avarice fought suspicion and fear. The girl was right, it would help to solve their problems, but a young man? Was there an ulterior motive in Rosemary's mind? After all the last thing she wanted to bring into their home was temptation. She glanced sharply at her daughter, but Rosemary met her gaze without guile. In any case, if they did take in a lodger, she thought, and she recognised it was an inspired idea, there was no way she'd want another woman in her house, interfering and busybodying. The thought of an older man, set in his ways, probably loud and coarse, repelled her. At least with this young lad, she'd be able to make him toe the line. For make no mistake about it, one foot wrong where Rosemary was concerned, and out he'd go!

'You'll have to make your mind up – he'll be out in a minute,' Rosemary muttered.

'All right, then.' Brenda clamped her mouth shut, her heart beating rapidly, as she watched Rosemary scribble their address on a scrap of paper.

'Of course, he may not be interested. We might be in the wrong area.'

'We're pretty central,' Brenda retorted. Now she'd made the decision, it was inconceivable that this, whatshisname, Tony Bartram, shouldn't be abjectly grateful.

Rosemary jumped up as Tony's tall, lanky figure reappeared in the doorway. Hurrying, she managed to catch him as he turned to leave the waiting-room.

'Hi,' he said and grimaced at her. 'I've broken it, I'm afraid. I'm just on my way to the Plaster Room.'

'Oh, I am sorry.' She hesitated. 'Look before you go, I wondered whether you might be interested in this.' She thrust the piece of paper into his left hand and at his startled look explained, 'It's our address. Only we're thinking of taking in a lodger, and after what you said earlier...' her voice trailed off lamely, and she flushed with embarrassment. It had all seemed so simple back in her seat, but now she felt an utter fool. Whatever would he think of her, accosting him like this?

Tony's eyes narrowed as he glanced with speculation at the scrap of paper.

'Poplar Crescent, Elston. Hey, that's quite near my job.' At Rosemary's enquiring look, he said, 'I work at that new supermarket, on the main road.'

Feeling flustered, Rosemary stammered, 'It's only a suggestion mind – I mean I don't know quite what you're looking for. But if you'd like to take a look...?'

'You bet I will. After all, I'm going to be a bit stuck with this,' he nodded toward his arm, and beginning to move away, said, 'How about tonight, say about seven o'clock?'

'That would be fine.' She watched him walk slowly down the main corridor and then returned

50

to Brenda, giving her the thumbs-up sign.

'He's coming tonight to have a look,' she said complacently.

'What?' Brenda blanched. 'But that little box-room's full of clutter, and it needs a good clean.'

'We've got until seven o'clock to give it a going over. He's been brought up in a children's home so it's not as though he's used to the Ritz,' Rosemary said, with more confidence than she felt.

'Oh, I do hope we're doing the right thing.' Brenda chewed on her lip.

'We're not doing anything yet, we're only exploring the possibilities. Look, I think you're next,' she added hurriedly. 'Leave your handbag with me.'

An hour later, Rosemary accompanied her mother, at her request, into the specialist's consulting room. Brenda handed him her doctor's letter and the large brown envelope containing the x-ray plates and they waited with apprehension as he examined them.

'Hmn. I'd like to have a look at you, Mrs Latham. Just go with Nurse here and undress to the waist.'

Rosemary remained where she was, and watched the tired-looking bespectacled man warily as, his fingers tapping the table, he once again studied the x-ray.

'Are you her daughter?'

'Yes.'

'Well, if my examination confirms what I fear, I'm afraid your mother is a sick woman.' He paused as Rosemary's face paled.

51

'Her doctor tells me he's told her to stop smoking. Has she?' he shot the question.

Rosemary shook her head. 'No. I keep telling her, but...'

Mr Merton sighed in exasperation, and went into the other room.

How many times have I told her about smoking, Rosemary railed in frustration as she waited, but would she listen, not her! Got to have my fags, was always her answer. Can't do without a smoke, it's the only pleasure I have. God, her mother could be so stupid!

After what seemed an eternity, but was only several minutes, the consultant reappeared, followed a few moments later by a subdued and anxious Brenda.

'Do sit down, Mrs Latham,' he ushered her to a chair. 'Now, I'm afraid as I have already told your mother,' he directed his remarks to Rosemary, 'she has severe emphysema, which means that the air-sacs of the lungs are enlarged and damaged. I'm afraid we can't cure this condition, but we can try to control it with drugs. However, any treatment we give her will be a waste of time if she continues smoking.'

'I won't have to have an operation, will I?' Brenda whispered.

'I'd like to avoid surgery if at all possible,' he said, 'but everything depends on how you progress.' He scribbled on a prescription pad. 'Nurse will show you where to go with this and will make you another appointment for three months. I want you to see your own doctor once a fortnight, and no smoking mind, or I won't answer for the consequences.' He nodded, the consultation obviously at an end.

'Right,' Rosemary demanded when they eventually arrived home. 'Give me any cigarettes you've got in the house.'

Brenda stared at her in horror. 'I can't just stop like that, I'll have to cut down.'

'No, you won't,' Rosemary snapped. 'We've been all through that before.' Her voice choked. 'Look, Mum, you're the only person I've got in the world. For heaven's sake, don't you realise you're killing yourself with your bloody fags!'

'Rosemary!' Brenda was shocked to hear her daughter swear.

'Give them to me,' Rosemary insisted.

Brenda hid her bag defensively behind her back, but Rosemary caught her arm and pulled it round to the front. Brenda reluctantly opened the bag and fished out a packet of cigarettes.

'And the rest,' Rosemary's tone was acid, and Brenda flinched.

'There's a packet by the side of my bed,' she muttered.

'And?' Rosemary challenged.

'There's some in the sideboard.'

'I'll have those as well. I'm sure someone in the office will take them off my hands.' Rosemary glanced at her watch. 'I've just got time for a sandwich and then I'll have to get back to work.' She looked at Brenda's despondent face and gave her an awkward hug. 'Don't look so worried. I'm sure if you do as the doctor says, you'll be all right. And think of the money you'll save.' Seeing that this statement did little to lift her mother's spirits, she placed five cigarettes on the table.

'All right, you can have these five to cut down slowly over the afternoon. But that's it, mind, you're finishing. Anyway, having to get the box-room tidied up will take your mind off things. Don't forget – he'll be here at seven o'clock.'

By five to seven they were ready and waiting, Rosemary attempting to watch TV and trying to ignore Brenda's irritability as she restlessly paced the room.

'I'm still not sure...' Brenda stopped as the gate clicked and a moment later the doorbell chimed.

'I'll go.' Rosemary stood up and hurried into the hall. Opening the door, she gave what she hoped was a welcoming smile as Tony grinned at her.

'Here I am, just like the proverbial bad penny!'

'How's your arm?' She led him into the lounge.

'A bit painful,' he said ruefully.

Brenda stood up, awkwardly smoothing her navy skirt.

'Hello, er I'm afraid I don't know your name,' he smiled.

'Oh, how silly of me,' Rosemary exclaimed. 'I'm Rosemary Latham, and this is my mother.'

'Pleased to meet you, Mrs Latham.'

Brenda gave a stiff nod. 'Yes, well, I expect you'd like to see the room.' With a lopsided grin, Tony followed her up the stairs, while Rosemary went into the kitchen to switch on the kettle. He was even better looking than she remembered. Oh, I do hope he likes it, she prayed, and then had a sudden thought. God, I hope he doesn't smoke!

Hearing their footsteps on the stairs, she went into the hall. One glance at their smiling faces and she said with relief, 'I'll make some tea.'

Tony followed her into the kitchen.

'Do you smoke?' she hissed.

'Yes, but only twenty a day, that's all I can afford,' he replied, looking puzzled.

Rosemary frowned.

'Is that a problem?'

'It could be. Look, would it be all right if we had a rule you could only smoke in your bedroom?' She looked at him anxiously.

After a moment, he shrugged his shoulders and said, 'If you insist.'

'That's okay then. I take it you liked the room. Are you sure it's not too small?'

Tony leaned against the cooker, wincing as he adjusted his sling.

'It's as big as any other I've been offered,' he said, 'and a darn sight cleaner than most. Anyway, when my arm's better I could always do it up a bit. That's if you don't mind?'

'Of course we don't mind, we'd be grateful.'

Over tea and biscuits, the terms were amicably agreed and it was arranged that Tony should move in the next day, subject to a reference from his present landlady.

'I've only a week's notice to give on my bed-sit,' he explained, 'and it'll be great to have my meals got for me.'

'I'm only a plain cook, nothing fancy, mind,' Brenda warned, a lump of anxiety forming in her throat.

'That suits me fine, Mrs Latham. I'll tell you

what's my favourite – egg and chips!' Brenda managed a weak smile, then Rosemary ushered him to the door.

'Come round in the morning and get settled in,' she said. 'I'll be at work, but I'll be home around six. Oh and Tony,' she looked earnestly at him. 'Don't get Mum any cigarettes, will you? Not even if she goes on her bended knees.'

He gave her a startled look, his blue eyes puzzled.

'It's her chest. The consultant says she's got severe emphysema and has to stop smoking. When I checked back at work at the Public Health Department, apparently if she keeps on, it could kill her.' Her brow puckered with anxiety as she waited for his reassurance.

'Don't worry, she won't get round me,' he promised, 'and I won't smoke in front of her either.'

With a feeling of relief, she watched him go. He'd told them he had the rest of the week off on sick leave, so at least over these crucial first days Brenda wouldn't be able to deceive her.

As Rosemary closed the door behind him, she leaned back, conscious of a sense of excitement. Despite her anxiety about her mother, all at once the future held a hint of promise, and it was with a spring in her step that she went to do battle with Brenda's nicotine addiction.

5

Two months later, 14 Poplar Crescent was a changed house. Gone was the repressive atmosphere which had lain like a yoke on Rosemary's shoulders since childhood. How he had done it, she didn't know, but Tony's easy charm was such that even Brenda had succumbed. Her narrow, pale face with its discontented mouth had softened, her glances even arch as she exchanged banter with the young man she insisted on calling her 'paying guest'.

To Rosemary's continued amazement, her mother, obviously frightened by the consultant's warning, had never touched a cigarette from that day. Nor had she whined or even been ill-tempered, at least not more than usual.

Mystified, Rosemary said one evening, 'I don't know how you've done it. People at work are always trying to give up.'

'I suppose those tablets could have helped.' Brenda put aside her knitting-needles and measured the length of a sleeve against Rosemary's arm.

Rosemary looked at the half-finished Aran cardigan with distaste. She'd told her mother umpteen times that no-one her age would be seen dead in home-knitted things, but she might as well have saved her breath.

'They're not supposed to stop you smoking,

they're supposed to stop you coughing and wheezing, but they don't seem to be having much effect,' she said.

'It's early days yet. The doctor says it takes time,' Brenda reassured her, bundling the knitting into a bag. 'Right, it's ten o'clock, my bedtime. I'll take my cocoa with me, so...'

'There's no need to disturb you,' Rosemary finished off her sentence. 'You say that every night these days.'

'You're not disappointed then, are you? Goodnight, Tony. Full breakfast, is it in the morning?'

'Yes please, Mrs L,' he replied from his sprawled position on the settee, Brenda's precious scattercushions tossed carelessly on to the floor.

Honestly, thought Rosemary, if I'd done that she'd have been on me like a ton of bricks! Still, she couldn't resent Brenda's laxity with him – Tony just seemed to have that effect on people. She watched her mother leave, feeling proud of her willpower, although she still went into every room on her return from work to sniff the air, feeling like a human bloodhound. She also searched the garden regularly for discarded butts, and the dustbin for cigarette ash, all to no avail. It was nothing short of a miracle.

Settling herself back into *Pride and Prejudice*, Rosemary was acutely aware of Tony's male presence a few feet away. He was watching television, seemingly oblivious to her. Colouring slightly, she watched him, her gaze lingering on the way his dark hair curled slightly on his collar. He had a nice nose, she decided, and she thought the cleft in his chin was cute. In fact, she sighed, he was absolutely fab, but was obviously not the slightest bit interested in her.

She'd had to suffer much ribbing at work once it was known she'd never had a boyfriend. It's been my own fault, she thought miserably, I've allowed my worries about things at home to take over my entire life. She really fancied Tony, but...

He turned suddenly, and his blue eyes locked with her own. 'Do you fancy going to the Palais on Saturday night?'

She drew a quick breath. 'Yes, I'd love to.'

'Great! I'd have asked you before, but I was waiting until I had my cast off.'

An ardent Liverpool supporter, he turned abruptly away as a goal was scored on *Match of the Day*, and Rosemary snuggled down into her armchair, Mr Darcy forgotten.

He'd actually asked her out! With panic she realised she hadn't got a thing to wear and quickly reviewed her finances. Yes, at last, she could just about afford something new, particularly if she went down to the market. Flared velvet pants, that's what she'd get, and a new tank top. Apparently hot pants were already on their way out. Oh, she couldn't wait to go shopping!

'What's he like then?' asked Lisa, the following morning.

'You'll see soon enough on Saturday.'

Lisa looked curiously at the older girl. 'He's done you good, this lodger of yours. You were much too serious before, if you don't mind my saying so.'

'All the same if I did!'

'Even so, I wish I had your brains,' Lisa said

59

wistfully. 'Look at you, taking your RSA Stage III already. My typing's rubbish!'

'You'll get better,' Rosemary assured her. She liked Lisa, liked her optimism and spunk. She cheeked everyone, and got away with it. It must be the result of coming from such a large family – nothing seemed to faze her.

Saturday night arrived at last, and Rosemary hardly recognised the glowing girl who smiled back at her from the mirror. It had taken her nearly two hours to get ready. A long scented bath, freshly washed hair, two coats of nail varnish, and at least three attempts to get her eyeliner right. The Palais, here I come, she gloated, preening in her new outfit, then ran downstairs.

Tony was waiting in the hall.

'You look great!' he said, admiring her bottle-green velvet flares and cream top.

'Thanks.'

Brenda came out of the lounge, and Rosemary turned to her. 'What do you think?'

'You look very smart.'

'Smart! I don't want to look smart!'

'You look very trendy,' Tony reassured her. 'Now come on, or we'll miss the bus.'

'Bye, Mum!' Rosemary grabbed her jacket, and followed him out of the front door.

As they walked along the road, Tony took her hand in his. 'You'll knock 'em dead in that gear.'

'That's the general idea!'

They burst into the house, full of laughter and high spirits, and to Rosemary's continued amazement at her change of attitude, Brenda was waiting up for them.

'Did you have a good time?'

'Smashing,' Rosemary said, still exhilarated from the music, crowds and heady atmosphere of the ballroom.

'You haven't been drinking, have you?' Brenda looked suspiciously at her flushed face. 'You're not eighteen yet!'

'One Dubonnet and lemonade, that's all, Mrs L,' Tony said, surreptitiously winking at Rosemary.

'Oh, well, I suppose that's all right.' Brenda looked sharply at Rosemary's bright eyes, before settling herself down in the lounge with her latest Mills and Boon.

'Aren't you tired? It's way past your bedtime,' Rosemary said irritably. Couldn't she see that she and Tony wanted to be alone?

'No, not really,' Brenda bent her head over her book.

Tony jerked his head, and Rosemary followed him into the kitchen. Pushing the door shut with his shoulder, he pulled her to him, his lips coming down forcefully to meet hers in a long, bruising kiss.

'You're so beautiful, hasn't anyone ever told you?' he whispered.

She shook her head, lifting it again to seek his mouth, her body straining toward him. Tony's hand moved down to cup her breast, and she could feel the heat of it through the flimsy material of her top. Could feel...

Brenda suddenly pushed open the door, and

they jumped guiltily apart.

'What's going on?'

'Nothing. I'm just making a cup of tea.' Rosemary averted her face, and busied herself at the sink.

'I couldn't get in the door!'

'I think it's sticking. I'll have a look at it tomorrow,' Tony said. 'Look, I don't think I want a cup of tea. I'll say goodnight. See you both in the morning.' His eyes searched for Rosemary's before swivelling upwards, and before her own could respond, he was gone.

She kept her back to her mother and poured the water on to the tea. Her breathing was quick, her body a maelstrom of new emotions, but her head was clearing. She might be without experience, but she wasn't that daft. She knew what that signal with his eyes meant, but he'd find a chair against her bedroom door if he tried that on. She felt a pang of disillusionment, then shrugged. She didn't suppose he was any different from the rest, not from what she'd heard the girls at work say.

Oh, but he was gorgeous! When she was with Tony she felt young and vibrant, she'd never had so much fun. Anxious to get to her room to relive the last wonderful few minutes, she said quickly, 'I'll take my tea up, Mum. See you in the morning for Mass.'

It felt strange the following day to be sitting in the same room with him, just as though nothing had happened. Tony didn't refer to the previous night, although Rosemary had seen her door handle turn just after midnight.

It wasn't until late afternoon that he approached her alone. 'What are you sketching?'

Rosemary looked up from the kitchen table and pushed forward her pad. 'Just a vase,' she said.

He looked around the room.

'Oh, I'm not copying one. I'm, well, just messing about really.'

He took the pad and skimmed through the pages. 'Hey, these are really good,' he said, admiring the graceful designs of bowls and jugs. 'Strange thing to draw, most girls would be doodling fashions or something.'

'They're not doodles,' she retorted. 'Anyway, I like drawing pottery. I like the feel of china,' she said reflectively. 'There's a wonderful shop in town, really expensive, but they have some beautiful pieces.'

He nodded. 'You must have been good at Art at school.'

'Yes, I was,' she said bitterly. She'd hoped to do a degree in Art & Design, but fat chance she'd had.

He put out a tentative finger and began to stroke her neck. 'I came along last night.'

'Yes, I know.' She twisted to face him. 'Let's get one thing straight, Tony. I'm not that kind of girl. One date and a few drinks won't get me into bed. If that's what you're looking for, you're shopping in the wrong market.'

He backed off, raising his hands in defence. 'Sorry, Miss. I thought you liked me, my mistake.'

She looked at him. 'I do like you, you daft toad.'

'No offence?' She could see his lips twitching

with amusement.

'None taken,' she smiled.

A couple of months later, Rosemary couldn't imagine life without him. They went everywhere together, to the cinema and dancing, ten-pin bowling and sometimes just walking, hand in hand. One day they'd gone for a day-trip to Westbourne, walking along the seafront, laughing as the salt spray whipped their hair and clothes.

I'm in love, she thought deliriously. Physical affection had never been part of her life, and to be held and caressed, the warmth of another body against her own, unlocked within her a depth of emotion she hadn't known she possessed. Tony had never again tried to enter her room, although now she wasn't so sure she'd be able to resist him.

But in some ways, Tony was an enigma to her. He was such a private person, obsessive about keeping the door to his room firmly closed. No-one was allowed to enter and he always changed his bed and cleaned it himself. Rosemary had asked him about his childhood, but he just said that his mother was still alive, but he never saw her nor had any desire to.

He was ambitious though. At the local supermarket he was training to be a manager, and worked long hours. In return for his rent, Brenda did his washing and provided all his meals. Rosemary ironed his clothes with her own. In turn, he sometimes did some weeding in the garden, and lately had taken to looking speculatively at the outside of the house, wondering whether he could repair the windows once his arm was stronger.

Friends at work teased her, saying she should get a ring on her finger – he was much too handsome to be on the loose.

Lisa, however, was reticent. 'How well do you really know him?'

'More than most girls know their boyfriends, seeing how we live in the same house,' Rosemary pointed out. 'What's the matter, Lisa, don't you like him?'

'Oh, he's very charming, it's just that ... oh, take no notice of me, I'm probably jealous.'

As her eighteenth birthday approached, Tony began to talk of getting engaged, either then or at Christmas. Rosemary began to panic. She wanted to, of course she did, but she could see her future stretching ahead, and it was so different from her dreams. Life would go on exactly as before. Once married, perhaps in another year, they would continue to live at 14 Poplar Crescent. Tony had already pointed out that it would be silly to take on a mortgage, even if they could save up a deposit. Anyway, he said he understood that Rosemary couldn't leave her mother, not with her health being so poor.

The only difference Rosemary could envisage was that they'd move into Brenda's bigger bedroom. Was that what she really wanted out of life? To carry on living in the house she'd grown up in, a house she'd never liked, in which she'd never been happy? However, Tony seemed so settled there. She supposed it was the only real home he'd ever had, and she had to admit it was convenient for his job.

She tried to discuss her doubts with her mother. But it appeared that Tony could do no wrong in Brenda's eyes.

'But don't you think I'm too young?' Rosemary said doubtfully. 'I haven't known him all that long either.'

'Long enough, you're made for each other. And no, I don't think you're too young, you've always been old for your age. You don't want to let a chance like this slip through your fingers. You won't get a better offer – and he doesn't drink – he won't be off down the pub like your dad.' She paused, and then added, 'As for his not being a Catholic, well, he doesn't seem to mind your going to Mass and, as for anything else, well, that's your business.'

Rosemary looked away. Such topics as birth control or even children had never been discussed. Tony's evasiveness on any serious topic sometimes disturbed her. Any misgivings she had, however, she dismissed as her own ignorance of the male character. After all, her only role model had been her father, and Tony was certainly an improvement on him. As to her mother's sudden change of heart, it mystified her. I'll never understand people, thought Rosemary wryly, they never react as you expect them to.

6

'You'll need a cardigan, there's a breeze getting up,' Brenda called.

'It's a lovely summer evening, Mum. Don't fuss!' Rosemary came into the lounge and waited until Brenda finished a bout of coughing, concerned to see her pallor and the dark circles beneath her eyes.

'I don't understand it, surely you should be feeling better by now,' she said with a worried frown.

'Don't you worry about me, it's probably the "change" on top of everything else.'

'Maybe. Anyway, when you see the specialist on Monday, I'm coming with you.'

'No, there's no need to take time off work, I'll be fine on my own,' Brenda insisted.

With a puzzled look, Rosemary said, 'Only if you're sure.' She adjusted the belt on her jeans. 'I'm off then. I'm meeting Tony from work and then we're going to the pictures. Are you sure you're okay?'

'I'm fine. Go on, or you'll be late.' Brenda watched her tall figure walk quickly down the road and waited until she turned the corner. She had the house to herself, thank God!

Slowly climbing the stairs, she opened the door to Tony's bedroom and sat for a moment on the yellow candlewick bedspread to get her breath back. Then, going over to the shabby chest of drawers, she took out a pack of cigarettes and a lighter, opened the window as wide as the hinge would allow, and settled herself on an old chair placed before it. Placing a cigarette between her lips, she lit up and inhaled deeply.

There was only one pack left, but it didn't matter. Tony would bring her some more tomorrow on his half-day. He said it was a perk of his job, they were old stock, but she didn't believe him for a minute. Still, if he wanted to treat her, she'd no objection. She'd never have been able to pull the wool over Rosemary's eyes otherwise – that girl was razor-sharp when it came to budgeting.

Tony had understood how important it was to her, right from that first day when he'd moved in and caught her smoking in the garden. No matter what the doctors said, there was no way she could give up, not after smoking for twenty-five years. Her nerves would never stand it. Such a help he'd been, listening with sympathy to her problems. It had surprised her really, how she'd found herself talking to him. It was the way he was – with his gentle questions he was so easy to confide in. He'd been very impressed to hear she owned this house outright. He'd looked at her with real respect; she'd liked that.

'You're a woman of property, Mrs L,' he said. 'You can make your own decisions about your life. Anyway, look at all the people who've never smoked in their lives, and then gone and died of bronchitis. The medical profession don't know everything.'

It was amazing how easy it had all been. Tony had worked it all out. She simply smoked in his bedroom. Rosemary never came in – she respected utterly Tony's insistence that his bedroom was sacrosanct. The evenings and weekends were the most dangerous – she really had to be on her guard then. Often she pretended to go to the toilet, only to nip in to Tony's room for a quick drag. She'd got around that one by saying her tablets made her constipated. She blamed those too for making her feel queasy, so that she had to have a constant supply of peppermints. Of course it was impossible to disguise that someone smoked in the house, but that was explained by Tony's few cigarettes, which as Rosemary had requested, he always smoked in his room.

The lad had been such a godsend. He'd thought of everything, even taking away her fag ends in an old sweet-tin to empty into a litter bin in the High Street.

All he asked in return was that she wouldn't interfere between himself and Rosemary.

'She's a lovely girl, Mrs L. I knew it the moment I saw her,' he said. 'I wouldn't take her away from you, not with a nice little house like this. We could all live together, nothing need change.'

After her initial panic, Brenda reasoned that she had to face facts. It was bound to come sooner or later, and better Tony than some stranger who might whisk her daughter miles away. He'd heeded her warning too. She wasn't born yesterday – she'd sussed his little game that

69

first time he'd taken Rosemary out. Well, he knew that any hanky-panky before the wedding, and she'd split on him, fags or no fags. Men! They were all the same.

Brenda stubbed out her cigarette and, flipping over the top of the pack, took out another. Her increasing shortage of breath and the way she struggled lately with the housework and cooking was a constant worry. But she couldn't give up, she just couldn't. At least if anything did happen to her, God forbid, this way she'd know her daughter was looked after. She glanced at her watch. Just time for another one and then she'd go and watch *Z Cars*. Perhaps she'd have a bath and an early night. She'd felt weary all day somehow, too tired even to feel resentment at being left on her own.

Rosemary and Tony descended the steps of the cinema and strolled hand in hand through the quiet, almost deserted streets of the small town. A few people, like themselves, stood staring into the illuminated windows of some of the shops, but most hurried on, anxious to get home. The evening was still warm although a light breeze arose as they paused before a jeweller's.

'Best time to shop,' Tony teased. 'Certainly the cheapest.'

Rosemary peered through the security grill.

'See anything you fancy as an engagement ring?' She didn't answer and he said plaintively, 'Why do you keep fobbing me off? Don't you love me?'

Rosemary quickly turned to him. 'Of course I

do, you know I do.'

'Then why don't you want to get engaged?' He put his arms around her and drew her to him. 'Shall I tell you what I want? I want us to get engaged on your birthday and then get married at Christmas.'

'Christmas!' Startled, Rosemary looked up at him, but he shushed her with his lips.

'Look,' his breath was warm on her cheek as he held her close. 'You're so sexy, do you know that? How long do you expect me to go on like this, you know, going so far and no further?'

'I ... don't know,' Rosemary said lamely.

'It's not good for a guy to be in a constant state of arousal and then, well, nothing. Trust me to choose a Catholic!'

Rosemary felt confused and guilty. Although the Church taught that sex outside marriage was a sin, no-one else in the world seemed to bother. The girls at work were all on the Pill and thought nothing of sleeping with their boyfriends. And look at all the pop stars and other famous people, the way they carried on. No-one seemed to think any the less of them. Tony had been really good about it too; he'd never put any pressure on her. It wasn't as though she didn't want to either. She was only too well aware that there had been times when only his control had stopped them. Mind you, it was a bit difficult with her mum always in the house. Honestly, the woman never went anywhere!

'What is it, Rosemary? Aren't you sure of your feelings? 'Cos if not, I'll shut up.'

'No, it's not that.'

'Well, tell me.'

'It's just that,' she hesitated, 'it's just that living at home for the rest of my life isn't how I'd seen my future. And don't ask me how I had seen it, because I don't know. I just don't want to stay at 14 Poplar Crescent all my life.'

'No-one's saying you've got to stay there forever,' he protested. 'Once I get to be manager, what with the money we'd get if we sold your house, we could move somewhere else, Westbourne for instance. You'd like to live near the sea, wouldn't you?'

'Oh, that would be fabulous. Tony, do you really think we could?' Suddenly Rosemary's mood changed. She'd been silly, worrying alone about all this. She might have known that Tony would understand.

'I don't see why not. Now, is there anything else?'

'Yes, there is.' She might as well get it all out in the open.

'Well, I'm listening.'

Rosemary took a deep breath. 'This might sound swollen-headed, Tony, but I've got brains and I want to use them. I was always top of my class at school, and if things had been different between Mum and Dad, then I'd have gone to University. If I get married now at eighteen, before I know where I am I'll be landed with babies, and that'll be the end of it.'

'You don't want kids, is that it?'

'No, of course I do. But oh, don't you see, not yet!'

He took her hand. 'Rosemary, there's no way

72

we could afford for you to get pregnant soon anyway. You'd have to go on the Pill. It'd be stupid not to.'

Rosemary bit her lip in confusion. From what she'd heard, the Pill didn't suit everyone. They didn't know yet about the side effects either. There were other methods though, all of them against the Church's teaching of course, apart from natural birth control. That might work, but the trouble was that by the time you found out it didn't, it was too late! Though as she saw it, if contraception was practised for the right reasons, especially within marriage, then she couldn't see anything wrong with it.

'Even if we did have kids,' Tony continued. 'Have you never thought about this new Open University? I think you can do that at any age.'

'You can, but it costs money.'

'So? If we're both working for a few years, we should be able to afford it. Anyway, how do you know we won't win the pools? Come on, Rosemary,' he coaxed. 'You can't plan your whole future, life isn't like that. You'll never do anything if you always think of the flip-side.'

Rosemary fell silent. Perhaps she'd misjudged him. After all, what he said made a lot of sense and it showed he did think seriously about things. She was being selfish, she could see that now. What did age matter? Lots of girls got married at eighteen. Tony was the best thing that had ever happened to her, and she was only too aware that she could easily lose him. She'd seen other girls attracted by his infectious smile and good looks – he wouldn't have to look far to replace her. Rosemary had a sudden vision of her life before they met, of the lack of physical warmth and affection, of her underlying loneliness.

'Okay then,' she said suddenly. 'You're on. We'll get engaged on my birthday and married at Christmas.'

Tony looked down at her with a satisfied smile. 'Whew, you certainly took some persuading.'

She snuggled up to him, oblivious of passers-by. 'Well, I'm worth it, aren't I?'

'I think so, thousands wouldn't.' He ruffled her hair. 'Come on, let's go and have a drink to celebrate, we'll just catch last orders.'

'But that'll make us really late getting home,' Rosemary objected. 'You know what Mum's like, she'll be watching the clock, working out what time the film finished.'

'For God's sake, Rosemary, you're nearly eighteen! She can't keep you tied to her apron strings all your life.'

Rosemary turned her head away. Did he think she didn't know that? But how could anyone else really understand her relationship with Brenda. Somehow she'd grown up feeling responsible for her mother, feeling that she needed to give her emotional support. In a way it was as though their roles were reversed. But Tony was right, she had to strike out for her independence, and perhaps now was the time.

'Okay then. But not the Dog and Gun.'

Brenda sat up in bed and glanced at her alarm clock. She'd come to bed early and nearly drifted

74

off to sleep. She mustn't do that, not until she knew Rosemary was home safely.

Too tired to read, she indulged in her favourite daydream, back to that triumphant day they'd first brought Rosemary home. She was a beautiful baby – how anyone could ever have given her up was beyond her. Nicely dressed though, in a flannelette nightgown, and handknitted matinee jacket. Brenda's lips curved in a tender smile as she remembered those perfect little toes in the lacy bootees. They'd had such hopes then, she and Keith. He with his good job, she with her new baby. Now look at Rosemary, thinking of getting married and yet still content to stay in her childhood home. She couldn't have done such a bad job. It was all down to her – Keith had never been a father to the girl. He'd even wanted to change her name, saying Rosemary was too posh; but she'd liked it – it was unusual.

She'd never regretted adopting, not for one minute. But oh, the shock when she'd seen Rosemary's name staring out at her from that advertisement in the paper, all those years ago. Never a newspaper had there been in the house from that day, not until Tony moved in and to her horror that first Sunday, bought a *News of the World*. But she needn't have worried, the notice wasn't in, and there had never been any sign of it since. No, she was safe now, no-one would ever take her daughter away.

I'll have to have a fag, she thought. Anything to keep me awake, and she padded wearily along to Tony's room to fetch a packet. It was breaking her rule to smoke in her own bedroom, but if she left the window open all night, she should be all right, just this once.

Life's strange, Brenda thought, as she settled back against the pillows and inhaled. I always dreaded the thought of Rosemary marrying, and yet look at me, planning how I'll give up my bedroom for them. Tony had better keep his promise, that's all, his vow that the three of them would live together.

She knew that Rosemary hadn't said 'yes' yet, but it was only a matter of time. He could charm the birds off the trees, that one. Oh, but she'd make a lovely bride, and Brenda determined to make sure she had the best wedding dress the Crescent had ever seen. She had the money, secretly hoarded in an empty chocolate box at the bottom of the wardrobe. It had always been for Rosemary, just a little bit at a time, squirrelled away. That daughter of hers could be too sensible for her own good, always thinking of security.

Fighting overwhelming fatigue, Brenda lit yet another cigarette. She'd just close her eyes for a minute – the film would have finished, so they couldn't be long now. She felt quite content with how things were going, and as her thoughts floated away, she dreamed that one day she might have a grandchild. It would be nice to have a baby in the house again...

Laughing together, Rosemary and Tony left the pub, and began the walk home, shivering slightly as the breeze quickened. She tossed back her long hair and smiled up at him.

'When can we get the ring, then?'

'I see, you only want me for my money, is that it?' he teased.

'Don't be daft...' she suddenly halted in mid-sentence. 'Tony, what's that? It looks like a fire!'

In the distance, they could see a black pall of smoke overhanging the rooftops, and a faint luminous orange glow in the sky.

'Can you see where it is?' she said anxiously.

'Not yet!' They quickened their step, trying to work out the location, and then as they turned the corner, the breath caught in Rosemary's throat.

'It's up near to...' she didn't finish the sentence, already her legs were moving of their own accord, as she began to run.

'Hold on, don't panic.' Tony caught her up. 'It could be any of the streets around there.' But Rosemary didn't listen – instinctive fear was already gnawing at her stomach. Please God, don't let it be our house, and please, Our Lady, she prayed frantically, wherever it is, don't let anyone be hurt.

As they drew nearer, they could smell the acrid smoke, and to her growing horror Rosemary could see that the fire was in Poplar Crescent. But oh, God, which side of the road?

She ran faster, her breath coming in hoarse gasps, and Tony sprinted behind her.

'It won't be, it can't be...' he shouted. She scarcely heard him, and then at last they reached the corner and ran into the grisly and harrowing scene which was to remain etched on her

77

memory forever.

Their vision was partially obscured by billowing smoke, but they could hear the devastating crackle and hiss of fire as crowds kept back by the Fire Brigade blocked their path.

'What number is it?' Rosemary screamed.

'14 ... hey, watch it!' A balding man moved resentfully to one side, as heedless of protests, they roughly forced their way to the front.

'Keep back there!' A burly fireman, his arms outstretched, barred their way.

'My mother!' Rosemary clutched at his arm and shouted in desperation, 'My mother was in there. Did you get her out?'

'That's your house?'

'Yes!' She struggled to get past him.

'Keep her back, can't you, son?'

But Tony didn't hear him. He stood ashen-faced, staring at the blackening shell of the house, as the firemen directed their hoses on the roof in an effort to control the raging blaze.

The fireman put his arm around Rosemary's shoulders. 'You say your mother was definitely in there?'

'Yes.' Her voice was a whisper. She looked up at him and saw the bleak answer in his eyes. Blue they were, she always remembered that. A startling blue in a smoke-blackened face, full of pity and compassion.

He shouted, 'Sir?'

A uniformed Fire Officer hurried over to them.

'This young lady says she lived there.' He lowered his voice. 'She says her mother was definitely in the house.'

The tall, grey-haired man nodded, and gently taking Rosemary's arm, drew her away from the crowd. 'I'm sorry, love. We did our best, but by the time we got here, it was too late to save anyone. It'd got a good hold by then, you see. It would have been quick, you know. People think the worst, but it's the smoke inhalation, it's deadly.'

He looked down at the slim girl beside him as, dazed with shock, she rubbed her smarting eyes, and sighed. 'Is there anyone with you? What about your father?'

She shook her head numbly. 'There's just my boyfriend.' She turned her head, her eyes searching for Tony in the crowd, desperate in her need for him. Where was he? Choking sobs rose in her throat. It couldn't be true, her mother couldn't be dead! Please God, don't let it be true, I can't have lost my mum, I can't! Her mother didn't deserve to die like this! Why should she die, she had everything to live for!

Tony was suddenly at her side. 'Do you know what happened, how it started?' he asked the Fire Officer.

'It's too early yet, but we'll let you know after we've done our investigations.' The Fire Officer touched his cap and hurried away as one of the firemen called to him.

Tony put his arm around her, his eyes bleak. 'Come on. There's nothing you can do here.'

Rosemary turned and stared at the crowd of onlookers. Suddenly, she hated them. Strangers morbidly gawping at the scene of her mother's death. What was it to do with them, the ghouls!

'Clear off,' she shouted. 'Clear off, the lot of you! The show's over, she's dead. Do you hear me, my mother's dead!' Her voice cracked as, on the verge of hysteria, she allowed Tony to lead her away from the tragic shell of the only home she'd ever known.

7

'14 Poplar Crescent hasn't been on Dave Thompson's round for the past two years, Miss Latham.' The manager of the insurance office was sympathetic but adamant.

Rosemary stared at him in bewilderment.

'But I don't understand,' she protested vehemently. 'I put the money out every week, I never missed. Are you saying there's no money at all, not even for a funeral?'

'I'm afraid not.'

Rosemary's eyes narrowed. Every Tuesday morning, she'd put out the weekly premiums on the sideboard ready for the insurance man to collect. Now she was being told that Brenda had no life assurance.

Seeing the suspicion in the blue eyes glaring at him, the manager pulled a grey folder towards him. 'I do assure you, Miss Latham, that this office is run on the most professional lines.' He opened the file. 'According to our records, there were three life policies taken out. One in the name of your father, Keith Latham, one in the name of your mother, Brenda Latham, and one in your own name.'

'Yes, that's right,' Rosemary said firmly.

'Well, I'm afraid your mother stopped paying the premiums on your father's policy in 1970. I believe he went to Australia?'

She nodded. She and Brenda had agreed to do that.

'The other two policies were allowed to lapse shortly afterwards, and any monies due were paid out.' He removed three forms and pushed them toward her. 'I think you will see everything is in order. That is your mother's signature?'

She scrutinised the handwriting, panic rising inside her. 'Yes,' she whispered.

His smooth pink cheeks creasing in concern, he leaned over the desk and placed one fat, pudgy hand over hers. 'I'm very sorry, my dear. It does seem that your mother used the money you say you allocated for the premiums for some other purpose. Perhaps she was saving for something?'

Conflicting emotions swept over her as she stared at him in shocked disbelief. Then, conscious of the dry, powdery touch of his skin, she removed her hand with distaste.

'I can expect nothing, then?'

'I'm afraid not.'

Rosemary rose shakily to her feet. She needed to get out of here, to try to absorb what was happening.

Humiliated, she muttered, 'Thank you,' then grabbed the handle of the door and flung it open, marching past the curious receptionist and out into the High Street. The bright sunshine seemed to mock her as, shocked and confused, she hurried straight to the coffee bar where she'd arranged to meet Tony.

The look of horror on his face was one she would never forget.

'But she told me...' he stopped.

'Told you what?'

'Oh, that first Tuesday morning I moved in. She was telling me what a good manager you were, showed me the money on the sideboard.' His voice began to rise. 'She even joked about it, said if it was left to you, she'd be worth more dead than alive! And all the time she was stashing it away behind your back!'

Rosemary flared with resentment. 'Don't talk about her like that!' She felt sick, things had been bad enough before, but now...

'I don't know what to do,' she said miserably. 'How can I afford a funeral? I've only got the gas-bill money. The funeral grant won't go anywhere.'

'You'll have to go down the Council and tell them what's happened,' Tony said coldly.

Rosemary could sense the anger emanating from him, and nervously put out a hand to cover his.

He gave no reaction, just sat staring into space, then suddenly hit his forehead.

'Oh, my God, what about the house insurance?'

She stared at him dully, still in shock, then as comprehension dawned, fear gnawed at her stomach.

'Did you pay it yourself?' he demanded.

She stammered, 'We paid that annually. I used

to put it in an old tea caddy, and then Mum would get a postal order and send it off, every October, I think it was.'

'Your mum used to pay it. I see.' His tone was sarcastic. 'And what about the renewal schedule, did you actually see it?'

'No,' she said slowly. 'Mum used to tell me it had come and she'd put it safely upstairs in her wardrobe. She used to have an old shoebox she kept all her papers in. You know, birth certificates, her marriage lines, the divorce papers...'

'All of which would have gone up in smoke!' He put his head in his hands. 'I don't believe it. I don't bloody well believe it!'

'Don't cross your bridges,' she snapped, struggling to control the panic rising within her. 'I've written to the insurance company, they should have their own copy of the policy. It doesn't go to say that because...' but she couldn't finish the sentence, couldn't face the enormity of its implications.

Tony's face was grey, and Rosemary looked at him with anguish. The last few days had been terrible for both of them.

'What was her life for?' she said brokenly. 'Married for twenty years, and we don't even know where Dad is to let him know she's died.'

Tony looked at her. 'Her life was you, you know that.'

She nodded, her throat too full to speak. Tears of desolation brimmed in her eyes, as she struggled to come to terms with her loss. Her mum was dead. She'd never see her again, never sense those possessive brown eyes watching her.

Even as a child she'd been conscious of her mother's constant surveillance, had been irritated and embarrassed by it. Now, she'd give anything to turn the corner to see her home with Brenda waiting inside with the kettle on. She just couldn't believe that life as she'd always known it had, in one short evening, changed forever.

'What do you think she wanted the money for?'

'We'll never know,' he said grimly. 'Not unless she opened a bank account somewhere.'

'Mum didn't believe in banks. God, how could she be so stupid!'

Rosemary lapsed into silence. She was seething with anger at her mother's deception, yet burning within her was a nagging sense of guilt. It was all her fault. She was the one who wanted to assert her independence by staying out late and going to the pub with Tony. If she'd gone straight home, she might have been able to get her mother out of the house, could have raised the alarm earlier.

According to the official report, the fire had started in her bedroom, most likely by a smouldering cigarette-end. The open window had fanned the blaze into an inferno, which when it spread downstairs had fed on the vinyl three-piece suite.

'Go up like torches, those things, and the fumes are deadly, it's the fillings in them,' a fireman had told Tony.

'But she hadn't smoked for months.' Rosemary had wailed. 'You know how I used to check up on her.'

Tony had remained silent.

'Oh, what's the use,' she said eventually, pushing aside her empty coffee cup. 'All the talking in the world won't bring her back.'

8

It wasn't a day of bright sunshine when Brenda was buried. It was grey and dismal. Rosemary's shoulders bowed in shame, and wearing a neighbour's old black coat, she walked slowly away from the travesty that had been her mother's funeral. A pauper's grave and she could count the number of mourners on one hand: herself and Tony, two women parishioners and neighbourly Mrs Jackson. Only five human beings in the world who cared enough to say a last farewell.

Father Kavanagh, the parish priest, touched her shoulder with compassion. 'She wasn't a woman for company, lass. I asked her more than once to join the Mother's Union or the Legion of Mary, but she wouldn't have any of it. Now, are you sure you're going to be all right?'

Rosemary nodded. 'Yes, thank you, Father. And will you thank everyone for the collection for me – they've all been so kind.'

'Aye, well, it's at times like this ... a sad business, a sad business indeed.'

He shook Tony's hand and stumped away, a short balding figure in his fluttering vestments, leaving them standing alone at the gates of the cemetery.

'Do you want to go into town for a bite to eat?' Tony asked.

She shook her head. 'No, you get back to work, you've had enough time off. I'll be okay. I'll go back to Lisa's and see if there's anything in the post from the insurance company.'

'They're taking their time,' he said bitterly.

Rosemary bit her lip. 'We're going to have to decide what we're going to do. I can't bunk down much longer in Lisa's room, it's not fair on her or her family. How long can you stay at Andy's?'

'Oh, he says there's no rush.'

'Well, I'll see you later, then.' Rosemary raised her face to his for a kiss, and then watched him walk away with his distinctive quick stride. Thank God she had Tony, although Lisa had been wonderful, a true friend. She'd never forget her family's immediate offer of a bed and their generous support in those devastating first days. But she was determined not to take advantage of their kindness. Now the funeral was at last over, she must find somewhere permanent to live.

She began to walk to the bus stop, intending to go straight to Lisa's, then suddenly changed her mind and, turning on her heel, walked rapidly in the direction of Poplar Crescent. She felt an overwhelming need to see her home again, to reassure herself of her identity, her roots. The searing knowledge that all her possessions and childhood treasures were charred to ashes was consuming her. Everything her parents had worked for had been in that house; it had been her security, her base. Now, she felt bewilderingly rootless, a piece of flotsam with nowhere and nothing to call her own. She was dependent on other people's charity for the very clothes she was wearing.

Rosemary turned the corner and walked slowly to where the remains of number 14 stood stark and isolated against a grey sky. Fortunately, the adjoining house had been empty, its 'For Sale' notice still leaning drunkenly against the gate. It had been smoke-damaged, but not structurally. Number 14, however, was a burnt-out shell.

She stood at the gate, gazing for a moment at the ruin that had been her home, and then walked slowly up the path, past her sparse patch of garden, its marigolds trampled roughly into the ground, and round to the back of the house. There, alone and unobserved for the first time since Brenda died, slumped against the smoke-blackened bricks, she allowed the tears she'd struggled so long to control, their release. Hot tears of anguish and grief, harsh tears of bitterness and loneliness, they poured unrestrained down her cheeks, as she sank desolately to the ground and buried her head in her arms.

'There's a letter for you!' Lisa's mother, her round features composed in what she considered a suitably sombre expression on the day of a funeral, came bustling forward as Rosemary entered the front door of the terraced house.

'Oh, thanks.' Removing the ill-fitting coat, Rosemary took the envelope, glanced at the postmark, and going into the untidy sitting-room sank into a shabby chintz armchair. At last, a reply from the insurance company. Nervously, she tore open the flap and extracted a single sheet of paper.

'Want a cuppa?' Lisa's mother popped her head around the door.

'Yes, please.' Rosemary answered automatically, her eyes swiftly scanning the few printed lines.

A few moments later, she raised her head and stared unseeingly into space. The letter simply stated that Policy PG144809 covering the buildings of 14 Poplar Crescent and its contents had been allowed to lapse in 1971. They apologised for the delay in writing; this was due to a recent move to new premises. It was with regret that they were unable to help her in this instance.

Rosemary clenched her hands to stop them trembling and fought nausea as she closed her eyes and leaned back against the soft cushions of the chair. For the sake of a weekly pittance, Brenda had left her homeless and destitute. Why? Why had she done it? Oh, you stupid, stupid woman! She banged her fist on the arm of the chair in frustration and anger, then got up and began to pace the room. She felt frightened, frightened of the future, scared too of Tony's reaction when he realised that what they had both dreaded had become a reality.

They met in the park, and sat on a bench in the cold and damp, the day a forerunner of the autumn soon to come.

Tony's face was expressionless as he read the letter. Silently he handed it back to Rosemary, only a whitening around his nostrils betraying anger.

'That's it then,' he said tonelessly.

'I'll never understand why she did it.' Emotionally drained, Rosemary turned to lean her head against his shoulder for comfort, but Tony didn't respond. He just stared bleakly ahead.

Eventually, she whispered, 'What are we going to do?'

'Do? We're doing nothing tonight.' He stood up and pulled her to her feet. 'Look, I'm bushed, and you look shattered.' Briefly, he gazed down into her anxious eyes, and then said, 'I'll walk you back to Lisa's. It's been a hell of a day, I think we should both get an early night, don't you?'

But exhausted though she was, sleep evaded Rosemary as she lay motionless in the narrow single bed, trying not to disturb the sleeping form of Lisa a few feet away.

In an effort to shut out the macabre image of her mother's body lying in the dark, cold earth, she tried to concentrate on the enormity of the financial problems facing her.

Outstanding bills for the replacement windows, for electricity, gas and rates, would all have to be settled – Brenda even owed money on her catalogue. But with what? She hadn't got any money! Oh, people had been so generous. Not only had there been a collection from church, but they'd had a whip-round at work. But she'd had to buy some cheap clothes and other essentials, so there wasn't much left. Frantically, she wondered whether the Health Department would give her a loan, but then dismissed the idea. It was public money, after all.

She wrestled with the problem and then it struck her. The land! Why hadn't she thought of it before. The house might be gutted, there might be no insurance money to rebuild it, but surely the land it stood on must be worth something?

'The land?' Tony stared at her, his forehead creased in a frown.

'Yes, the land? Don't you see, it must be worth something!' Rosemary clutched his arm as they walked slowly around the park, which was the only place they could meet in privacy without spending money. Unlike the previous day, the evening was warm, the air still and heavy. She drew Tony down to a nearby bench.

'I mean, I know there's debts,' she continued, youthful optimism surfacing, 'but surely there'll be something left to give us a start.'

'Debts.' Tony's voice was flat. 'What debts?'

Rosemary went through the list, finishing with a flourish. 'I've already got enough for the gas bill, so that's one less.'

Tony turned on her. 'You're a bloody idiot!'

Rosemary flinched as if she'd been hit.

'You're small-minded and stupid, do you know? "I've got enough for the gas bill, Tony,"' he mimicked. 'As for the land that pathetic house stood on, yes of course it's worth a bit. But don't you realise, you're going to have to pay back the council for the funeral out of that, not to mention all these other debts you say that stupid mother of yours left. And there's that shell of a house. It's unsafe and it'll cost a bomb to have it demolished. Who do you think is going to pay for that, eh? Well, I'll tell you, it'll come out of the money you get for the land. So, little Miss Hopeful, seeing as you don't earn enough yet to support yourself, there's going to be bugger all left after that lot!'

Rosemary's face whitened as his bullying tirade washed over her. 'Why are you being like this?'

'Like what?' His voice was like a whiplash.

'So ... so nasty! I thought...' Deeply shocked and close to tears, she stared at him in growing bewilderment.

'Well, you thought wrong. It's off, Rosemary. You can forget it all – the engagement, and certainly the wedding.'

Rosemary felt as though she'd been punched in the stomach. 'But why, Tony? What have I done?' Her voice rose in hysteria.

'You haven't got a clue, have you? You're so naïve, Rosemary. Do you really think I'd go ahead and marry some penniless, homeless eighteen-year-old? Get myself saddled with a mortgage at my age? No way! I saw enough of what crippling debts can do when I was a kid. Repossessed, my mum was, that's how I ended up in care.'

'What happened to her?'

'Last I heard, she was on the game,' he said with a shrug.

At Rosemary's sharp intake of breath, he sneered, 'Shocked you, did I? God, you've got a lot to learn about the world.'

Rosemary stared at him in shock and confusion. This cold, unpleasant young man bore no resemblance to the Tony she thought she knew.

'So you might as well face it,' he said brutally, 'It's finished between us. It was one thing to marry you and have a nice little home all paid for, not to mention your mother's so-called life insurance, but I'm not taking you on now!'

Stunned by his scathing words, Rosemary struggled to take in exactly what he was saying. Did he mean he only wanted her because of the prospect of security, was that it? But she and Brenda weren't even comfortably off. Then she realised that to someone from Tony's background, their modest home and prospects must have seemed a heaven-sent opportunity.

But despite all his cruel words, there was one question she had to ask, even though she despised herself for doing so. 'All those times you said you loved me, did you ever mean it?' She held her breath waiting for his reply. She couldn't bear the humiliation of that rejection also and, as hot tears stung her eyes, she brushed them roughly away with the back of her hand.

Tony turned and looked at the girl sitting beside him, slim and almost beautiful with that creamy skin with its dusting of freckles. He gazed speculatively into her wide-set blue eyes, brimming with tears and then said, 'Love's a funny word. You're a nice enough girl, Rosemary, a good looker as well. But let me tell you something, you're too serious by half. A bloke wants a girl with more spark to her, like Lisa for instance.'

'So what you're saying is that you never meant

any of it.' Rosemary's voice was hoarse with disbelief.

'Do I have to spell it out? As I've said, you're so bloody naïve. You should get about a bit more.' He looked down at her full breasts. 'With a figure like yours, you'll never have any difficulty with men fancying you. Words don't mean anything. A man doesn't have to love someone to want sex, but if that's what the girl wants to hear...' He shrugged.

With growing horror, Rosemary realised just how wrong she'd been about him. Thank God they'd never gone all the way. When she thought of how near she'd been to losing her virginity and perhaps even getting pregnant, to this – this creep! As Tony's scathing dismissal of their relationship finally penetrated, anger began to surface within her, bitter and sour. She'd only buried her mother the day before, yet he could do this to her. He, who more than anyone knew how devastated she was by the tragic events of the past weeks. Knew she hadn't anywhere to live, had no family to turn to.

Full of bitterness, she stood up and looked down at him with contempt. 'You bastard! I feel sorry for you, Tony Bartram. You'll never be a complete human being. Do you know why? Because there's something missing in you. You're flawed, do you know that?'

His face stony, he didn't even look at her.

Blindly, Rosemary turned and walked swiftly away along the tree-lined path and out through the park gates. Her bruised spirit longed for solitude and refuge and her steps led her like a homing pigeon to St Augustine's. There, in the cool, dim church, she sank on to a pew. She sat in the silence, and at last the tears came. So many tears she had shed in the last few days, and now they were tears of despair and utter hopelessness. Later, she got up and knelt before Our Lady's altar. She prayed for her mother, prayed for herself. For she had to face the stark reality that, on the eve of her eighteenth birthday, she was totally alone in the world.

9

'You're to stay until after Christmas, and I'll hear no more about it!' Lisa's mother was adamant.

'It's really kind of you, Mrs Bennion. Are you sure Tracey won't mind my taking her bed for so long?' Rosemary said anxiously. The offer was a godsend – at least it would give her a breathing-space until she got herself sorted out.

Dot bristled. 'All the same if she does. She can double up with our Sandra for that long. Young Debbie's managing all right on the camp bed. She's only little – they can sleep on a clothes-line at that age. But you see how it is love, I can't offer you a home permanently, we just don't have the room. When this next one comes, we'll be bursting at the seams.' She chuckled, her double chin wobbling with merriment. Nothing seemed to faze Dot Bennion, not even a late pregnancy, and Rosemary was fascinated by the way this jolly woman ran her home. Oh, you didn't have to look at the dust, and she could just imagine what Brenda would have said about the state of the bathroom! But Lisa's mother sailed through her chaotic days with earthy humour and a blithe disregard for anything more than token housework. And yet, the atmosphere in that untidy house was a much happier one than Rosemary had ever known.

Stirring another spoonful of sugar into her mug of coffee, Dot Bennion sighed. Trust their Lisa to land her in this pickle, as if she hadn't enough on her plate.

Jim was certainly not too pleased about it, saying it was one thing to offer the kid refuge when her home was burnt down, but another to land them with another mouth to feed for the next three months.

'There's enough women in this house already,' he grumbled. 'It'd better be a lad this time.'

He was a daft sod at times. But what else could she do? Of all the rotten hands, this girl had been dealt the worst. No family, no home, and now her boyfriend had not only let her down, but from what Lisa said, had kicked her in the teeth as well. Dot's eyes narrowed as she watched Rosemary sitting tensely at the drop-leaf red formica table wedged against the kitchen wall. She was an unusual girl – there was class there too.

'Are you sure you can't find out how to get in touch with your dad? I know Australia's a big place, but surely someone must know?'

Rosemary shook her head.

'When Mum died, I even went to the pub where he and that Shirl used to work, and asked there. Apparently, they told no-one. They wanted a fresh start, I suppose.'

Dot's lips pursed in contempt. Pure selfishness, that's what she called it. Who wouldn't at times like to take off, free as a bird, ditching all their responsibilities? God knows, at times she felt like it herself. But to leave your kid behind, with no way of getting in touch ... well, that was criminal.

'When is it you go back to work?'

'Tomorrow. I shan't be sorry, to tell you the truth. I'll pay you board, Mrs Bennion, and I'll do my own washing and everything. I could give you a hand if you like,' Rosemary hesitated, she'd better not mention cleaning in case she gave offence, 'with the ironing or something.'

Dot beamed. 'That would be great, I can't stand it myself. Now about your board ... you can pay me the same as Lisa, that'll cover your food. I don't suppose you've got any future plans yet?'

Rosemary shook her head. 'Not really. The only thing I have done is to enrol for evening classes three nights a week at the Tec. I can't go to day-release any more, 'cos I've had my two years. That's all you're allowed.'

Dot looked at her with interest. 'What are you studying then?'

'I'm doing shorthand, and "O" level English and Commerce.' Rosemary explained, 'I've got a lot of catching up to do as far as qualifications are concerned. I might as well spend my evenings doing that – I don't suppose I'll be doing anything more exciting!'

'You don't want to talk like that, an attractive girl like you. There's plenty of other fish in the sea, you know. You'll soon meet someone else,' Dot chided.

'No thanks!' Rosemary said shortly. 'I've had my fill of the male species.'

'Try telling that to our Lisa. It's a different boy every week with that girl.' Dot heaved herself up from the table and went over to the sink, filling it with water in readiness to peel potatoes. Rosemary got up to help her.

'Oh, you don't need to worry about Lisa, Mrs Bennion.'

'Thanks, love. It's nice to hear you say that. I've tried to bring my girls up to know what's what. They may not be brilliant at school, but they've plenty of common sense and that's what counts in the end.'

Rosemary paused, peeler in hand, as the statement struck home. Mrs Bennion was right, and perhaps if she'd had a bit more, she wouldn't have been taken in so easily by that rat Tony!

Looking back, the signs had been there. Subtle hints, if only she'd had the intelligence to notice them. For instance, offering to paint the outside of the house only a few weeks after he'd moved in. What single young man of his age could be bothered to do that, unless he had a vested interest? He must have planned it all, and how gullible she'd been! Hot shame swept over her as she realised he must have thought her a pushover. No wonder he'd called her naïve.

Well, now she was forewarned. She'd be on her

guard in future, not that she had any intention of getting involved with anyone else! She'd more important things to think of, like getting herself a better-paid job and somewhere to live.

But for the moment, Rosemary was still having difficulty coming to terms with her mother's death, and it was with a heavy heart that she plunged her hands into the cold water.

A couple of hours later, Lisa flung herself into the warm kitchen, her face flushed with urgency.

'Guess what!'

'Just a minute, girl, can't you see we're dishing up!' Dot bustled around the table, handing out plates of nourishing stew, while Rosemary placed a heaped dish of mashed potatoes in the middle of the table.

'Come and sit down, you're late.' Dot's voice was sharp. If there was one thing she couldn't stand, it was people being late for her meals.

Lisa sat down obediently and opened her mouth to speak.

'You heard your mother. Now get stuck in, your news will keep.' Jim Bennion liked his dinner in peace. He worked hard at his job as a welder in a local engineering firm and considered he deserved a bit of comfort when he got home. The trouble with women was they were always chattering – a man couldn't hear himself think.

Lisa let out an exasperated sigh, and rolled her eyes at Rosemary.

'Tell you later,' she mouthed, but it wasn't until the table was cleared and they were alone in the kitchen, that she actually spoke.

'It's Tony!' she announced dramatically. 'You

98

know Jack, in the stores at work? The one with the long hair – fancies himself?'

Rosemary nodded impatiently. Now what?

'His youngest girl, Jane, works at Hellman's supermarket. Apparently, Tony's been filching hundreds of cigarettes every week for months. They only found out 'cos he suddenly stopped about three weeks ago...' She put a hand to her lips, her eyes widening, 'I never thought, but that's when...'

'The house caught fire!' With a tea towel clutched in her hands, Rosemary leaned back against the cooker. 'What else did he say?'

Lisa chewed her lip. Surely her friend had suffered enough ... but then if she didn't tell her, she'd only hear it from somebody else.

She took a deep breath. 'I'm sorry, Rosemary, but it seems that as well as everything else, Tony was two-timing you.'

'What...?' God, how much more had she to take?

'Yeah, so he says, with Jane. Jack had the shock of his life when he found out. She works in the cigarette kiosk and was so infatuated with Tony she'd been turning a blind eye to his goings-on. The manager was already suspicious when he caught the pair of them snogging in the stockroom and faced them with it. Jane panicked and told him everything. Apparently, Tony had convinced her it wasn't really stealing, 'cos he was planning to pay it all back from some money he was expecting from an insurance policy.'

'An insurance policy?' Rosemary frowned. Tony was too young to have an insurance policy mature, surely? 'Lisa,' she said slowly, 'how long did you say he'd been stealing these cigarettes?'

'Since about March, I think.'

March. That was when he'd first come to live with them. When Brenda had been forced to give up smoking. Rosemary's thoughts raced ahead. Tony only smoked twenty a day, and he'd been cutting down on those. Brenda, on the other hand, had smoked sixty a day. But what if she had never really finished smoking? Suppose that cigarette she'd been smoking on the night of the fire hadn't been just an odd one, after all. Rosemary's throat tightened with horror, as her logic revealed with cold clarity how Tony had manipulated her mother for his own avaricious ends. She'd been the one he wanted the cigarettes for, knowing that in the end they'd kill her. He'd known she had chronic emphysema, had been after her life insurance.

Of course, he'd have had to marry her daughter to get it, and then with Brenda dead, he'd have been in clover. A house all paid for, a naïve wife, and plenty of money to spend. When she thought of what a fool she'd been... They'd both been lying to her, Tony and her mother.

'Hey, watch what you're doing with that, it'll be fit for nothing!' Coming into the kitchen, Dot glanced sharply at Rosemary.

Rosemary looked down and saw that in her distress she'd twisted the threadbare tea towel into a crumpled rag.

'Sorry,' she said, flushing.

'Debbie,' Dot said, turning to her youngest who'd followed her in. 'Go and play, there's a good girl.' She waited until the child had disappeared and then leaned against the sink, her arms akimbo. 'What's going on? Come on, out with it, Lisa. I can see by your face something's up.'

Lisa glanced at Rosemary, who nodded. Then she related her story again.

'Well, I'll be blowed! You picked a good 'un there, girl.' She looked sideways at Lisa. 'Didn't you pick up any wrong vibes about him?'

'Lisa never took to him, Mrs Bennion. She just didn't want to hurt my feelings,' Rosemary said.

'Perhaps you'll learn next time, Lisa,' Dot looked reprovingly at her daughter. 'Sometimes you have to speak out and shame the devil. It might have saved a lot of heartbreak.'

'Oh, you can't blame Lisa. I probably wouldn't have listened anyway. He was a right charmer, you know,' Rosemary protested.

'They're always the worst kind. Look at my Jim now – he's not much to look at and couldn't charm a rice pudding, but he's steady and he's dependable.' Dot picked up the kettle and went to the sink to fill it. 'That's what you want in a man, you two,' she said over her shoulder. 'Never mind the fancy manners and flowery words, they don't last!'

But Dot's homespun wisdom flowed over Rosemary's head, which was full of turmoil. What should she do? Should she say something? Voice her suspicion that Tony had tried to kill her mother by encouraging her to smoke herself to death? But then, what would be the point, she thought wretchedly. People would only say Mum had a free choice, he didn't force her to smoke the damn cigarettes. Had Brenda known they were stolen? No, never! It hurt though, that her mother had deceived her, lied to her, connived with Tony against her own daughter.

'Do you think he'll go to prison, Mum?' Lisa asked, as she filled the kettle and plugged it in.

'It's more than possible.'

'Good, I hope they throw the book at him.' Lisa caught her mother's eye and indicated Rosemary's pallor.

Dot reached up for her purse, which she kept on a high shelf in the kitchen. 'Nip round the off-licence and bring a miniature bottle of brandy.'

While Lisa grabbed her coat and hurried out, Rosemary buried her head in her hands. She was beyond tears. If this was what life was like, one blow after another, then she didn't know if she wanted any part of it.

'Chin up, love. It can only get better,' Dot murmured. 'Come on, I'll make a nice pot of tea and put you a good dose of brandy in it. You'll come through it all, you'll see.'

Rosemary raised her head and smiled bleakly. 'I've no other choice, have I?'

It was not until early in the New Year, when Brenda had been dead for four months, that young Debbie's childish questions roused Rosemary from her stony grief. Oh, she went to work, she studied hard at evening classes. She dutifully practised her shorthand every night, but inside she was frozen, distanced from the outside world and its inevitable problems.

'It's nature's way,' Dot explained to Lisa. 'She needs this time to recover from the shock of all that's happened.'

It took a seven-year-old child to pinpoint what everyone else had missed.

'Rosemary,' Debbie said, as they played Ludo quietly in the kitchen, while the others watched TV and indulged in beer, pop, crisps and popcorn.

'Yes, pet?'

'Where's your granny and grandad?'

Rosemary stared at her in surprise. 'I thought I told you – my mum was brought up in an orphanage.'

'I know,' the little flaxen-haired girl was thoughtful, 'but what about your other granny and grandad?'

Rosemary frowned. 'I don't know them. My dad had an argument with them before I was born.'

'You could go and find them,' Debbie pointed out, as she shook the dice. 'Just because they were cross with him, it doesn't mean they'd be cross with you. I bet they'd be really glad. My granny's always pleased to see me. She says I'm a poppet.'

'And so you are, Debbie,' Rosemary smiled. 'Ludo! There, that's one game each. Didn't you say you wanted to play snap with Tracey?'

'Ooh, yes!' Debbie raced off, yelling for her sister.

Distracted, Rosemary remained in her chair. She could hear the raucous laughter from the front room at *Are You Being Served*, but had no

103

desire to join the others. The recent Christmas in the Bennion household had been a revelation. The banter, the jollity, the squabbles and noise, it had been so different from the tense atmosphere at Poplar Crescent, and yet she'd felt so apart from it all. Oh, she knew it was too soon after the fire and her mother's death to expect to feel happy, but it hadn't been just that. It was the knowledge that this would be her life now, she would always be on the outside, no family, ultimately alone.

She stared unseeingly at the wall of the kitchen, facing her bleak future. Debbie's innocent words had pierced her self-imposed shell, and within her flickered a faint hope, perhaps even a sense of excitement. They might be unaware of her existence, they might not be interested, but she vowed that no matter how long it took, she would find her grandparents.

10

Lounging on her bed, Rosemary watched Lisa's attempts to paint her bitten fingernails with black nail varnish.

'Shit, I've smudged it!' She dabbed frantically with remover at the offending nail.

'What's all this in aid of?'

'I've got a date, haven't I?' Rummaging on the cluttered dressing-table, Lisa hastily re-applied another coat. 'There!' She tiptoed back to her rumpled bed and reclining against a propped pillow, held out her hands and fluttered her fingers. 'Mum would have a fit if she knew, but Kevin's taking me to see *The Exorcist* at the Odeon.' She slanted her eyes at Rosemary. 'You've been quiet at work today. What were you doing on the switchboard, going through the phone book?'

'Honestly, you can't do anything in that place without being spied on!' Seeing Lisa's eyes narrow at her sharp tone, Rosemary added, 'Sorry, it's just that...'

'What?' Lisa raised her finely plucked eyebrows.

'It was something your Debbie said. It set me thinking and, well, I've decided to try and find my grandparents on my dad's side.'

'You mean the ones you've never met?'

'Yes. It was only after Dad left that Mum told me they were still alive. So, Miss Noseyparker, all I was doing was checking how many Lathams there are in the telephone directory, just to see how common a name it is.'

Lisa grinned. 'Go on, then. How many were there?'

'Seven.'

'Hey, that's not too bad. It's not as though it was Smith or Jones.'

'It might as well be,' Rosemary complained. 'Dad came from London. Think about it, seven Lathams in a population of twenty thousand. How many do you think there are in a population of nearly seven million?'

'Don't ask me, I was hopeless at Maths.' Lisa grimaced. 'How do you know all these figures?'

'I had a look in the library when I went to change my books. Anyway, if you work it out as a percentage, it goes into thousands. I can't really believe that – I mean, some names are regional, aren't they? But there's probably hundreds,' she said glumly.

'Do you know which part of London?'

'I don't know anything, except that there was a huge row and Dad never spoke to them again. It all happened years ago, before he met my mother.'

Lisa blew on her nails and examined them. 'Must have been some row! So they don't even know you exist?'

'I can't see how they could.'

'I know, you could hire a private detective,' Lisa suggested.

'Oh yes, what with?' Rosemary retorted.

Pulling a face, Lisa swung her legs from the bed and, slipping off her skirt, changed it for a black leather one. 'How do I look?'

'Fantastic, as usual.' Rosemary watched with a pang of envy as Lisa dabbed Avon perfume behind her ears.

After Lisa left, Rosemary finished reading *Watership Down*, then reluctantly began to tidy her half of the messy room.

'Damn!' Her one bulging drawer jammed and, objecting to her giving it a yank, fell out spilling everything on the floor. Grabbing a small box before it rolled under the bed, she realised with a pang of guilt that she'd almost forgotten the rosary beads nestling inside. They'd been a present at her Confirmation. All the children had

106

been given them – mother of pearl for the girls, black ones for the boys.

Rosemary leaned back on her heels thoughtfully. Her parents were both cradle Catholics. When they'd first moved to Staniforth, they would have gone to Mass and introduced themselves. Father Kavanagh had been the Parish Priest for as long as she could remember. With a bit of luck he might remember their previous parish.

The following Saturday afternoon, Rosemary walked through the crowd of busy shoppers in the town centre, in keen anticipation of her appointment at the presbytery. She was almost an hour early, but that had been deliberate, for before she began this new phase in her life, there was something she'd been steeling herself to do.

As she approached the gates of the park, her steps faltered. Then taking a deep breath she walked slowly along the tree-lined path. It was the first time she'd returned to the park since the day after the funeral. Now the lake was a cold, grey expanse of water, so different from the summer months, when tiny children fed the ducks while small boys sailed their boats. She saw no-one.

Rosemary halted at the familiar seat, the one she and Tony had so often used after Brenda's death. She looked down at the green flaking paint, at the signs of rust on the supports. Such a pathetic little bench, and yet it had played such a vital part in her life.

Wrapping her second-hand coat around her, she sat down, her hands cold inside the thin woollen gloves, and closed her eyes. As she had planned, she played through her mind that ugly scene once again, analysing every cruel syllable Tony had spoken. Despite the chill wind, she remained lost in thought until, at last, she felt able to put the whole degrading and bitter experience behind her.

'Come in, come on in, child.' Father Kavanagh rubbed his hands together in welcome. 'You'll be wanting a cup of tea, now.' He shot a shrewd glance at Rosemary's cold, pale face and called, 'Mrs Hanrahan, would you be so good as to bring us tea in the study!

'Would you like a choccy biscuit? Only she makes an exception when I've got a visitor.' He looked at her hopefully.

Rosemary smiled, and suddenly felt more relaxed than she had for weeks. 'I'd love one, Father.'

'Sure, you're an angel!' He hurried away.

Rosemary took off her coat and, seating herself in a worn, brown-leather chair, looked around the room. A brown study, she thought, and then smiled at the pun. It was a square room, simply furnished with a well-worn brown and cream Axminster carpet, surrounded by brown linoleum. Bookshelves lined the walls, not all of them books on theology or Lives of the Saints, she noticed. There were quite a few detective novels, and several of the classics. A cosy log fire in a rather fine mahogany fireplace was surrounded by a well-polished old brass fender. A grand-father clock ticked quietly in one corner and Rosemary felt a sense of peace and security. It's so quiet, she thought, so tranquil, but then anywhere would be after the Bennion household.

'Right, refreshments will be along in a minute. Now then, Rosemary, how are you managing?'

Father Kavanagh's keen eyes noted both the intelligence and the shadows in the blue eyes which met his own, and sighed. The ways of the Lord were a mystery to him even yet.

'I'm fine, thank you, Father.'

'You're still living at your friend's?'

'Yes, but it was only until after Christmas. I've got to look for somewhere else now.'

He nodded. 'Would you like me to see if there's anyone in the parish who'd be willing to take you in?'

Rosemary winced. He made her sound like a bundle of dirty washing! The thought of being a lodger again in someone else's family didn't appeal one bit. The alternative would be to live with some kindly but pious widow. I'm young, she thought in panic. If I can't have a proper home then I want my independence, my freedom. The trouble was that every poky bed-sit she'd seen so far had been way above her tight budget.

'Thank you, Father. Could you give me a little time first, just to see if I can find anything myself?'

'Of course. Ah, here's the tea.'

His housekeeper carried in a tray and put it on a coffee table. Then before leaving, pointedly

109

turned it round so that the plate of chocolate-finger biscuits was furthest from the priest.

'Are you going to be mother, now?' said Father Kavanagh.

Rosemary offered him the plate of biscuits.

'She thinks I'm too fat,' he confided. 'Can you believe such a thing?'

She shook her head, smiling.

They drank their tea, chatted, and shared the biscuits, then the affable priest sat back in his chair.

'Well now, what exactly can I do for you?'

Rosemary explained, telling him of her hopes of finding her paternal grandparents and of her predicament.

'You see, Father, it'll be like looking for a needle in a haystack unless I can pinpoint which part of London they lived in before they moved here.'

He took off his rimless glasses and polished them, his forehead creasing in a frown. 'I can't help you, child. I know that for a fact, because you were my first baptism when I joined the parish.' He chuckled. 'I remember it well. A bit heavy with the holy water I was, and you squawking like a stuck pig, your mother glaring at me as though I was the devil incarnate!' He replaced his glasses and leaned forward. 'It would have been Father Egan before me, but he's long gone to join his Maker, God rest his soul.'

Disappointment hit Rosemary like a lead weight. She didn't even know her grandfather's initials. It would take months, even years to search, not to mention a fortune in phone calls.

She also had to face the fact that they might not still be alive – after all she had no way of knowing their age. There was no guarantee either that they even had a telephone.

Father Kavanagh watched the fleeting expressions on the young girl's face and racked his brains. There must be something he could do to help her.

'Look,' he said gently. 'Let's talk this through, step by step. If you were able to find the people you thought might be your grandparents, what were your plans?'

She looked at him and hesitated. 'I'd go and see them. After all, they could only shut the door in my face.'

'But Rosemary, put yourself in their place. A strange girl turns up on the doorstep and says she's their granddaughter. How do they know you're not one of these "con merchants". There's been a lot in the papers recently about people tricking their way into the homes of elderly people, only to rob them or worse. You do have your birth certificate?'

Rosemary shook her head, feeling confused. She'd been so obsessed with the idea of tracking down her grandparents, she'd never thought of it from their point of view.

'Everything went up in the fire.'

He gazed at her reflectively, then going over to the bookshelves, removed a thick reference book. Leafing through the pages, he scanned a few paragraphs and said, 'Ah, here it is. Yes, seeing you were born here, the local Registry Office is the place to go. You know where it is, in

111

Hamilton Street?'

'Yes.'

'There's a small fee to pay, but they should be able to provide you with your birth certificate without any problem. It might be an idea to request a copy of your parents' marriage certificate, as well. That will show your grandfather's name and profession. You've no idea where they were married, I suppose?'

As Rosemary shook her head, he raised his eyes to Heaven. It never ceased to amaze him how families could live together and yet never communicate. 'You'll need to know their full forenames then.'

Rosemary thought a moment, then admitted, 'I only knew them as Keith and Brenda, but I suppose they might have had other names.'

'In that case, I'd apply for the birth certificate first. Their full names will be on that. In the meantime, I'll ask around some of my older parishioners, see if they can remember anything.'

'Thank you, Father. I'm really grateful.' Rosemary stood up and picked up her coat.

'Not at all, child.'

She looked at him. 'I am eighteen, you know, Father.'

'Ah, you're all God's children to me. Go in peace now, and say a prayer for me.'

'I will.'

Buoyed with purpose, Rosemary began to walk briskly back to the Bennions. It was more than likely that Keith and Brenda had got married in London, and once she had her grandfather's initials, she could begin her search in earnest.

Lost in thought, she didn't notice a middle-aged man weaving along the pavement in her direction, until he barred her path.

'Don't I know you, darlin?'

She turned her head in distaste at his sour ale-filled breath, and tried to move past.

'I don't think so,' she said icily.

'Aw, come on. A tasty little bird like you wouldn't miss one little kiss!'

He leered at her and staggering moved closer, his beer belly hanging obscenely over his trousers.

Rosemary recoiled at his bloated face as he thrust it forward, his bulk blocking her attempts to dodge out of his way. Breathing heavily, he pushed her against a wall and with a quick movement pinned her arms against her sides.

Rosemary glanced around in panic. The street was deserted except for a lone mongrel busy relieving itself against the park gates.

He grinned in triumph, his bloodshot eyes mocking her, but Rosemary hadn't lived with Lisa for four months for nothing.

'Piss off, you pervert!' she spat, and brought up her knee sharply with all the strength she could muster.

Her attacker doubled up like a punctured balloon, and she shoved him off balance and ran, her breath coming in hoarse gasps of relief.

Slowing down, she looked fearfully over her shoulder and saw him sitting on the ground, knees under his chin like a child, as he rocked to and fro in agony. She hurried away from the scene with a shudder, anxious to be among people, to feel safe.

Although shaken by the unpleasant incident, it was with a sense of elation that she eventually turned into the main shopping area of the town. Not only did she have a plan and hope for the future, but she'd proved she could cope on her own, could handle herself in a crisis. It's just as well, she told herself, because there's no-one else to do it for you.

11

Standing in the doorway of the tiny bedsit, Rosemary concealed a shudder as she looked around the squalid room, at the sparse furnishings, worn linoleum and flaking brown paintwork. An ominous grey patch adorned one corner of the grimy ceiling, while the limp curtains at the small window defied any guess as to their original colour. A beaded curtain hung before a recess, which when examined revealed an ancient cooker, single sink unit, small water geyser and one wall cupboard.

'There's a lavatory you can share on the next landing. Baths are once a week on a strict rota, otherwise most tenants wash down in their kitchenettes to save queuing.' The landlady, a Mrs Forbes, rattled off her sales spiel in a lacklustre voice, then cast a curious glance at the young girl before her. She looked too respectable for this place.

'How many bedsits are there?' Rosemary asked.

'Eight. Mainly working men. I don't often get young women. I'll have to say this. If you take it I don't hold with any sort of carrying on. No,' she held up a hand, 'don't take offence and I admit you don't look the sort, but I want no trouble with either the police or the Social. You've got a job, I take it?'

'Of course. There are other women here, though?'

'There's a couple. They live together on the top floor.' Mrs Forbes rolled her eyes suggestively, but Rosemary didn't notice, she was too busy wrinkling her nose at the pervading stale odour.

'I'd expect four weeks' rent in advance. There's a meter in the corner for gas and electric. Take your time,' she said wearily.

Rosemary glanced at her, sensing her impatience. Mrs Forbes reminded her in a way of Brenda. A woman in her late forties, thin, with restless darting eyes and a sallow, lined complexion. I bet she smokes, she thought suddenly, and looking down saw the tell-tale nicotine stains on her fingers.

She bit her lip, trying to come to a decision. If she wanted to be independent, what other choice did she have? This room was the cheapest she'd found and it was already the middle of January. Although Lisa's parents hadn't said anything, she was well aware that she had outstayed her welcome, particularly where Jim Bennion was concerned.

'I'll take it. I'll pay you a deposit now, and the rest when I move in on Saturday.'

Mrs Forbes nodded in agreement. Jerking her head to indicate their business was finished, she ushered Rosemary out, locking the shabby door. She shuffled in her slippers down the narrow, oilcloth-covered stairs, while Rosemary followed, wondering just what she'd let herself in for.

It's only temporary, she promised herself, as she hurried along the mean street, taking care to give a line of overflowing dustbins a wide berth. A dustcart wound its way slowly along, as binmen emptied the bins' contents in its gaping maw.

She checked her watch. If she hurried, she'd have enough time to grab something to eat before the end of her lunch-hour. The nearest takeaway was in the High Street and, with a few minutes to spare, she paid for a corned beef and pickle cob, and turned to leave.

'Rosemary! Hi, how are you?'

Two girls of her own age faced her, fresh faces beaming above their striped university scarves.

'Sarah! Maria! Hi!' Rosemary's gaze swept enviously over their trendy clothes. 'It's ages since I've seen you.'

'Sorry about your mum and all that,' Maria said awkwardly. 'I meant to come round, but I didn't know where you were.' Her voice trailed off, and Rosemary forced a smile.

'That's okay. There's not much you can say, really. What are you two doing now, or need I ask?' She looked pointedly at their scarves.

Sarah laughed.

'We're both at Bristol. I'm reading History and Maria's doing English.' She hesitated. 'We always

116

thought you'd end up at either Oxford or Cambridge – it's a damn shame you had to leave early.'

Rosemary shrugged. 'Luck of the draw.'

'What are you doing now?'

'I work at the Public Health Department.'

'What, in the office?' asked Maria.

'Yes. It's not too bad, and I'm going to evening classes to try and get some qualifications.'

'Good for you!' Sarah smiled.

Rosemary said quickly, 'Sorry, I've got to rush, I'm due back at work.'

'We must get together sometime,' Maria called as they turned away.

'Great!' Rosemary knew it wouldn't happen, their lives had taken a different direction. Although she'd been friendly enough with the other girls at school, it had been difficult to sustain a close relationship with anyone, given her home circumstances. Lisa was the nearest she'd ever had to a 'best friend'. You're just jealous, Rosemary Latham, she thought as resignedly she pushed open the heavy doors into the Health Department. Jealous as hell, but there's nothing you can do about it. You haven't a hope in heaven of getting a university education.

'When are you going to the Registry Office?' Lisa asked that evening.

'Tomorrow lunchtime. They said about five days, so it should be ready.'

Despite the extra expense, she'd requested a full birth certificate hoping it would provide more of the information she so desperately needed.

117

'I'd come with you, but it's my day at the Tec.' Lisa yawned. 'God, I'm tired, I don't really feel like going out.'

'I don't know how you stand the pace,' Rosemary teased.

'Better than staying in like you, sobersides, practising your shorthand. And yes, before you ask, I'll test you on your short forms later. Was this a fab Christmas present or what?' She nodded toward her record player, where Pink Floyd's *Dark Side of the Moon* was playing.

'It's great!'

'Yeah.' Lisa drew up her knees and hugged them. 'I'll miss you, you know.'

'I should hope so.' Rosemary grinned at her. 'Still, I think your Mum and Dad will be glad to have the house to themselves again. I'm so grateful, Lisa, for all they've done.'

'Forget it, you'd do the same for me.'

Rosemary looked at her earnestly. 'Promise me that whatever happens in the future, if you ever need help, you'll get in touch. Promise me, Lisa.'

'Hey, okay! Don't get so heavy, babe.' Lisa threw her a cheeky grin. 'Seriously though, Rosie, isn't it time you started living again? Why don't you come down to the Palais on Saturday? You needn't worry about bumping into Tony, no-one's seen him for ages.'

'I wish you wouldn't call me that,' Rosemary said crossly. 'You know I hate it. The kids at infant school used to do it, only they made it "Nosy Rosie"!'

Lisa giggled. Rosemary did stand on her dignity somewhat. It was that funny upbringing,

118

stuck in the house all the time with only her mother for company.

'Anyway,' Rosemary said with embarrassment, 'I haven't got anything to wear. I've only got a couple of outfits suitable for work.'

'It's a pity you're not the same size as me. But I thought you'd had the money from the Council for the land, and you've been saving hard from your wages. You've hardly spent a penny on yourself.'

Rosemary looked down and began to fiddle with her nails. She hadn't told Lisa that she'd been back to 14 Poplar Crescent, nor of her grief and bitterness on seeing the demolished site of what had been her home. How could all three lives have been lived on such a tiny patch of earth? Three people with their ambitions, struggles and heartaches had lived within the shelter it provided. Yet all that remained was a forlorn patch of derelict land strewn with rubble and encroaching weeds.

She frowned. 'The money wasn't as much as I'd hoped. They deducted a lot for the demolition, and by the time all the debts were paid and Mum's funeral expenses, there was not a lot left.' She looked despairingly at Lisa. 'I don't think you understand. Once I'm living on my own, I've got to pay for everything. I've got to fork out a month's rent in advance, and that's only the beginning. There'll be bedding and towels to buy, and I don't expect there's much in the kitchen that I'll fancy using. The state of the kettle alone was enough to put me off – it was gross and I daren't even think who last slept on the mattress.'

'Can't you get any help with it all? Surely you're entitled to some handout from the Welfare State?'

'Why should they? I'm not a child, I'm in full employment and have been for three years. In any case, I don't want charity. It was bad enough after the fire, grateful though I was. No,' she lifted her chin, 'I'm strong and healthy, I'll manage.'

'There's a second-hand stall on the market, they might have something you can afford,' Lisa suggested.

'I know,' Rosemary said. 'Just let me get settled in first.'

'Are you still thinking of looking for another job?'

'I've got to. I need more cash, it's as simple as that.'

Lisa giggled. 'You could always go on the streets!'

'Oh yeah! You'd be better at it than me!'

'What, with my boobs!' Lisa looked disparagingly at her small bust. 'No chance, they'd fall for your cleavage every time – not that you ever show it off. Now if it was me...'

'It'd be plunging necklines down to your waist!' Rosemary laughed. 'No thanks, the only thing I'd catch is a cold! As for men, I'm not interested!'

Lisa looked at her shrewdly. 'It's only a matter of time, you know.'

'Perhaps,' Rosemary shrugged. 'You'd better get off. And Lisa...'

'What?' She swung her legs off the bed and wriggled into a pair of jeans.

'Watch out for yourself in that pub.'

'If you mean they pass pot around, so what? You can get it anywhere these days.'

Lisa's tone was flippant, but Rosemary detected a defensive note.

'You haven't!' She sat upright, staring at the younger girl with concern.

'A few times. Everyone smokes it. There's no danger, you know, it's not addictive.' She glanced sideways at Rosemary. 'You should try it – your problems wouldn't seem half so bad.'

'That's not the point!' Rosemary was becoming alarmed. 'Look, Lisa, people begin with cannabis then they progress to harder drugs. What if you get offered amphetamines or LSD? For God's sake, I thought you'd got more sense!'

Lisa pulled on a skimpy top. 'The trouble with you, Rosemary Latham, is that you're an old woman in a young girl's body. You don't know how to have fun. I'm going to make the most of my youth. I want to experience everything, not to go through life half-alive like most people. Anyway, how come you know so much about it?'

'I read, don't I? If you think it's nothing to be ashamed of, why have you kept so quiet about it?'

'You're not my keeper, you know! I don't have to tell you everything,' Lisa flared.

Rosemary flushed. 'No, of course you don't.' She hesitated and then said, 'Do your parents know?'

'Don't talk crap, they'd freak out!' Then, always quick to recover her good humour, Lisa grinned at Rosemary's worried expression. 'Calm down, I'm not stupid, you know.'

No, thought Rosemary, as she watched her leave. You're not stupid normally, but how about when your mind is altered by drugs? Not that she knew too much about them, but did Lisa really understand the risk she was taking?

The following day, Rosemary went to collect her birth certificate, and stood in a small queue before the glass-fronted enquiry desk at the Registry Office. It was situated in a municipal building at the far end of the town, and the precious minutes of her lunch-break were ticking away. There was an air of unhurried calm in the square room, and she idled away her time reading the various notices on the walls, with their racks of application forms for various official documents.

When her turn came, the middle-aged clerk glanced up and leaned forward. 'I wonder if you could step into that room for a moment, Miss Latham. Mr Cummins would like to have a word with you.' She picked up a telephone and indicated a door opposite.

Puzzled, Rosemary went inside and seated herself before a small table. The room was bare and chilly, suggesting it was not in continuous use and she glanced at her watch anxiously, hoping she wouldn't have to wait long.

She didn't. The door opened and a thin man with a grey moustache entered. He held out his hand.

'Miss Latham?'

She nodded.

'I'm Robert Cummins. There's nothing to

122

worry about, I assure you, but we've had a bit of trouble tracing your records. This means we can't supply you today with your birth certificate, but if you wish us to do so, we can conduct a General Search. There is an additional fee for this, I'm afraid,' he added. 'I've brought an Application Form with me if you decide to go ahead. You can apply by post, if you prefer.'

Rosemary felt bewildered. 'Does this often happen?'

'Oh, it's not unknown. Are you sure you gave the correct place of birth?'

She considered. Brenda had always told her she'd been born at home. She'd said she didn't trust hospitals not to get the babies mixed up. Could it be possible she'd meant a previous address? She knew her parents had only moved to Staniforth in that same year.

'I think so, but I suppose I could be mistaken.'

'Oh, that could explain it then,' he smiled reassuringly.

'I'll take the form with me, if that's all right?'

She held her hand out and, taking the form, put it in her bag. She didn't have enough money on her to pay an extra fee – she'd have to get a postal order tomorrow.

'How long will it take?' she asked.

'Oh, they'll try not to keep you waiting. The form will have to go to the Office for National Statistics in Southport, and they will mail your birth certificate directly to you.'

Rosemary thanked him and made her way thoughtfully back to work.

That evening, after savouring one of Mrs

Bennion's filling steak and kidney pies, she walked briskly through the town and out to St Augustine's church. Going round to the presbytery, she rang the bell.

Father Kavanagh answered the door himself, a small glass of whisky in his hand. 'Ah, you've caught me at it, Rosemary. Me secret's out at last!'

She laughed. 'Everyone knows you like a tipple, Father.'

'Sure, are ye telling me I'm the talk of the parish now?' he joked. 'Come along in and tell me what I can do for you.'

After they had settled in front of his log fire, she explained what had happened at the Registry Office and then said, 'I wondered if you could tell me the date of my baptism, so I could work out how old I was at the time.'

'I can tell you that off the top of my head. It was the first Sunday after I joined the parish, and that was on the 1st November.'

'So I'd be three months old,' Rosemary murmured. 'Then I suppose I could have been born elsewhere. That would explain why they couldn't find any record of me.'

Father Kavanagh regarded her, his expression impassive as he looked intently at the tall, slender young girl who sat gazing into his log fire. He thought of Keith Latham with his short stature, sandy hair and coarse, florid features. Remembering Brenda, with her narrow face, long nose and mousy hair, he mentally compared Rosemary's tall figure, her lustrous dark hair, fine bone structure and widely set blue eyes. She had a good brain too. Sister Marie, the headmistress at the school, had been devastated when the child had to leave without taking her exams. God forgive him for his lack of charity, but he'd never rated the Lathams highly in the intelligence stakes.

'Would you excuse me a moment? I'll just check on that date and make absolutely sure.'

He left the study and went into the small room he used as a parish office. Taking down a leather-bound book, he leafed through the pages and ran his finger down a column. No, there was nothing there to indicate that Rosemary wasn't the Lathams' natural child, and yet that could explain the problem at the Registry Office. Of course, if the adoptive parents had submitted a short birth certificate at the baptism, then no-one would have been the wiser. He sighed. Surely the child had suffered enough? This would be a sore blow to her. Please God he was mistaken and, as she believed, it was merely a case of a different district for the birth.

He returned to the study with a wide smile.

'No, that's absolutely right, so it's just a question of waiting now.'

'Thank you, Father. Oh, by the way, this is my new address. I'll be there from Saturday.'

After Rosemary had left, the priest unfolded the square of paper and, on scanning the address, sat down heavily in his leather armchair. 'Mother of God!' he exclaimed, and took a swallow of whisky. Independence was an admirable quality, but combine it with poverty and naïveté and you had a recipe for disaster. For sure, he'd include the girl in his prayers that night.

12

Rosemary dumped the large bin-liner in the middle of the floor and, breathless from the climb up two flights of stairs, turned to face Lisa's father. 'Thanks, Mr Bennion. I'm really grateful for the lift and everything.'

Jim Bennion put down the suitcase he was carrying and looked around the squalid room with its drab furnishings and cramped accommodation. Cheap, she'd said. Cheap and cheerless was nearer to the truth. You couldn't get much lower than this!

'Sorry Lisa couldn't come to give you a hand,' he said awkwardly, 'but with Dot having the 'flu, I need her to look after the kids.'

'Of course, I wouldn't expect anything else. I'll be okay. You'd better be off, or you'll miss the kick-off.'

Rosemary smiled at him, unaware of the attractive picture she made, her face flushed with exertion, her dark hair in disarray. She slipped off her coat, flinging it on to the sagging armchair, and rolled up her sleeves. 'See, I'm all ready to get started. I've enough soap and bleach in that bag to clean a battleship.'

Jim grinned and ran his hand through his hair. My, but she was a fetching piece! He was damn glad to get her out of the house, not that he could fault her, mind. She'd always kept herself covered up, even when going to the bathroom. Not like his own kids, who wandered around skimpily dressed, but then that was different. He averted his eyes from the swell of Rosemary's full breasts, remembering how the blokes at work had ribbed him from the start.

'A nubile young eighteen-year-old as a lodger? Come on, Jim, pull the other one,' they'd bantered. 'Don't tell us you're not getting a bit?'

But Jim prided himself on being a family man. He'd never do anything to hurt Dot. But a man could only stand so much, and what with her being pregnant and right off sex, Rosemary's constant presence was something he could do without.

Rosemary picked up the suitcase and, putting it on the dilapidated bed, turned round, her smile fading as in that one unguarded moment she saw the expression in Jim's eyes.

She flinched, shocked and embarrassed, and then, feeling flustered, ushered him to the door, gabbling, 'Thanks again for everything, Mr Bennion.'

'That's okay. And thanks again for Dot's flowers, she was thrilled to bits.'

Rosemary hustled him out of the bed-sit and locked the door. For a fleeting moment she wondered whether she'd imagined it. But her intuition told her otherwise. Lisa's dad fancied her! Oh, he'd always treated her well, if in an offhand way, but she'd always felt uneasy in his presence, and now she understood why. Some day she'd find a way of repaying Dot's kindness, but no matter how bad things got, she could never go back to live there.

Despondently, she gazed at the crumpled black bag and the small suitcase. The suitcase contained her meagre wardrobe. The plastic bag was filled with a stained flock pillow, a couple of threadbare sheets and pillowcases, a cheap towel and tea towel, and an old grey blanket, all donated by Lisa's mother.

Three hours later, she was still cleaning. Tackling the kitchen area first, she'd found the oven rancid, the cupboards and drawers stained with mould, while the sink defied description. She scraped and scoured, pouring bleach down the plug-hole, washing every inch of paintwork and disinfecting the floor. One glance inside the furred and rusting kettle deterred her from drinking any of the water, but she boiled it and scalded the few paltry items of crockery and cutlery.

At last, drying her reddened hands, Rosemary pushed back damp tendrils of hair from her forehead. She needed to go to the loo though she dreaded what she'd find up there. Clutching her door-key and a towel, she climbed the narrow stairs and found the lavatory next to a damp-smelling bathroom. Inwardly cringing, she wrinkled her nose and got out as quickly as possible. It's no worse than the public toilets in the market place she told herself, choosing to forget that she normally wouldn't go near them.

Hearing footsteps trudging toward her up the stairs, she waited on the landing. A grizzled head came into view as a workman wearing greasy overalls grunted with relief as he reached the top.

He glowered at her.

'Who the hell are you? Not another Nosey Parker from the Social, are yer, 'cos if you are I've only borrowed these togs. I've been helping a friend with his car, see.' He glared at her belligerently.

'No,' she said quickly. 'I'm nothing to do with the Social. I've just moved into number six.'

He peered at her with suspicion.

'Honestly, you can ask Mrs Forbes.'

With a scowl, he shoved her roughly out of the way and lurched into the lavatory.

At least the natives are friendly, she thought sarcastically, and hurried back to her room. She'd got more to worry about than morons.

What next? Food, of course. She was absolutely starving. Rosemary began to write a list. One electric kettle, one pint of milk which would have to be sterilised as there wasn't a fridge. Tea, sugar, bread and marg. She added honey, then crossed it out as too expensive. Eggs, baked beans, tinned soup, bacon, potatoes and cabbage. She'd have to get her own loo roll, the one upstairs was useless. Only buy bare necessities, she told herself firmly, there are sure to be expenses you haven't thought of.

There were. After two weeks of bleak hours spent in solitary silence, Rosemary delved into her savings. First, fed up with drawing on old scraps of paper, she bought a sketch pad. The creative urge was still strong within her, and sometimes she thought only that and her visits to the public library kept her sane. Then, torn between a television set, radio, or record player, she bought a small second-hand transistor radio. Televisions needed a licence, record players needed records, neither of which she could afford.

She missed the hurly-burly of family life in the Bennion household more than she'd ever thought possible, but despite Lisa's assurances that her mum would always find her a bed in an emergency, she knew there was no going back. She'd lost her bolt-hole.

It was a week later, when the pavements were grey with compacted snow, that Rosemary first saw the official envelope. It lay sideways in the normally empty cubbyhole allocated to number six. With a sense of excitement, she picked up the long envelope and hurried up the stairs.

But her steps slowed as she saw a man lurking outside her door. He was in his early thirties, unshaven and wearing a dirty pair of jeans and a black leather jacket.

'What do you want?' she said sharply. She cast an uneasy glance over her shoulder, but there was no-one in sight.

He leaned against the doorframe, his gaze sweeping insolently over her. 'You in 'ere, then?' He nodded toward the number of the door.

'Yes!'

'Bit of a come-down for a girl like you.' His tone was provocative and he grinned, displaying surprisingly white teeth.

'I don't see it's any of your business,' she snapped, while edging near to the door, key in hand.

'Hoity, toity!' He wagged a finger at her. 'That's

no way to speak to your next-door neighbour.'

'You mean you're in number seven?'

'Yeah! Could be quite cosy, couldn't it?' he leered, running his tongue suggestively over his lips. He moved a fraction toward her.

Rosemary felt a flicker of fear. Not another weirdo! Was she the only normal person in this place? No wonder it was so cheap. She'd never seen the women from the top floor, but as for the men, they gave her the creeps. After the first few days, she'd taken to wedging the armchair against her door at night, and even then she didn't feel safe.

'Don't flatter yourself!' she snapped.

Thrusting the key into the lock, she opened the door just wide enough to squeeze through, slipped inside and quickly slammed it. I can't stay here, she began to panic, I'll have to move and soon.

She flung her coat on to the bed, sat in the shabby armchair, and with eager anticipation slit open the envelope. This was the first step in her search. Only the hope of finding her grandparents had compensated for the dreary isolation of the past few weeks.

Rosemary unfolded the birth certificate, and glanced down at the handwritten entries. It was all there, her date of birth, her full name, Rosemary Elizabeth. Her father was stated as Keith Latham, sales representative of 14 Poplar Crescent, Elston, Staniforth, her mother as Brenda Latham of the same address. She frowned, puzzled. She had been born in Staniforth. So what had been the problem, why had it taken so long? Then for the first time she saw the printed heading. Certified Copy of Entry from Adopted Children's Register. Adopted Children's Register? What did they mean, Adopted Children's Register? Bewildered, she checked the handwritten entries to make sure there was no mistake. She read the heading again, reading the words slowly, her brain struggling to accept their meaning. Then she saw the official signature. Juvenile Court, Staniforth.

She was adopted! Brenda and Keith had adopted her as a baby ... that meant they weren't her real parents.

Rosemary put down the long, narrow piece of paper with a trembling hand, and leaned back in the chair. All those years and they'd never told her. Why? She thought of Keith Latham, that blustering, coarse man she'd been unable even to like, let alone love, no matter how much she'd tried. He hadn't loved her either, his final rejection had made that perfectly clear. And yet he'd fed, clothed and sheltered her for fourteen years, even though she wasn't his child. It was an aspect of his character which surprised her. He hadn't been a charitable man, either with his money or in his dealings with other people. It must have been Brenda whose longing for a family had prompted them to adopt a baby.

Rosemary thought with a pang of the difficult, possessive woman who'd brought her up, the woman she'd always thought of as her mother. Brenda had loved her. In the dismal atmosphere in which they'd lived, Brenda's love had been the only warmth. She hadn't been a demonstrative

132

woman, hugs and cuddles were rare, but Rosemary had always known that to her mother she had been the most important person in the world. Had that been the reason why Keith had looked elsewhere, she wondered. If so, that could explain his cold resentment of her, which as a young child had hurt so much. A cuckoo in the nest, Rosemary Latham, that's what you were, she told herself sadly.

Numbly, she got up and moved toward the kitchenette and, hardly aware of her actions, began to fill the kettle. Hot sweet tea, that was what she needed. Something to steady her, for she was beginning to feel a bit shaky. She managed to make the tea, but, as she lifted the teapot, her hand began to tremble so much it slipped and crashed on to the floor, breaking and spilling its hot contents. The minor accident was the final straw. Weak tears sprung to her eyes as she crouched to clear up the mess, and then she slumped against the wall. She couldn't be bothered. What did it matter? What were a few tea leaves when she'd just found out her whole life had been based on a lie? She closed her eyes, feeling unutterably weary, and then got up and made her way back to the armchair.

Picking up the birth certificate, she stared once again at the printed heading. Adopted. That meant that her real mother, the one who'd given birth to her, hadn't wanted her, had rejected her own baby and given it away to strangers. And what of her real father? Hadn't he cared either?

'I hate them!' she spat aloud the words, as hot tears of rejection began to flow down her cheeks.

133

'I hate them, whoever they are.'

She leaned miserably back in the threadbare chair. In the last five months, she had coped with her mother's death, with the loss of her home, with Tony's treachery. But never before had she felt such despair. The bald fact was that she belonged to no-one, for she also had to face the bitter truth that the grandparents she had intended to find weren't even related to her. Her search, the focal point of her dreams, would be pointless.

I suppose I was lucky, at least I had Brenda, she thought miserably. She was a mother to me, she was the one who looked after me when I was ill. She might have been possessive, but at least she had cared. Her real mother hadn't given a damn, had probably forgotten her very existence.

She brushed the tears from her face and glanced at her watch. It was almost nine o'clock, she'd sat here over two hours. If she didn't get a move on she'd miss her weekly turn on the bathroom rota. She could just about manage the rest of the time with a good wash, but she couldn't miss her weekly soak.

Then, going into the kitchenette, the smashed teapot lying in a mess on the floor, the brown trickles of tea down the front of the cupboards, brought Brenda's memory back so vividly, that once again she fought tears.

Struggling to control herself, Rosemary cleaned up, then collected her toilet bag and a clean pair of knickers. She'd have to get dressed again afterwards, but she couldn't risk walking around in a dressing-gown, not in this God-

134

forsaken place.

As she cleaned the bath with distaste after its previous occupant, Rosemary muttered defiantly, 'What the hell! So what if my mother didn't want me! What do I need other people for anyway? I'll manage, I have so far and I will in the future!'

But as she waited for the limited hot water to run, Rosemary knew that despite her brave words, her life had changed forever. She'd lost her roots, and she'd lost her identity. She didn't even know her real name.

For pity's sake, she thought despairingly, why did I have to find out?

13

'I don't know what you're so upset about,' Lisa said airily, as she turned the key in the door. She held it open for Rosemary to precede her into the hall. 'Just think, you could be the illegitimate child of royalty, or someone famous. You could even be related to a pop star!'

'You do talk rubbish sometimes, Lisa. How would you feel if your mother had given you away?'

'Don't think I'm not tempted sometimes, even now!' Dot Bennion appeared from the kitchen, her face wreathed in smiles. In her eighth month of pregnancy, she leaned awkwardly toward Rosemary and kissed her cheek. 'Good to see you again, love. You've left it far too long.'

Rosemary evaded her gaze. She'd waited until she was sure the football team Jim Bennion supported was playing at home before she visited.

'Make some tea, Lisa, while I have a chat with Rosemary.' Dot ushered Rosemary into the small sitting-room, and heaved her bulk on to a chair. Rosemary looked at the familiar clutter, contrasting its cosiness with her own bleak surroundings.

'Where are the kids?'

'They've gone to the pictures, thank God. Never mind them, how are you?'

'I'm okay.'

'I was sorry to hear your news, love. It must have been a terrible shock. You know, I think it's better to tell a child it's adopted, once it's old enough to understand. Mind you, there's plenty of people wouldn't agree with me.'

Rosemary looked at the woman to whom she owed so much, and swallowed a lump in her throat. 'What really hurts is that my real mother could give me away, as though I was a bit of cast-off clothing or something. She obviously didn't want me.'

'You were probably such an ugly baby, she couldn't stand the sight of you,' Lisa shouted from the kitchen.

'Oh, shut up, Lisa, it's no joke.' Dot reddened with annoyance. That girl was getting above herself, she took nothing seriously.

She looked at Rosemary's set face, read the misery in her eyes, and sighed. 'Look, love, you don't know what the circumstances were. People

136

do things for all sorts of reasons. I don't think any woman could give her baby away without a lot of heartache. You mustn't feel bitter. I thought your lot preached "judge not lest you be judged".'

'I didn't know you knew the Bible, Mum,' Lisa said, as she brought in a tray with tea and biscuits.

'There's a lot you don't know, young lady.'

'Perhaps she was raped. I wouldn't want to keep a child of someone who'd raped me!'

'Lisa!' Dot Bennion's face was thunderous. 'If you can't be a bit more sensitive, then clear off upstairs.'

'Sorry! I was only trying to help.'

'And it's helping, is it, to try and tell the girl her father could have been a rapist?'

Unperturbed, Lisa took a digestive biscuit and began to munch. 'The thing is,' she said, through the crumbs, 'Rosemary's been going round with a face like a funeral ever since she found out. All I'm trying to say is that perhaps her mother had a good reason, or thought she had. After all, we don't know what happened, do we?'

'Precisely, but that sort of talk doesn't help.' Dot offered Rosemary the biscuits and decided to change the subject. 'How have you settled in?'

'Oh, fine.'

'I've told you, Mum, it's the pits!' Lisa grimaced.

'It'll do for now,' Rosemary said hurriedly. 'I don't intend to stay there for very long. As soon as I get a better job, I'm moving.'

Dot nodded, thinking that once Rosemary left

Lisa should be promoted to receptionist. Perhaps a bit more responsibility would steady her down a bit.

Three months later, Rosemary was still living in the bed-sit. Despite all her searching, she could find nothing better for the rent she could afford. At times, she almost capitulated and appealed to Father Kavanagh to find her lodgings in the parish, but pride and a determination to keep her independence held her back.

An underlying bitterness about her adoption still lingered, despite acknowledging the truth in Dot's advice not to let it fester. Father Kavanagh had also talked to her, his compassion not preventing him from speaking sternly.

'Hatred is a terrible thing, Rosemary. You can't possibly hate someone you don't know. I'm surprised you can't find more charity. It's been a shock, I know, but at least you were adopted and not left in an orphanage all your life. You must practise forgiveness, child.'

Only then did Rosemary see the parallel between herself and Brenda. Now, when it was too late, she began to understand Brenda's brittle nature, her discontent, her restlessness. Had she gone though life resenting her unfortunate childhood? With sudden perception, Rosemary realised that she could develop those same traits if she continued indulging in self-pity.

She could never pinpoint exactly when the idea came to her. It lay quietly in her subconscious, emerging only after she'd finished taking her examinations. Perhaps it was that she was now devoid of a goal – perhaps her empty evenings and weekends left more time for reflection. But one Sunday morning at the end of June, waking to see the sun streaming through the tiny window, she knew with absolute certainty what she was going to do.

She was going to find her origins. She was going to seek out her natural mother, and through her, her natural father. She wanted – no, needed to know her true identity.

Although she realised there was the possibility that she was an orphan, logic convinced her that if this been the case, then Brenda would have told her. It would have been a bond between them, and Brenda would never have missed an opportunity to bind her daughter to her. In any case, there was only one way to find out.

'You do think I'm right, Father?'

The priest examined the birth certificate. 'Yes. The court's jurisdiction would only cover this diocese, that's true enough.'

'So, if you could let me have the names of all the Catholic orphanages and Mother and Baby Homes, then I could make some enquiries. Oh, and the address of the Catholic Children's Society as well.'

He looked at her with concern. 'Rosemary, you're looking for heartache. The authorities won't tell you anything – they're not allowed to by law.'

'Then it's a stupid law.' Rosemary's jaw set mutinously.

'It's to protect the adoptive parents.'

139

'Don't the children have any rights?'

'I'm afraid not,' he said sadly. 'I'm not saying I'm in full agreement with it – in fact there's talk it might change in the future. But as the law stands at the moment, that's the position.'

'So, who would know about me?'

He hesitated. 'I suppose the Court would, but sure they'd never tell you.'

'Is there any way you could find out? Just whether I was an orphan or not?' Rosemary wheedled.

Father Kavanagh looked at her thoughtfully. If that could be established, then the child would settle down and forget all this nonsense. Understandable though it might be, her obsession could have catastrophic effects. Who knew what scandal she might uncover, causing not only herself but others untold harm.

He said warily, 'I don't suppose there would be any harm in that. But don't be getting your hopes up now. I don't want to bring you more disappointment.'

'How long do you think it will take him?' Lisa was squatting on the floor in the bed-sit.

'He said to give him a fortnight,' Rosemary said, looking down at her red varnished toenails and wiggling them. 'I always think sandals look better if your toenails are painted.'

Lisa grinned. 'Glad you've actually got a pair. I was beginning to think you were going to wear those black things forever.'

Rosemary pulled a face at the shabby black court shoes she wore for work. 'I'm sick of the sight of them. It's a pity my feet are bigger than yours, or I could have had your cast-offs.'

Lisa looked at her curiously. 'What answer are you really hoping for?'

Rosemary frowned. 'I don't really know. I mean, if I am an orphan then at least I won't have to live with the fact that I wasn't wanted.' She paused, her expression bleak. 'That really hurts, you know.'

'And if you're not?'

Rosemary's face hardened with determination.

'Then I won't give up. Somehow I'll trace my mother. I'll want a few answers when I find her, as well.'

'You'll only get hurt,' Lisa warned.

'I'm hurt now, so what's the difference,' Rosemary shrugged.

'Anyway, have you finished tarting yourself up yet?' Lisa scrambled up and pulled down her black leather skirt. She looked critically at Rosemary's blue ethnic dress.

'I know you had to buy something you could wear for work as well, but couldn't you find anything sexier?'

'You're sexy enough for both of us. If that neckline was any lower you'd fall out!' Rosemary shook her head at the shocking-pink boob-tube.

'I wish I had more to fall out,' Lisa grumbled.

'Go on, you know you like people calling you "Twiggy".'

'I wish I had her money!'

Rosemary locked the door carefully behind them. Not even Lisa knew how she hated returning to the dimly lit rooming-house late at night. Her heart pounded as she scurried up the stairs to the dubious sanctuary of her room. Even after all these months, she still felt threatened, still placed the armchair behind the door. At least twice she'd seen the door-handle move after she'd gone to bed, and had lain there hardly daring to breathe with fear. But she'd determined she wasn't going to hide away in the evenings like a scared rabbit.

Much as she loved being part of the throng again at the Palais, Rosemary had another reason for going on Saturday nights. Worried about Lisa's casual approach to drugs, she could keep her eyes open, watch if anyone tried to supply her with purple hearts or worse. Her fear was that now Lisa had crossed that first barrier, she might be tempted to experiment further.

Later that night, Rosemary lay awake, unable to sleep. She'd had a great time, but her thoughts were of Lisa. Lisa, surrounded by a group of high-spirited lads, on a high, sparking and flirting, while joints were surreptitiously smoked. Lisa, glimpsed in a dark corner with a pasty-faced youth, their heads together, whispering. Lisa, with secretive eyes, avoiding Rosemary's searching look as she returned to their table. It was not until dawn that eventually sleep overcame her.

Two weeks later, Rosemary walked slowly to the presbytery, deep in thought. She'd just been for another interview for a secretarial job, only to find that the salary was scarcely more than her present one. It was the same story every time.

Her age was the barrier. No-one wanted to pay an eighteen-year-old the same salary as someone in their twenties. The injustice incensed her. They accepted she was capable of doing the same job, so why couldn't they pay her the same salary?

She squared her shoulders as the church came into view, and tried to calm her nerves. Despite her brave words to Lisa, she knew she'd be devastated to find that both her parents were dead. The news might take away her feeling of rejection, but it would mean the end of her dream. Only she knew how much she longed to find her natural family. It would have been different if Brenda was alive, she told herself. Even if I'd known I was adopted, she would always have been my mother. But, oh God, she prayed as she walked up the path, you took Brenda away from me, please let me at least find and meet my real mother or father. Let me belong to someone.

'Come along in now.' Father Kavanagh bustled forward and ushered Rosemary into his study.

She waited expectantly, her stomach fluttering with nerves. The priest filled the bowl of his pipe with tobacco from a small tin, and she watched with impatience and frustration while he applied a taper and sucked on the stem. Not until it was glowing to his satisfaction did he raise his eyes to meet hers.

'Well, Rosemary, you've led me a merry dance, I must say. Got my knuckles rapped too, in the process. The nuns don't take kindly to enquiries of this sort, you know.'

'Did you find anything out, Father?'

'Yes, I found out just as much as they were willing to tell me, and sure I'd rather get blood out of a stone.'

'And?' She could hardly breathe.

'Your mother was alive and well at the time you were adopted. That was a long time ago, of course, and only the good Lord knows what's happened to her since.'

Rosemary scarcely heard his last words. She wasn't an orphan! Okay, so her mother had given her away, but at least she was alive.'

'What about my father?'

Father Kavanagh shook his head at her question.

'I can only tell you the father wasn't named.' He held up a hand. 'Now, there's no use you quizzing me further, for I don't know any more. It's only because of the extenuating circumstances in your case that I was given this much information.'

But Rosemary persisted, 'If I wasn't an orphan, then I must have been adopted from a Mother and Baby Home.' She shot a quick glance at the priest and saw from his expression that she'd hit on the truth.

'Come on, Father,' she coaxed. 'Surely you can tell me which one. That's not against the law, is it? I can always go to every one in the diocese, but I don't want to make a nuisance of myself.' She added with a glint in her eye, 'Particularly after you've already made enquiries.'

Father Kavanagh stiffened. The last thing he wanted was complaints over his involvement with her case.

Seeing his annoyance, Rosemary bit her lip. 'Sorry, Father. I'm really grateful for all you've done. But surely you can see that I can't leave it there? I've got to try and trace her, and if it takes me months I'll explore every possible avenue.'

Father Kavanagh turned his head aside and continued smoking his pipe while he considered the problem. Had he the right to keep this information from her? In any case, she would find Sister Mary Ignatius a worthy adversary. He mentally shuddered at the memory of his own icy reception. Merciful heavens, the woman had made him feel more like a guilty schoolboy than a responsible parish priest. No, let her deal with Rosemary. It was out of his hands now.

'I'll tell you, but you'll be wasting your time,' he said with some misgivings. 'I did warn you about the law in these cases.'

Rosemary nodded. 'I know. But I've got to try.'

The priest wrote the name and address of the Home on a piece of paper, and as an afterthought included the telephone number and the name of Sister Mary Ignatius.

He watched Rosemary leave with a spring in her step, determination written in every movement, and shook his head. You just wait, child, he thought grimly. Sure, that woman will make mincemeat of you.

14

The following Saturday the nine-thirty train, crowded with holidaymakers, pulled in to Westbourne station. Rosemary alighted and followed the crowd along the platform and out into the glorious sunshine. She laughed at two small children stumbling along with their brightly coloured buckets and spades, remembering the Bank Holidays during her childhood, when Keith and Brenda would bring her to the beach. At least she and Brenda had played on the sands – Keith had spent most of his time in the nearest pub.

Seeing a long queue at the bus stop outside the station, she decided it would be quicker to walk to the seafront. She could find her directions from one of the maps she remembered being displayed on the promenade. As her appointment wasn't until eleven o'clock, she had plenty of time.

The tide was just coming in when eventually she reached the sea wall, and for a few moments she leaned against the railings watching the encroaching waves. She could taste the salt in the air, while the cries of the gulls echoed her own longings. There was such a happy holiday atmosphere, with a clear blue sky, and warm caressing sun. A perfect day, for at last she was on the brink of finding out who she really was. It wouldn't make sense to refuse to tell me, she told herself stubbornly.

But for all her bravado, it was with a distinct sense of nervousness that Rosemary walked up the long tree-lined drive to the Home. My mother walked up here, she thought. I wonder how old she was, what she was thinking? Had she decided even then to give up her baby? Rosemary had read somewhere that mothers in such circumstances fed and looked after their babies for the first six weeks. She could only imagine the horrific wrench it must be when their child was taken away from them. That's if, of course, the baby was loved or wanted in the first place, she thought bitterly.

The Home was a large, ugly Victorian redbrick building, with blank and secretive windows. The doorway was massive, framing double oak doors. There was an old iron bell-pull and, with a sense of foreboding, Rosemary clutched the cold ring-handle and tugged it. She looked round at the wide porch where she was standing. The red and black tiles were clean and polished, although several were sunken and cracked. The doors too, although badly in need of new varnish, were free of dust. Poor, but well cared for, she judged. In fact the Home was exactly as she'd imagined it to be. She flicked back her hair and lifted her chin with more confidence than she felt as the heavy door swung open.

A fresh-faced nun stood facing her.

'I have an appointment with Sister Mary Ignatius at eleven o'clock.'

'And your name is?'

'Rosemary Latham.'

The nun stood aside, and Rosemary stepped into a wide reception hall. It was cool and white, dominated at one end by a huge wooden crucifix.

'I won't keep you a moment.'

She bustled away and Rosemary watched her figure in its sombre black habit retreat down a long corridor. She looked down at her own cool floaty skirt, bare legs and sandals, wondering how anyone could bear to be confined in those heavy clothes and close-fitting wimples in this heat.

She waited, her apprehension heightened by the silence. A few minutes later the nun returned with a beaming smile.

'Sister will see you now.'

Rosemary followed her along the same narrow corridor, acutely conscious of the noise the soles of her sandals made on its polished floor. Everywhere was so quiet, she could only suppose the maternity wards were on the other side of the building. Her impression was one of coolness and order, as they passed two alcoves set in the wall displaying a statue of Our Lady and one of St Joseph, each adorned with a small bowl of roses. They paused outside an imposing door. The nun opened it and ushered Rosemary inside, closing the door behind her.

Sister Mary Ignatius sat behind a large, uncluttered desk before a square bay window. Her eyes like pebbles behind her thick, rimless glasses, she indicated with a hand that Rosemary should seat herself in the chair opposite.

Watching the young girl approach, her shrewd gaze summed up the blue ethnic dress, simple sandals and inexpensive handbag. None of that heavy eye make-up so many girls wore nowadays. But years of experience had taught her that appearances could be deceptive. Then her eyes met frank but anxious blue ones, and she sighed. She believed in eyes, truly they were the windows of the soul. What she saw in Rosemary's made what she had to do just so much harder.

She drummed her fingers on the file on her desk. It was all before her time, of course, but this case bothered her. When Father Kavanagh had explained the circumstances, she'd furnished him with the information that the girl had been born here, and her mother had been alive and well at the time of the adoption. Her intuition told her that he had hoped for different news.

She glanced up at Rosemary.

'You had a good journey?'

Rosemary was determined not to let herself be intimidated by the nun's curt attitude. 'Yes, thank you, Sister. And thank you for seeing me.'

The nun nodded. 'It is not my practice to refuse to see anyone. My role here is to help and advise wherever I can.'

She waited, her long, pale face expressionless.

Rosemary took a deep breath. 'I wondered, Sister, whether you could give me some information about my mother. I believe you've already spoken to Father Kavanagh about me.'

'That I have, and I also told him I could help no further.' Her tone was terse.

Rosemary leaned forward pleadingly. 'But, Sister, please help me. My adoptive mother died last year, and my adoptive father left us years ago.

149

He lives somewhere in Australia. So finding my real mother can't harm them.' She swallowed. 'I haven't anyone, no relatives at all. If I could just find my mother or my father...' She looked at the forbidding countenance of the nun, trying to communicate her distress. 'Even if they don't want to know me, there might be someone, grandparents, or brothers and sisters or even cousins. Can you imagine what it must be to go through life never belonging to anyone?'

'I am bound by the law not to divulge such information.'

The nun's expression was implacable, but Rosemary continued in desperation. 'I wouldn't tell anyone. I just want to know my real identity, and to find my mother. I'd be very discreet, and if she isn't interested, I'll accept it. But I've got to try. Did you know her, do you remember her?'

Sister Mary Ignatius shook her head. 'It was before my time.' She rose and walked to the window. Gazing into the garden, she watched several young girls hang terry-towelling nappies on clothes-lines, while others sat in the warm sunshine nursing their babies. She knew of her reputation, but her stern exterior was her only defence. Did people think she didn't suffer with the young mothers when they had to relinquish their babies? Did anyone understand the responsibility she felt when faced with the joy of adoptive parents receiving their longed-for child? She had to keep faith with them, just as she kept faith with the young mothers who came to her for help.

But this case posed a moral dilemma. Since

reading Rosemary's records her mind had been troubled. Knowing the contents of that file, now safely locked in her drawer, common sense dictated that she reveal the whereabouts of the girl's mother. Here was a situation where the girl's family were desperate to trace her. Did she have the right to keep them apart? Her predecessor, a woman of great integrity, had no doubts. Even when promised a large donation by the grandfather, she had refused to sacrifice her principles. And they were good people, for even after their disappointment, a donation had been received.

She had prayed upon the matter, but knew there was only one answer. Her vocation was to help these unfortunate young girls. The adoptive father was still alive. The law was clear, and any infringement of it, no matter how well intentioned, could put in jeopardy the valuable work they did here.

She turned. 'I can only repeat that the present law forbids me to reveal the information you seek. Many people involved with adoption feel that the law should be changed and are working toward that end. I can only advise you to be patient.'

She looked at Rosemary's crestfallen face, and fingered the heavy black rosary hanging from her belt.

'Would you excuse me a moment,' she said abruptly. 'I have something I must attend to.'

Angry and bitterly disappointed, Rosemary sat motionless as the nun's skirts swished past her. She heard the door close and like a magnet her

151

eyes were drawn to the file on the desk. The struggle with her conscience took only seconds and then she was on her feet, leaning over the desk and turning the green folder toward her.

She opened it. It contained one single sheet of paper headed *Admission Form*. Her heart hammering in her chest, she glanced over her shoulder in panic and then ran her eyes quickly down the page, each word searing itself on her memory. Then, at the bottom of the page, confirmation. Normal labour, no complications. Girl, name Rosemary Elizabeth, weight seven pounds. Date of birth, 3rd August, 1956. Every nerve attuned to sound, she heard footsteps approaching along the polished corridor and hurriedly replaced the file.

Rosemary struggled to remain calm as Sister Mary Ignatius rejoined her.

'I'm afraid I have a very busy schedule, so...'

'Of course.' Anxious to leave, Rosemary stood up and held out her hand.

'Thank you again, Sister.'

As Rosemary's slim figure departed, the nun looked down at the folder. With an inscrutable expression, she removed the single sheet of paper, unlocked the desk drawer, and replaced it carefully in the Sherwin file. The information the Admission Form contained was minimal, but in all conscience, she reflected, I can do no more.

15

Rosemary went out from the cool, dim interior of the Home into the midday sun and shielded her eyes. Pausing, she rummaged in her bag for her sunglasses and, with a spring in her step, began to walk triumphantly down the leafy drive.

She'd done it! She'd found out who she was. Her brain feverishly repeated the information she'd read on the top of the Admission Form.

Her mother's name was Elizabeth Sherwin. Elizabeth Mary Sherwin. Did that mean that her own name was really Rosemary Sherwin? She said it aloud, tasting the sound of it, relishing the words. Happily, she turned into the main road which led to the seafront, walking briskly despite the heat, as adrenalin surged through her.

Not only did she know her mother's name, she'd found a valuable clue! On the Admission Form, her mother's current address was given as The Presbytery, St Gregory's RC Church, Westbourne. But surely that was enough! The priest was bound to have kept records, and all she had to do was to persuade him to give her an address. Rosemary dismissed as irrelevant his possible refusal. She hadn't got this far to give up now. I'll find out somehow, she vowed, by fair means or foul. She grinned at the thought of herself as a cat burglar, dressed in black and crawling over the presbytery roof.

In buoyant spirits, she walked along the promenade scanning the cafés. She needed to get something to eat, but not at these prices. As the cafés gave way to elegant hotels, she decided to try one of the back streets and turned right to face the one person she'd hoped never to meet again.

He stared at her, she stared at him.

Tony was the first to speak.

'Rosemary! What are you doing here?'

She looked at him coolly. 'Having a day out, how about you?'

He hesitated. 'Oh, I'm meeting someone for lunch.'

Rosemary's gaze swept over his immaculate appearance, summing up his expensive trousers and trendy shirt. Doing quite well for himself was Tony, but on whose money?

'Three months in prison doesn't seem to have done you much harm,' she said.

His eyes narrowed. 'Come on, there's no need to drag that up. Okay, I made a mistake, but I paid for it.'

'No, Tony,' she said bitterly, 'my mother paid for it and not with a few months in jail – she paid with her life!'

'Hey, you can't blame me for that!' he protested.

'No?' she countered angrily. 'Maybe not for the fire, but I'm not the naïve girl I used to be. I've had to grow up and fast. I know what you were up to, and if the fire hadn't killed her, you'd planned that smoking would. So you see, Tony, indirectly I hold you responsible for her death.

154

How does it feel, knowing that someone thinks of you as a murderer?'

Tony's face paled, and then he mocked, 'Hell hath no fury, eh? You're just bitter because I jilted you.'

'Think what you like,' she snapped. 'You'll get yours someday. I only hope I'm around to see it happen!'

'I wouldn't hold your breath, sweetie!' He looked over her shoulder, the venom in his expression suddenly changing to one of smiling welcome. He began to move past her, and she turned to see him hurry toward a white Aston Martin as it drew slowly to the pavement before a glass-fronted luxury hotel.

Tony hurriedly opened the passenger door and helped a young girl to alight, bending to kiss her cheek. He gave a friendly wave to the silver-haired man at the wheel, and began to escort his companion up the steep steps to the hotel entrance. Rosemary watched him as he portrayed the very picture of charm and concern and felt a sour taste in her mouth. The bastard was nothing but a con merchant, only this time he was aiming for the jackpot. So, she wasn't the only one he'd hoodwinked. In a way, Rosemary found this a comfort, although reading the mouth-watering menu at the front of the hotel did little to curb her resentment. Whoever said crime didn't pay lived in a different world to hers!

For a few moments she hovered outside, unsure whether she should find some way of warning the young girl. But what could she say? Tony's prison sentence was his own business. He might already have spun her some tale about that, probably wrongful imprisonment or something. Her fears about Brenda? She had no proof and, as he said, her words could be interpreted as spite because he'd jilted her. No, much as she'd like to ruin his plans, there was nothing she could do.

Ten minutes later, she found a modest café and despite the heat ordered egg and chips, the cheapest meal on offer. As she sipped her earthenware mug of strong, hot tea, she was relieved to find that Tony's old attraction for her had vanished completely. Her overriding emotion was one of contempt. What a base, shallow character he was! She was well rid of him. Dismissing him from her mind, she concentrated on her plan of action.

The dour café proprietor gave her directions to St Gregory's church and, at two o'clock precisely, she approached the arched door and, turning the heavy handle, walked slowly up the deserted aisle. It was a small, modern church with oak rafters, the cream walls blending harmoniously with green carpeted altar steps. The stations of the cross adorning the walls were simple and plain in polished wood, while the church brasses gleamed with loving care.

Rosemary knelt at the end of a pew on the right-hand side for a few moments and then sat in the silence, deep in thought. She tried to imagine her mother, a young girl perhaps, like herself, sitting in this same pew, alone and fearful of the future. From the Admission Form she knew that Elizabeth Sherwin had been only seventeen when she gave birth to an illegitimate daughter. No father had been named, so he'd probably done a runner, Rosemary thought bitterly. Getting up, she placed a coin in the small black box before a statue of Our Lady, and lit a candle for Brenda before letting herself out into the bright sunshine.

The presbytery, a pre-war detached house with two large square bay windows, was next to the church. Several windows were open and she breathed a sigh of relief. That meant someone was at home. She pressed the bell. Footsteps sounded on the path at the side of the house and a woman came round the corner.

She was slim and in her late thirties, and was wearing a pair of gardening gloves.

'I wondered if it would be possible for me to see the parish priest?' Rosemary smiled hopefully.

The woman put her head to one side and wiped her forehead, leaving a grubby smudge.

'Well now, if you can see across the water, you can.' Her voice had the soft lilt of southern Ireland.

'Sorry?'

'Sure he's away visiting his folks. It'll be another two weeks before he's back.'

'Oh.' Rosemary's spirits plummeted. At that moment two weeks seemed like an eternity.

'Is there anything I can do to help?'

She hesitated. 'Are you the housekeeper?'

'Yes.' She smiled. 'Actually I'm also Father Burke's cousin from Cork. It's better when a young priest has a relative as a housekeeper, if you know what I mean. Saves gossip!'

'He hasn't been here long, then?' She'd been

157

hoping for an old priest, fond of reminiscing.

'About three years.' Seeing Rosemary's crestfallen expression, she offered, 'Would you be wanting a nice cold drink now? It's unbearably hot.'

Obediently, Rosemary followed her round to the small, neat back garden, where a table and two wooden chairs were set out in a shady spot. She looked up at the back of the house, wondering which of the bedrooms her mother had slept in, and then smiled her thanks as the housekeeper came out with two glasses of lemonade.

'Thank you. My name's Rosemary, by the way, Rosemary Latham.' She coloured and then said painfully, 'Although I've just found out it's actually Rosemary Sherwin.'

'I'm Maureen Donnelly, and sure there's been plenty of times I've wished I could change mine, what with six brothers back at home.' She gave a low infectious chuckle, then waited curiously.

Rosemary haltingly began to explain. 'I've recently found out I was adopted, and apparently my mother was staying here at St Gregory's until she went into the Mother and Baby Home. I'm trying to trace her.'

'When would that be now?'

'1956. I was born early in August. Do you know who the parish priest was before Father Burke?'

'Ah, that would be Father Cotton, but I did hear the poor man had a nervous breakdown. In any case,' she frowned, 'aren't details of adoption supposed to be confidential?'

'Yes, they are,' Rosemary admitted.

Maureen drained her glass. 'If you're hoping

that Father Burke will let you see any parish records, I can tell you now, he won't. I've never met a man more a stickler for the rules than that one.'

'I suppose,' Rosemary said diffidently, 'there's no chance...'

Maureen frowned. 'I couldn't in all conscience do such a thing – it would be a betrayal of trust. In any case, the records are kept in a safe and I haven't a key.'

'Oh.'

Seeing the stark disappointment in Rosemary's eyes, Maureen asked, 'Don't your adoptive parents mind you searching for your real mother?'

Rosemary told her how Keith had deserted them, and described what had happened to Brenda. Maureen, remembering her own warm, boisterous family, felt a rush of sympathy for the lonely dark-haired girl facing her.

'1956,' she said thoughtfully. 'Wait a minute, let me look something up.'

She came back a few minutes later, her expression eager. 'I suddenly remembered something. Father Cotton was here in 1956, but only as assistant to Father Murphy while he was ill. He didn't become Parish Priest until after Father Murphy died.'

'So it would have been Father Murphy then,' Rosemary said in disappointment. The whole thing was hopeless. She'd already looked in the local telephone directory, but there were no Sherwins listed in Westbourne. This had been her only chance.

Maureen held up a hand. 'Sshhh. Let me think.' Various expressions flitted across her face and then she clapped her hands.

'Mary Flanagan! Oh, what a shame you didn't come sooner!'

'Mary Flanagan?'

'She'd be the housekeeper at the time,' Maureen explained. 'I'm afraid she passed away a few weeks ago, God rest her soul. Sure wasn't she the most garrulous person you ever met, and that's saying something coming from an Irishwoman! Now, she spent her last years with her niece down in the town. She's a friendly soul and if Mary ever mentioned your mother, she'd be sure to tell you.' She leaned forward, lowering her voice, 'There'd be no need for you to go into details now, and don't let on why you need to know.'

'I won't,' Rosemary said quietly, and then added, 'I can't thank you enough.'

'You may have nothing to thank me for – it's only a shot in the dark,' Maureen warned. She got up. 'It must be God's own will you came today, for aren't I off tomorrow back home for me wedding?'

'Oh, congratulations!'

'Aye, well, with Seamus for a husband, I'll need all the good wishes I can get, but we've known each other since childhood and I have a yen to be cleaning me own home.' She went into the kitchen and returned with a scrap of paper. 'That's the address. Now, go back to the promenade, follow the directions to the town centre, and you'll find the road on the right.'

Rosemary held out her hand. 'Thank you again, and good luck with the wedding.'

Maureen watched her go, admiring her tall slender figure and then, looking down at her own dumpy frame, sighed. Still, the Lord had been good to her in other ways, and to be sure she didn't envy that lass one bit.

20 Silverdale Road was a tiny terraced house, its gleaming red door fronting the pavement of the short, slightly run-down street.

Rosemary raised the heavy black knocker and rapped twice. A few minutes later, the door was opened by a flustered-looking woman in her mid-fifties.

'Yes?'

'Mrs Egan?'

'Yes?'

Rosemary had rehearsed her story on the way.

'Maureen up at the Presbytery gave me your address. I'm trying to trace an old friend of my mother's, and she thought your aunt, Mary Flanagan, might have mentioned her. My name's Rosemary by the way, Rosemary Latham.'

'You'd better come in out of this heat. I'm at sixes and sevens, mind.' She ushered Rosemary into the parlour.

Rosemary gave a wry smile, as she saw the impeccably neat room with its rust moquette three-piece suite, Axminster carpet and goatskin hearthrug. By the pristine condition of the antimacassars, it was obvious the room was only used on special occasions.

Mrs Egan indicated that Rosemary should take

161

a seat, and then perched stiffly on one of the armchairs.

'What was her name, this friend of your mother's?'

'Elizabeth. Elizabeth Mary Sherwin. She stayed at the Presbytery once in 1956.'

Mrs Egan frowned. 'I didn't move here until 1964 after my husband died.' She tucked a few stray grey hairs into place. 'You say your mother's lost touch with her?'

'Yes, she moved to another part of the country – you know how these things happen.' Rosemary felt the heat rise in her cheeks. Would the other woman guess that she was lying?

But Mrs Egan had her eyes raised to the ceiling as she searched her memory. 'No, love. I can't say I remember Mary mentioning her. Mind you, if it was parish business then she wouldn't. For all she had a tongue on her, she could be as close as the grave at times.'

Rosemary tried not to let her feelings show, but seeing the stricken expression in her eyes, Mrs Egan pursed her lips. 'Let's see now. I've gone through most of her things – in fact only yesterday I burnt all her letters, and a bundle of old newspaper cuttings. You've never known such a body for hoarding. There's still an old shoebox in Mary's wardrobe though. Full of old cards, theatre programmes, train tickets, all sorts of rubbish. I was going to do that tomorrow. You could have a look through if you like – there might be something.'

'Oh, please, Mrs Egan. That's if you're sure Mary wouldn't mind?' Rosemary crossed her

162

fingers, a surge of hope flooding through her.

'Ah, she'll not be minding anything where she's gone. A good woman was my aunt, and one who'll have found peace with her Maker. Just you wait there and I'll fetch it. Now would you like a nice cup of tea?'

At Rosemary's acceptance, her homely face relaxed and she smiled, 'It's nice for me to have a bit of company. Mary was a great one for the crack, you know, and it's a poor soul who isn't missed.'

A few moments later she handed Rosemary a bulging shoebox, and after asking whether she took milk and sugar, went off to make the tea.

Rosemary began to sort through the faded pile of mementoes, taking out a pile of old birthday cards and postcards and placing them to one side. The rest were mainly old receipts, programmes, and cuttings of recipes, household hints and health remedies. Discarding these, she shoved everything back inside the box and began to concentrate on the cards.

She was peering at the scrawled signatures, trying to decipher the handwriting, when Mrs Egan came back with a tray, where the tea was already poured into two flowered and fluted cups.

'Have you found anything?'

'Not yet. There are so many!'

'Here, let me help.'

For several minutes they both worked their way through the pile, Mrs Egan exclaiming over familiar names, her eyes growing moist as some of the cards brought back memories.

'There's nothing here, love,' she said. 'How about you?'

'Not yet,' Rosemary murmured. Sipping her tea, she scanned the names on old postcards from Ireland, Blackpool, London, and most seaside resorts in England.

'Did she never throw anything away?' she asked, noticing one card was dated 1930.

'Not much.' Mrs Egan picked out a couple of old photographs and handed one to her.

'That's Mary with Father Murphy.'

She looked at the faded black and white image of an elderly priest standing next to a small woman with tightly permed grey hair, and then offered it back.

Mrs Egan waved her hand. 'Keep it if you like, I've got plenty of others.'

Without much hope, Rosemary picked up one of the few remaining cards. The handwriting was well-formed, the signature clear: *Beth*. She sighed and pushed it to one side. Then she stopped. That could be short for Elizabeth, surely? She picked up the card again, and read the message.

'I promised to send you a card from my home town. Well, here it is! Thank you again for all your help and support over the past weeks.

Love, Beth.'

Excitement already rising within her, Rosemary quickly turned over the card. The picture on the front showed a large bottle-kiln against a background of factories. At the bottom was written: *The Potteries, Stoke-on-Trent.*

'Have you found something?'

'I'm not sure.' She peered frantically at the indistinct postmark. Everything depended upon the date!

'Beth can be short for Elizabeth, can't it? If only I could read the date!'

Mrs Egan got up. 'Wait a minute.' Bustling away, she returned with a round magnifying glass.

With a fervent prayer in her heart, Rosemary pored over the postmark. Nervously trying to decipher the faded ink, she magnified the print until she could just make out the blurred date. Then she saw it. The postmark was dated the 2nd November, 1956. She'd been born on the 3rd August, so Beth would just have returned home after the adoption. There was absolutely no doubt in her mind that she was holding in her hand a postcard written by her natural mother.

Her hand began to tremble and she kept her head down to hide the vulnerable tears which threatened to overwhelm her. Tears of sadness, yes, for it was a strange feeling to read those words, to see that handwriting. But also tears of exhilaration and hope.

After a few moments, she put down the magnifying glass and said,

'It's signed Beth, and the date's about right. If you wouldn't mind my taking it?'

Mrs Egan glanced at the card and then handed it back. 'Not at all, it's no use to me.'

After impatiently scanning the few remaining cards, Rosemary finished her tea and put the postcard and photo safely in her handbag. She stood up, wanting to be on her way.

'Thank you so much. Let's hope it will be of some help.'

On an impulse she bent and kissed Mrs Egan's cheek, and she flushed with pleasure before ushering her out on to the pavement.

In a state of euphoria, Rosemary made her way back to the station.

It had been a hugely successful day. Not only had she found out her mother's name, but she also knew that she came from Stoke-on-Trent. Then, when she was sitting in the noisy, crowded railway carriage on her way back to Staniforth, the true significance struck her.

Her mother's name was Elizabeth Mary. Her own name was Rosemary Elizabeth. Now why would anyone name her baby after herself, unless she cared about her?

16

'Stoke-on-Trent?' Lisa queried. 'Never heard of it!'

'Come off it, Lisa, you must have heard of the Five Towns,' Rosemary protested.

'I never listened in geography,' Lisa grinned. 'I used to read comics behind my atlas.'

'Oh, you're hopeless!'

'What did he look like?' Lisa asked.

'Who?'

'Tony, dimwit! You know, when you bumped

into him yesterday.'

'Same as before,' Rosemary shrugged.

'Funny,' Lisa mused. 'You'd think prison would change someone.'

'Well, it hasn't changed him.' She looked searchingly at Lisa, frowning.

'What's wrong with your eyes?'

'Nothing, why?'

'They just look a bit red, that's all. You've been smoking pot, haven't you?'

'So, I had a quick puff in the park on the way here,' Lisa retorted. 'Don't try to run my life, Rosemary, I've told you before. If you're going to start lecturing me, I'm off!'

Grabbing her jacket, Lisa made for the door and, without a backward glance, kept to her word.

Wishing she'd kept her mouth shut, Rosemary collected their empty Coke cans and slung them into the rubbish bin.

'Well, well! Quite a cosy little pad you've got here.' The deep voice startled her and she swung round in alarm to see the man from next door.

'I can't remember inviting you in,' she said coldly. Damn Lisa. She mustn't have closed the door properly!

'Now that's not very neighbourly, is it?' He moved toward her, blocking her way.

Rosemary looked at his unkempt appearance and unshaven face with distaste, then saw his dilated pupils and felt a flicker of fear. This was just the sort of situation she'd striven to avoid.

'Come on, chick, you and I could do the business. I've got some smack if you like?' he

167

leered, and lunged at her, his hand groping for her breast.

Rosemary gave him a violent shove, twisted away and swiftly grabbed a knife from the kitchenette.

She thrust it in front of her. 'I'm warning you, come one inch nearer and I'll have you!'

He edged forward and she threatened him, baring her teeth.

'Aw what the hell, you're an ugly bitch anyway!' He spat on the floor, turned and slouched out of the door.

Rosemary rushed at it, slamming it shut, shot the bolt and dragged the armchair to wedge it under the door handle.

Only then did she allow her terror to surface and sat on the bed, shaking. Horrified, she stared at the steel blade of the knife lying where she had thrown it. Deep down, Rosemary knew that her instinct for self-preservation had been paramount, and she would have used it. What am I going to do, she thought wildly? It was only a matter of time before one of the drop-outs in this hell-hole caught her off guard. Now that the two women from the top flat had moved out, she was the only female in the building.

'You left the damn door open,' she accused Lisa the following day. 'I could have been raped, or worse. Or was he one of your junkie friends?'

Lisa flushed. 'Don't be stupid!'

'Yes, well, be more careful next time, or better still don't come round unless you're in full control of your wits!' Rosemary snapped, still shaken by the incident.

'Sorry.' Lisa looked sheepish and then said, 'What time is your check-up, only I'm covering you.'

'Two o'clock,' Rosemary said shortly.

The morning had been busy, giving her little time to concentrate on her personal problems, and in one way it was a relief to sit in the silence of the dentist's waiting-room. Rosemary tried to bring order into her chaotic and elated thoughts. Somehow, she had to find a way of tracing her mother, but that meant going up to Stoke-on-Trent. The journey would take half a day; anyway, she'd need far more time than that. But even if she managed the train fare, she couldn't afford to pay for anywhere to stay. There was just no answer to it.

Collecting a couple of magazines from a central mahogany table, she indulged in fantasy for the next fifteen minutes as she leafed enviously through *Country Life*. Then with a sigh, she turned to the other magazine and flicked it open. A few moments later, she raised her head, her eyes blazing with excitement. Why had she never seen this magazine before? A live-in job, that's what she needed. It was the perfect answer. Avidly, she began to read the advertisements.

Most were for nannies, au pairs, and mothers' helps. She frowned. Apart from living with Lisa's family, she'd had no experience with children at all. As for taking care of a baby, she'd never even changed a nappy! But there were some jobs advertised she could do. Being a companion and taking care of someone's home, for instance. Now if there was one in Stoke-on-Trent, that

169

would give her a base...

'Rosemary Latham?' The nurse's voice broke into her thoughts, and with a hasty glance at the magazine's title, Rosemary followed her into the surgery.

Twenty minutes later, she was in the nearest newsagent's, scanning the shelves.

'Can you find what you want?' A bored-looking assistant wandered over to help.

'I'm looking for *The Lady.*'

'You're a bit late for this week, love. Try next Wednesday,' she yawned.

The following week, in an agony of impatience, Rosemary hurried home with the magazine and scoured the advertisements. Just reading them gave her a fascinating glimpse into a privileged way of life she'd hardly known existed. The problem was that nearly all the jobs were based in London. It was the same the following week, and the week after that – hardly any jobs in the provinces.

No wonder they call Londoners soft, she thought. They seem to be the only ones who can afford domestic help.

Then, just when she was beginning to give up hope, she saw it. Not in Stoke-on-Trent – in North Staffordshire, but surely that was near enough.

"*Girl Friday wanted,*" ran the wording. "*Recent move to new country and new home equals chaos. Reliable help needed, to live in. Must like dogs. Ability to type essential.*" There was no name, just a telephone number.

It was perfect, tailor-made for her. As for

liking dogs, she'd only ever passed them in the street, but she could like anything, barring snakes, if it got her out of that bedsit and up to the Potteries.

'If you could possibly get your head out of that magazine for a moment?' The sharp voice made her jump guiltily.

'Sorry, Miss Pritchard.'

'Hmn. Well, if anyone wants me, I'll be back at four-thirty.'

Rosemary watched the erect figure depart and hastily rang through to Lisa.

'Can you cover for me?'

When a curious Lisa arrived, Rosemary hissed, 'There's a job in! I'm going to use the phone in old Pritchard's office.'

She got an outside line and, heart pounding, dialled the number given in the magazine.

'Sally Ann Ford.' The husky voice had an unmistakeable American drawl.

'You're advertising in *The Lady* for a Girl Friday,' Rosemary began.

'That's right, honey.'

Rosemary hesitated, 'Could you tell me, are you situated anywhere near Stoke-on-Trent?'

'I'm in Newcastle-under-Lyme, which to me is the same thing. But don't quote me to people hereabouts! You English sure are insular in your ways.'

Rosemary swallowed, her throat suddenly dry.

'I'd like to apply for the post.'

'And your name is...'

'Rosemary Latham.'

'Right, Rosemary, tell me about yourself.'

171

Rosemary listed her qualifications and experience. 'I may be young,' she added, 'but I'm independent and I've supported myself for the past year.'

'I see. And how soon would you be able to start?'

'I have to give one week's notice.'

'I'd need two references, Rosemary. Can you do that?'

'Would my parish priest and my employer do?'

Sally Ann chuckled. 'I would think so. Look, you're my first applicant, so I'd like to give it a bit longer. Why not ring me again tomorrow about three.'

'Thank you. And Mrs Ford—'

'Oh, I'm not married, honey. Call me Sally Ann, most everyone else does.'

'I'd just like to say that I'm really keen on this job,' Rosemary said desperately.

'I never knock enthusiasm. Bye for now.'

Rosemary put down the phone, surprised to find her palm wet with perspiration.

Lisa was incredulous. 'A complete stranger! You'd go all that way and live with someone you've never met? How do you know she's not an axe murderer?'

But Rosemary was in no mood for caution. This was her big chance. Who knew when another job in the Potteries might come up? After an agonising wait the following day, she managed to find an empty office and, promptly at three, made her phone call.

'Sally Ann Ford.'

'This is Rosemary Latham. You asked me to

172

ring at three o'clock?'

'Oh yes, Rosemary,' Sally Ann's voice was warm. 'The other applicants hadn't your typing qualifications, and what the hell, I liked the sound of your voice. So what I'm saying is, I'd like to offer you the job subject to certain conditions.'

Rosemary waited in suspense.

'I'm willing to take you on without interview to save time, but just in case we hate the sight of each other, it will be on a trial basis for one month. Now about your salary,' she named a sum which was slightly less than Rosemary's present wage, then added, 'Of course that's on top of your keep. Does that sound acceptable to you?'

Dizzy with relief, Rosemary forced herself to sound calm and level-headed. 'That sounds fine.'

'Great. Now give me the phone number of that priest of yours, and a number on which to reach you.'

By the time she replaced the receiver, Rosemary could hardly contain her exultation. It was fate, it had to be. That this particular job came up at this time had to be a good omen for the future.

Lisa was dumbstruck.

'You mean you're actually leaving, you're going up to this place?'

'I am. Oh, Lisa, isn't it wonderful!'

Rosemary, still on a high, was surprised to see Lisa blink away tears. 'Hey!'

'We'll lose touch, perhaps won't ever see each

other again,' Lisa wailed.

'No, Lisa, you're wrong.' Rosemary gave her a hug. 'I told you, I'll never forget how you and your family stood by me when I needed help. Anyway, I might be back sooner than you think.'

Lisa gave a weak smile. 'Maybe.'

'And don't forget – you made me a promise!'

'I haven't forgotten, and the same goes for you too.'

Her head full of plans, Rosemary found it almost impossible to get off to sleep that night. One more week and she would actually be in the Potteries. Then her search could really begin. She gazed again at the postcard, trying to analyse the personality behind the firm handwriting. Like a talisman, she tucked it beneath her pillow and closed her eyes. With such a crucial phase of her life before her, she needed to be strong and full of energy, for she had no illusions about the difficulties ahead.

17

A perspiring middle-aged woman heaved herself into the railway carriage at Euston and sat opposite Rosemary.

'What a crush! Going far, love?'

'Stoke-on-Trent.'

'I'm just going as far as Watford. I always go this time of year to visit my sister.' She took a flask and packet of sandwiches out of her shopping bag and began to unwrap them.

Looking politely away, Rosemary stared out of the window, thinking of the previous day when she'd gone round to the Bennions to say goodbye.

'There'll be no-one to keep an eye on our Lisa, when you've gone,' Dot had complained.

Rosemary looked at Dot's kind, homely face, wondering whether she should confide her fears to her.

'Did you want to say something, love?'

'Just that, will you promise you'll let me know if...' she hesitated.

'If what?' Dot glanced at her sharply.

'Oh,' Rosemary muttered, 'you know, if there's anything I can help with.' She leaned forward and kissed Dot's cheek. 'Thanks again for storing my box up in your loft.'

'Come and see your Auntie Rosemary.' Jim Bennion, his face wreathed in smiles came in, carrying his long-awaited baby son.

'Hello, Kevin!' Rosemary held out her arms and cuddled the warm little body.

'Never thought I'd see it happen,' Jim said proudly. 'It must be my reward for putting up with all these women for so long.' Rosemary laughed. She watched Jim place an affectionate arm around Dot's shoulders, and wondered whether her intuition had been wrong on the day she'd moved out. Perhaps it had all been in her imagination. In any case, the family were obviously happy and thrilled to bits with their new addition.

Oblivious to the crowded carriage, her fellow passenger suddenly let out a noisy belch. 'That's better. Always feed the inner man, or woman in this case,' she chortled. She screwed up the greaseproof paper and bundled it into her bag.

'Tickets, please.' The collector stood at the door of the carriage.

Rosemary fumbled in her purse, hoping her new employer was true to her word and would refund the cost.

According to Father Kavanagh, Sally Ann was on a cultural exchange with an English professor at Keele University.

'She said she found it a hoot to be grilled by a Roman priest,' he chuckled, when Rosemary went to see him. 'But why Stoke-on-Trent?'

'I went to see Sister Ignatius.'

'And?'

'I managed to see my mother's Admission Form.'

He looked at her suspiciously, then his lips twitched as Rosemary flushed and avoided his gaze. So, the old dragon had a heart after all.

'All right, you don't need to tell me any more,' he said. 'And do you know your real name?'

Rosemary nodded. 'It's Sherwin. Rosemary Elizabeth Sherwin.'

'So, isn't it a blessing that you still carry the name your mother gave you,' he said softly. 'God go with you, child, and I wish you the best of luck.'

I'll miss him, Rosemary thought, he's been a good friend to me.

176

As the train drew into Watford Junction, the friendly Londoner said goodbye and struggled with her bags out into the corridor. Glad of the extra space, Rosemary stretched her legs, and discreetly eased off her shoes.

'Excuse me.'

She hurriedly scrabbled her feet around. 'Sorry.'

Legs even longer than hers preceded their owner's athletic body into the vacant seat opposite.

Embarrassed, Rosemary leaned forward, 'My shoe...' she pointed to the floor where her left shoe lurked behind his foot.

'Oh!' He bent down, picked it up and silently passed it to her.

'Thanks.' She flushed, conscious of the worn leather and scuffed heels.

He gave a slight smile, and retrieved a paperback from his briefcase.

Covertly, Rosemary watched him. In his late twenties, he was immaculately dressed in a blue pin-stripe suit, crisp white shirt and blue silk tie. With a long, angular face, he was undeniably good-looking. Dark hair flopped on to his forehead and he lifted a hand absently to brush it away.

Suddenly, he looked up and she found herself staring into green eyes which held more than a hint of amusement. Mortified, she realised he'd been aware of her scrutiny all along.

She looked away quickly, and stared out of the window. Then, a few minutes later, stole another glance. He was immersed in his book, and she craned her neck to read the title. It was *The Day*

177

of the Jackal.

Again, he glanced up.

She smiled at him, nodding at the book. 'Good, isn't it?'

'You've read it?' He looked surprised.

'Yes, last year.'

'I wouldn't have thought it would appeal to a girl,' he said, raising his eyebrows.

'Why not?'

He lowered his voice, 'Sorry, do I sound like a male chauvinist?'

'I'll forgive you,' she smiled.

He smiled back, then continued reading, while she watched the passing scenery. Rosemary was surprised to see how rural it was. The word 'Midlands' had always conjured up images of industrial towns, grime and smoke. Yet here were green meadows, streams, horses and cattle grazing. It just showed how ignorant she was, after all – the furthest she'd ever travelled was to Westbourne, twenty miles from home.

She glanced again at the young man opposite. He was so lucky, she thought enviously, to be able to buy books, even paperbacks. She should have splashed out and bought a magazine, anything to stop the thoughts from whirling round in her mind.

One possibility she had to face was that her mother could have moved to another area, leaving no forwarding address. She could have married, built a new life, in which Rosemary's unexpected appearance would be merely an unwelcome embarrassment. Sick to the stomach at the thought of rejection, Rosemary knew that only one option was worse. Her mother could be dead. The thought lay like a stone within her. For over the past months her life had been fuelled by her search. Without that beacon of hope, the future stretched bleakly before her. Eventually, she leaned back and closed her eyes in an effort to switch off. It had been a long day, the bustle of the unfamiliar Underground had been exhausting, and she stifled a yawn as she began to doze.

'We are approaching Stoke-on-Trent,' the loudspeaker crackled.

With a start, Rosemary blinked, grabbed her handbag and stood up to reach for the overhead rack.

'Here, let me help.' She stood aside gratefully, as her travelling companion hauled down her shabby suitcase.

'I wonder...' a gentle voice murmured, and he turned as one of the two nuns in the carriage pointed up at her luggage behind him.

'Of course,' he said and lifted down her case, only to see the other nun nodding and smiling at him with a similar request.

The train halted, and Rosemary fumbled awkwardly with the window. Opening the door, she cast a regretful backward glance as she carefully negotiated the high step and stepped down on to the platform. The station was busy and she was jostled by other passengers leaving, preventing her from catching his eye.

She wondered idly where he was going. Crewe perhaps? Or was he changing there for somewhere else. Ah well, she sighed with regret, she'd never know.

Simon Oldham, briefcase in hand, tried desperately to ease his way past the two nuns, but, with black habits flapping, they dithered so much about disembarking he relieved them of their cases yet again. Once on the platform, their effusive thanks meant that precious minutes were wasted. Wasted because he was cursing himself for his slowness. What a peach of a girl! Her face as she'd slept had been so beautiful and yet with a vulnerability which he'd found oddly moving. He'd assumed she was travelling further, and reluctantly resigned himself to the inevitable. If his interview at the North Staffordshire Royal Infirmary was successful, as a Registrar he'd have no time for making long journeys. But if she was local...

He quickened his stride through the exit tunnel under the railway lines until he reached the main entrance of the station. Anxiously, he scanned the crowds. There was no sign of her.

Simon gave a resigned shrug as he joined a queue at the taxi rank. Perhaps it was just as well. In any case, he might not be appointed, and if he was, the last thing he needed was any form of romantic entanglement. It was only by being single-minded about medicine that he'd come so far so soon. It was a pity though, he thought with a tinge of regret. He had an uncomfortable feeling that this particular girl wouldn't be so easy to forget.

18

First in the taxi queue, Rosemary handed the driver the address, as Sally Ann had instructed, and clambered in after her suitcase. As they waited for an opening in the traffic, she peered eagerly out of the window, anxious for her first sight of her mother's home town. Opposite stood an imposing building, The North Stafford Hotel, and she could just make out that the large statue before it was of Josiah Wedgwood. Then they were travelling along a busy road, turning left under a railway bridge, and right up a steep hill.

She leaned forward to speak to the driver.

'If this is Stoke, are the other four towns close?' she asked him.

'Five.'

'Sorry?'

'Five other towns. You've forgotten Fenton.'

'But...'

'Arnold Bennett missed it out, didn't he? There's six towns. Longton, Fenton, Stoke, Hanley, Burslem and Tunstall.'

'Oh.' Rosemary paused. 'But Newcastle-under-Lyme is near to them?'

'Newcastle,' he corrected her. 'It's the borough of Newcastle. Nobody gives it the full title, not round here. No, it's just up this hill.'

Rosemary peered out of the window as they

passed a church and school on the right, and the sign to a hospital on the left. Her spirits rose as they drove up a wide tree-lined road into the town centre. Why, it's full of character, she thought in surprise, as she glimpsed an open-air market on cobbles. The taxi turned into a maze of side streets, eventually stopping outside a square-bayed Victorian terrace house in a quiet avenue.

She climbed out of the cab, paid the driver, and then as he drove away stared with dismay at the peeling paint and grimy brickwork. She checked the name on the lintel over the door. Balmoral. Yes, it was the right place.

Tentatively, she opened the rusty gate, walked up the tiny path, and rang the bell.

It opened immediately.

'Honey! You got here. Well done!' Sally Ann's warm, friendly voice did much to ease Rosemary's fears, and in a couple of seconds both she and her suitcase were standing in the red and black diamond-tiled hall.

Rosemary stared at Sally Ann in astonishment. She didn't know what she'd expected, but this tall, emaciated woman with a long cigarette-holder wasn't it. Her brown eyes peered out from a wrinkled face so camouflaged with heavy foundation that Rosemary found it difficult to judge her age. But the most bizarre aspect of her appearance was her hair. It was short and stood in spiky orange tufts. But through smudged, clashing crimson lipstick, her smile was welcoming.

'Well now, look at you,' she drawled, her gaze sweeping over Rosemary. 'I've got myself an

English rose.'

'They're usually fair,' Rosemary smiled, 'and without freckles.'

'Fair, dark, what does it matter? Anyway, freckles are cute, ask any American. Now you settle yourself in, while I rustle up some coffee.' She ushered Rosemary into a sitting-room.

'Aw, sorry, honey, would you rather have tea?' she called over her shoulder, as she went into the kitchen.

'No, coffee's fine,' Rosemary answered, and looking around the room for somewhere to sit, moved a pile of books to one side and sat gingerly on the edge of a dusty velvet chair.

It was a large and well-proportioned room with elaborate plaster cornicing, and a fine centre rose. Averting her eyes from the cobwebs in the corners, Rosemary admired the handsome mahogany fireplace. Although some of the green-patterned tiles were cracked, and the hearth was littered with cigarette ends, nothing could detract from its elegance. There was a drooping cheese plant in one corner, a huge shabby green velvet sofa, and books. Fusty and tattered, pristine and new, hardbacks, paperbacks, they overflowed from the shelves lining the walls, on to small tables, and lay carelessly on the faded and worn Axminster carpet.

She turned as Sally Ann came back into the room carrying a tray.

'It's instant, I'm afraid. One of my first purchases must be a percolator. I do miss real coffee in this country of yours.'

'How long have you been over here?'

'About six weeks. Cream and sugar?'

'One please.'

Handing over a cup and saucer, Sally Ann perched on the sofa. 'So, how was the journey?'

'Fine.' Rosemary sipped her coffee, hesitated and then helped herself to a chocolate biscuit.

'Hungry?' Sally Ann smiled.

'Starving,' Rosemary admitted. It was several hours since she'd eaten anything more than a small packet of biscuits.

'Good,' Sally Ann said approvingly. 'I've made a pot roast and I'd hate it to go to waste. You can cook, I take it? When semester begins I'd be glad if you'd take over that side of things. Oh, sorry, you call it term over here, I keep forgetting.'

'I manage,' Rosemary said. 'But mainly everyday things really.'

'Oh, that's all I'll need, just something to tuck into when I get home. I expect they'll feed me well on campus.'

She glanced sideways at Rosemary. 'You're very young, but that priest of yours said you were a resourceful young lady, so I'm sure we'll get along real fine. Once you've unpacked, I'll introduce you to Homer.'

'Homer?'

'The dog. I've shut him outside. He's not mine, I've sort of inherited him while I'm here. Your quarantine laws stopped him going to the States, although he'd have gone down a bomb over there.'

At Rosemary's look of enquiry, she grinned and said, 'You'll see, but I sure hope you like 'em big and hairy.'

Rosemary's bedroom was small, simply furnished in beige and brown, with a single bed, wardrobe, dressing-table and chair. To Rosemary's relief, the dust which seemed to pervade the rest of the house was mercifully lacking. The window looked out on to the car-lined road and a large silver-birch tree on the opposite pavement.

'Okay, honey?' Sally Ann queried. 'I cleaned it up special. The professor I swopped with was no dandy when it came to house maintenance, but that's academics for you. I've had neither the time nor the inclination, but now you're here I hope you don't mind doing the cleaning.'

'Of course not,' Rosemary said quickly.

Twenty minutes later, feeling refreshed after a wash, she ventured down the stairs.

The sitting-room was empty, so she hesitantly opened the kitchen door.

'Homer, come here, damn you!' Sally Ann grabbed the dog's collar as he leapt toward Rosemary. 'Is he Lassie's double or what?' she grinned.

His tail wagging furiously, Homer struggled to get to Rosemary, and she tentatively put out a hand to pat his head.

To her surprise, he immediately sat as she gently stroked his silky fur and, with a long pink tongue lolling to one side, gazed at her with soft brown eyes.

'Oh, he's gorgeous,' she exclaimed with delight.

'Sure, he's the biggest softie in the world. Good, he's taken to you. You'll need to walk him three times a day, once first thing, and then again at lunchtime and in the evening,' Sally Ann instructed, and waved a hand toward an old kitchen table. 'Food's ready. Let's eat, and then I'll fill you in on everything.'

Apart from attending Mass at Our Lady of Good Counsel, the Catholic church a few minutes' walk away, it was a week before Rosemary had even a minute to herself. Despite her zany personality, Sally Ann was a hard taskmaster, and in addition to her other duties, Rosemary struggled to decipher, type and bring order to piles of scribbled research. And Sally Ann was always there, leaving her little opportunity to pursue her own aims.

Unable to contain her impatience, she'd looked up Sherwin in the telephone directory on her first morning. Her heart leapt as she found the name, and then she'd ran her eye down the page with disbelief. There were literally dozens of entries. She kept reminding herself that Beth could now be married – she could even be living somewhere else, but it seemed logical to assume that she might have family in the area.

Undaunted, Rosemary worked out that if she made at least four calls a day, then by the end of her month's trial, she should have an answer. Wondering what that answer would be was one reason why she was finding it so difficult to sleep.

Her frustration grew as the busy days passed. Was Sally Ann never going to leave her on her own? Then one day, she announced she would be out for the morning.

'I've got to pop into the university, honey, to get things set up for the new intake. I'll bring in

186

some shopping at the same time. Now are you sure you can manage?'

'Absolutely,' Rosemary reassured her.

'Great. Could you give my room a good clean while I'm out?'

'Of course,' Rosemary promised. She'd been desperate to get into the chain-smoking American's bedroom ever since she arrived. Although just how she'd react if she did find out that Sally Ann smoked in bed, she wasn't sure. Perhaps in her subconscious that worry was another reason why she was sleeping so badly.

Full of adrenalin, she whizzed through her chores, anxious to get them out of the way. At eleven o'clock, relieved not to have found a single fag-end in Sally Ann's chaotic room, Rosemary put away the Hoover and dusters.

Now, she planned, her brain buzzing with excitement and trepidation, I'll do it now! It's a good time, just before lunch.

Carrying a kitchen chair into the hall, she placed it beside the hall table. Awkwardly balancing the telephone directory on her knee, she held her forefinger beneath the first entry. Her heart racing, she dialled the number.

It was ringing! Once, twice, three times, and then suddenly she was shaking and replacing the receiver in panic.

This was stupid; she'd waited so long for this moment, had dreamed of it.

Going into the kitchen she made herself a coffee and tried to control her nerves. After a couple of sips, she could wait no longer and went and dialled the number again.

This time it was answered immediately.

'Yes?' The voice was male and impatient.

Rosemary's voice was hoarse.

'Could I speak to Beth, please?'

'Who?'

'Beth, Beth Sherwin.'

'Never heard of her,' he snapped.

'Sorry, I've got the wrong number,' she gabbled.

It was a few minutes before she felt calm enough to try again. She dialled the next number. No answer.

The third call answered on the fourth ring, repeating the number in a quavering voice. Obviously an old lady, Rosemary decided.

'Could I speak to Beth, please?' she said gently.

'Who did you say, dear?'

'Beth, Beth Sherwin.'

'There's no Beth here, I'm afraid.'

'Thank you. I'm sorry to have bothered you.'

'Goodbye, then.'

Rosemary let out a deep, ragged sigh and tried again. She had never imagined it would be such an ordeal.

'Hello?' A woman's breathless voice answered above the sound of a baby crying.

'Could I speak to Beth, please?'

'Yer've got the wrong number, duck.'

'Sorry,' she replaced the receiver, and jumped as Homer thrust his long nose on to her lap.

'Yes, all right. Just one more, then I'll take you.'

His tail thumped and he settled down at her side, watching the door with patient eyes.

Rosemary dialled again. She daren't be on the

phone too long in case Sally Ann tried to ring. She didn't want any awkward questions at this stage.

'Hello?' It was a man again.

'Could I speak to Beth, please?'

There was a pause and then he said, 'Just a minute, I'll fetch her.'

Rosemary felt as though she was suspended in time. Her hand began to shake and she put up her other hand to steady it, pressing the receiver hard against her ear. With a dry throat and taut nerves, she strained to hear what could be the first sound of her natural mother's voice. She tried to prepare herself for disappointment, that it would be a different Beth Sherwin, but the few seconds she waited seemed an eternity. Then she heard movement, and the receiver being picked up.

'Here she is, duck.' It was the man again.

'Sorry?' Rosemary said sharply, every nerve on edge.

'Our Bess. Cleverest cat in the Potteries, only she doesn't usually get phone calls,' he guffawed.

'You stupid idiot,' Rosemary screamed, 'I said Beth, not Bess!' She slammed down the phone. 'Moron!'

Flinging the directory back into its drawer, she carried the chair into the kitchen, and grabbed Homer's lead. 'You've got more sense than him! Come on, boy, let's get out of here!'

Fighting tears of bitter disappointment, she strode through the streets to a nearby recreation ground, half-dragging the collie behind her.

'No, you can't stop and sniff,' she told him. 'I'm

189

not in the mood!'

But the fresh air and sunshine helped her to calm down, and eventually she was able to smile at Homer's joy in his freedom. As he bounded towards her as she called him to heel, Rosemary bent and ruffled his fur. 'Soon, we'll have the house to ourselves,' she muttered. 'Then just watch me, I'll really go for it.'

19

In warm sunshine on Saturday afternoon Rosemary browsed around the stalls on Newcastle's cobblestoned market. There were some good bargains and, knowing she'd soon be needing warmer clothes, she wished she could afford to buy something. Sally Ann hadn't refunded her travelling expenses yet, nor had she paid her. Did her employer expect her to wait until the end of the month's trial?

As she moved among the crowds, Rosemary couldn't resist glancing furtively at any woman she saw in her late-thirties. It was weird to think she and her natural mother could unknowingly walk past each other. Once she caught her breath as she saw a freckled profile, but as the woman turned to face her, she realised she was too old. You're daft, she told herself, things like that don't happen in real life.

Loth to return too soon to Sally Ann's demands, she dallied until the shops closed, before walking slowly back. This was the first time she'd had off since arriving, and she'd had to ask for it. Surely she wasn't expected to be available seven days a week?

But it seemed she was. On Sunday afternoon, Sally Ann presented her with a pile of papers, covered with her crabbed writing, to be typed up ready for Monday morning.

'She certainly wants her pound of flesh,' Rosemary muttered resentfully, as later that evening she wearily stacked up the sheets of typescript. The tiny spare room which had been turned into a study was cramped and airless, and she yawned, her eyes watering with strain.

Sally Ann appeared in the doorway and gave a crooked grin. 'You sure look whacked. Work 'em to death, that's my motto! Want a nightcap?'

'Nightcap?'

'A drink, kid. Bourbon's my poison, what's yours?'

'Er ... I usually drink Martini, or Dubonnet.'

'Right. Come on down and we'll talk.'

An hour and two Martinis later, Rosemary went to bed exhausted, but relieved. In return for agreeing to work in the evenings, Sally Ann had said she could have weekends free. That would give her time for her search. And, she'd refunded her train and taxi fares.

'Anything else, I'll settle at the end of the month,' she said firmly. Rosemary was too embarrassed to protest. It was only as she was drifting into sleep that she realised why the wily American was withholding her wages. What better way of ensuring you weren't left in the lurch, than by owing your Girl Friday money?

As Sally Ann began to spend more time at the university, Rosemary began her telephone calls, spacing them at intervals over the day. If Sally Ann phoned, she didn't want her to hear a continuous engaged tone. The cost didn't worry her – they were only local calls and very short. In any case, she considered she deserved a perk. The days were busy and it was rare that she finished much before ten at night.

I'm beginning to understand why domestic service went out of fashion, she thought grimly. Although I suppose servants in those days didn't have to type up manuscripts as well as do the housework. Not that she was complaining; the job was a godsend.

On Sunday night she despondently counted up her calls. Twenty frustrating attempts so far, only to have her hopes dashed. But her determination didn't waver. If her mother was out there, she'd find her. If she wasn't ... but she couldn't even face that possibility.

'Rosemary?' Sally Ann called upstairs the next morning.

'Yes?' Rosemary leaned over the bannister.

'Aw heck, doesn't anyone call you Rose or something? It's such a mouthful!'

'Does anyone call you Sal?' Rosemary retorted.

Sally Ann raised an eyebrow.

'We *are* a bit cranky today. Tell me, does this scarf go?'

Rosemary looked down at her. Sally Ann's dress sense was eccentric to say the least. She loved flowing scarves, which she wound endlessly around her long neck. Her gaunt trousered frame, in its check pants and embroidered waist-coat, was so garish Rosemary was convinced she was colour blind.

'Well,' she said tactfully, 'I think purple's a bit strong against the orange. Cream would look better.'

'You think so?' Sally Ann looked at her doubtfully. 'Okay kid, throw me one down.'

With a sense of relief, Rosemary closed the front door behind her. Perhaps she was a bit down today, but who wouldn't be?

Then, returning from Homer's walk, she found a single blue envelope waiting for her.

'Someone's remembered after all,' she told the dog, guessing who it was even as she tore open the envelope.

'Bless you, Lisa!' She sat on the bottom step of the stairs reading the familiar scrawl, and then glancing with pleasure at the book token, went up to her room.

Putting the card on display on her window-sill, she made a mental note to hide it in a drawer later. If Sally Ann knew it was her birthday, there would be all sorts of awkward questions.

Then halfway downstairs she paused, Sally Ann's comment on her name echoing in her mind. Rosemary. Why had her mother called her Rosemary? Had it simply been a name she liked, or was there a reason? Something niggled at the back of her mind, and deep in thought she went into the sitting-room and curled up on the sofa. Think, think how you would react if you had a baby and had to give it away. How would you

193

name it? Wouldn't you try to give your child a family name?

Her second name being Elizabeth proved that. Could she be called after someone called Rosemary? Then she remembered that her mother's second name had been Mary. Could she possibly have been named after someone called Rose?

As she went about her work, tidying, sorting out laundry, the thought played around in her mind. Rose was an old-fashioned name. Could it … could it possibly be the name of her grandmother? Excitement surged within her. Why hadn't she thought of it before? It was a long shot, she knew, but she decided to skip some of the initials in the telephone directory, and go down to R. Then she paused in doubt. But wouldn't the entry be under her grandfather's name? Though he might not still be alive. Anyway, it was definitely worth a try.

At eleven o'clock, she ran her finger down the page. There were six names beginning with R. Most had two initials, but the first one was simply R Sherwin, in a place called Minsden.

Rosemary dialled.

It rang four times before a woman's voice repeated the number.

Her mouth suddenly dry, Rosemary moistened her lips.

'Could I speak to Beth, please?'

'Sorry, you've just missed her – she left about twenty minutes ago.'

Stunned, Rosemary could only stare down at the mouthpiece in silence.

'Hello, are you there?'

'Who am I speaking to?' she managed to whisper.

'Rose Sherwin, I'm Beth's mother. Can I take a message?'

Her voice suddenly hoarse, she swallowed nervously.

'No, it's all right. Thank you.'

Rosemary slowly replaced the receiver and, as though in a dream, went back into the sitting-room. It had all been so simple, she couldn't believe it. That must have been her grandmother! She'd actually spoken to her grandmother! It had to be – surely anything else would be too much of a coincidence? She frantically tried to recall her voice, replaying the short conversation over in her mind. She'd missed her mother by twenty minutes. Not that she'd have spoken to her, not yet. She just wanted to hear her voice. Tears of relief seeped beneath her closed lids, slow weak tears, stemmed during months of loneliness. She'd found her family. Even if they wanted nothing to do with her, at least she'd know who she was, where she came from.

For the rest of the day, she was jumpy and restless. Grudgingly, she did her chores, all the while her mind racing with plans. Should she ring again, tonight perhaps? But suppose Rose Sherwin didn't know about Beth's baby. Could someone be pregnant and their mother not know? Why, for instance, had Beth gone all the way to the south coast to give birth, unless she was trying to keep her pregnancy secret? Or was it simply to protect the family's good name? The questions whirled round in her mind until she

195

felt emotionally exhausted.

I can't, Rosemary agonised, I can't simply announce who I am over the telephone. The last thing she wanted to do was to explode a bomb in everyone's midst. She could write a letter, but she couldn't risk it getting into the wrong hands. Suppose Beth had only been visiting? Suppose she was married and her husband knew nothing of her past?

Eventually, she came to a decision. She needed to know more, and the only way to do that was to go to this place called Minsden. Then, she'd take it from there.

20

The week dragged on, with Rosemary's impatience growing stronger every day. She looked up Minsden in the A-Z, relieved to find she could catch a bus directly from the centre of Newcastle, and planned to set off early on Saturday morning.

At last Saturday arrived. As Rosemary was about to leave, Sally Ann came into the hall. 'Where are you off to, all dressed up and so bright and early?'

Not knowing what else to say, Rosemary admitted, 'I'm going to look up my relations.'

'That's great. I have to admit I've wondered about you a few times,' she said, wagging her finger.

'How do you mean?'

'Well, a kid like you, on your own all the time. I know your father's in Australia and your mother died, but no-one ever phones or anything. After all, that's why you wanted to move up here, you said – to be near your family.'

'I just wanted to get settled in first,' Rosemary said shortly.

Sally Ann held up her hands in mock horror.

'Okay, I'm not prying.' She cast a speculative glance at Rosemary's flushed face. She liked a girl with spunk, and this one had plenty.

The journey on the front seat of the double-decker bus was a revelation to Rosemary. Fascinated, she watched the industrial landscape unfold as she travelled through Stoke, then Fenton and Longton. She didn't see many bottle kilns like the one on Beth's postcard, but there were old and forbidding factories lining the main road. Impressive buildings were few, but Longton boasted a fine Town Hall, even if it did overlook a railway bridge. As the bus gradually filled with passengers, Rosemary heard for the first time the true Potteries dialect. She'd become accustomed to the flat vowels of the Midlands, but this was different.

'Ah thowt they were goin up 'Anley,' a thin-faced woman greeted another as, laden with shopping bags, she sat beside her.

'Ah changed me mind, didner'a.'

Rosemary strained her ears to listen to their good-humoured banter, trying to make sense of it.

'Could you tell me when we get to Minsden,' she asked a woman in a chiffon headscarf who

197

squeezed in beside her.

'Which stop do yer want?'

Rosemary hesitated.

'I don't know exactly. I'm looking for Elm Grove.'

'Jus gerrof when I do, duck.'

Rosemary smiled her thanks and peered out of the window. Apart from one or two tiny shops, the narrow road was lined once again with large china or earthenware factories, their grimy blank windows staring back at her. I wonder whether my mother or father worked in one of these? That was another thing she wanted to know – who her father was. But that could come later, much later. Whoever he was, it was obvious he'd taken no responsibility either for herself or her mother. His name wasn't even on her birth certificate. Probably married already, or a bad lot, she thought miserably. But what did that say about her mother? Not for the first time did Rosemary wonder whether she was going to open a can of worms. Would she, at the end of it all, wish she'd never found out?

As she neared her destination, she felt her stomach tighten into knots. At last she was going to see where her family came from, although she still hadn't any idea what she was going to do when she got there.

The bus began to climb a hill, and then the woman stood up. Staggering along the stuffy upper deck, Rosemary followed her down the stairs and out into welcome fresh air.

'Straight up, first on the left,' the woman directed. 'Tar-rah!'

'Bye, thank you.'

Fortunately, the day was fine and dry, although a cool breeze made Rosemary glad she was wearing her jeans. She'd agonised over what to wear in case by some miracle she actually met her mother. But she also wanted to be inconspicuous, and with her navy sweater she was hoping she would just blend into the background.

She walked slowly up a slight incline into what appeared to be an estate of rented houses. Small and semi-detached, they screamed working-class respectability. All seemed well cared for, if in some cases the paint was flaking. A few were obviously in private ownership, with new front doors and different paintwork, but most looked identical. So much for Lisa's fantasies, thought Rosemary wryly, I'm certainly no duke's daughter!

She turned the corner into Elm Grove and paused. Number two was the first house on the opposite side. Her eyes fastened on it hungrily. She began to walk along the short cul de sac, gazing at the flat leaded windows, the tiny rockery at the front, the side path edged with a profusion of flowering hydrangeas.

Compared with some of its neighbours, number two displayed freshly pointed brickwork and gleaming white paint. The lined curtains looked expensive, in fact the house looked extremely well cared for. Rosemary was a fine judge of such things, having lived with Keith Latham's neglect for years. Perhaps her grandfather was still alive. She was only assuming he was dead. After all, his name could also begin with R. Anyway, her grandparents lived comfortably, even if their home was modest.

She crossed back to the corner and stood just behind a hedge, giving her a vantage point where she could see without being seen. If anyone approached, she bent to adjust the clasp on her sandal, worrying that if she stayed too long, it would arouse curiosity.

She stared avidly at the house, wondering how long Rose had lived there. Was this where her mother had grown up? Had she lain in one of those bedrooms, unable to sleep, terrified when she'd realised she was pregnant? Had she been an only child? She could have an aunt, or uncle, or cousins. If Beth was now married, she could even have half-brothers or sisters. That ordinary home held the answer to so many of her questions.

As she stood there, feeling self-conscious and frantically wondering what she should do next, a door opened at the side of the house and she suddenly drew further back. A woman came out pulling a small shopping trolley. She locked the door behind her, walked stiffly down the path and out of the wooden gate. Panicking, Rosemary froze for a moment, then turned and began to walk swiftly away. She mustn't draw attention to herself, not at this stage. Breathing rapidly, she went a hundred yards or so before daring to glance over her shoulder. The woman she was assuming was her grandmother was going in the opposite direction. Rosemary began to follow. Minsden centre seemed to consist simply of one busy road, lined with shops, with smaller streets of terraced houses or council houses leading off.

It didn't seem a very prosperous area and as Rose went to the chemist's, the Co-op and the butcher's, Rosemary studied her face. She looked in vain for any resemblance to herself, watched her smile and joke with shopkeepers, and carefully count her change. About sixty-five, her grey hair stylishly permed, practically dressed in good-quality clothes, she looked a very sensible sort of person. Definitely not a poor, old granny. Rosemary slid into the doorway of a jewellers as Rose walked past, pretending to look at the rings.

Now what do I do, she wondered? She walked slowly at a safe distance behind the stiffly moving figure until she reached her home.

For a few minutes, Rosemary stood uncertainly, then spinning on her heel went quickly to find the nearest telephone box before she could lose her nerve.

She rang the number and waited.

Rose answered, her voice slightly breathless. 'Hello?'

'Could I speak to Beth, please?'

'Sorry, she's not here.' There was a pause. 'Who's calling?'

This was it! Rosemary steadied herself. So much depended on her grandmother's reaction.

Slowly and distinctly, she said, 'Would you tell her,' she stressed her name, *Rosemary* called.'

There was sudden silence. Her words hung heavily in the air as seconds ticked by. Rosemary could hardly breathe as, fraught with anxiety, she waited for Rose to speak.

Then came the whisper, 'Did you say ... Rosemary?'

'Yes.'

Another silence followed. She knows, Rosemary realised, her heart thudding. She knows I exist! In confusion, she hurriedly replaced the receiver and slumped weakly against the glass of the telephone kiosk. 'She must know,' she muttered, 'or she wouldn't have reacted like that.'

Now what? Her nerves on edge, she jumped as a young girl knocked on the glass.

'Sorry,' she mumbled, as she pushed open the heavy door, and stood uncertainly on the pavement. Every fibre in her strained to go back to Elm Grove, to walk up that side path to the door she'd seen Rose use, and just knock. She longed for human contact, for warmth and love; she was so sick of being alone, without any roots. Or, on the other side of that door, would she face embarrassment, coldness and rejection? Life had taught her not to expect any favours.

Despondently, she went back to a small café she'd noticed, and sat brooding over a cup of hot, sweet tea. On the other hand, Rose would know what her mother's circumstances were – she might even be willing to act as a go-between. Should she risk it, take a chance? Then her shoulders slumped. She couldn't just turn up on the doorstep and announce she was her long-lost grandaughter! For all she knew, Rose could have a bad heart. That would be just my luck, she thought bitterly, to lose my grandmother as soon as I find her. Then my mother would really be pleased to see me! And what if my grandfather's there, and he doesn't know anything about me?

No, she'd have to wait. Reluctantly, she came to

the conclusion that she'd have to give Rose time. Time to think, to decide what she should do. Somehow, she'd have to control her impatience, then phone again in a few days.

21

Trembling, Rose replaced the receiver and going into the small living-room, sat back in her winged chair. Hearing that name suddenly, unexpectedly, had given her quite a turn. But, she tried to tell herself, Rosemary wasn't that unusual a name, it could just be someone who knew Beth.

But as her breathing became easier, every instinct told her this was no normal call, no ordinary message. She could still hear that tremulous young voice, the emotional tension in the way the girl had emphasised her name. And why would a stranger ring here?

Hope began to flicker, slowly at first and then gathering momentum. Hope that she had long since dampened down. Rosemary would be nineteen now. Rose glanced up at the perfect scarlet rose she'd placed in a glass stem vase. She'd never told anyone, not even Beth, but she'd planted that rose bush specially. Remembrance it was called, not that she needed to be reminded. For only six of those nineteen years had she known she had a granddaughter, but never a day went by that she didn't wonder whether she was well, whether she was happy.

She looked for reassurance at her late husband's photograph on the mantelpiece.

'I'm going to have to go up, Harry. I can't tell them something like this on the phone.'

Glancing up at the cuckoo clock, she realised it would be sensible to have something to eat first. She was going to need all her strength for the next few hours. Her mind and emotions in turmoil, she sliced cheese and laid it on the fresh oatcakes she'd just bought, then put them under the grill. Trying to keep calm, she leaned against the tiny kitchen table and prayed. If God would grant just this one blessing, she'd never ask for anything else, ever again.

The Rushtons were relaxing after a late lunch when the doorbell rang. The large, split-level lounge was bathed in early afternoon sunshine and, in a tranquil mood, Beth sat watching her two small children playing in the garden.

'Are you expecting anyone?'

Immersed in the *Financial Times*, Michael shook his head.

Beth tilted her head and listened.

'Maria's seeing to it.'

Hearing faint voices in the hall, Beth looked expectantly at the lounge door, then jumped up in surprise.

'Mum! How did you get here?' She hurried forward to kiss Rose's cheek.

'Taxi.'

Michael put down his newspaper.

'Why didn't you ring, Rose? You know one of us

would have fetched you.'

'Are you all right?' Beth asked.

'I'm fine. I could do with a cuppa though.'

'Of course, I'll ask Maria.' Beth went quickly to the door.

'Where are the boys?' Rose queried as she sank on to the down-filled chintz sofa.

'Out in the garden.' Michael leaned forward in concern. 'A taxi, Rose? That's not like you.'

'It certainly isn't,' Beth said, as she came back into the room. 'Come on, Mum, there must be something wrong for you to come up suddenly like this. Are you sure you're not ill, or anything?'

'No, love, honestly. Look it's nothing like that, and before you ask, our Gordon's all right as well.' Rose hesitated, her stomach twisting in knots. 'I'll just wait 'til Maria's not likely to come in ... then I've got something to tell you.'

Beth and Michael exchanged a mystified glance, Beth looking in alarm at her mother. Rose's eyes were feverishly bright, her expression tense.

'The garden's looking nice,' Rose said, gazing out at the extensive grounds.

Michael folded his newspaper and placed it to one side, his brow furrowing. His mother-in-law was one of the most level-headed women he knew. She hadn't splashed out on a taxi and come here to talk about their garden. He frowned with impatience.

'How long does it take to make a cup of tea?'

'She's got to wait for the kettle to boil,' Beth pointed out. She noticed her mother's hands, how she was twisting them nervously on her lap, and felt anxiety rise in her throat. If she wasn't ill, then what on earth could it be?

It was with relief that Beth turned to see Maria bring in the tray.

'Thank you. Maria, would you like to take the children to play further down the garden? There's no need to tell them yet that Mrs Sherwin is here.'

'Yes, Mrs Rushton.' The Italian au pair gave a shy smile and, going out of the room, closed the door quietly behind her.

'She's been a great success,' Rose said.

'Yes, the boys are already picking up odd words.' With another anxious look at her mother, Beth poured her a cup of tea.

Rose took a few sips, put down her cup and looked at their worried faces. She didn't know how to begin.

Seeing her mother's mouth tremble, Beth went to sit beside her.

'Mum, what is it?'

'I've ... I've had a phone call.'

'Not a threatening one?' Michael said quickly.

'No, no.' Rose shook her head and taking Beth's hand in hers, held it tightly. 'I don't know ... I could be imagining things ... it was a young girl, in a call box.' Her voice broke. 'Oh Beth love, I think there's a chance, just a chance, it might have been,' she swallowed, finding it difficult to say the word, 'Rosemary.'

There was a stunned silence. Beth reached out blindly to Michael, and then he was at her side, holding her close as Rose gabbled, 'Of course I could be wrong. I mean, do you know anyone

206

else with the same name, someone who'd ring you on my number?'

Speechless with shock, Beth could only shake her head.

'Think, Beth, are you sure?' Michael urged.

They both waited as Beth struggled to think clearly. Slowly, her head moved in denial.

Michael turned to Rose.

'What exactly did this girl say?'

'She just said, "Could I speak to Beth, please?" I remembered something else coming in the taxi. I'm sure it's the same girl who rang earlier in the week. It was the same thing, "Could I speak to Beth, please?" Only that time, she didn't leave her name. But she did ask who she was speaking to.'

'And what did you tell her?' Michael asked quietly.

Rose paused, trying to remember.

'Just that I was Rose Sherwin, Beth's mother. I didn't think anything of it at the time.'

Beth stared at her mother in a curiously detached way.

'The second time she rang, did she say anything else?'

'When I said you weren't there, and could I take a message, she said,' Rose's eyes filled with tears, as she remembered the pathos in that young voice, 'she said would I tell you "Rosemary" called. Oh, it was the way she said her name, deliberate like.' Rose looked at them both, and said brokenly, 'I'm not an imaginative woman, but deep down inside, I know, I just know it was her.'

Michael stood up abruptly.

'You've had a shock, Rose. I think a drop of brandy would be a good idea. And you, darling?'

Beth nodded, and said in a wavering voice, 'I'll make some coffee as well.'

Slowly, her legs feeling strangely heavy, Beth made her way into the kitchen and, as though in a dream, switched on the percolator, and reached for cups, saucers, cream and sugar. Only then, when the tray was neatly set, did she allow Rose's words to surface in her mind, did she face up to their implications. Suddenly, she was gripping the edge of the sink, fighting for control, breathing slowly and deeply. She couldn't believe it! So many times she'd dreamed of a phone call, a knock at the door, a letter. Now, on an ordinary Saturday...

How on earth had Rosemary found her? Trembling, her hand sought the tiny gold locket nestling inside her blouse, and her thumb caressed it in the familiar gesture she'd made so many times. Nineteen years. Nineteen years of not knowing whether her child was alive or dead. Torturing herself with images of possible neglect, or even worse, cruelty. And for twelve of those long years, she'd born her heavy burden of guilt and regret in secret.

'It would never have happened if your dad had been alive,' Rose had said sadly, when at last Beth had told her.

It was true, for if Harry had lived, then that fateful decision would never have been made. At seventeen, overcome by shame, it had seemed to be the only one possible at the time. She'd

208

needed to protect the recently widowed Rose, and it was only later that Beth had come to realise the enormity of her sacrifice. And what of Rosemary? What of her little girl? How often had she lain awake at night, remembering the feel of that silky baby skin, those piercing blue eyes gazing into her own. She could still feel the painful wrench when six weeks after her birth, the nuns had taken Rosemary away. It had been a dreadful mistake to give her up for adoption, she knew that now. Oh, at the time she'd convinced herself it was better for the baby, but with maturity had come clearer insight.

'We'd have managed, somehow,' Rose had said, shocked and distressed, and Beth knew that by not confiding in her all those years ago, she'd unwittingly hurt her mother deeply.

'Are you all right?' Michael came into the kitchen.

'Oh, Michael, can it be true? Can it?'

Michael looked down at her eyes, shining with excitement, and gathered her to him. As he stroked her soft, dark hair, he waited for the tears he knew must come, and then Beth began to weep, deep rending sobs, as all her pent-up emotion spilled over in tears of overwhelming joy.

Michael held her close, knowing that if ever there was a time his wife needed him, it was now. No matter how happy their marriage, and these past few years it had been very happy, there had always been a tiny shadow. Ever since she'd told him about Rosemary, he'd known that Beth would never feel complete while her daughter was lost to her.

'Come on,' he murmured. 'Come and have a brandy.'

Beth nodded, and shakily poured the coffee, and Michael carried the tray back into the lounge.

Rose turned anxiously as they entered.

'Are you all right, love?'

'Yes, I'm fine.' Beth dabbed at her eyes, then sipped at the glass of cognac Michael urged on her. Slowly, the warm golden liquid soothed and restored her, and she leaned forward eagerly.

'So, what do we do now?'

'There isn't anything we can do,' Michael said. 'Not until she gets in touch again.'

He looked at Beth, at the fervour in her eyes, at Rose, with her expression of loving concern, and felt a stir of unease.

He frowned.

'If it is Rosemary,' and he held up a hand. 'Now don't both of you look at me like that. Remember that other time?'

'But that was different,' Beth said. 'That was years ago when your father advertised in all the newspapers.'

'She could have found an old issue,' Michael suggested.

'But where did she get my number?' Rose said. 'That wasn't in the paper.'

'She could have written to the box number. I wouldn't put it past Father to keep it to himself.' Michael said tersely.

'Oh, surely not,' Beth protested. 'Since he found out he was breaking the law by advertising,

210

he's been quite reasonable about things.'

'Anyway,' Rose shook her head. 'Robert wouldn't have passed on my number – he'd have wanted to be first in the queue!'

Michael couldn't help grinning. 'Spot on, Rose. You're right, as usual.'

He stretched out his legs and remained silent. He needed to think this through, to look at the situation logically. But God in heaven, if this girl was Beth's daughter, then her appearance could have drastic consequences for the whole family.

'Don't get your hopes up too much, Beth,' he warned. 'I don't want you getting hurt. I've every faith in your mother's intuition, but we can't be sure this girl's genuine.'

Beth looked down as her spirits plummeted. Suppose this was another heartless chancer like the other time? That girl had sounded so plausible in her letter, but her claim had easily been disproved. But then this girl knew her name, had actually traced Rose and spoken to her. No, this was different, she just knew it was.

'I wonder if her parents know,' she said suddenly.

'How do you mean?' Rose said.

'That she's trying to find me. The fact that she rang from a call box makes me wonder.'

'They must have told her she was adopted,' Rose pointed out.

'Yes, but that's a different thing from her wanting to find her natural mother,' Beth said.

'Philip was telling me the other day at Rotary,' Michael said slowly, 'that they're changing the law on adoption next year. If anyone over eighteen

211

wants to find their natural parents, then they'll get counselling and help to contact them.'

Beth stared at him.

'I didn't know that.'

'No, I've been meaning to tell you,' he admitted. 'I was putting it off, knowing how it might affect us in the future.'

'We'll face that when it comes,' Beth said quietly. 'Andrew has always known he's adopted, and so will Ben when he's old enough.'

'Speaking of the boys,' Rose said with a smile. 'I can see them heading this way.'

'Yes, they'll be wanting to come in.' Beth got up and began to walk restlessly around the room.

'Suppose she wants to meet me? I mean, she could be ringing from anywhere in the country.'

'Why not let Philip deal with it first, like last time,' Michael suggested. 'Putting it in the hands of solicitors saved us all a lot of heartache.'

'No!' Beth turned swiftly to face him. 'It's Mum she's contacted. It's me she's asking for. No, Michael, I shall go, no matter where it is.'

Rose remained silent, watching them both.

Michael looked at Beth's flushed, determined face, and knew it would be a waste of time to argue.

'All right,' he said. 'But if you do, then I'm coming with you. And Rose,' he gazed at her intently, 'whatever you do, don't give her this number, or Beth's married name.'

At Beth's gesture of protest, he explained, 'There's too much involved, Beth. Until we know she's genuine, the less this girl knows the better. God knows how, but she's got hold of your mum's phone number, and I think for the moment, we'll keep it at that.'

'It's all right with me,' said Rose hurriedly, as they heard childish voices in the hall. 'But you'll have to tell me what to say...'

22

'Whatever's the matter with you?' Sally Ann snapped a couple of days later.

'Sorry,' Rosemary muttered, taking back notes to be retyped. She couldn't concentrate on anything – how could she when her whole future lay in the balance? The forty-eight hours since she'd spoken to Rose had seemed endless.

'Time of the month?' Sally Ann glanced at her sharply. She hoped it was, for sometimes she wondered whether the girl wasn't hiding something. She was so evasive and vague about these supposed relatives she'd moved to be near. And what girl with looks like hers didn't have a boyfriend in the background? She was a good kid and worked hard, but she was obviously capable of a better job than this. Call it a sixth sense, but there was more here than met the eye, she'd swear on it.

But Rosemary was immersed in her own thoughts, her mind in an agony of uncertainty. The spectre of Beth rejecting her, of refusing even to meet her was ever present. If that happened, what would she do with her life, where would she go? Her month's trial period would soon be up, and it would be stupid to spend the next year as someone's glorified skivvy, without a reason to stay.

Later, on her way to the fish and chip shop on the main road, she paused outside a babywear shop and studied the tiny outfits displayed in the window. Beth must have knitted for her, must have chosen vests, nappies, a shawl perhaps. Surely she couldn't have just forgotten about her own child, surely she would want to see her daughter, even if only out of curiosity? Her own longing to meet her mother had grown to consume her every waking moment. Wouldn't Beth, in even a small way, feel the same?

There was a sudden noise behind her, and Rosemary turned to see the door of a pub opposite open, its golden light and music spilling on to the pavement. A group of young people stumbled out, their high spirits filling the quiet street. Rosemary watched with a pang as a boy and girl started to dance along the pavement to the strains of *'I'd like to teach the world to sing...'* She loved the lyrics of the New Seekers' famous hit. The girl, her long dark hair lifting in the breeze, leaned back and laughed, a deep throaty laugh of sheer joy of life. The boy swung her round into his arms, his face alight with love as they kissed. Then they were running to join the others, their laughter floating back along the deserted pavements to where Rosemary stood, half-hidden in the shop doorway.

As they disappeared and the door of the noisy pub swung shut, Rosemary felt strangely bereft, depressed even. You're just lonely, she told herself, and continued on her errand. At least she'd decided she could now contact Rose again.

After a restless, anxious night, the morning finally arrived. At a quarter to eleven, Rosemary put Homer out into the garden, made herself a cup of tea, and watched the grandfather clock slowly tick away the minutes. Then at eleven o'clock precisely, she went into the hall, picked up the telephone, and dialled.

Rose answered on the second ring.

'Hello?' Her voice was strained, questioning.

'It's Rosemary. I rang before?'

There was a sharp intake of breath.

'Rosemary?' Rose's voice was steady now. 'Can you let me have your number? Is there some way I can contact you?'

Rosemary floundered. She looked down in panic at the number on the telephone. Suppose Beth rang when Sally Ann was within earshot?

'No, no, I'm sorry,' she faltered.

'Oh.' There was a pause. 'I gave Beth your message,' Rose said slowly.

A suffocating ache closed Rosemary's throat, and her next words came out thickly.

'Does she want to see me?' She shut her eyes in an effort to build a wall between herself and despair.

Rose hesitated, and then said in a measured tone, 'Beth said she'll meet you wherever you suggest.'

Rosemary's heart somersaulted painfully, and leaning back against the wall for support, she blinked away tears and pressed a hand to her lips in an effort to stop them trembling. Oh, thank you, God, she whispered, thank you!

'Rosemary?'

'Yes, yes, of course,' she stammered. So it wasn't to be Beth's home, or even that of Rose? Quick, quick, think of somewhere! Somewhere quiet, private.

'The church,' she blurted. 'Tell Beth I'll meet her at the church.'

'The church? Which church, Rosemary?'

'Our Lady of Good Counsel.'

'Let me write that down – Our Lady of Good Counsel,' Rose paused and frowned, but dismissed the thought. She couldn't possibly mean... 'Where, Rosemary, what town?'

'Newcastle.'

'Newcastle-upon-Tyne?'

'No, no, Newcastle-under-Lyme.'

Rose's voice sharpened in disbelief.

'Here, in Staffordshire?'

'Yes, that's right.'

There was a pause. 'When?'

Rosemary thought hurriedly. When was the most unlikely time for a service to be taking place?

'Sunday,' she said. 'Sunday at one o'clock.'

'This coming Sunday?'

'Yes. Will that be all right?'

'I'm sure it will be. I'll make sure Beth has the message.'

Rose's voice was carefully controlled, almost distant, making Rosemary want to scream 'Say something, I belong to you too, you're my grandmother for heaven's sake!'

Instead she said politely, 'Thank you.'

There was silence, and after waiting a few seconds, Rosemary replaced the receiver.

Unsteadily, she made her way back into the sitting-room and curled up on the sofa. Ignoring the sound of Homer whining outside the back door, she closed her eyes and replayed the whole conversation, examining every tone, every nuance of Rose's voice. With a sickening lurch of her stomach she realised why it had been different. That warm friendliness had been missing. And she hadn't suggested a meeting at her house in Minsden, nor had there been an invitation to Beth's home. They were willing to meet her, but were keeping her away, at a safe distance.

Even the knowledge that she was to meet her mother at last couldn't prevent Rosemary's heartbreak, as slowly, painfully, she began to cry, knowing she was crying like a child for her mother in the dark, but she was too disappointed to care.

Rose felt like an executioner as she slowly put down the telephone. That young, vulnerable voice, it had torn at her heart. While she'd done exactly as Michael had instructed, it had been hard, very hard.

'It's very important,' he impressed upon her, 'to keep your voice calm, and non-committal. Keep your distance, Rose, until we know more about her. You can't afford to give anything away.'

Of course, in the circumstances he was right. Beth had to be protected, and not only Beth but the whole Rushton family.

'Eeh, Harry,' she murmured to her beloved photograph, 'there's something to be said for being ordinary folk. Money brings its own problems, I've always said it.'

Reaching out for the phone, she dialled.

'Mum! Have you heard anything?' Beth's voice was tight with tension.

'Yes.'

'Thank God! What did she say?'

'Well, she wouldn't give me a phone number, but she wants to meet you on Sunday.'

Beth's heart leapt.

'Where?'

'One o'clock at Our Lady of Good Counsel in Newcastle.'

'What ... our church ... here?' Beth was astounded. 'Are you sure?'

'That's what she said. I wanted to ask her more, but it was really difficult to talk to her in the way Michael said. I felt awful, being so cold. I never want to have to do that again.'

'Never mind, Mum – if it really is Rosemary, we'll make it up to her.'

'You can never make up for hurt feelings, love.'

Beth flinched and then said flatly, 'You're right, of course. But you know what Michael's so afraid of...'

'Blackmail.' Rose said the ugly word with distaste. 'Yes, I know.'

'How did she sound?' Beth said forlornly.

'Young and ... a bit lost.'

Tears, so near the surface since Rosemary's original contact, welled up in Beth's eyes. 'Do

218

you still think...'

Rose hesitated, and then said, 'Yes, love, I do. There's just something about her, don't ask me what it is.'

'I hope to God you're right,' Beth said quietly. 'I just couldn't bear...'

'I know love, neither could I,' Rose said with a heavy sigh. 'But as I always say, time will tell.'

At midday on Sunday, Michael drove Beth into the centre of Newcastle and parked the car a considerable distance from the church.

'I know you were worried about someone recognising the Rolls, but surely my car would be safe,' Beth protested.

'We're taking every precaution,' Michael said grimly. 'I still can't work out why or how she knew about your parish church. I mean, if she doesn't know where you live, or your phone number, how come she chooses the main Catholic church in Newcastle? It would have made more sense if you'd had to go to her home town.'

'I don't know.' Beth twisted her hands in her lap. She didn't want to be bothered with talking about it. All she wanted to do was to go and sit in solitude in the church, and wait. Wait for the most important meeting of her life. She loved her adopted little boys, of course she did, but always there had been that deep and hidden sorrow that she hadn't a child of her own. The discovery that he couldn't father children had almost destroyed Michael, had threatened their marriage, and Beth was careful not to reveal the extent of her own disappointment. The knowledge that somewhere in the world a young girl was growing up, a girl who was her daughter, her own flesh and blood, had been like a knife in her side.

'Let's go,' she said abruptly.

'We've plenty of time.' Michael glanced at her, noting how pale and strung up she was. 'Beth...' he warned.

'I know, you've told me.' She turned to him and held out her hand for his support. 'I'll be very careful and logical. I'll ask for proof, I'll ask questions.'

'And...'

'I'll try not to be emotional, clouding my judgement.' She looked down. 'I'll try, Michael, but I can't promise.'

'No, I know.' He looked approvingly at her simple navy summer dress and lack of jewellery. She'd chosen well – there was no indication there of her wealthy background.

Michael leaned his head on the headrest as they sat in tense silence, waiting for the minutes to pass. He closed his eyes, remembering with pain that traumatic day six years ago, when, their relationship in turmoil, he and Beth had bared their souls. The shock of Rosemary's existence, and the circumstances surrounding her birth had rocked the whole family. Now, in the next hour, her reappearance, if it was true, would once again cause not only ripples, but a minor earthquake in the Rushton dynasty. Did he really want that turmoil in his life again? You can be a selfish bastard at times, he thought wearily.

220

'Come on, Michael. I can't sit here any longer,' Beth muttered.

They locked the car and walked along the main road to the church. It was half past twelve. Opening the oak door, Michael, as they'd planned, mounted the stairs to the choir stall and, hidden in the shadows at the back, chose a seat with a clear view.

Beth walked slowly down the side aisle to Our Lady's altar, the tapping of her heels on the wooden floor echoing in the large, empty church. There, as she had done every week of Rosemary's life, she lit a candle for her daughter. Only this time, her prayer was different.

'As a mother you know how I feel,' she whispered. 'Please let this be Rosemary, please give me another chance.'

She knelt with her head bowed for a few moments, then heart pounding turned and looked indecisively at the pews. Where should she sit? Finally, she chose a pew three rows from the front and sat at the end of it near to the centre aisle. Now she could only wait.

Rosemary set off at twelve thirty exactly. After days of dithering over what to wear from her meagre wardrobe, superstition had finally won. The blue ethnic dress, and her now shabby sandals had brought her luck on her visit to Westbourne. It seemed fitting somehow to wear them again for the journey which was to find its end in the next half hour. She'd prayed desperately for a fine day, and on seeing the blue sky that morning, had almost wept with relief.

Stomach churning, she stared searchingly in the mirror before leaving, wondering whether there would be any resemblance, worrying whether Beth would be disappointed.

The street was quiet, and there was little traffic on the main road as she walked along. She remembered Brenda, her adoptive mother, saying once that if ever England could be invaded it would be on a Sunday lunch-time. Her lips twisted wryly at the memory, knowing that Brenda's ultimate nightmare would have been the meeting which was so shortly to take place. Or now, knowing how alone her daughter was, would she have given her blessing? I hope so, Mum, Rosemary thought sadly, I do hope so.

As she drew near to the church, the knot in Rosemary's stomach tightened into a ball of steel. Gazing at the building ahead, she tried to picture the scene inside. Was her mother, that shadowy figure, already in there, waiting?

She glanced at her watch. It was a quarter to one. Hesitantly walking the last few yards to the church door, she turned the heavy iron handle and, her heart thudding in apprehension, stepped into the cool interior.

23

Rosemary closed the heavy door behind her and, dipping her fingers into the font of holy water in the vestibule, made the sign of the cross. She waited a moment in an effort to calm her nerves, then resolutely pushed open the inner door to the church.

In the silence and lingering musky scent of incense, a woman was sitting alone in a pew three rows from the front. Dusty shafts of sunlight filtering through the stained-glass windows illumined dark hair so uncannily like her own that Rosemary's breath caught in her throat. For a moment she was unable to move, then nervously, the crepe soles of her sandals squeaking on the polished floor, she began to walk up the aisle toward the waiting figure.

Beth forced herself to remain absolutely still. She'd heard the door open, with every sense acutely aware of Rosemary's presence. Now she waited, her heart thumping painfully as the hesitant footsteps approached. Not until Rosemary drew level did she move, then slowly, very slowly, she stood and turned to face her.

The next moment stretched into eternity as mother and daughter stared at each other in profound silence.

'Rosemary?' It was the softest of whispers.

Rosemary could only nod, her throat closing

with unshed tears as she fought for self-control. She gazed wordlessly at the slim, poised woman before her, a woman who looked far younger than her thirty-six years, a woman who avidly searched her eyes, her features. For one heart-stopping second, Rosemary saw in their depths a yearning and longing equal to her own and then dark lashes were lowered, and when she looked again it was into a veiled blank expression.

Beth was valiantly struggling to hide the emotional turmoil which threatened to over-whelm her. None of her fevered imaginings had prepared her for this. This tall young girl whose anxiety leapt out at her from eyes so very like her own. Dark hair and blue eyes she'd been prepared for, had hoped for even, but never had she expected the heartbreaking impact of those freckles. Oh my God, James! Her soundless cry winged its way upwards. James, if only you could see her...

For Beth knew in that first glance, knew in her innermost soul, that at last she had found her daughter. This was her child, this was James' child, and neither Michael nor anyone else would ever make her doubt that truth. Trembling with relief and overwhelming joy, she fought the compulsion to look again into those wideset eyes and, afraid of revealing her exultation, turned and went back into the pew. She moved further along the bench and silently placed a hand on the empty space.

Shakily, Rosemary sat beside her. She felt tongue-tied, unnerved by Beth's blank, tense expression. Desperately, she searched for the right words to say, but it was Beth who broke the silence.

'Why did you ring my mother?' Her voice was strained.

Taken aback by the stark question, Rosemary stammered, 'Surely you know!'

'I'd like you to tell me.'

Rosemary twisted in her seat to look at her mother, trying to meet her eyes, but Beth resolutely looked ahead, her eyes fixed on the altar.

'I was trying to find you.'

The poignant words smote into the depths of Beth's soul. Michael, she thought brokenly, I don't think I can do this. Then she steadied herself. The situation wasn't only between herself and Rosemary – there was so much more at stake.

'Tell me about it,' she said in a low voice.

Falteringly, Rosemary explained how a year ago she'd found out she was adopted, that her search for her real identity had taken her via her parish priest to the Mother and Baby Home in Westbourne.

'The Mother Superior said they weren't allowed by law to give any details, but when she went out of the room, I sneaked a look at the file on her desk and saw your Admission Form. That's how I found out my real name was Sherwin.'

When Beth showed no reaction, Rosemary stared at her in misery, wanting to say something, anything, to disturb that calm, expressionless face. This wasn't at all like she'd imagined. Oh, she hadn't been naïve enough to think they'd fall into each other's arms, but she'd hoped, prayed for more than this. Conscious of Beth waiting for her to continue, she stumbled on.

'The Form said your current address was St Gregory's Church in Westbourne. But Father Murphy and Mrs Flanagan who would have known you were both dead. The housekeeper sent me to Mrs Flanagan's niece in the town, and she showed me a postcard. That's how I knew you came from Stoke-on-Trent.' Fishing in her handbag, she handed it to Beth.

Beth looked blindly down at the words she'd written so many years ago. Westbourne, the Mother and Baby Home ... at the familiar names, painful memories long suppressed began to surface. She pushed them away, knowing only that a frightened seventeen-year-old girl had entered the Home, to emerge six weeks later a young woman with a burden of guilt she'd carried all her life. For God help me, she thought, I'll never forgive myself. Ever conscious of Michael's presence, she held the muscles in her face rigid, knowing that if she once looked at Rosemary, then her resolve would collapse.

As Beth made no gesture toward her, no smile, no attempt to establish even eye contact, Rosemary's heart sank further. Her mother wasn't even going to admit to their relationship. Rejection had been her constant nightmare, but not even to be acknowledged...

Close to tears, she rummaged again in her handbag.

'And this is my birth certificate.'

With trembling hands, Rosemary unfolded the

long form and spread it out to show her mother. Beth looked at the heading: *Certificate of Adoption.* It was so familiar to her – there were two similar ones in a little box at home. Slowly, she read the handwritten entries. Keith and Brenda Latham. So they were the people who had brought up her child. Did they know their adopted daughter was here, with her?

Rosemary, now almost in despair, made one final attempt to break through the invisible glass wall which Beth had erected.

'I also thought you might like to see this.' She handed over the slightly creased photograph of Father Murphy and Mrs Flanagan.

Beth looked down at the familiar faces. So many years ago, and yet she'd never forget their kindness. And Father Murphy ... how much she owed to his guidance and fine brain. He'd opened her eyes to a world of literature she hadn't known existed, he'd taught her to question, to dissect, to think for herself.

Not a single reaction, Rosemary thought bitterly, not even a comment. Well, I've answered all her questions, I'll give her five more minutes, and then I've some of my own! She can at least tell me why she gave me away, and who my father is. She owes me that much!

Beth carefully folded up the birth certificate and placed the photograph on top.

'Tell me, Rosemary,' she probed, 'have you told anyone else about this? About your telephone calls, about our meeting?'

'No!' Rosemary said angrily. 'I'm not stupid. No-one knows. I've always wanted to protect you

– I didn't know what your circumstances were.' Despite all her efforts, her voice broke as she muttered, 'I don't want to make any trouble for you, I just...'

At the sob in Rosemary's voice, Beth's hold on her self-control crumbled into tiny pieces. In God's name, what was she doing to this young girl? A girl she knew was the daughter she'd almost given up hope of finding. She'd asked the questions, she held proof. Surely, she'd already kept her promise.

At last she turned, only this time there was no careful façade and what Rosemary saw was a woman whose emotions were as overwrought as her own. Suddenly, hope flickered, slowly, painfully, and she sought Beth's eyes for the reassurance she so desperately needed. And what she saw was her undoing, for her mother was gazing at her with such joy and love that Rosemary to her horror began to weep. All her pent-up emotions, all her fear, anxiety and loneliness were in those tears, and Beth, anguished at her distress, placed a tentative arm around her shoulders. Not wanting to relinquish this first physical contact, she brushed away her own tears with the back of her hand. But scarcely aware of her mother's light touch, Rosemary leaned forward, reaching blindly to her bag to find a handkerchief. Unsure of herself, Beth withdrew her arm.

'I'm sorry,' Rosemary mumbled, feeling ashamed and embarrassed.

'No, I'm the one who should be sorry,' Beth said intensely. 'Sorry I've been so distant, behaved so coldly toward you. You must have felt very hurt. There was a reason, but it doesn't matter now. Oh, Rosemary, have you any idea what it means to me to have found you again?'

Impulsively, Rosemary moved her hand a fraction, and after a second's nervous hesitation, Beth covered it with her own.

'Your hand's much slimmer than mine,' Rosemary said, in an effort to regain her composure.

Beth looked at her daughter's square, capable fingers, and murmured, 'Yours is like my mother's.'

For a moment they were both silent, lost in their own thoughts, and then Beth pulled herself together.

'Do you have plenty of time? I mean, before you have to get back?'

'All day.' Rosemary glanced down at the slim gold band on Beth's finger. 'Does he know?'

'Yes, he knows,' Beth said quietly. 'But before you ask, I met him long after you were born. You'll have lots of questions, Rosemary, and I'll tell you the truth. Let's take it one step at a time, but not now.' She hesitated. 'And you? Have you been happy?'

Rosemary looked down in disquiet. Had she?

Beth saw the forlorn expression in her eyes, as she answered, 'At times. I've lots to tell you, too.'

Stricken, Beth wondered how much more guilt she could bear and turned her head away, fighting treacherous tears. Then suddenly she had a need to move, to get out of the church and into the fresh air. Only this time, she would be taking her daughter with her. Forget the dark side, she told herself, this is a day for rejoicing, for happiness.

'Would you mind waiting a moment, there's someone I want you to meet. It's my husband, Michael.'

Startled, Rosemary could only nod apprehensively, as Beth moved past her to walk back down the aisle. Did she mean he was actually here, at this minute?

Michael, who had watched intently the sunlit tableau from his vantage point, was fighting his own battle. To his shame, he knew he was half hoping this girl's claim would prove to be false. And that was being a traitor to Beth, for he should be supporting her, should be happy not only for her, but for what this would mean to his mother, his father, and to Rose. But long-buried feelings of jealousy and anger must have been simmering in his subconscious, for now they were being resurrected, and with them memories which were best forgotten. He was fearful too, and with just cause, for if this girl was Rosemary, then the problems which lay ahead were such that the threat of blackmail paled beside them.

Michael suddenly tensed as he saw the young girl sitting next to Beth collapse into tears and then with a heavy heart he saw Beth's arm encircle her. Involuntarily, his hands clenched until the knuckles whitened, and it seemed a lifetime until Beth moved out of the pew and began to walk down the aisle toward him.

She glanced up at the choir stall and her face was so alight with happiness that his throat contracted. For a moment his shoulders bowed in defeat, and then he straightened up, moving forward to meet his wife as she came to him with wet, shining eyes. She stretched out her hand to take his.

'Michael, everything's fine. Come on, I want you to meet my daughter, and your niece.'

Rose waited until the cuckoo-clock struck two, before putting the vegetables on a low light. A leg of lamb was crisply roasting in the oven, the potatoes above it browning on the top shelf. The narrow working surface at the side displayed her baking, an apple pie and a custard tart. Everything was organised.

She tidied her hair in the mirror, then stood by the front window watching for the car to turn the corner.

Oh, she'd listened without comment to Michael's plan. It was all very well in theory, but that was the trouble with men, they didn't understand a woman's emotions. And if ever there was a sensitive soul, it was their Beth. She knew her daughter. If that lass was who she claimed to be, and Beth knew it, then she'd not be able to deny her, Michael or no Michael.

So Rose made her own preparations, and there in the middle of the table stood a vase holding a single scarlet rose, although she hadn't tempted fate by laying an extra place.

'What do you think, Harry?' she murmured. 'Are we going to have our granddaughter with us after all these years? Or will it be just Beth and Michael, wanting to talk out of earshot of the boys. Well, we'll soon know, for they won't be long now.'

And so she waited, hardly daring to hope, remembering that young hesitant voice on the telephone. Then suddenly they were there, and her eyes strained, searching through the tinted glass until she saw the outline of a figure on the back seat of the car. With a heartfelt prayer of gratitude, she moved away from the window and hurriedly set that vital extra place, and then, her pulses racing with excitement, stood in the middle of the small living-room, and waited.

Rosemary got slowly out of the car outside the modest semi-detached house that had been her mother's childhood home. She could hardly believe that, no longer an outsider, she was actually going through the gate and walking up the side path. From the open door wafted the appetising smell of roasting meat, and then she was in the kitchen and being ushered by Beth into a warm, cosy room. In the centre stood the woman she knew was her grandmother.

She hesitated on the threshold, then seeing the flushed, lined face, the moist eyes smiling in welcome, moved awkwardly forward, holding out her hand in greeting.

But Rose, unhampered by her daughter's burden of guilt and misgivings, simply stretched out her arms. Not normally demonstrative, she could recognise a need when she saw it, and if she couldn't hold her granddaughter, then who could?

While Beth watched, her face radiant, Michael stood by the door. Rosemary's resemblance to both Beth and James had been a shock, but it was unmistakable. However, he still intended to double-check her story. His own feelings he'd have to deal with, but for now his main concern was how Rosemary would react when she not only found out her father was a rapist, but that her mother had married his brother.

24

'Someone's sure lit your candle!' Sally Ann exclaimed, when Rosemary returned early in the evening.

'Sorry?'

'You're absolutely glowing. Do I detect a boyfriend?'

Rosemary, still on a high from the day's events, reddened.

'No,' she said shortly, 'nothing like that.'

Sally Ann held up her hands in defence.

'Okay, I was only asking.'

'Actually,' Rosemary lied, 'I've got a bit of a headache.' She turned toward the stairs, desperate to reach the privacy of her bedroom. She was longing to lie on her bed, to relive every second of that momentous scene in the church. And then there were the past few hours to savour. Hours of warmth and welcome as Rose had fussed over her, pressing on her helpings of food until she couldn't eat another mouthful. With her newly-found grandmother at her side, she'd pored over photographs of Beth and her brother Gordon as children, of her grandfather Harry, and faded sepia ones of her great-grandparents. Beth had watched quietly, her eyes soft and reflective, but Michael's expression had been difficult to read, and she needed to think about that...

'Right, you have a lie-down, I'll see you later.' With a frown, Sally Ann watched the lithe figure run up the stairs and turned slowly back into the sitting-room. She'd bet her bottom dollar that girl had no headache. Something had happened since she left that morning, and from the look of her, it was the Fourth of July and Thanksgiving rolled into one! She could only hope it wouldn't affect their working arrangement, for she'd struck gold with that kid.

But Rosemary readily agreed that evening to stay on now that her month's trial was up. For a while anyway, she thought, just until her future became clearer.

She found it impossible the following morning to settle into her usual routine, too restless even to write to Lisa. Looking at the clouds scudding across the blue sky, Rosemary ignored the muddy paw-prints on the kitchen floor, the untidy bedrooms and pile of ironing, unhooked the dog's lead and grabbed her anorak.

With exhilaration, she walked briskly to the recreation ground, the collie prancing beside her as she played with him, laughing at his delight.

'I've got a family, Homer, a real family!'

Then when she let him off for a run, she ran with him, swerving and dodging, teasing and chasing. Never in her life had she felt so alive, as the breeze whipped tendrils of her hair across her face. Opening her arms wide, the delirious dog leapt into them, knocking her to the ground, and she shrieked with sheer high spirits as they rolled over in an ungainly heap, before he scrambled up, panting, eager for more.

'Enough, enough, I surrender,' she gasped.

The young man standing in the large bay window overlooking the recreation ground grinned as he watched the exuberant antics of the girl and the dog. Then she bent and, clipping a lead on to the sable and white collie, began to walk toward him, tossing back her tousled hair. About to turn away, Simon stopped and narrowed his eyes. Surely ... he waited until Rosemary drew nearer and then ... it was, it was the girl from the train! What a stroke of luck!

Swiftly, he turned on his heel, muttering, 'Would you excuse me a minute,' to the other man in the room, and ran quickly down the stairs. Fumbling with the unfamiliar lock on the large, heavy front door, he hurried through it to the arch in the tall hedge which screened the double-fronted detached house. The girl and the dog were approaching a few yards away. Simon stepped out on to the pavement and waited.

With amusement and some satisfaction, he watched Rosemary's eyes widen with startled recognition.

'Hi!' he smiled. 'Remember me? From the train?'

Rosemary could only stare at him in confusion

and disbelief. Remember him? Her problem had been trying to forget him!

'Of course I remember you. But what are you doing here? I mean, in Newcastle?'

'I got the job.'

'What job?'

'Sorry, of course you wouldn't know. When we met on the train I was coming up for an interview. You are now looking at the new Surgical Registrar at the Infirmary. My name's Simon Oldham, by the way.'

'I'm Rosemary,' she hesitated, 'Rosemary Latham.'

'Now we've been introduced so to speak, what about you? Do you live near here?'

'Yes, at the moment.'

Simon bent and patted Homer, then said impulsively, 'Look, you couldn't do me a favour, could you? I'm just viewing this flat. That's where I saw you, there's a bay window overlooking the recreation ground. I'd really appreciate a second opinion.'

'Of course.' Overcome with embarrassment, Rosemary tied Homer's lead to a sapling safely inside the front garden, and began to follow him into the house. God, he must think she was a nutcase, leaping all over the place like that. And just look at the state of her, no make-up, hair all windblown, scruffy jeans...

'Just a friend to help me decide,' Simon told the young estate agent, who stood patiently waiting, clutching a folder.

'This is the third one I've looked at, and it's by far and away the best,' he said to Rosemary.

'What do you think?'

She looked at the large, airy room, at the open view, and silently wandered around. The kitchen was practical and recently re-fitted, the two bedrooms spacious and well furnished. There was even a full-size bathroom. No grime, no dingy ceilings and rusting window-frames – what a contrast to the squalor she'd had to endure!

She smiled at Simon. 'I think it's great.'

'You do? Right, I'll take it.'

With relief, the young man ushered them both out, locked the door and got into his car, waiting for Simon to join him.

'There are only two flats,' Simon explained to Rosemary. 'The ground floor's occupied by a headmistress, so I'll have to watch my step!'

'Oh yes, I've heard about you young doctors!'

'Don't believe a word of it,' he grinned. He fished in his inside pocket and produced a biro and diary.

'Anyway, give me your phone number. Or am I treading on someone's toes?'

Rosemary shook her head, her pulses racing. 'No, not at all.' She watched him scribble down the number and then he got into the passenger seat, waved and was gone. Bemused, she walked home in a dream, hardly able to believe what had just taken place. He must have got off the train at Stoke station after she did, only she'd been in such a hurry to find a taxi, she'd missed him!

'You know what, Homer?' she murmured to the dog as she bent to release him. 'I think my luck's changing.'

Beth turned anxiously as Michael came into the lounge.

'Did you speak to the parish priest?'

'I did.' Michael sprawled in the armchair and rested his head on the high velvet back.

'And?'

'Every word she said was true.' Michael's voice was flat, and Beth glanced sharply at him.

'Well, tell me, Michael. I want to know exactly what he said.'

'He simply confirmed what Rosemary told us. Her father disappeared to Australia, and her mother died a year ago in a fire which destroyed her home. Yes, he knew she'd come up here looking for you, and was relieved to hear that she was safe and well.'

'Anything else?'

'He just said that she was a very determined and resourceful young lady. Also, he hoped her reappearance in your life wouldn't cause us any problems. If only he knew,' he said bitterly.

Beth stared at him in dismay.

'Michael...?'

He looked at her wearily. How could he admit to the demons which had haunted him over the past twenty-four hours. The very sight of that face, so reminiscent of James, had brought with it such painful and disturbing images that last night he'd lain awake by his wife's side, unable even to touch her. Please God it would be a temporary insanity, for he'd fought this battle once before and won. Only then, there hadn't been a constant reminder before him.

'It's all right, Beth,' he said. 'It's just that it's

been a bit of a shock. And you have to admit, it is a complicated situation.'

'Yes, I know,' she said quietly. 'We're going to have to take it one step at a time.'

'Have you thought about the practical side? What it will mean? For instance, how will you explain Rosemary to the children? And that's only the beginning. The first thing we must do is to go over to Linden Lodge. I've got a meeting this afternoon, so it will have to be this evening.'

'Yes, I'll ring Sylvia later.'

'Don't say...'

'I won't say a word, but you know your mother. She's going to be over the moon when she finds out.'

'Can you imagine Father's reaction?' Michael said grimly. 'I think I'll have a stiff drink first.'

'I'm so happy, I'll cope with anything,' Beth smiled.

'You know how overbearing he can be!'

'Yes, but while he may be her grandfather, I happen to be her mother. She's my responsibility, not his.'

'Have you never thought that Rosemary might think she's her own responsibility, Beth? Don't make any assumptions – she strikes me as a very independent girl.'

'She's also a lonely one,' Beth said softly. Then as the telephone rang, she got up and went into the hall to answer it.

Michael glanced at his watch. Nearly time for Maria to bring Ben back from nursery school. He'd have a spot of lunch and then get back to the office.

'It was Mrs Hurst,' Beth said as she came back into the room. 'The doctor's signed her off, so she'll be here in the morning.'

'Good. Although how you can stand her constant warbling, I'll never know.'

'It drowns out the noise of the vacuum cleaner,' Beth smiled. 'Besides, she cheers me up. Now, how about some home-made soup and a salad?'

'Fine.' Michael closed his eyes against the glare of the midday sun as it filtered through the huge picture windows. So, it was all about to start. This evening was only the beginning. God alone knew where it would all end, and he was powerless to stop it.

Rosemary too was thinking. Thinking of Beth's husband, that tall quiet man who she supposed was her stepfather. She doubted that he welcomed such a role. She'd felt uneasy with him, nervous even. How she'd longed to ask Beth about her real father, but obviously it wasn't a subject she could bring up in front of Michael.

What had happened? Had he been a married man? Had he been a young boy in his teens like Beth, who'd abandoned her when he'd found out she was pregnant? And why hadn't Beth kept her baby? Who or what had persuaded her to have it adopted? Surely not Rose, the warmth of whose welcome had acted like a soothing, healing balm. Her grandmother wasn't the sort of woman who would let her daughter down in time of need.

Soon, when she saw her mother alone, she would ask all these questions, and remembering Beth's frank blue eyes, and her promise,

Rosemary felt sure she would be told the truth. Instinctively, she liked Beth, was drawn to her, but until she knew the full story, her mind shied away from examining her true feelings. So much depended upon Beth's explanation. Rosemary knew she needed to find it in her heart to forgive, for while she could see the offer of love shining in Beth's eyes, as yet her own feelings were more difficult to define.

But for now, she thought as she put away the ironing board, I'm going to concentrate on writing to Lisa. I'd love to see her face when she reads it.

Dr Simon Oldham ... and he had been interested, she knew he had. Mrs Simon Oldham, she mused. Then laughing at her own silliness, she ran upstairs to fetch a writing pad, her every sense full of anticipation. Perhaps he would ring tonight, or if not, tomorrow...

25

At eight o'clock that evening, Beth sat quietly in the passenger seat as the Rolls Royce purred along the busy main road toward the outskirts of Newcastle. Michael too was silent, only the clenching of his hands on the leather-covered steering wheel giving any hint of the tension she knew he must be feeling.

She gazed reflectively out of the window, as the car swept along exclusive leafy residential avenues to the home of her parents-in-law, remembering her first sight of Linden Lodge all those years ago. Even now, she never failed to be impressed by her first sight of the huge opulent house. At that time, it had seemed to the girl who'd grown up in Minsden like a scene from a film. Beth smiled, recalling how she'd stood at the white pillars, almost turning back in panic. The long tree-lined drive, the lights and music streaming from the gracious ivy-covered windows...

That New Year party had been her introduction to a way of life and a class of people completely alien to her own working-class upbringing. But it hadn't been easy. Robert Rushton had been furious when a few months later his eldest son had announced he wanted to marry one of his employees. It had taken many years to overcome her father-in-law's prejudice and bigotry, and the insidious snobbery of many of his social circle. Proud of her background, defensive of her Catholicism, Beth had fought back, finding an unexpected ally in Michael's mother. Sylvia, with her privileged background and exquisite manners, had been a perfect role model. With her support, Beth had gradually mastered the social skills deemed essential in the wife of the son and heir of the prestigious Rushton family.

Michael glanced at his watch as the car drew to a halt outside the double oak doors.

'At least we're punctual, that should please him.'

'Michael...' Beth warned. Since her father-in-law had recovered from a long period of clinical depression five years ago, his temper had been even more volatile than before. Robert's illness had been a catalyst. Only then had Beth confessed not only to Michael and his parents, but also to Rose, the secret of Rosemary's existence. Only then, knowing that now he had an heir, had the formerly powerful and domineering man found the strength and incentive to claw his way out of the black hole into which he'd sunk. Still chairman of the family firm at seventy, his refusal to consider retirement and his constant meddling in Michael's administration was a cause of much friction between them.

Beth caught at Michael's sleeve.

'Let's not dwell on the problems, not at first. This is such wonderful news for them.'

Michael touched her hand. 'I know.'

The door opened even before they rang the bell. Sylvia, elegant as always in a cream silk dress, greeted them with a smile and raised eyebrows.

'This all sounds very mysterious,' she said. 'I've done as you suggested, and given Mrs Hammond the evening off. She's gone to visit her sister.'

Beth breathed a sigh of relief. The Rushtons' well-ordered existence depended greatly on their resident housekeeper, who, with daily cleaners and a gardener, ran their household with unobtrusive efficiency.

Michael bent and kissed his mother's cheek.

'You're looking tired,' she remarked.

He shrugged. 'I'm all right. How are you?'

'Fine. Your father's in the drawing-room.'

Robert Rushton was waiting for them, having

taken up his usual stance before the marble fireplace, where even on this warm evening a fire was laid in case it turned chilly.

'Beth,' he nodded in greeting. 'How are the children?'

'They're fine,' Beth smiled. She was no longer intimidated by the man she'd first known as an arrogant and distant figure, referred to in awe as a 'master potter' by his older employees. Not that the term inferred any artistic ability, merely the inherited wealth to own one of the largest and most successful potteries in Staffordshire.

'Coffee?' Sylvia inclined her head gracefully over the tray.

'Thanks.' Michael reached out and took the fluted cup. 'I still think this is one of our best designs,' he commented.

'Couldn't agree more,' said Robert briskly. 'That's why I'm against some of these more modern ideas. Classic shapes, that's what people want.'

'Of course,' Beth said, 'and they always will. But the younger generation are looking for stronger colours, bolder shapes. Surely it's only good business sense to cater for both markets.'

Robert glanced keenly at his daughter-in-law. He'd learned over the years to respect her astuteness. 'I suppose you could be right,' he admitted grudgingly.

Michael threw Beth a grateful glance. 'Glad to hear you agree, Father, particularly as I've just set on a new young designer.'

'Robert, I'm sure Michael and Beth haven't given up their evening to come here and talk shop,' chided Sylvia gently.

'No, of course not. Well, let's have it. What is it that Mrs Hammond can't overhear?' he demanded. 'Not that she's in the habit of eavesdropping.'

Michael glanced at Beth and waited for her to speak.

Looking directly at Robert, she said, 'Do you remember five years ago, when you were so ill?'

He drew his grey bushy eyebrows together.

'Everyone says I was,' he said abruptly. 'Can't remember it myself.'

Beth's eyes met Sylvia's, remembering the stooped, broken man hunched in his armchair, not caring whether he lived or died.

'Telling you of Rosemary's existence gave you the strength to recover, we all know that. Do you recall how you vowed never to abandon your search for her?'

Robert stiffened.

'I didn't abandon it,' he snapped. 'It was those damn lawyers, telling me my advertisements broke the law.'

'They didn't achieve anything anyway,' Sylvia said sadly. 'Is that what you've come to talk about, Beth? The new Adoption Bill they're proposing?'

Beth shook her head, her mouth suddenly trembling now that the moment had actually arrived.

'We've come to tell you...' she stopped, unable to continue.

'Tell us what?' Sylvia said with concern. She leaned over and took Beth's hands. 'Take your

245

time, sweetheart. It can't be that bad.'

'It's not bad at all,' Beth said through her tears. 'It's wonderful!' She looked at them with wet, shining eyes. 'We've come to tell you that you can forget your vow, because she's here, she's found us! Rosemary's here, in Newcastle!'

'What?' Sylvia gasped. 'What did you say?'

Robert moved swiftly to sit beside Michael on the leather chesterfield.

'Are you telling us...?' His expression was one of incredulity.

'Are you saying you've actually seen her?' Sylvia's voice was breathless.

Beth nodded as she dabbed at her eyes with a handkerchief.

'We both have, yesterday.'

'But when did all this happen, why didn't you say anything to us?' Robert demanded, getting up to pace the room, his head thrust forward belligerently. 'Have you checked? Is this girl genuine? I don't need to tell you, Michael, that this is a very sensitive situation. We're sitting targets here for blackmail!'

'Oh, for heaven's sake, father, what do you take me for?' Michael said irritably. 'This is exactly why we didn't say anything to you, not until we were sure, particularly after last time.'

Robert sat down again and stared at his son. 'You mean you've actually found her? You're sure? It really is Rosemary?'

Beth interjected, 'As I said, she found us. You'll only have to see her to know she's your granddaughter.' Her eyes flickered to a silver-framed photograph on the baby grand piano. It

246

was of James, Michael's younger brother and Rosemary's father, taken with his Italian wife Giovanna on their wedding day. The resemblance was unmistakable.

'She's definitely Beth's daughter,' Michael said quietly. 'I'll make sure you see her birth certificate as soon as possible.'

'But how ... when?' Sylvia leaned forward, her face alight with excitement. 'Tell us everything, right from the beginning. Oh Beth, what is she like?'

'She's lovely. Tall, with dark hair, blue eyes and ... well, wait until you see her.'

'When will that be? Why haven't you brought her with you?' Robert demanded, bristling.

'It's not as easy as that,' Michael pointed out. 'All she knows at the moment is that she's found her natural mother. Once Beth's told her about James, then of course we'll bring her to see you.'

'So she doesn't know about us?' Sylvia said, her eyes wistful.

'No, not yet.'

'Well, you'd better tell her, and quickly,' Robert said abruptly. 'Come on now, we want to know everything, right from the beginning.'

As Beth began to relate the events of the past two weeks, Michael wandered out of the drawing-room and slowly climbed the broad staircase. Going to a room at the end of the first landing, he opened the door and stood on the threshold. The bedroom was still furnished as James had left it. Photographs were on the walls of his form at prep school, of him grinning on the front row of the Cricket XI at his public school,

247

of looking suitably academic on his graduation from university. A studio portrait of Giovanna, dark-haired, beautiful and laughing, taken when they became engaged. Michael had often wondered at his mother's wisdom in refusing to change her younger son's bedroom, but for the first time, he began to understand why. Somehow, there was a calm there, an acceptance, a comfort.

'Oh, James,' he muttered, 'that damn party had a lot to answer for.' But Michael knew that however bitter his own feelings, his brother had paid a far heavier penalty. With a heavy heart, he closed the door and slowly made his way down the familiar staircase back to the drawing-room.

Robert confronted him.

'So, a granddaughter of mine, a Rushton, is working as a glorified skivvy less than three miles from here?'

'She is,' Michael said tersely.

'Then what are you doing about it?' he demanded.

'We can't do anything yet,' Beth said. 'Rosemary doesn't know she is a Rushton, in fact she doesn't even know my married name.'

'You mean she has no idea...?'

'None whatsoever,' Michael said.

'The next time I see her, which must be very soon, she's going to be asking questions,' Beth said with anxiety. 'And I promised her in the church that I'd tell her the truth.'

Sylvia paled, and her hand fluttered to her throat in distress.

'You don't mean...'

'I have to, Sylvia,' Beth said huskily. 'I have to make her understand all the circumstances, why I didn't keep her.'

'These people who brought her up, has she said much about them?' Robert asked.

'Not a lot,' Michael said. 'But we did gain an impression that she hadn't had an easy time.'

'So,' Robert probed, 'you don't think she comes from this sort of background?' He waved a hand at the luxuriously furnished room.

'I'd very much doubt it,' Michael said drily.

Sylvia began to gather up the cups and saucers, her hands trembling as she piled them on to the tray.

'I could do with a drink, I don't know about you, Michael,' muttered Robert.

'I'll have a brandy.' Michael followed his father to the elegant Edwardian sideboard at the far end of the room.

Beth got up to take the tray out to the kitchen.

'I'm sorry, Sylvia,' she said quietly. 'I know how painful it is for all this to be dragged up again. But I've got to tell her the truth about James.' Her voice broke. 'Can you imagine how it felt to find my daughter after all these years, and then to see hurt and resentment in her eyes. I have to try and make her understand. I don't want any more lies, any more secrecy. I lived with that burden for years, I'm not going through it again.'

'I know,' Sylvia whispered.

Robert poured himself and Michael a generous measure of Remy Martin, and then said, 'I know Sylvia will have one, but what about Beth?'

'Do you want a brandy, darling?' Michael called as Beth came back into the room.

'Yes, please.' She turned to Sylvia. 'Sorry we didn't let you know sooner, but we didn't want to raise your hopes. In fact, Michael was really worried about the prospect of blackmail.'

'And you?'

Beth shook her head.

'Not really, not after seeing Mum's reaction. She just had this feeling...'

'Rose must be so thrilled,' Sylvia said wistfully.

Beth touched her hand. 'You won't have to wait long, I promise.'

'And I think you'd both better give some thought to our strategy in all this,' Michael said, as he brought the drinks over. He looked at his parents, his forehead creasing in concern.

Robert glanced at Sylvia, who bit her lip and looking away, stared steadfastly at the oil painting over the fireplace.

'Yes,' he said heavily, 'there are going to be difficult times ahead. But first I want to see this girl, find out what she's made of.' He drummed his fingers impatiently on the arm of the chair.

Beth, her expression carefully blank, stared straight ahead. Would Rosemary be a match for her grandfather? As Rose always said, only time would tell.

26

'Yes, I'm sure I can get tomorrow afternoon off...'

'Good. I'll pick you up at two o'clock. Bye then, Rosemary.'

'Bye...' Floundering over what name to call her newly-found mother, Rosemary put down the receiver.

She went back to her typewriter, but instead of trying to decipher Sally Ann's manuscript, sat with her hands resting limply on the keyboard. Thinking.

Her reaction to the phone call was mixed. Relief that Beth had been in touch so soon and wanted to see her, anxiety as to the outcome of that meeting. It was only in the last few hours, as her initial euphoria faded, that Rosemary had come to realise that her mother had told her nothing, not even her married name. Neither had Beth written down her telephone number. It was almost as if Sunday hadn't happened, for Rose was still her only contact. Slowly, uncertainly, fear began to grow within her. A dread that Beth, who was obviously guarding her privacy, wanted to keep her family life apart from her illegitimate daughter. Was that what Beth was going to tell her? That despite her joy in being reconciled with her daughter, their lives had to be separate?

There was something else that was odd too. While Rose had proudly displayed a family wedding photograph of Beth's brother Gordon and his wife Val, there had been no photograph of Beth and Michael's wedding. Also, when she'd plucked up the courage to ask Beth and Michael if they had any family, Beth had murmured that they had two little boys. Yet on the upright piano there had only been a photograph of Gordon's two little boys, Paul and Carl, and she recalled how it had stood alone, almost as though some other ornament, vase or even photograph had been removed.

Rosemary frowned in concentration, remembering how Rose had shown her an album filled with photographs of Beth and Gordon as children, and of Harry their father. There had also been photographs of his mother, a thin, sharp-featured woman referred to as Grandma Sherwin, and of Rose's own mother, who'd recently died, a smiling, plump woman called Granny Platt. But there were no up-to-date photographs, or at least she hadn't been shown them. Why?

When the shrill ring of the telephone punctured her anxious thoughts, she jumped up quickly in relief, her mood changing with a sudden rush of adrenalin. Let it be him! Oh, please let it be him!

'Hello, Rosemary?'

'Yes?' She tried to make her voice cool and sophisticated.

'It's Simon. Remember me?'

'Of course.'

'I wondered if you'd like to meet for a drink?'

'I'd love to.' Her heart thudded with excitement.

'Any chance you're free tonight?'

'Tonight?' she echoed. 'Well...' Rosemary hesitated, then deciding she could handle Sally Ann, said nonchalantly, 'Yes, I am as it happens.'

'Good, I'll pick you up. What's the address?'

Rosemary told him. 'It's just around the corner from your new flat, you can't miss it.'

'Fine. About eight okay?'

'Great.'

'See you then.' He hung up.

Ecstatic, Rosemary raced up the stairs to her room and flung open the door to the single wardrobe. She sighed with exasperation. The only thing she could possibly wear was the same blue ethnic dress she'd worn on Sunday. She glanced at her watch – nearly four o'clock. Time to finish off the typing, take Homer for his run, and to wash her hair. To get Sally Ann in a good mood she'd make her a bread and butter pudding. Real English nursery food, the American called it.

'But you never go out in the evenings,' she objected, when Rosemary made her request. 'That was part of the deal, remember? Besides I wanted to go through these notes with you. I need them typed up for the morning.'

'We could read through them now, and I'll get up early in the morning and do it.'

Sally Ann glanced at her sideways. 'Do I take it you have a date?'

When Rosemary nodded, Sally Ann sighed. She might have known it was too good to last, a good-looking kid of her age.

'I guess I'm not so old I can't remember how

that feels. A local boy?'

'He's a doctor at the hospital. I met him on the train coming up and bumped into him yesterday,' Rosemary explained.

'A doctor! Gee honey, that's the idea, aim high. I never knew a poor one!'

Rosemary reddened.

'Okay, off you go, but don't be too late, I don't want you oversleeping. And I'd rather you didn't make a habit of it, honey.'

Simon glanced at his watch. It was twenty past seven.

'Are you nearly finished?'

'I won't be long,' his mother answered serenely, reaching up and checking her measurements of the width of the bay window.

'It's a nice open view out of here, over the recreation ground,' she commented.

'Yes,' Simon said impatiently, 'so you already said. I don't know why you didn't do all this earlier.'

Christine Oldham ignored him. She glanced down at her only son. Had to pick up a friend at eight o'clock, he'd said. She could always tell if Simon was meeting a girl. It was the only time he fussed about his appearance and, judging by the time he'd spent in the bathroom, this one must be pretty special.

Well, she'd go the same way as the others if she had anything to do with it. Simon fooled himself that his dedication and single-mindedness about his career in medicine had kept him free from entanglements, but Christine knew better. She was determined that her only son's advancement should be right to the top. He had the brains to be a specialist, for Harley Street even. And he needed time for research, for cultivating the right people, not for playing happy families in the suburbs.

Christine smiled ironically. It had all been so easy. She'd always been a good manipulator. Also, poison could be dripped in many subtle ways, and obligingly Simon had always brought his girlfriends home. But now, she mused as she closed her notebook, he's in a new responsible post and alone in a new town. A dangerous combination.

'I'll just measure the sofa. Loose covers would brighten it up no end,' she said.

Simon, who could see nothing wrong with the sofa, sighed in exasperation.

'Can't you do that next time?' he coaxed.

'No,' Christine said airily. 'It won't take long.' Slowly, she took her time with the tape measure.

'How about a cup of tea before I go,' she suggested.

'You do know you'll miss your train?'

'Oh, that doesn't matter, I can always catch another one. Besides, I've had second thoughts about those bedroom curtains.'

'I'm going out in about twenty minutes!'

'That's all right, you can drop me off for the train after you pick up your friend. You did say it was only round the corner?'

'Yes, but...'

'Don't fuss, Simon. The station's only five minutes in the car.'

Rosemary, not knowing what type of car Simon drove, was peering out of the window as the white Ford Capri cruised up the street. As it drew to a halt, Simon got out, leaving a woman sitting in the passenger seat.

When Rosemary came out of the gate, he muttered, 'Sorry about this, I've just got to drop my mother off at the station.'

'That's okay.'

He pulled back the driver's seat for Rosemary to climb into the back.

'My mother's come up to give the flat the once over,' he explained, switching on the ignition. 'This is Rosemary, Mum.'

'Nice to meet you, Mrs Oldham.' Rosemary smiled.

'You too,' Christine said coolly over her shoulder, glancing disparagingly at the Victorian terrace house. What a dump – it looked as if it hadn't seen a lick of paint for years! If this was her background...

'And what do you do, Rosemary?' Christine asked as they drove down the hill. 'Are you a student, or are you working?'

'I'm working,' Rosemary said.

'What sort of work?'

'Mum, she doesn't want the third degree,' Simon interrupted.

'It's okay,' Rosemary said quickly. 'At the moment I'm working as a Girl Friday for a professor at Keele University.'

'Girl Friday! What exactly does that entail?' Christine kept her tone one of mild interest.

'I live in, Mrs Oldham,' Rosemary said. 'I type her manuscripts and look after the house and dog. She's an American over on a year's exchange.'

'Sounds fun,' Simon smiled. 'Smashing dog.'

Christine didn't comment. Instead, she murmured casually, 'I expect you're having a year out.'

Rosemary frowned. 'Sorry, I'm not sure what you mean.'

Christine's lips tightened. As she'd thought, the girl was not only poor, judging by that cheap dress, but also uneducated. As for this Girl Friday job, she knew exactly what that meant. The girl was nothing but a cleaner and common typist for God's sake! Had her son neither taste nor sense, or was he like so many men – kept his brains in his trousers?

'Look, question time over, we're here,' Simon said with relief, drawing up outside Stoke station.

Rosemary looked up at the imposing entrance opposite The North Stafford Hotel, remembering her arrival. Was it only four weeks ago?

'No, don't bother to see me off,' Christine smiled sweetly at them both. 'I've taken up enough of your time already. Nice to have met you, Rosemary.'

'And you,' Rosemary smiled back, but uneasily. She watched Christine lean over to kiss Simon's cheek. She was an attractive woman in her late forties, smartly dressed in a lightweight tweed suit, her blonde hair cut bluntly in a fashionable bob. The nicotine stains on her red-tipped fingers revealed she was a heavy smoker.

A minute later, she walked briskly away, an expensive overnight bag in her hand.

'Sorry about that,' Simon said, as he drove back into Newcastle. 'She came up to measure for curtains and things. I thought she'd have left ages ago.'

'No problem,' Rosemary smiled. 'Where are we going?'

'Someone said the best pub around here is out on the Whitmore Road,' he said. 'I expect you know it?'

'No, I don't know much at all,' she confessed. 'I've only been here a few weeks.'

He glanced sideways at her. 'I guessed wrong then. I thought you'd been away on holiday or something, when I saw you with your suitcases that time.'

'No, I'm new to the area, just like you.'

'Where do your parents live then?'

'I'm on my own,' she said shortly.

Simon shot a look at her set face and took the hint.

'I originate from Chalfont St Giles, in Buckinghamshire,' he said, 'but I've been working at Guy's in London for the past couple of years.'

'It's a very famous hospital.'

'Yes, and full of people like Sir Lancelot Spratt, too,' he grinned. 'Or are you too young to have seen the "Doctor" films?'

'What, at nineteen? I've seen them on TV. I suppose you see yourself as Dr Sparrow!' she laughed.

'If only,' he moaned. 'I wish I had his luck with women.'

'I've come out with you, haven't I?' Rosemary teased.

'Ah, but you're too young and innocent to be a good judge.'

'You don't know anything about me,' she protested.

'I can see it in those lovely blue eyes,' he grinned, then turned off the main road to park the car outside a black and white timbered pub.

The bar was smoky and crowded, so Simon led the way into a cool lounge and found an empty table in one corner.

'What would you like to drink, a gin and tonic or...?'

'Gin and tonic will be fine,' Rosemary smiled.

'I must tell you about this guy who came into Casualty today,' Simon began, when at last they'd been served with their drinks. 'It would have been hilarious if he hadn't been in so much pain.'

Rosemary leaned back, cautiously sipped the unfamiliar drink, and listened with growing amusement as Simon recounted, and she suspected exaggerated, various incidents at the hospital.

'You obviously enjoy your work,' she said. 'Have you always wanted to be a doctor?'

'Yes,' he said, 'right from when I can remember. My father was a GP, although of course my mother thought he was wasted.'

'Wasted? Why?'

'Oh, because she was ambitious for him, I suppose. Mum's always been one for social status,' he grimaced. 'Whereas Dad, well, all he wanted was to look after his patients and do a bit of fly fishing.' He looked down. 'He died, three years ago.'

'I'm so sorry,' Rosemary said.

There was a short silence, then she asked, 'And you? What's your ambition?' She watched his eyes narrow as he considered.

'I think I want to specialise,' he said. 'Carcinoma is on the increase you know, both with men and women. Cancer,' he explained. 'If I'm good enough, I'd like eventually to become a surgeon, that's if I can get a consultancy.'

Rosemary gazed at him, noting the keen intelligence in his eyes, now serious with thought. Then she looked away, her own eyes shadowing. Laughing and joking with Simon was one thing, and she knew he found her attractive, but she had to face facts. Not only was he several years older than herself, but it was obvious there was a world between them in terms of education and experience.

'What about you,' he said suddenly. 'What do you want to do with your life?'

She paused. Now would be a good time to tell him about her background, about Brenda's death in the fire which destroyed her home. Her search for her natural mother would explain her lack of plans for her own future, but remembering the intensity of Beth's question in the church, she felt constrained, not free to reveal any personal details.

Simon watched the consternation on Rosemary's face as she struggled to find a reply. God, she was a mystery this one! He'd backed off immediately from asking her about her family, and now she was dithering about answering a perfectly simple question. His gaze wandered over her wide, intelligent brow, her deepset blue eyes which could be so open one minute and secretive the next. With that creamy complexion and stunning figure, she was the most beautiful girl he'd ever seen, and so intriguing. Who'd have thought she was only nineteen for instance, a discomforting thought. He'd had her down for at least twenty-two.

'I'm not sure,' Rosemary confessed at last. 'Perhaps I'm still searching.'

Simon found her confusion touching, and reached over the small oak table to take her hand in his.

'You've got plenty of time,' he said gently.

Rosemary gazed down at their joined hands, liking the feel of his skin against hers, delighting in the sudden warm stirring of her senses.

For a moment there was silence, and then Simon murmured, 'Would you like another drink?'

'Just a soft one this time,' she said. 'Lemon and lime or something.'

By the end of the evening, Rosemary felt she'd known Simon all her life. Relaxed with each other, they talked of books, music, of Simon's passion for football, of her own neglected interest in drawing and design.

'Once I've sorted myself out, I might go to evening classes or something,' she confided.

Simon wondered what she had to sort out? Yet he already knew that if he asked she'd clam up. No matter. Perhaps when she grew to trust him, he'd learn all about this nineteen-year-old girl/woman. He winced. Nineteen, he must be mad! But then as he looked into Rosemary's candid eyes and held her gaze, Simon knew the decision was made for him.

'I'm off duty this weekend. Are you any good at shopping?' he asked.

'Am I female?' she laughed.

'I can vouch for that,' he grinned. 'You wouldn't like to come and help me on Saturday, would you? Only I need a few things for the flat. We could get a ploughman's lunch or something to fortify us.'

'I've always been told never to go shopping with a man, they get bad-tempered,' she teased.

Simon scowled at her.

She laughed. 'Sounds a great idea to me,' then glanced at her watch. 'I'd better be going, I've got to be up really early in the morning to type up some notes.'

'Bit of tartar is she, this American woman?'

Rosemary shook her head. 'She just expects her money's worth. I'm only there temporarily anyway.'

'Oh?' Simon raised his eyebrows, but as he half expected, Rosemary didn't elaborate.

'Okay,' he said. 'Let's go.'

He drove Rosemary home along the darkening country roads back into Newcastle, and pulled up outside the house.

'I'll pick you up about twelve then, on Saturday.'

'I'll look forward to it,' Rosemary smiled, then quickly leaned over and kissed his cheek. 'Thanks for tonight, Simon, it was great.'

Simon watched her unlock the door, and then thoughtfully put the car into gear. Was he wise to get involved? And yet, as he drove away, the memory of a pair of blue eyes lingered, and it was with difficulty that he switched his mind to the full operating list awaiting him in the morning.

27

The following day Rosemary waited in an agony of impatience for Beth to pick her up as promised. Ready well ahead of time, she'd been standing at the window for half an hour when at last the small red car drew up. Her stomach churning with nerves, Rosemary grabbed her bag and let herself out of the front door.

'Sorry I'm late,' Beth apologised. 'The phone rang just as I was about to leave.'

Rosemary got into the passenger seat and glanced at her. Although dressed in a cool summer dress, Beth looked flushed and ill at ease.

'Thank goodness it's a fine day,' she said, as she drove through the town centre.

'Why, where are we going?'

'I thought Trentham Gardens would be nice. It's not far, about ten minutes or so.'

Not to her home then. Rosemary's spirits fell. So, her fear had been justified.

'Originally,' Beth explained, 'it was part of the

Duke of Sutherland's estate, but now it's quite a famous beauty spot.'

Disappointed, Rosemary remained silent. She stared bleakly out of the window as they passed a hospital, a Catholic church, and then several large houses built high above the road.

'That's the River Trent on the right,' Beth told her. She pulled over and parked the car in a shady side lane. In the warm sunlight they walked slowly through an imposing gateway to a long tree-lined drive. A few minutes later, Rosemary gave an involuntary cry of delight.

'Lovely, isn't it,' Beth commented. 'This part is called the Italian Gardens.'

'I hadn't expected it to be so huge,' Rosemary exclaimed. Before them stretched a lake, the only sound on its shimmering surface a small motor launch cruising along.

'Oh, this is only a small corner,' Beth said, 'but I thought we could be private here. There are things I want to tell you, Rosemary, that I wouldn't want anyone else to overhear. Otherwise I would have taken you home.'

Rosemary glanced at her, startled. Did that mean that after today, she would?

There were few people about on that weekday afternoon and they strolled along a path until Beth halted at a secluded seat under large beech trees. She sat down and waited for Rosemary to join her.

For a few minutes neither spoke.

Beth looked down at her hands, deliberately bare except for her slim gold wedding band. Nervously, she twisted it round, seeking the right words.

'Do you have to tell her?' Rose had questioned, upset and worried.

'She's not a child, Mum,' Beth pointed out. 'And if I don't tell her the truth, then how is she going to understand why I gave her away?'

'You could say you had an affair with James.'

'Yes, I could. But once she meets Robert and Sylvia and sees the background he came from, any excuses I had wouldn't hold water. Don't you see, I've got to make her understand how it was.'

Rose bit her lip, her forehead creasing in worried lines.

'Don't expect too much from her, lass, not yet.'

'I know. I've got nineteen years to make up for.'

Now, with her daughter beside her, Beth closed her eyes and willed herself to resurrect the traumatic memories of that one eventful year, 1956.

'You want to know about your father, and how I came to give you up for adoption, don't you?' she eventually said.

Rosemary answered quietly, 'Yes, I think I have a right to know.'

'Yes, I think you have.' Beth took a ragged breath. This was going to be one of the hardest things she'd ever had to do. She gazed straight ahead, above the formal flower-beds, over the stone balustrade, out on to the silver water.

'What I'm about to tell you is a shocking thing for any mother to tell her child,' she said slowly, desperate to find the right words. 'I just want you to know, Rosemary, that I loved you from the

265

first moment I held you in my arms.' Beth turned to face her daughter. 'Your father was a fine man,' she said with intensity, 'and what he did was completely out of character. I want you to try and understand that.'

Rosemary nodded, her eyes meeting her mother's in an effort to reassure her. She could see the anxiety there, almost feel the tension in Beth's body.

Beth looked out again over the water.

'I suppose it's apt in a way that we should be here. If I hadn't come to a dance at Trentham Gardens Ballroom, on that one particular night, you would never have been born. A boy we met invited my best friend Valerie and me to a party the following week.' Beth sighed. 'Such insignificant things at the time and yet how they influence our lives! Anyway, at the last minute Val was ill, and as we didn't want to let people down, I went on my own. At seventeen and still at school, I'd only been to parish socials before, and was green enough to believe someone when they said a bowl of punch was non-alcoholic.'

She paused, her face paling as slowly, painfully, she described to Rosemary the events of that fateful evening. How, exhilarated with the music and party atmosphere, she drank glass after glass, ignorant of the effects until it was too late.

'I was so naïve, so stupid,' she said bitterly.

Feeling ill, and in an effort to get away from the crowd, she'd staggered upstairs to lie on a bed in a darkened room. When four youths had burst in the door, her vision had been so blurred that it was only when one shouted 'Heigh ho, Silver!'

that she realised they wore masks and were in fancy dress as Lone Rangers.

'They'd gatecrashed the party and were even more drunk than I was,' Beth said.

A trickle of fear ran down Rosemary's spine, as her mind tried to grapple with the scene and its implications and she whispered in horror, 'Four of them?'

'Oh, it was only one, the others left him to it.' Beth closed her eyes, even now nausea rising within her at the memory of the stench of beer on her attacker's breath, his heavy body ramming into her.

'Oh, I fought, Rosemary. I struggled and clawed at him, but I'm slightly built, I didn't stand a chance. Afterwards...'

She turned her head away, trying to shut out the vision of herself, vomiting on the floor beside the bed, then stumbling in shock to a bathroom to clean herself up.

'I didn't know who he was, not then, not for years. He never even spoke, just lurched out of the room.'

Rosemary sat as though turned to stone, her face ashen with shock. Why did I have to ask? Why in God's name did she have to tell me? Bitter, despairing tears welled in her eyes. How can I live with something like this?

'Is that why you had me adopted?' she whispered. 'Because I was the result of rape?'

'I suppose that must have influenced me in some ways,' Beth admitted. 'I was so ashamed. I felt so dirty. I told no-one, not even my mother. Not then, and not when I found out I was pregnant.'

'You mean Rose didn't know about me?'

'She didn't know until six years ago. But I'll come to that later.' She turned and said intensely, 'You've got to understand what it was like then. To have an illegitimate baby was the ultimate disgrace at the best of times, but for a schoolgirl to get pregnant...' Beth's eyes shadowed, remembering the sheer misery and terror of those early months. 'Dad had recently died,' she tried to explain. 'Gordon was away doing his National Service, and Mum and I were only just making ends meet. Not only that but it was a terrible struggle to keep me at the grammar school. Even my grandmother was using her savings to buy my uniform and books. How could I let them all down? And as for Mum, well, the shame would have killed her. Or that was how I felt at the time.'

'But how did you manage to keep it a secret?'

'I was lucky,' Beth said simply. 'I didn't show very much in the early months. I wore a loose gymslip in the week, and a sloppy Joe sweater at other times. No-one suspected anything, they had no reason to. Eventually, I knew I had to do something so I went to confession and told my parish priest. He arranged for me to spend the last three months of my pregnancy in Westbourne.' She paused. 'I think you know the rest.'

Rosemary remained silent, still struggling with the treacherous tears. Shock at Beth's traumatic revelation warred with compassion for that young seventeen-year-old girl. Slowly, the anger and resentment simmering inside her began to slip away. Who was she to judge, for how would she have reacted in similar circumstances, even now, when the stigma of illegitimacy had largely disappeared?

'You said "then",' she said at last.

'Sorry?'

'You said you didn't know who he was "then".'

'No, I didn't, not for a long time. No-one knew who the gatecrashers were. It was not until...' Beth took a deep breath. She glanced anxiously at her daughter, seeing her pallor, the tension in her shoulders. It isn't over yet, my love, she thought with despair. 'It took me many years to get over the rape, at least as much as you ever get over something like that. Then, when I met Michael and we got engaged, I agonised over whether I should tell him. It was wrong of me not to, I know that now, but at the time I was terrified of losing him.'

Nervously, she got up and said, 'Shall we walk a bit?'

Rosemary nodded, and they walked slowly side by side in the dappled sunlight, physically close and yet still with an invisible barrier between them.

Beth, her expression one of sadness, continued. 'It was on Boxing Day, 1968, when I found out who your father was. Michael had a younger brother, James, who was married to an Italian girl. They'd come over to England for Christmas, and there was a terrible car crash. Giovanna was killed instantly, and James...' Her voice faltered and Rosemary waited with growing apprehension until she was able to continue.

Slowly, with difficulty, Beth told Rosemary of that scene at the hospital which would forever be etched on her memory. How she'd overheard James confess his fear that he might have raped a girl. 'From what he told Michael, how he described what happened,' Beth said, 'I knew without any doubt that he was the one.' Her lips twisted. 'My own brother-in-law.'

Rosemary stared at her, hardly able to believe what she was hearing. Michael's brother had been the one? Michael's brother had actually raped her mother? She wanted to speak, to say something, anything, but dazed with shock, she turned her head away.

'When Michael left the room, to try and contact his parents,' Beth eventually continued, 'I told James that I had been that girl. Oh, Rosemary, if you could have seen how distressed he was! All those years I'd thought of him as a monster, yet in his own way he'd suffered just as I had.' She paused, remembering that earnest, freckled face, how his eyes had beseeched her forgiveness. 'I understood at last that he was drunk,' she said simply. 'As I was. So drunk, he thought at the time I was willing. It was only afterwards he realised what he had done.'

'Did you tell him about me?' Rosemary turned toward her and held her breath, waiting for the answer.

Beth nodded. 'I thought it would comfort him to know he was leaving behind a child. He and Giovanna were just making plans to have a family, but,' her eyes filled with tears, 'it wasn't to be.'

'You said "leaving behind",' Rosemary whispered. 'You mean...'

Beth turned toward her, longing to hold her daughter, to comfort her, but sensed that the time was not yet right.

She said quietly, 'James died shortly afterwards.'

For a few moments they walked in silence, and then Beth said intensely, 'Before he died, I promised James that if I ever found you, I would tell you that your father was a man to be proud of. And I'm not just saying that – he was, Rosemary. Despite what happened, your father was a good and kind man. I want you always to remember that.'

As she finished speaking, they drew level with an empty bench, and as if by mutual consent they turned to sit in the warmth of the sun.

After a few minutes, Beth opened the clasp on her handbag, and placed a photograph face down by her daughter's side.

She stood up.

'There's a café just over there,' she said shakily. 'I need a cup of tea, and I think you need to be on your own. Take your time and come and join me when you're ready.'

Without a backward glance, she walked quickly away.

Rosemary stared down at the white oblong and put out a hand to restrain it as a breeze gently stirred the leaves above. For several minutes she tried to calm her trembling nerves, to banish from her mind the brutal image of her conception. And to accept that her unknown father

271

was dead.

Then, with her heart beating rapidly, she picked up the photograph and gazed at the image of the man who had given her life.

28

The phone was ringing as Beth opened the front door.

'How did she take it?' Sylvia's voice was low and anxious.

'I'm not sure,' Beth glanced round but the kitchen door was firmly closed. 'She was very quiet, but so would anybody be.'

'It must have been very painful for you, Beth. Did you tell her about us?'

'Not yet.'

'But she does know that James was Michael's brother?'

'Yes, I told her that.'

There was a short silence, before Sylvia said, 'When are you seeing her again?'

'Well,' Beth said slowly. 'I gave her my phone number and told her to ring me when she felt ready to talk. I'm sorry, Sylvia, but I just don't think I can rush things.'

'Oh.'

There was a wealth of disappointment in Sylvia's voice, and with a sudden rush of compassion, Beth said, 'I know how you feel. But we have to remember Rosemary's only nineteen.

She's already lost her mother and her home in the last year or so. I didn't want to swamp her with everything at once. Not after learning about James. I mean, I'm still shaky after telling her, God knows how she feels.'

'You're right, of course. Let me know...'

'Immediately,' Beth promised. She replaced the receiver, then turned as the kitchen door opened.

'Mummy, you're home!' Ben raced toward her and Beth held out her arms to hug her three-year-old son.

'And that's another thing,' she murmured as she buried her face in his fair, curly hair. For how would Rosemary feel, when she discovered that after giving her own baby away, Beth had gone on to adopt two other children?

After an uneasy night's sleep, Rosemary awoke the following morning, heavy-eyed and with a splitting headache.

Sally Ann, who'd noted with concern her strained face the previous evening, offered advice.

'You're coming down with something, honey. Have a couple of aspirin and go back to bed. Oh damn! Homer needs to be taken out. Do you think you can manage that?'

'Of course I can, the fresh air will do me good. But I'll take it easy today, if that's okay.'

'You do that, kid.'

After Sally Ann had gone, Rosemary forced herself to tidy the kitchen, then took the impatient dog for his morning walk on the recreation ground. As the collie trotted off, she stared up at the back of Simon's flat, wondering whether he was there, perhaps sleeping after being on call at the hospital.

How would he react if she told him the truth? That he was with someone who was the result of a forced drunken coupling between two complete strangers? Her cheeks burned with shame and turning sharply away she called Homer to heel.

'Come on, that's enough. I need to get back.'

Ten minutes later, she curled up on the sofa and slept heavily for the next two hours. The snap of the letterbox disturbed her, and she lay dozing for several minutes before sitting up to find with relief that her headache had eased.

'A bacon sandwich and a mug of hot, sweet tea, that's what you need,' she muttered, and got up to go into the kitchen.

One letter lay on the doormat, and she picked it up, turning it over to see Lisa's distinctive handwriting.

She waited until her bacon was crisping under the grill, then ripped open the envelope.

'*Write to me*,' Lisa urged. '*You must have some news by now. Was Rose really your grandmother? Did you find Beth?*' She went on to detail snippets of local office gossip, and ended, '*Mum sends her love, and the kids say they miss you. Don't stay away too long, I need your steadying influence.*'

Rosemary felt a sense of unease at the last sentence. Was that just a lighthearted comment, or a genuine plea? One never knew with Lisa.

After she'd eaten, Rosemary sat with her hands cupped around her warm mug of tea, slowly mulling over Beth's words. She knew she would

274

never forget that scene in Trentham Gardens, knew too that hearing the truth had, in a strange way, eased her. For she finally understood just what had driven her mother to give her up for adoption. As she'd watched Beth struggling to tell her story, Rosemary had felt her heart soften, had even had to restrain an impulse to reach out, to take Beth's hand.

She got up and went to fetch her handbag, once more taking out the photo of James. There before her were the hated freckles, the wideset eyes. How strange and sad that she would never know this man she resembled so closely. She began to pace around the room, her mind racing with questions. Why had Beth kept her secret all those years, only to disclose it after James had died? And who exactly had she told? She'd mentioned that Michael had left the room at the hospital to contact his parents. Did they know?

Impulsively, Rosemary searched in her bag for the number Beth had, at last, given to her.

What am I waiting for, she thought. Why not take advantage of my free afternoon? Beth did say to contact her as soon as I was ready. Suddenly, she was tired of all the waiting, of feeling that her life was on hold while she searched for her origins. I need to find out whether I can build my future here, in the Potteries, she determined. I've marked time long enough.

An hour later, when Rosemary got into the car, Beth told her they were going to her home.

'The children aren't there at the moment,' she added, 'but you'll meet them another time.'

'Do they know about me?'

'No, not yet,' Beth said briefly.

'Oh.' Rosemary felt a pang of disappointment. 'Is it far?'

Beth smiled at her. 'Would you believe Newcastle?'

'Really. And the only job outside London advertised in *The Lady* happened to be where you live! Don't you think that's weird!'

'No,' Beth said quietly. 'Because every week since the day you were adopted, I've lit a candle to Our Lady to keep you safe, and return you to me. If you believe in the power of prayer, Rosemary, there's your answer.'

Rosemary felt her scalp tingle.

'All those years?' she whispered.

'All those years. Also, the church where we were reunited is where I got married, and where I go to Mass every Sunday.'

Rosemary shook her head in disbelief. 'I've been going to Mass there too and I've lit a few candles myself,' she admitted.

'There you are then,' Beth smiled, as she paused at a junction. Leaving the main road, she drove up a wide tree-lined avenue, and indicating left, turned into a small cul-de-sac. There seemed to be only one house, its green tiled roof just visible behind a screen of tall beech trees, and Beth swung the car into a white gateway. Rosemary glimpsed a brass plate with the name, *The Beeches*, then as they drove up a long circular drive her eyes widened as at last she saw Beth's home. The house had obviously been specially designed, with white shutters framing large picture windows. Before them lay immaculately kept flowerbeds and lawns. But it was the sheer size of the house which made her catch her breath.

Beth switched off the ignition and opened the car door. Rosemary nervously followed her to the polished oak double door and waited. Beth rummaged for her key, offering a prayer of thanks that on this particular afternoon, neither the housekeeper nor Maria were at home. As for the children, Andrew was at school, while little Ben was at his playgroup.

'Go on through, Rosemary,' she said. 'I'll just put the kettle on.'

Subdued, Rosemary walked across the parquet floor of the square hall, and into the largest room she'd ever seen. Split level, it was expensively furnished in a modern style, with cream leather sofas and pale golden furniture. Light poured in from windows lining one wall, and she walked slowly across to look out over a beautiful landscaped garden to a tennis court at the end.

She stood still, the memory of the mean, sparsely furnished house she'd grown up in, the sordid bed-sit she'd been forced to endure, contrasting starkly with these spacious, comfortable surroundings. She thought of all the petty economies, the constant self-denial, the worry about bills. How unjust it all was! Why were some people able to live like this, while others, no matter how hard they worked, remained forever just above the poverty line? What did Michael do, for God's sake, that he earned this sort of money?

Rosemary was so wrapped up in her own

thoughts that she didn't hear Beth approach until she said wryly, 'It's a bit much for a girl from Minsden, isn't it?'

'What does Michael do?' Rosemary's question was sharper than she intended.

'He's a managing director.' Beth turned evasively, saying, 'Would you like to see the kitchen?'

Rosemary followed her into the sort of kitchen she'd only ever seen on American films, or in magazines. Gleaming work surfaces, Wedgwood blue and white units, a honey pine breakfast table and chairs, pretty curtains...

'Do you take sugar?'

'Just one, please.'

Beth glanced at her, put some biscuits on a plate, and then carried the tray back into the sitting-room.

'I have some questions,' Rosemary said abruptly.

Beth handed her a cup of tea. 'Fire away.'

Rosemary bit her lip.

'Go on,' Beth said gently. 'I'll answer if I can.'

'I was wondering,' Rosemary said nervously, 'what made you suddenly tell Michael and Rose about me? I mean, after keeping it secret all those years.'

'I rather thought you'd ask that. It ties in with what I want to tell you, anyway. Not long after James died, we found out that Michael couldn't have children.' Beth saw the surprise on Rosemary's face and said softly, 'Yes, that's something else for you to come to terms with. Our two little boys are adopted.' Her eyes met Rosemary's in appeal as she said, 'Michael would have liked a girl the second time, but I just couldn't. Not when my own daughter was out there somewhere. I'd have felt so disloyal to you. Can you understand that?'

Rosemary felt tears prick her eyelids. She nodded.

'Coming on top of losing his other son, the news hit Michael's father very hard. He'd always had this dream of a family dynasty, of grand-children to carry on the family name. He became ill, severely depressed, a shadow of his former self, and medication wasn't helping. Also Michael felt he'd let me down, was carrying all this guilt about my never having a child.' Beth's eyes shadowed as she remembered how she'd struggled with her conscience, how frightened she'd been that her relationship with Michael, already under strain, wouldn't survive the shock of her revelation.

'So, you felt you had no alternative but to tell them?'

'Yes. I told Michael the truth – then, before we went to see his parents, I told my mother.' Beth looked away, not wanting to relive the pain of those scenes, the trauma of knowing she was hurting the two people she loved most in the world.

'Does anyone else know?'

Beth shook her head. 'No, not even Gordon and Val. We decided to keep it between ourselves and the grandparents.'

Rosemary put down her cup with an unsteady hand.

'Can I ask you something else?'

'Of course.'

'Did you tell them about the way it happened, you know, about the party?'

Beth gave a deep sigh. 'Yes. They know everything. As you can imagine it was a terrible shock, especially for Sylvia and Robert.'

'Sylvia and Robert,' Rosemary repeated. 'So they must be my grandparents.'

'They are,' Beth smiled. 'And dying to meet you.'

'Did knowing about me help Michael's father to get better?'

'He never looked back. In fact he became obsessed with searching for you. I'm surprised your parents didn't see his advertisements in the newspapers.'

Rosemary stared at her in astonishment.

'He advertised to find me?'

'Frequently. He only stopped because he found out it was against the law. Just a minute, I'll show you.'

Rosemary slumped against the soft cushions. So that was why Brenda had forbidden newspapers in the house. She remembered how the paper boy had suddenly stopped delivering, how Brenda had said the money they saved would help to pay for a colour television.

Beth returned with a white envelope and took out a newspaper cutting.

Rosemary held out her hand, took it and slowly read,

SHERWIN, *Rosemary Elizabeth. Would anyone*

knowing the whereabouts of Rosemary Elizabeth Sherwin, born on 3rd August, 1956 at Westbourne, Hants, please contact Box No...

She looked up, her face pale.

'Mum must have seen this, that's why she suddenly cancelled all the papers.'

'Perhaps she was afraid of losing you,' Beth said. 'Although, as you were legally adopted, her rights would have been protected. But you see, Rosemary, all those years, you weren't forgotten. Never a day went by that I didn't think of you, and once Mum knew, she was the same.'

Rosemary gazed at her, then looking down again at the newspaper cutting, found she couldn't speak.

Beth, seeing her distress, busied herself collecting up the teacups and taking the tray back into the kitchen.

'Come on,' she said eventually. 'Let me show you the garden.'

They walked along paths between carefully tended herbaceous borders, where Beth pointed out the shrubs and saplings she and Michael had chosen.

'We were so lucky with this land,' she explained. 'It was part of a large estate, so we're blessed with all these mature beech trees. Usually, with a newly-built house, you have to start a garden from scratch.'

'It must take a lot of work,' Rosemary said, seeing an extensive kitchen garden in the distance.

'Fortunately, we have a very good gardener.'

Beth glanced with a pang of guilt at Rosemary's carefully controlled features. As yet Rosemary had only told them the bald facts about her adoptive parents, but she'd gained an impression that her daughter's childhood hadn't been easy, and certainly she appeared to have little in the way of material possessions.

'So,' she asked, 'how do you feel about meeting Michael's parents? Is it too soon?'

Rosemary shook her head. 'No, I'd like to. But it won't be easy for them, will it? I look so much like ... him!'

They turned to walk back to the house, Beth thinking of that ugly scene when she'd made her confession at Linden Lodge all those years ago. Robert had practically accused her of lying about James, of trying to palm off her bastard as a member of his family. Now, one look at Rosemary, and any lingering doubts he might hold as to her identity would be laid to rest forever.

'Don't worry about that,' she said. 'They'll be as proud of you as I am.'

Rosemary smiled at her uncertainly, remembering the strain on Michael's face, her unease in his presence. Now that she had an insight into the reason, she could understand it. Would she be such a painful reminder to his parents?

29

The phone rang the following morning just as Rosemary was finishing off a long and detailed letter to Lisa. Hurriedly, she licked the flap on the envelope and put it on the hall table ready to post.

It was Simon.

'It's about Saturday.' He sounded in a hurry.

Rosemary's spirits plummeted. He'd thought better of seeing her again – she'd known it was too good to be true.

'Yes?'

'It's just that Mum phoned. I told her I was going flat-shopping with you, but she says there's no need, she's already got all the stuff I'll need. So, as I'm not on duty this weekend, she wants me to go down to fetch it.'

Rosemary said quietly, 'That's okay, Simon.'

'The thing is, I wondered whether you'd like to come?'

'To Chalfont St Giles?' She felt almost giddy with relief.

'Yes. We needn't stay over, and perhaps we could get a Chinese or something when we get back? What do you think?'

'Won't your mother mind?'

'Of course she won't.'

'Then I'd love to.'

'Great. We'll make an early start. I'll pick you

up at eight, okay?'

Rosemary replaced the receiver and turned to go back to a pile of ironing, only for the phone to ring again. This time it was Beth. She wanted to arrange a meeting with Robert and Sylvia on Saturday.

Awkwardly, Rosemary explained why she couldn't come.

'Don't worry about it,' Beth said. 'I'll check with them and come back to you.'

Beth put down the phone, a frown creasing her brow. Why hadn't it occurred to her that Rosemary might have a boyfriend? She could just imagine Robert's reaction.

She was right.

It was Michael's Rotary evening, so after the children were tucked up in bed, Beth drove alone round to Linden Lodge.

Sylvia greeted her with a smile of sheer delight.

'I just can't wait to see her. What time is she coming? It's such a nuisance this business thing tomorrow, I wish we could get out of it.'

Beth followed her into the drawing-room where Robert was enjoying his after-dinner cigar.

'She can't make it on Saturday,' she explained.

'Can't make it? Why ever not?' demanded Robert.

Sylvia was crestfallen. 'Did she say why?'

'She's already arranged to go to Chalfont St Giles. Apparently a friend of hers has just moved into a new flat, and they're going down to pick up some things for it from his mother's.'

'His?' Robert seized on the word immediately.

284

'That's what she said.'

'But she's only been here a matter of weeks – you're not telling me she's got herself a boyfriend already?'

'I don't know whether he's that.'

'Of course he damn well is. She wouldn't go all that way otherwise,' he snapped.

'She's nineteen, Robert,' Sylvia said. 'It's only natural she should be interested in boys.'

'Yes, well, it's one more complication, isn't it? I mean, if we're to keep this thing under wraps, the fewer people involved the better,' muttered Robert.

'Is that what you mean to do?' Beth said with bitterness. 'Sweep it all under the carpet?'

'I don't know what the hell we're going to do.' His bluster collapsed and he looked gloomily down at the carpet. 'I just want to meet her first – I can't seem to think beyond that.'

'Do you think she'll be able to come on Sunday?' Sylvia's tone was wistful.

'I'll ask her. But not for lunch, Sylvia. I want this to be as easy and informal as possible for her. I think I'll bring her on Sunday afternoon. Michael too, if he wants to. Although I don't think any of this is easy for him.'

'Of course it isn't.' Sylvia looked with sympathy at her daughter-in-law. 'It must re-open a lot of old wounds for you both.'

Beth's eyes met hers, and the two women exchanged a look of understanding.

'Rose rang me yesterday,' Sylvia said. 'She was saying what a lovely girl she is.'

Beth smiled. 'She reminds me of Mum in some

ways, very sensible and level-headed. You'd think she was older than nineteen, somehow.'

'She's been through a lot. It's bound to have affected her, made her grow up more quickly.'

'We could have lost her, you know,' Robert said abruptly. 'She could have perished in that house when it burnt down. Did she ever say what caused the fire?'

'Apparently Brenda was a chain-smoker, and it started in the bedroom,' said Beth. 'She hasn't said very much yet about her childhood. She seems reluctant to talk about it.'

'There are things I shall need to know,' Robert declared. 'What education she's had, what her aptitudes are.'

'Well, don't give her the third-degree the minute you meet her,' Beth said. 'You can be a bit intimidating you know, Robert.'

'I think I know how to conduct myself, thank you, Beth.'

'We all know that,' Sylvia intervened. 'But Beth's right. Rosemary has to get to know us, learn to trust us. She'll open up when she's ready.'

'Just be patient, Robert,' Beth pleaded despairingly. But experience had taught her that where Robert Rushton was concerned, his single-mindedness and ambition overruled any advice.

'Are you going to tell her?' Sylvia asked, her blue eyes troubled.

'About Rushton's, you mean?'

'Yes.'

'I don't know what to do. Strangely enough, she hasn't asked about her father's surname. I don't

286

even know if she'd make the connection – after all, Rushton's not that uncommon a name.'

'Probably not,' Robert suggested. 'It isn't as if she'd been brought up in the Potteries.'

'Rushton china is famous throughout the world, Robert,' Sylvia said.

'That's true. Though how much longer we can remain an independent family firm is debatable.' He frowned, thinking of how many smaller potteries had been swallowed up by the large conglomerates. So far, they were holding their own, but what they needed was continuity and depending on what his granddaughter was made of, she could be the answer to their prayers. Good staff were necessary of course, and valued, but in Robert Rushton's mind, family involvement was essential – it meant solidarity and confidence. Now, from the tragedy of the loss of his younger son, had come this girl, carrying in her the Rushton genes. There would be much to put right of course – she wouldn't have had the right upbringing – but if there was a spark of intelligence there, he'd see that she was groomed to take her rightful place. His mind shied away from the crucial and seemingly insurmountable problems which lay ahead. He just needed to see her, talk to her, grasp her mettle, then he'd find some sort of solution.

Seeing Robert's brooding expression, Beth raised her eyebrows at Sylvia and stood up to go.

'Just a minute, Beth, I've got something for the boys.'

Sylvia came back with an Action Man outfit for Andrew, and a pack of felt-tip pens for Ben.

'You spoil them,' Beth laughed.

'That's what grandparents are for,' she smiled. 'Give them my love – tell them I'll see them soon.'

'Sunday?' Rosemary said, in answer to Beth's call the following day. 'Yes, that's fine.'

'Right. I'll pick you up about three o'clock. Have a nice day in Buckinghamshire.'

'Thank you. Bye.'

Rosemary put down the phone thoughtfully, thinking about the proposed trip to Simon's home. She hoped he was right, and that his mother really didn't mind.

Saturday dawned bright and sunny, and Rosemary was ready and waiting at a quarter to eight. Yet again, she was wearing the ethnic blue dress, the colours of which were now beginning to fade from constant washing. Clothes were becoming a major headache. Her summer sandals were past their best and, with winter coming, she was going to need something more decent to wear than a second-hand anorak. What if Simon wanted to take her somewhere really nice? It was true Sally Ann had now paid her, but she was still too scared to spend much of it. Rosemary glanced with distaste at her cheap vinyl bag. She'd held a leather one once in a shop, loving the smell of it, stroking its smooth surface. Then, seeing the price tag, she'd replaced it with resentment, knowing that it was far out of her reach and likely always to be so. It wasn't fair, she thought, surely everyone loves beautiful

288

things, yet only the rich can afford them. It was like the lovely china she used to see in exclusive shops and try to sketch from memory. How she'd longed to hold a piece in her hands, run her fingers over its graceful shape, but always there had been notices saying *'please do not touch'*. Suddenly, she realised she hadn't done any drawing since she'd arrived in Newcastle, and yet the shops here were full of wonderful figurines, vases in new intriguing shapes, designs of teapots and bowls, all waiting to inspire her. Perhaps now she wasn't so focused on finding Beth, the urge to draw would come back to her.

Simon tooted his horn, rousing her from her reverie, and quickly she let herself out of the front door and hurried to the white Ford Capri.

'Hi.'

'You're ready,' he said approvingly.

'Of course, what did you expect?'

'To sit waiting while you titivated, of course.'

'Some of us don't need to!'

He laughed, and Rosemary settled back into the low-slung seat as Simon cruised to the end of the side road, and then accelerated away. He put out a hand to touch hers briefly as it lay on her lap.

'It's good to see you,' he said.

'You too.' She glanced sideways at him, feeling suddenly shy. Somehow, in the early morning light, he looked older, yet in a way even more attractive. She watched his hands on the steering wheel, seeing the tiny dark hairs on his wrists, the capable fingers. A doctor, and a surgeon. Her heart quickened at the prospect of being with him for the whole day. Would he get bored with her? What would they talk about? It had seemed so easy the other night in the pub – he'd been in a lighthearted mood, teasing her, laughing and joking. Now, his profile was serious, intent as he drove. A map lay open on the dashboard.

'How long do you think it will take us?' she asked.

'It depends on the traffic, but at least two hours,' he said. 'Would you like some music?' He switched on the radio to the sound of Charles Aznavour's sensuous voice singing *'She'*.

'Mmn,' Rosemary said dreamily.

'You're just an old romantic,' he accused.

'Hardly old!'

'No, that's true. When are you twenty, by the way?'

'Next August.'

So, she was only just nineteen, he thought.

'You seem older. I can say that as you're so young,' he grinned, 'but just wait a few years, you'd floor me if I made that comment.'

'I've always felt older than my age,' she admitted. 'But I hope you're not inferring that I look old and wrinkly!'

'You look absolutely gorgeous, and no, it's nothing to do with your looks, it's just ... oh, I don't know, just something about you. Maybe it's in the eyes.'

Rosemary looked away and Simon shot a swift glance at her, sensing again her withdrawal. It was just like the first time. As soon as he touched on a personal nerve, she pulled down the shutters.

Eventually, she said, 'Sometimes you have to grow up too quickly, Simon.'

He waited, but Rosemary didn't elaborate, and resignedly Simon concentrated on the road ahead.

They drove for some time in companionable silence. Then Rosemary said, 'Was there a reason why you didn't drive up for your interview?'

'My car was in dock,' he explained. 'I'd got a few days off anyway, so it seemed a good time to have it repaired at a garage I could trust. Mum drove me to the station, so it wasn't much bother.'

'Do you remember me scrabbling around for my shoes?' she laughed.

'I certainly do. And I remember the once-over you gave me when you thought I wasn't looking.'

'I didn't,' she began to protest indignantly, then seeing him laughing, she accused, 'That was nothing to the way you stared at me when I was asleep.'

'You're making that up, you couldn't possibly have known!'

He stopped as she teased, 'There you are, you've admitted it!'

He grinned. 'Okay, I'm guilty. Now, my sweet, let's listen to the music while I try not to get lost.'

Rosemary nestled back in her seat, feeling a warm glow at Simon's endearment. She was looking forward to seeing Simon's home and learning more about the environment he'd grown up in.

Chalfont St Giles was delightful, with several

half-timbered cottages and a church grouped around a green. Rosemary peered out of the window at a sign where St Giles was depicted as the patron saint of lepers, cripples and animals.

A minute later, Simon touched her arm and pointed out Milton's Cottage at one end of the main street, telling her it was where he finished *Paradise Lost* and began *Paradise Regained*.

'He came here,' he said, 'as a refuge from the Great Plague in 1665.'

'It seems a lovely place to grow up in,' Rosemary said wistfully.

'Yes, it was.'

A few minutes later, he was turning into a short drive and pulling up outside a mock-Tudor detached house, its leaded windows reflecting the sun's morning rays.

Christine Oldham appeared immediately at the front door, her smile of welcome freezing for a second as she saw Rosemary in the passenger seat.

Simon swung his long legs out of the car and enveloped her in a bear hug.

'What a great morning!' he said.

'Don't talk too soon,' she replied. 'They're forecasting rain later.' She turned to face Rosemary, who was struggling to her feet.

'Hello, this is a surprise.'

After greeting Simon's mother, Rosemary glared at him. He merely shrugged, grinned and reached out for her hand.

'Come and see the house. We're dying for coffee, Mum.'

Christine followed them both into the house,

inwardly fuming. She'd thought to put a spanner in the works by getting him down here. It hadn't occurred to her that he'd bring the wretched girl with him. Just look at her, wearing that same tatty dress again, and as for that handbag, well she'd have trouble selling it at the church jumble sale!

Simon took Rosemary into a cool hall and through to a large chintzy sitting-room. French windows overlooked a lawned garden, surrounded by formal rose beds, and hedged with tall privet. At one side of the lawn a table covered with a white lace cloth was set out. There were just two chairs.

'You didn't tell her I was coming,' Rosemary hissed at him.

'Mum always cooks enough to feed a regiment.'

'That's not the point!'

'The coffee smells wonderful,' Rosemary ventured, as Christine came in and invited her to sit on the sofa.

'Yes, I can't bear that instant stuff, can you? Mind you, I do keep a jar in for the workmen.'

Rosemary, who'd never tasted anything else, was at a loss how to reply, when Simon interjected.

'You'll have to drink it if you visit me.'

'Not if I buy you a percolator for your birthday,' Christine said tartly.

'Oh yes,' Rosemary said when she'd gone out of the room. 'And how old will you be this time, forty?'

He threw a cushion at her, laughing, which missed and landed on the floor just as Christine returned with a tray.

'Stop horsing about, Simon,' she said abruptly, 'and pick that up.'

He grimaced at Rosemary, but she didn't respond, impressed by the white and gold coffee service and solid silver tray. She began to feel uncomfortable, conscious of her cheap, scuffed sandals and bare legs. Straightening her skirt over her knees, she tucked her feet out of sight and took the translucent china cup from Christine.

'What a lovely service,' she said.

'Yes,' Christine said. 'It belonged to my mother.'

'So, what's for lunch?' Simon asked. 'I hope you've pushed the boat out.'

'Don't I always?' Christine smiled at him, and Rosemary saw the pride in her eyes as she gazed at her son. 'I thought we'd eat in the garden. What do you think? It might be the last chance we'll have this year.'

'Absolutely,' Simon said, swallowing his coffee. 'I'll go and put another chair out.'

Rosemary sipped her own drink slowly, unsure whether she liked the strong, slightly bitter taste. She wished she'd put in more sugar, but felt too nervous to take more.

'I'm sorry Simon didn't let you know I was coming, Mrs Oldham,' she said. 'I hope it hasn't put you out.'

'Oh, I'm used to it,' Christine smiled, though her eyes were cold. 'It wouldn't be Simon if he didn't turn up with a pretty girl in tow.'

The words hit Rosemary like a brick. How stupid she'd been, thinking he thought she was

294

special, that the day meant as much to him as it did to her. She was over-reacting, she knew that – of course Simon would have had lots of girlfriends, would have often brought them home. But some of the joy had gone out of the morning, and she turned her head away not wanting Christine to see her disappointment.

Christine's carefully outlined lips pursed with satisfaction. Just a word here and a word there, it always worked. But she'd have to be careful with this girl, for from the light in Simon's eyes when he looked at her, her son was besotted.

Rosemary looked up as Simon returned.

'Okay, then, Mum, what have you got for me?'

'They're in the kitchen,' she said. 'Come on, I'll show you. Some are things I don't need, and the others you can count as a flat-warming present.'

'You're too good to me,' he said, putting his arm carelessly around her shoulder as they went out of the room. Then, as Rosemary remained uncertainly where she was, he turned and held out his hand. 'Are you coming?'

She got up to join them, feeling reassurance in the warm clasp of his fingers.

Christine had provided an electric kettle, various saucepans, an array of silver-plated cutlery, towels and tea towels, and some sheets, blankets and an eiderdown.

'I'm changing over to duvets,' she explained.

Rosemary looked at all the top-quality, clean and new items, and felt a pang of envy. What must it have been like to grow up in a lovely home like this, surrounded by every comfort, and no worries about bills or debts? She and Simon, their backgrounds were so different, how could their relationship go anywhere? And always there was within her the sick realisation of her own beginnings. The fact that she owed her very existence to an act of violence haunted her. No matter how she tried to push it from her mind, the shame of it was there, lying just beneath the surface.

Lunch was a revelation. Christine was obviously an adept hostess, and from the smoked salmon mousse to the delicious lemon chicken, followed by Black Forest gateau, Rosemary was entranced. She'd never realised that food could taste so sublime, that flavours could be so subtle. As they sat in the peaceful garden with the warm sunshine lying like a blessing on the white cloth and fresh flowers, she began to relax, enjoying the affectionate banter between Simon and his mother. Naturally, she was excluded from much of it, as Christine gossiped about mutual friends and acquaintances, but she was perfectly content just to sip her glass of chilled white wine and let her gaze rest on Simon.

'Have you two been seeing a lot of each other?' Christine asked.

'Stop fishing, Mum,' Simon grinned. 'Anyway, you know I'm working most of the time.'

'This is the second time,' Rosemary smiled at him.

Christine looked at them. Seeing their transparent happiness in each other's company, one would have to be blind not to know that they were falling in love. What a pity Rosemary was so unsuitable, for despite herself she liked the girl.

There was an honesty about her, a dignity. Exactly how old was she? She must remember to ask Simon later. For a fleeting moment, Christine felt a pang of conscience, then hardened her resolve. It was her duty to protect her son, to guide him to achieve his full potential. Unlike his father, Simon was ambitious, had acknowledged to her the unpalatable truth that often success depended on the right contacts. What he needed was a wife with those contacts, perhaps the daughter of an eminent specialist or at least the social background suitable for furthering his career. But she'd have to be subtle, for Christine was well aware that her son was older now, his perceptions sharper.

As she began to collect the dessert plates, she was already planning ahead. The first seed may have been sown, but it would need careful nurturing, and her problem was, how could she do that from a distance?

Rosemary was quiet on the journey home, so Simon, sensing her mood, turned the radio on low, and concentrated on his driving.

Eventually, he said, 'Are you okay?'

She smiled. 'I'm fine. It's been a lovely day.'

'Tired?'

'A little.'

'I didn't realise the journey would take so long. I wish all these people wouldn't bring their cars out when I'm on the road.'

She laughed.

'Thanks to Mum, I think I've got everything I need for the flat,' he said with satisfaction.

'You're very lucky.'

He glanced at her. 'You still haven't told me much about your family, just that you're on your own.'

Rosemary turned her head away and stared out of the window. How much should she tell him? It was obvious that she couldn't go on being secretive for ever, not now he'd taken her to his home, and she was sure Christine would have been quizzing him. Let's face it, she thought, if I want anything to develop out of this, and I do, then I'm going to have to be more open, give Simon a chance to know and understand me. Or was she flattering herself, imagining the special feeling which seemed to flow between them? Was she just another of his pretty girlfriends, as his mother had insinuated, a casual distraction? Lisa always told her she was too serious – she was probably dippy for trying to read so much into such a short acquaintance. She stole a glance at him – just looking at him gave her pleasure, and she knew she was longing for him to take her in his arms, to kiss her, to...

Simon, still waiting for an answer, turned and seeing the look in her eyes impatiently notched up an extra ten miles on the speedometer. 'Well, Rosemary,' he said, 'are you going to tell me, or do I assume you're an escaped criminal?'

His joke broke her tension and she began, 'I am on my own, Simon. My father ran off to Australia with the local barmaid when I was fourteen. My mother died in a fire which destroyed our home in Hampshire, just over a year ago.' She stated the facts baldly.

Involuntarily, he reached out and touched her hand. 'I'm so sorry.'

She gave a weak smile. 'I can't deny things have been tough. Also, my background is not at all like yours. There was never enough money, and even though I wanted to go to university, once Dad had disappeared I couldn't even stay on at school to take my exams. So you see, Simon, you are in the company of a complete ignoramus.'

'People often confuse education with intelligence, my sweet. You must never make that mistake.'

'I know,' she admitted, 'but a decent education is essential if you want to improve your lot, and once I get myself sorted out, I mean to do something about it.'

'How do you mean, sort yourself out?'

'Oh,' she said vaguely, 'decide where I'm going to settle, that sort of thing.'

He frowned. 'What brought you to Newcastle?'

'A live-in job. If you could have seen the squalid bedsit I was in, you'd understand,' she said with bitterness.

'You mean there wasn't any money?'

'No,' she said, feeling ashamed. But he might as well know, it would save explanations later. 'No insurance, nothing. All I had were the clothes I stood up in.'

'God, you poor kid.'

'I managed,' she said, relieved that she'd managed to tell him so much without revealing Beth's secret.

'I can understand now why you were so reluctant to talk about it. It must been devastating, I mean not only losing your mother, but also your childhood home, your security.'

'I wouldn't wish it on anyone,' she said bleakly.

They drove in silence for a while, then he glanced at his watch.

'We should be home in about fifteen minutes. I told Mum we were going to get a Chinese takeaway, but she insisted on giving us tea, telling me you'd be too tired after the journey. Are you? Or do you fancy coming back for a coffee?'

'I'd love to.'

Half an hour later they were in the flat, Simon apologising with a grin that the coffee was only instant. 'The best brand, mind,' he declared. 'None of this supermarket stuff.'

He produced a tin of chocolate biscuits. 'No-one can say I don't treat my guests royally.'

'I should hope so,' she said, taking first one and then another.

'Not watching your figure, I see.'

'Why, should I be?'

'Not from where I'm sitting.' Putting down his mug, he moved over to the sofa to sit beside her. 'You really are something, did you know?' he said softly.

Her eyes searched his, then seconds later she was in his arms, and as Simon brought his lips down to hers in a long, deep kiss, she felt such a sense of belonging that when at last they drew apart, her eyelashes were wet with tears. He touched them wonderingly,

'What's wrong?'

She shook her head, not wanting to speak, not

knowing what to say. Then reaching up she brought his head down again, wanting his lips on hers, loving the feel of his arms around her. Starved for so long of any form of physical affection, Rosemary knew that this wasn't just her own need. Even with Tony, she'd never felt like this. As though she'd come home, that here with Simon was where she belonged.

This time their kiss was even deeper, and she nestled closer as Simon gently kissed her eyelids and the tip of her nose. He smiled down at her. 'See me tomorrow,' he murmured. 'Spend the day with me.'

Stricken, she said, 'I can't. I've already promised...'

'Whatever it is, can't you break it? Or have you had enough of me for one weekend?' Simon tenderly pushed her hair away from her face.

She shook her head. 'It's not funny. I want to see you but I just can't...'

'Is that slave driver making you work on Sundays now?' Simon felt annoyed. After all, it wasn't every weekend he had off duty.

Rosemary seized on the excuse. 'It's just this once. Sorry, Simon.' It's not really a lie, she told herself as she looked away. It wasn't her fault that she couldn't tell him the truth.

'What about the evening?' he persisted. Suddenly he couldn't bear the thought of not seeing her for several days.

'I could probably manage that.' She smiled at him with relief. 'I'm not sure what time, but I'll come round as soon as I can.'

'Great. Come on then, I'll walk you home.'

Sally Ann, about to draw her bedroom curtains, saw them coming and drew back to watch them walk hand in hand down the road. This was a Rosemary she hadn't seen before – animated, laughing, the light from the streetlamp shining on her upturned face. As the young couple paused by the gate and merged into one shadow, she turned tactfully away, strangely moved. A few minutes later, hearing Rosemary open the front door and creep up the stairs, she called out, 'Had a good day, honey?'

'Oh, yes,' came the reply. 'I've had a wonderful day.'

30

On Sunday morning, careful to avoid the earlier children's Mass in case Beth had taken the boys, Rosemary walked slowly to the church just before eleven o'clock. And when she walked back an hour later, it was to realise that she hadn't heard a word of the sermon. All she could think about was Simon, and if she wasn't daydreaming of that fantastic time in his flat, then she was worrying about the afternoon, when at last she would meet her grandparents, Robert and Sylvia. She tried to imagine what they would be like. Michael was older than Beth, so they might be white-haired and frail. I hope it won't be too much for them, she thought. My presence is bound to bring it all back, what James did all those years ago. Yet they'd wanted her in their lives enough for Robert to try to find her.

The thing was, what could she wear? She searched the sky for clouds, deciding it might or might not rain, which meant she ought to wear that grotty anorak, but she damn well wasn't going to.

'I'm not turning up like second-hand Rose,' she muttered, 'even if it is true.'

The next couple of hours were spent in frustration, as after grabbing a sandwich and washing her hair, Rosemary flung first one garment, then another down on the bed. The heap was pitifully small. She hadn't realised just how much she'd relied on that blue dress, but after yesterday it wasn't fit to wear.

'I might be poor, but I'm clean,' had been one of Brenda's frequent sayings, and Rosemary knew what she meant. It was a question of pride.

'Going anywhere nice?' Sally Ann was reading in the sitting-room, when Rosemary went down at five minutes to three.

'Just to meet some friends,' she evaded, waiting at the window. She could feel the heat rising in her neck as she lied. How she hated all this subterfuge – surely Beth must make a decision soon whether to publicly acknowledge her or not? The subject hadn't been mentioned since that appeal for secrecy in the church, but Beth still hadn't revealed her married name, nor introduced her to the children.

Then suddenly she saw an opulent silver saloon

cruising up the road, and as it drew nearer Rosemary saw the famous emblem on the bonnet. She drew back in disbelief as she recognised Michael at the wheel, with Beth in the passenger seat. Rosemary had only ever seen a Rolls Royce on the films, or through a polished showroom window and, flustered, she went out and climbed self-consciously into the back. Sinking into the soft leather, she caught a glimpse of Sally Ann's startled face at the sitting-room window.

To Beth's surprise, Michael had insisted on using his own car.

'We could use mine,' she'd suggested. 'I'll drive.'

He shook his head. 'No, Beth. Rosemary knows where we live, and once she's been to Linden Lodge, we're all in her hands. There's no need for pretence any more, don't you see? Whatever we decide to do, and I still don't know how we're going to resolve it, she's the one holding all the cards.'

'I'm sure we can trust her.'

'Let's hope so.'

It was the first time Rosemary had seen Michael since that eventful day in the church, and although he greeted her pleasantly, she could still sense the constraint there. Not that she could blame him. Of everyone involved in this reunion, he was the outsider. He might be her uncle, but he must hate to be reminded of it.

Beth, aware that Rosemary was unnaturally quiet, tried to ease the tension.

'Did you like Chalfont St Giles?' she asked.

'Yes, it was lovely.'

Silence.

Beth tried again. 'How are you feeling?'

'I'm a bit nervous,' Rosemary admitted.

'There's no need to be – they're dying to meet you.'

The car sped along a quiet exclusive avenue and turned in between two white pillars proclaiming Linden Lodge. Then they were driving up a long tree-lined drive to what to Rosemary looked almost like a manor house. It was breathtaking, with russet ivy-covered windows, a huge porch and massive oak double doors.

She felt stunned by the sheer size of it and, knowing how she felt, Beth said, 'The first time I came here was to a New Year Party. I was on my own, hardly knew Michael, and I'll never forget walking up this drive. I nearly turned round and went home.'

Michael laughed, the first time Rosemary had heard him do so.

The front door was already opening as they got out of the car, and a slim elegant woman stood waiting on the porch.

'There's Sylvia now,' Beth murmured and ushered Rosemary forward. Rosemary smiled hesitantly, but Sylvia couldn't even speak. She just gazed at that young anxious face looking at her with Beth's eyes. For he was there. Her son so cruelly taken from her was there, in the freckles, in a resemblance which was almost unnerving. She stretched out her hands to hold, to welcome his daughter.

Rosemary put her hands into Sylvia's and felt herself drawn into cool, scented arms, felt a kiss on her cheek, tears on her skin.

'I can't tell you what this means to me, to both of us,' Sylvia managed to say. 'Come along, come and meet your grandfather.'

With Beth and Michael following, Rosemary was taken into a huge oak panelled hall and through to the imposing drawing-room. There, standing before an Adam fireplace, stood a tall, well-built elderly man. As she walked uncertainly toward him, he didn't move, his silent gaze sweeping her from head to foot, his eyes beneath their bushy eyebrows almost blazing in their intensity.

She lifted her chin and said clearly, 'Hello.'

Robert said gruffly, 'Hello.'

Sylvia joined them, her happiness transparent. 'Just look, Robert, she's so like James, can't you see it?'

'Of course.' He turned away and went to the heavy sideboard, his hand shaking as he poured brandy into a glass. See it, of course he could see it, and by God, it was a shock. There was no doubt about it, this girl was a Rushton, and only now did he admit that despite the evidence, he'd still harboured doubts.

Rosemary, invited to sit on the leather chesterfield next to Sylvia, felt confused. She'd been told Robert had tried to find her, that knowing of her existence had brought him back from depression, yet his welcome had been almost cold. She looked at Beth, who smiled reassuringly. Michael sat on a burgundy winged leather chair and said nothing.

Sylvia shot a concerned glance at Robert's

back. Accustomed to her husband's reactions, she knew his curt manner was due to embarrassment. Showing emotion or weakness was anathema to him, and not until he was fully in control would he rejoin them.

She looked again at Rosemary and struggled for her own composure.

'It must have taken a lot of courage to leave your home town to come here and try to find Beth,' she said.

'I wasn't leaving very much behind,' Rosemary admitted. 'It was sheer luck that this job was advertised in *The Lady*.'

'Do you like it?'

'It's okay – it was a means to an end really.'

There was an awkward pause, and then Michael, seeing his mother's polished social skills deserting her, said, 'Did you put anything on ice?'

'Of course, perhaps you'll open it for me.'

Michael followed her out into the kitchen and put his arms around her, holding her close.

Sylvia leaned against his broad shoulder, her eyes wet with tears. Such a lovely girl, and yet James would never see her.

'Just think of the good things,' Michael murmured. 'You know you always wanted a daughter, and look how good you were with Beth.'

'I know,' she whispered, 'and you're right, I know that. But oh, Michael, I don't think anyone understands how I grieve for him, even now.'

'So do I.' Michael's eyes were sombre. James had not only been his brother, he'd been his closest friend. It was only because Michael had left to start his National Service that James had got involved in gatecrashing that blasted party. 'If', he thought, the biggest word in the English language. If we hadn't been driving along the Whitmore Road at the same time as that drunk driver, James and Giovanna would still be alive. And if their car had been the one in front, then the fatalities would have been himself and Beth. Life was all chance; it was useless to try to make sense of it.

'Come on,' he said gently. 'A couple of glasses of champagne will relax all of us. It is supposed to be a celebration, after all.'

'Of course it is. And what about you, are you able to cope?' Sylvia dabbed at her eyes and, looking up at her son, saw the strain in his eyes.

'I just need time,' he said. 'You don't need to worry about it.'

Sylvia opened the fridge, and took out two bottles of Bollinger. 'The flutes are already in there, and I'll bring through some canapés.'

Rosemary watched Sylvia place a tray on the sideboard, while Michael began to pour the champagne. How graceful she was! She must be in her sixties, yet she was still attractive, her hair a perfect silver frame, her manicured nails polished in the exact shade of her soft lilac dress. She brought two flutes across to Rosemary and Beth, then returned for her own. Michael passed one to Robert and, seeing the empty brandy glass, glanced sharply at him, but knew better than to offer any support.

Robert, who'd now taken up his customary stance before the fireplace, cleared his throat.

'I don't suppose many families ever celebrate an occasion like this. Sylvia and I are proud to welcome at last our granddaughter to Linden Lodge. To Rosemary and the future...'

They all raised their glasses and, embarrassed to be the centre of attention, Rosemary took her first sip of champagne. It tasted odd, almost sour. She watched as the others sipped theirs, smiling at her, and tasted it again, the bubbles tickling her nose. Sylvia offered her a plate of small unfamiliar savouries, and she hesitated, then chose one topped with smoked salmon and cream cheese. It was mouth-watering, and she wondered if it would be considered bad manners to take another.

Robert watched her. Obviously ill at ease and out of her depth, perhaps after another glass of champagne she'd relax a bit more. There was so much he needed to know and it was all right for Michael and Beth to say take it slowly, but he was no longer a young man. One thing advancing age taught you was that there is not always tomorrow.

In an attempt to give Rosemary a breathing-space, Beth was talking to Sylvia about the children, telling her of their comical sayings.

'This morning in church, Ben decided he'd had enough and just when everywhere was quiet at the Consecration, he piped up, "I don't like church! Can we go home, Mummy?"'

Sylvia laughed.

Rosemary, who was hungry after her meagre

lunch, took another canapé. While the others were talking, she let her gaze wander around the large, richly furnished room, admiring the elaborate cornicings and beautiful rose in the ceiling.

At one end of the room was a massive mahogany display case and, as she was looking at it, Sylvia said, 'There's some more food on the sideboard, please help yourself.'

Glad of the excuse to move, Rosemary put down her half-empty champagne glass, but before going to the sideboard walked curiously over to the display case.

Four pairs of eyes swivelled to watch her as she stood before it. Robert, his eyes keenly watching for her reaction, noted that this was no cursory glance: the girl was taking an interest, inching slowly along the cabinet, peering through the glass. He glanced over at Michael, who was also closely observing, then at Sylvia, then at Beth. They all waited. Just as Rosemary began to turn away, Robert strolled over to her.

She looked up at him. 'What a wonderful collection,' she said.

'You like it?'

'Oh yes, I've always loved Rushton china.'

The simple sentence, so unexpected yet dreamed of, sent a rush of adrenalin through his veins.

'I wondered though,' Rosemary said shyly, 'why you have only individual pieces. I mean, most people collect whole dinner services, or tea sets. You seem to have an enormous range, but only one of each.'

Robert deferred answering her question, and

instead asked one of his own. 'You say you've always liked Rushton china – does that mean you're interested in pottery?'

'I've always liked sketching the shapes,' she told him. 'Not that we ever had anything like this at home,' she indicated the display, 'but I used to go into a shop in Staniforth, and get inspiration there.'

Silently, Robert unlocked one of the doors and took out a slender, white vase.

'This is one of my favourites,' he said. 'It's one of the earliest pieces.'

Rosemary took it from him, holding it carefully in one hand, while her fingers reverently traced the outline. The delicate china was almost translucent, cool and smooth to the touch, and with delight she turned to smile at him. 'It's beautiful.'

Robert, who had been noting the sensitivity of her hands while she handled the fragile object, took it from her and replaced it in the cabinet, then touching her on the shoulder, indicated that they should join the others.

'Rosemary just asked me why we only collected one item of china from each range,' he said evenly. 'I think we should tell her, don't you?'

But Rosemary was looking at the three concerned faces before her. Beth's eyes showed profound relief, Sylvia's a smiling pride, while Michael simply watched his father. She thought of the secrecy, Michael's wealth, this magnificent house, and suddenly she knew.

With a startled expression she swung round to face Robert, who nodded.

311

'I see you've guessed. Yes, James was a Rushton – and so, my dear, are you.'

Silence hung in the air, an expectant silence, and Rosemary knew everyone was waiting for her reaction. Stunned, not knowing what to say, her eyes instantly sought Beth's, who explained with an apologetic smile,

'Your grandfather wanted to meet you, before telling you himself.'

Rosemary sat down and, on reaching for her champagne, in her confusion swallowed too much. Spluttering, her eyes began to water, and feeling an absolute fool she searched for a hanky. With sympathy, Beth passed over her own.

'That's your first lesson learned,' Robert said briskly.

Sylvia frowned at him, then to take the attention away from the young girl next to her, said, 'Beth, how is Rose? Has she recovered from her 'flu?'

'Oh, she's much better thank you, Sylvia. Disappointed, of course, that she hasn't been able to see Rosemary again.'

'Never mind, there will be plenty of time.' She smiled gently at Rosemary. 'Champagne's an acquired taste, I always think. I hated it at first, and did exactly the same as you. Just small sips, and drink it sparingly – it's more intoxicating than it seems.'

'Thank you,' Rosemary said, still feeling dazed. The name of Rushton was famous. No wonder Beth had been intent on proof that first day in the church.

'So,' Robert said, rubbing his hands together,

'now that's out in the open, we need to plan for the future.'

'Perhaps today isn't a good time,' Sylvia remonstrated. 'After all, Rosemary needs to get to know us.'

'I don't agree,' he said briskly. 'Time doesn't wait for anyone – the academic year, for instance.'

Rosemary stared at him. What was he talking about?

He looked back at her, his gaze keen. 'I gather you had to leave school early?'

'Yes, but...'

'So am I right in thinking you have no qualifications at all?'

'No,' Rosemary said defensively. 'I went to evening classes and did "O" level English and Commerce. I've also got RSA certificates in shorthand and typing.' Gosh, she thought, this is like an interview.

'Capital. Shows she's got initiative!' He directed the last remark to Michael.

Beth intervened, 'Robert, please, she's not one of your employees.'

Michael simply leaned forward, his fingers interlaced. He might have known this would happen. The old man couldn't wait, could he? He looked across at Rosemary, her face flushed with the champagne, seeing a glint of resentment in her eyes. Well, if he would pass remarks like that about the girl, what did he expect?

But Robert was set on his course. 'Tell me, Rosemary. If you'd had the choice, what would you have done?'

'Stayed on, of course,' she said. 'Hopefully gone to university to study Art & Design.'

Robert shot a triumphant glance at Michael. He knew it! From the first moment he'd seen her rapt expression at the display case. By God, she'd got the Rushton genes, and he'd damn well make sure she had every opportunity to develop her potential.

'Now do you see why we can't pussyfoot about?' he challenged. 'No Rushton has ever lacked a decent education. It's not too late, she's only nineteen, but we can't afford to let this year go to waste.'

'Hang on a minute, Robert,' Beth said angrily. 'You can't just lay down the law about Rosemary's future. Perhaps she has some plans of her own.'

'Have you?' he shot.

'No, not really.' Rosemary looked round at them all. 'I'm sorry,' she said slowly, 'it's come as a bit of a shock, so perhaps I'm not thinking clearly. But could I ask a question of my own?'

Beth leaned forward saying, 'Of course you can.'

'It's just that I understand more now, all the secrecy and everything. But it doesn't change the fact that I'm still a skeleton in the family cupboard, so to speak. My grandfather talks of the future, of my education, but what I'd really like to know is...'

They all waited.

'Is it possible for me to become a real part of the family – you know, in the circumstances and everything?' Her face grew red with embarrassment, as she avoided looking at Sylvia.

There was an awkward silence, then Michael said, 'Thank you, Rosemary. You've pinpointed the exact problem, and it's no use glowering, Father, it's got to be faced. Any plans for Rosemary are secondary to finding an acceptable solution.'

Beth shot a worried glance at Rosemary. 'I'm not sure we should be talking about this at the moment.'

'If you mean while Rosemary is here, then I think you're wrong, Beth,' Michael said. 'Don't underestimate her, she's had to stand on her own feet and overcome tragedy early in life. She's adult enough to understand what's at stake here.'

Rosemary looked at him in grateful surprise.

Robert cleared his throat. 'It's a thorny problem, I don't deny that.'

'The resemblance doesn't help,' Michael said quietly.

'No. It does complicate matters.' Robert knit his brows together. 'I've gone over and over this in my mind. For all sorts of reasons, business and personal, Rosemary has got to be acknowledged as a Rushton – it's just how to do it.'

'I've also been racking my brains,' Sylvia said. 'Couldn't you come up with a fictional long-lost relative or something?'

'You mean that Rosemary could be Father's great-niece?' Michael asked.

'That would explain the resemblance,' Sylvia said.

'It would have to be a close one,' Robert

315

muttered. 'For me to have a brother would be ideal, but people round here have long memories.'

'Aren't you both forgetting something?' Beth's tone was stiff with anger. 'The way you're all talking, it's as if there's only your family to be considered. What about me? What about my mother? Is our relationship with Rosemary to be ignored?'

'Beth...' Michael leaned forward.

'No, Michael. Look, we can skirt round this for hours, but the fact is that I've denied her for nineteen years, and I'm not prepared to go on doing so. Also,' she said, fiercely protective, 'don't you realise you're suggesting Rosemary loses her own identity. She is who she is, whether it's convenient or not. Do you want her to live a lie for the rest of her life?'

'What do you suggest then?' Robert snapped. 'Okay, so we want to protect James's memory, but what about Michael? Do you think your husband wants everyone to know you had a child by his brother?'

Beth flinched and, seeing her distress, Michael threw his hands in the air.

'God, I don't know what the answer is.' He got up and strode to the other end of the room, turning his back on them to gaze blindly at an oil painting.

Rosemary, watching and listening, felt increasing horror. The whole scene was an absolute nightmare. And no-one was asking her opinion, it was almost as if she'd become invisible!

But in that she was wrong, for Beth suddenly

316

said, 'Rosemary, I do apologise. We've been so busy arguing that we haven't heard your point of view.'

Aware that everyone had turned to look at her, Rosemary could only shake her head helplessly.

Then Beth said gently, 'Just say what is important to you.'

Rosemary looked at her, and to her dismay her eyes filled with tears.

'I just don't want,' she said in a choked voice, 'it to be public knowledge that I was conceived in rape. I don't think I could live with that.'

There was absolute silence for a moment, and she began to fumble in her bag for a handkerchief.

Beth longed to put her arm around her daughter's shoulders to comfort her, and Sylvia, understanding her hesitation, quickly stretched out a hand and covered Rosemary's with her own.

Beth looked at Michael, who was now gazing at Rosemary with an inscrutable expression. With sudden determination, she got up and went over to him. 'I need to talk to you in private,' she whispered. 'How about if we go into the morning-room?'

Michael, his shoulders rigid with tension, gave a slight nod.

She returned to the others.

'Would you mind excusing us for a little while?' Anxiously, she looked at Rosemary, who smiled reassuringly.

Sylvia said, 'No, not at all.' She watched them both leave the room with a worried frown, then suggested, 'I think now would be a good time for the tea tray. I could certainly use a cup. How about you, Rosemary?'

'Yes, please.'

With a warning glance at Robert, Sylvia left grandfather and granddaughter together.

'Sorry about all this,' Robert said gruffly.

'It's all right.'

'I meant it, you know, what I said earlier, about your education.'

Rosemary frowned. 'I'm not sure what you had in mind.'

He came over and sat beside her on the leather sofa.

'It's obvious. We need to make up for lost time, that's all. With the right crammer, we can get you through whatever exams you need in quite a short time. Then, with qualifications behind you, you can choose which university you wish to attend.'

She looked at him sideways. 'How do you know I have the brains for all this?'

'Because you're a Rushton,' he answered firmly. 'In any case, I'm a great believer in my own judge of character, and you're an intelligent girl. Tell me, how did you do at school?'

'I was top of my class,' she admitted.

'There you are then,' he said with satisfaction. 'Now the first thing is to get you out of that demeaning job. Can't have a member of my family charring, you know.'

'Is that what I'm doing?' Rosemary said, then added despairingly, 'But there just doesn't seem to be an answer.'

31

Beth led the way into the morning-room and, once Michael was inside, closed the door. She walked over to the large bay window overlooking the garden, and stood for a moment blindly gazing out before turning to him.

'Michael, we have to talk, to face this. Do you think I don't know how traumatic all this has been for you, that I haven't noticed how it's affecting our relationship? I'm sorry, but I can't change the situation. Rosemary's here, she's in our lives, and we've got to deal with the problem together. Don't shut me out, please.'

Michael slumped in an armchair, and looked despairingly at her.

'I don't mean to, Beth. I just feel...'

'What do you feel? Tell me.' Beth went to him and crouched at his knees, taking his hands in hers.

'I thought,' Michael said with difficulty, 'I'd come to terms with what happened between you and James. That it was all in the past. But somehow Rosemary has changed that. I can't help it, Beth. Her presence has somehow made it real. Every time I look at her, my mind fills with a horrifying mental vision of you both. Don't you understand, it's because of the violence of the act – that it was my own brother makes it almost unbearable.'

'And when you look at me, how do you feel?'

'Nothing but love, I promise you. It's a physical thing.' Michael drew her to him, and looked down into her anxious eyes. 'Just give me time, I'll deal with it.'

'And can you deal with Rosemary?'

'I'll have to, won't I?'

Beth got up and went to sit on the velvet chaise-longue opposite him. Her eyes brimming with tears. 'I do wonder whether I did the right thing in telling her the truth about James – it's an awful burden for her to carry.'

Michael looked at Beth's downcast face and drew her into his arms.

'It was absolutely the right decision,' he said gently. 'If she's to be a member of this family, then she needs to know of the skeletons also. How else is she to understand the decisions we make? In any case, surely there should be only truth between a mother and daughter? But I still don't know what we're going to do.'

'I do,' Beth said quietly. 'Let's face it, Michael, I'm her mother, she's my responsibility. Not yours, not your parents. There's no way out of this without someone being hurt, and I'm determined it isn't going to be Rosemary. I at least owe her that.'

'So, what are you saying?'

'I think we would all wish to protect James's memory,' she said, 'and anyway what would be achieved by telling the truth? At the moment, the only people besides ourselves and Rosemary who know what happened that night at the party are my mother and your parents, and I propose we keep it that way.'

'I'm not sure I understand...' Michael leaned forward, his eyes fixed on Beth's, waiting impatiently as she struggled to explain.

'Well, suppose I'd had a teenage fling with your younger brother. I kept the pregnancy secret and had the baby adopted. You knew about it when we got married, and it was all in the past, until Rosemary found us. Now, your parents are over the moon to have a granddaughter, and as for us, we're delighted to welcome her into our family. It's 1975, Michael, not such a big deal any more. It'll be a seven-day wonder, that's all.'

Michael stared at her. It all sounded so simple, put like that. This way, his parents wouldn't have to face the shame of people knowing about the rape. Only Beth, who wouldn't sleep with him even when they were engaged, was faced with lying, telling the world she'd had pre-marital sex, making public her guilt at giving away her baby.

'No, Beth, I can't let you do this,' he said angrily. 'Why should James's reputation be protected at the expense of yours? There must be some way we can keep your name out of it.'

Beth looked at him in despair.

'Not if I want to give Rosemary her rightful place as my daughter. I don't want to be part of a pretence, Michael. I'm not ashamed of being her mother, I'm proud of it. I've been given a second chance, and this time I'm determined to do the right thing.'

Michael sat with head bent, looking down at the floor. He hated not being able to protect Beth in all this, but what could he do? Eventually he

321

looked up at her, his face taut but resigned.

'Are you sure?'

'What alternative is there? And I'm not just protecting James's reputation either. Like Rosemary, I can't bear the thought of people knowing about the rape. As for my reputation, well, I'll just have to hold my head high and ride it out. As I've said, there's no real alternative, and don't forget there's the business to think of. Yes, I'm sure.'

Michael rose and took her in his arms, burying his face in her soft dark hair. He didn't think he'd ever loved her more. They could get over this, he could get over this. What was past had gone, let it stay buried.

'I love you, Elizabeth Rushton,' he murmured.

'I love you, Michael Rushton!' She raised her head and kissed him on the lips.

'Come on, let's go back to the others.'

They returned hand in hand to the drawing-room, where Sylvia looked up from pouring tea to search their faces. Beth immediately looked for Rosemary. She was once again gazing into the windows of the display cabinet. Robert was sitting in the chair Michael had vacated. Beth sat on the chesterfield, caught Rosemary's eye and put out her hand to squeeze her daughter's as she joined her. Michael took up his father's stance before the fireplace.

'I think I may have found a solution,' Beth began, and slowly outlined the plan she'd discussed with Michael.

In the silence that followed, Robert gazed in profound gratitude at his daughter-in-law. When he thought of how he'd objected to this marriage, the way he'd sneered at Beth's motives, her poor background, her religion! It had taken many years for him to fully accept her, but once again, she was proving to be his salvation. The word humility was not one which played a large part in Robert's vocabulary, yet as he saw the quiet integrity in Beth's face, he felt ashamed.

Sylvia was the first to speak, her heart full of relief that James would not be remembered as a man who'd committed the vile crime of rape.

'Have you cleared this with Rose?'

Beth nodded. 'She agreed it was the only possible solution. Her actual comment was that she was old enough and tough enough to withstand any tittle-tattle in Minsden. In fact, she also said,' she added wryly, 'that one or two would be glad to see me brought down a peg or two.' She turned to her daughter. 'You'll always find someone who's jealous if one of their own kind "gets on", so to speak. It's human nature.'

'It hardly seems fair on her. I know how proud she is of the way she brought you up.' Sylvia's tone was concerned.

'Yes, I know,' Beth said sadly.

'But what about your brother and his wife?' Sylvia persisted.

'We talked about that, and it won't be easy not telling Gordon and Val the truth. But we have to think of Rosemary's feelings. To put it bluntly, the fewer people who know how she was conceived, the better, and apart from anything else, I think we should keep the truth to ourselves. That way, we know both the family's reputation and, indirectly, that of the business, will be safe.'

'It's just yours...' Sylvia's eyes stung with tears. It was her own son who'd caused all this trauma, her laughing, affectionate boy. What he did that night would always haunt her.

'Sylvia, I haven't any choice,' Beth said gently, 'and let's face it, what would have been a huge scandal years ago, will be regarded with much more tolerance now. Times are changing – the sixties saw to that.'

'Yes, but this area's always slow to change,' said Sylvia. 'I don't think the permissive society ever reached here.'

'Certainly not in the way it hit London,' Michael commented, 'but I think Beth's right. I think we'll be surprised how easily people will accept what she tells them.'

'And you?' Sylvia asked. 'Are you happy with your role in this?'

'I'm not happy about any of it, but I can't see any other way.'

Rosemary, who had been avidly following the conversation, said quietly, 'Does this mean that I can tell people who I am?'

'Yes, of course.' Beth turned to look at her. 'Has this been causing you problems?'

'Some,' she admitted.

'But you'll stick to the story we've outlined?'

Rosemary nodded, glad that Beth understood how she felt. She wanted no-one, not even Simon, to know that she owed her existence to violence. There were times that she felt shame and, strangely, guilt that she'd ever been born.

'So,' Robert said suddenly, 'now we can plan

for the future.' His eyes alight with purpose, he leaned forward. 'Rosemary has already told me something of her schooldays...'

Michael glanced at his mother, saw the strain on her face, and interrupted, 'Perhaps we'd better leave it to another day, father. Give us all a chance to mull things over. I think we're all a little tired, and Beth and I need to get back to the boys.'

'But...'

'Michael's right, dear,' Sylvia said. 'I do think another time would be better.'

'At least the main decision has been taken,' Beth said, getting up and kissing Robert on the cheek. 'We'll bring Rosemary again as soon as possible, I promise.'

Rosemary stood up too and, seeing her hesitation, Sylvia signalled to Robert with her eyes. He bent awkwardly and pecked his new granddaughter on the cheek, while Sylvia simply held her close for one long moment.

'Goodbye, my dear,' she murmured. 'Seeing you has brought two people tremendous joy.'

Rosemary flushed with pleasure, then with a last lingering smile followed Beth and Michael out to the car.

When they dropped her off, it was with the arrangement that they would take her again to Linden Lodge, hopefully during the next couple of days.

'Father's right,' Michael told her. 'Time is of the essence. Give your future some thought, Rosemary – decide what you want to do with your life. Remember, there will be no obstacles in the way.'

Beth got out of the passenger seat to say good-bye, and stood facing her daughter. Rosemary's growing affection for her mother was now tempered with respect and admiration. She was beginning to feel proud of being Beth's daughter and moving forward impulsively hugged her.

Aware of Sally Ann hovering at the window, Rosemary opened the gate and inserted her key into the front door.

'Hi, honey.'

Rosemary turned in surprise at the slurred speech, and saw Sally Ann leaning against the doorframe, her face flushed, her eyes suspiciously bright.

'Had a good day out with the nobs, did you?'

Rosemary took a step backwards.

'Are you all right?'

'Never better, sweetheart, never better.' She lurched into the hall. 'Just been on a bender, that's all. Happens sometimes, don't worry about it.' She waved the bottle in her hand. 'Want a drinkie?'

'No thanks.' Rosemary tried to slip past her, but found her way blocked. She knew Sally Ann liked a drink, but she'd never seen her in this state.

'Has anything happened?' she probed. 'Have you had bad news or something?'

'Nope.' She tried to sit on the stairs, but missed the tread and landed heavily on the bottom step. 'If you're wondering why I've hit the bottle, kid, perhaps it's because it's my birthday, and not a goddamn soul has even remembered. How's that for a successful life?' Tears of self-pity began to trickle down her cheeks.

With embarrassment Rosemary said, 'I'm sorry, I'd have done something if I'd known.'

Sally Ann grimaced. 'I suppose even a card from the hired help would have been better than nothing.' She sat with her head down, a pathetic figure with smudged lipstick, and her scalp showing through the sparse orange-tinted tufts of hair.

'Let me make you some coffee,' Rosemary suggested.

'Yuk! What I need is another drink. I might be under the influence, but not nearly enough, honey, not nearly enough.' She struggled to get up and weaved her way to the kitchen, leaving Rosemary staring hopelessly after her. There was nothing she could do. If Sally Ann wanted to drink herself into oblivion, then she might as well leave her to it. At least she was safe in her own home.

'I'll just go and have a bath,' she called. She glanced at her watch. It was only half-past six. Plenty of time for her to relax, take in and mull over all that had happened in the past few hours, and then switch her mind to delicious anticipation of spending the evening with Simon. At least now she could be open with him, tell him what had really been happening in her life over the last year.

Having sneaked some of her employer's bath salts, Rosemary lay in the scented water, feeling happier than she could ever remember. I can't wait, she thought, to tell Lisa the thrilling news.

An hour later, she went downstairs in some trepidation, unsure of what she'd find. But Sally Ann was still in a talkative mood, a half-empty bottle of whisky by her side.

'So,' she drawled, 'the socialite returns.'

Rosemary disregarded the sarcasm.

'I'm doing some cheese on toast, do you want some?'

'What, and soak up this lovely booze?' She began to cackle at her own joke.

Glad to get out of the room, Rosemary went into the kitchen and got herself something to eat. It was awful the way people lost their dignity when they drank too much. She remembered how Keith used to blunder about the house when he returned from the pub, laughing at his own puerile, coarse jokes.

'It's not going to happen to me,' she muttered. She was never going to smoke, either. After all, with Brenda and James, she had two prime examples to learn from. After drinking her coffee in the kitchen, she went warily back into the sitting-room.

'I shouldn't be too late,' she began.

'I told him,' Sally Ann said thickly.

'Who?'

'Your knight in shining armour. Told him you weren't working for the wicked witch at all – you'd been out gallivanting in a Rolls Royce. By the way, who was that, honey? Your sugar daddy?'

Rosemary ignored the jibe, as anxiety flared. 'Told who? Did Simon ring?'

'That was his name, I couldn't remember.' She

328

began to grin, *'Simple Simon, met a pieman...'*

Rosemary interrupted sharply, 'What did he want?'

'To know what time you would finish working. Have you been telling porkies, honey?'

Rosemary stared at her in growing horror and disbelief.

'I told him, "She never works on Sundays, she's leading you up the garden path, my boy!"' She wagged a playful finger at Rosemary. 'Good thing to make them jealous, you know, keeps them on their toes.' She gave a lopsided smile and took another swig directly from the bottle.

At first, Rosemary could only stand in stunned silence as her mind grappled with the implications of Sally Ann's words. Then, grabbing her coat she rushed out of the door. Hurrying, almost running, she made her way to the double-fronted house where Simon had his flat, looking anxiously up at the top-floor windows as she approached. The flat was in darkness. She pressed the bell next to his name. There was no answer. She pressed it again, more urgently, and retreated back a few steps, staring once again up at the darkened windows. Whatever must he think of her, discovering she'd lied to him, deceived him that she was working, only to have gone off with someone else! At least that was what Sally Ann had implied, and goodness knew what else she'd said, the state she was in. How stupid could anyone get, to blab like that to a complete stranger? As if it was any of her business, anyway!

It began to rain, a fine drizzle which soaked her

hair, her shoulders, but Rosemary hardly noticed. She shouted up at the window, '*Simon!*'

The curtain moved in the downstairs flat and the other tenant – the headmistress, peered out, the television flickering behind her. Rosemary quickly moved to one side, out of sight, and then suddenly realising that if he was in, the car would be there, went out into the street, checking the line of parked vehicles. There was no sign of Simon's Ford Capri. So, he'd actually gone out, stood her up without even giving her a chance to explain! How could he do that? It just showed how much he trusted her, Rosemary thought bitterly.

Smarting at the injustice of it all, she stood for moment then shrugged and began to walk back in the now driving rain. There was nothing she could do tonight, she'd just have to phone him tomorrow.

She was sure that when he heard the truth, he'd understand. Rosemary made one resolve: she wasn't going to let the misunderstanding spoil today. The memory of Linden House, and all that had been revealed there was one she wanted to hug close, to mull over, to secrete away in her heart. But tonight and the next few days, she had some serious thinking to do. She had to decide exactly what she wanted out of life.

32

The following morning, it was a shame-faced Sally Ann who came downstairs.

'Gee, honey, I hope I didn't disgrace myself last night?'

Seeing her ravaged face, Rosemary thought, what's the use? Having a row wouldn't achieve anything, and she probably wouldn't remember Simon's phone call anyway.

'No,' she said curtly, 'of course not.'

Once she was on her own, however, she paced up and down, wondering whether to ring the flat. When she'd walked Homer that morning, the curtains were still drawn so she knew Simon wasn't on duty. It'll be okay, she kept telling herself. Once I explain everything, I'm sure he'll forgive me. By eleven o'clock, she couldn't wait any longer.

He answered on the second ring.

'Dr Oldham.' His voice was curt, professional.

'Simon, it's me, Rosemary.'

'I'm just about to leave for the hospital.'

Dismayed at the coldness of his tone, she said quickly, 'I just wanted to explain...'

'There's no point,' he interjected. 'As I said, I haven't time to talk.'

'I'll ring you later then.'

'You'll find it difficult to catch me – this is a busy time.'

Rosemary heard the click of the receiver being replaced, and with a suddenly shaking hand, put down the phone. The blatant snub both hurt and shocked her. Damn Sally Ann! It didn't help that it had been her own fault in the first place for not telling Simon the truth.

But she didn't have time to brood because almost immediately there was an unexpected call from Dot Bennion.

'Rosemary? I'm ringing from a phone box. Have you got a minute?'

'Yes, of course. How are you all, is anything wrong?'

'We're okay. It's our Lisa. I'm worried sick about her.'

There was panic in her voice, and Rosemary said quickly, 'Give me the number, I'll ring you back if we get cut off.' She scribbled it on the pad.

'Right, tell me what's been going on.'

'I was trying to find a pair of knickers to fit Tracey, she's growing so fast I can't keep up with her! Anyway, I had a look in Lisa's drawer, and,' Dot stumbled over the next words, 'hidden at the bottom I found these white tablets!'

'What sort of tablets?' Did Dot mean Lisa had gone on the Pill?

'I don't know what they are, but I do know they were never prescribed by a doctor – you can tell.'

Rosemary caught her breath. Drugs! God, she'd only been away from Staniforth a few weeks. Not that Lisa would necessarily have listened to me, she thought bitterly.

'It's drugs, isn't it? Did you know?' Dot asked

332

sharply. 'I want the truth, mind.'

'No, no, of course not.'

Dot picked up on her hesitation. 'But you knew something?'

'I knew she smoked dope,' Rosemary admitted.

'What, both of you?'

'No, honestly, Mrs Bennion. I never have.' The pips went, and she gabbled, 'I'll ring you back.'

Hurriedly, she dialled the number and Dot picked it up immediately.

'Have you told her dad?'

'I haven't told anyone yet, I only found them this morning. I don't know how to handle this, Rosemary,' Dot's voice broke. 'If I do the wrong thing, I could make matters worse. It's not only worrying about Lisa, it's a criminal offence, isn't it?'

Hearing the desperation in her voice, Rosemary said quickly, 'Can I help at all? Would you like me to come down, talk to her?'

'Oh, could you?' Dot's relief was palpable. 'She might listen to you. I daren't think what Jim'll say.'

'Go ballistic, I should think. What did you do with them?'

'What? Oh, the drugs. I flushed them down the toilet. Apart from anything else, I don't want that sort of stuff in the house with the kids about!'

'Of course not.' Rosemary's anger was growing. 'I'll come down as soon as I can get a train.'

'Thanks, love.'

'I only hope I can help.'

Putting down the receiver, she thought for a moment, then went into the sitting-room. Going

333

to the bookshelves, she ran her finger along the spines. Yes, she thought so. There was a reference book about social trends in America and when she looked in the index, a section on drug abuse. She put a bookmark in the page to read later once she was organised.

Ringing Stoke Station, she found there was a London train with a good connection to Staniforth at two o'clock.

'You'll be all right, won't you?' She bent to Homer, lying in the middle of the hall and ruffled his fur. 'She'll just have to get up early and take you out before work.'

Running upstairs, she rapidly packed a change of clothes in her suitcase, grimacing at its unsuitable size. Then she made a couple of cheese sandwiches and grabbed an apple from the fruit bowl to eat on the train.

What next? A note for Sally Ann of course, and she'd better ring Beth. But there was no answer from The Beeches. Rosemary decided to ring Rose.

'Rosemary, how lovely to hear from you!'

Hearing the pleasure in her grandmother's voice, Rosemary felt guilty that she hadn't rung before. 'Are you feeling better?'

'Yes, I am, thank you, dear.'

'I wondered if you could give Beth a message for me? Only there's no reply from her house.'

'Of course I will.'

Not giving any details, Rosemary told her she had to go to Staniforth.

'I should be back in a couple of days.'

'I'll tell her. Is there anything wrong, Rosemary.

Can I help in any way?'

'Thank you, not really. I just need to go and see a friend.'

'Oh. Well, good luck, I hope to see you soon.'

Rose slowly replaced the receiver. Now what was all that about?

Their knowledge of Rosemary's previous life was sketchy as yet, Beth insisting that her newly-found daughter would tell them more when she felt ready. Thoughtfully, Rose continued her task of polishing her brasses. She was always intending to part with them, but Harry had liked them, particularly the little Royal Marine Artillery hat which had been made out of a shell case and doubled as a tiny ashtray. It had belonged to his father. Automatically, she lifted the lid and ran the tip of her finger in the corners, searching for remains of his cigarette ash. A futile gesture, she knew, but one which – in an odd way – made her feel closer to him.

She carried on rubbing, thinking of the difficult days ahead. Oh, there'd be a few round here who wouldn't be sorry. Those who were jealous of the money Beth and Michael had spent on improving her home. But most liked Beth, appreciated how she'd never forgotten her roots, would remember how her generosity had helped many local causes. Mind you, she thought frowning, our Gordon's going to have a shock. Val too, for before she'd married Gordon and moved away, she and Beth had been inseparable. They'd both be hurt that Beth hadn't turned to them all those years ago. Upset too, that once Beth did reveal the truth, Rosemary's existence had still been kept secret from them. That had been to protect the Rushton name, to shield them from any scandal. Well, it was all going to come out now, even if it was watered down. Typical though, that Beth should be the one to take the brunt of it. Nothing changed, money had always talked and always would. Rose sighed. Much as she liked the family her daughter had married into, give her the simple life any day – it was far less complicated.

Lisa was already home from work, when Rosemary, having lugged her suitcase from the station, stood outside the front door and rang the bell.

Seven-year-old Debbie answered the door, her face splitting in a huge grin as she saw who was there.

Rosemary put her finger to her lips. 'Ssh! It's a surprise,' she whispered.

With exaggerated caution, Debbie let her in and closed the door quietly. Rosemary followed her into the familiar untidy hall, one hand pushing back her windblown hair. Debbie, revelling in her dramatic role, flung open the door to the sitting-room.

'Guess who's behind me?'

'Jimmy Osmond,' said Lisa, without lifting her head from her magazine.

'No!'

'Donny Osmond, then.'

'No, silly. Look, it's Rosemary!'

Startled, Lisa jumped up and stared in

astonishment at her friend.

'Hey, it really is! Hi!'

The two girls hugged.

'What's brought you here all of a sudden,' Lisa demanded. 'Are you all right?' She looked with concern at Rosemary's carefully controlled expression. 'Don't tell me your mother's rejected you? The selfish cow, I could–'

'No, everything's fine,' Rosemary interrupted. 'There's no problem at all.'

'Well, that's a relief. Give Debbie your coat, and while you're at it, Debbie, tell Mum and Dad we've got a visitor. They're upstairs, baby-worshipping.'

'How is little Kevin? I bet he's grown.' Rosemary removed a pile of clothes waiting to be ironed from a chair.

'Most remarkable baby ever born. God, the fuss they make of him, just because he's a boy! I'm changing sex next time, I've decided.' There was an underlying note of bitterness in her tone, and Rosemary glanced at her in surprise.

'Go on then, bring me up to date,' Lisa urged.

Rosemary hesitated, feeling that perhaps now wasn't quite the time to tell Lisa her thrilling news. Then fortunately she was saved from answering by Dot's appearance in the doorway.

'Rosemary! Go on, Lisa, make the girl a cup of tea, she must be frozen to death after travelling!'

When Lisa went out of the room, she lowered her voice and said rapidly, 'I've told Jim to get the kids upstairs once *Coronation Street*'s finished, then he's going down the pub out of the way.'

'So you've told him?'

She nodded grimly.

'Soon as he came in from work. I thought he was going to have a stroke, he was so mad. He's kept out of her way, says he won't be responsible for his actions 'til he's calmed down. So, the plan is that we'll talk to her first, see if she'll open up, and he'll deal with her later.' She stood back as Lisa returned with the tea, and said, 'Hey, what about a biscuit?'

When Lisa went back to the kitchen, she hissed, 'Why didn't you let me know she was smoking dope?'

'I wanted to, but...'

Lisa came into the room, offering a plate with two Jaffa cakes on it.

'Thanks.' Rosemary sipped the hot tea gratefully. She was ravenous, but she knew that at nearly seven o'clock the Bennions would already have eaten.

But Dot Bennion hadn't catered for a large family without being aware of others' needs.

'There's some casserole left,' she offered, not mentioning she'd made an extra portion. 'I could heat it up if you like.'

'That would be great,' Rosemary said with relief.

'Just like old times, this,' Lisa said, draping herself over the arm of a chair, as her mother left the room.

'Yeah,' Rosemary grinned at her, glad to be with someone of her own age again. She looked admiringly at Lisa's clothes. They might be cheap, off the market probably, but the younger girl always managed to keep up with the latest fashion.

'I like your outfit,' she said.

'I see you haven't bought anything new.'

Rosemary pulled a face, and suddenly it was as if they'd never been parted.

It was not until after eight that the two girls had a chance to talk alone.

'Right!' Lisa switched off the TV. 'Now you can tell me what this is all about.'

'What?' Rosemary said.

'Come on, I wasn't born yesterday. You turn up without any warning like this – there has to be a reason.' She looked warily at the older girl. 'You're not in any trouble, are you?'

'I'm not, but apparently you are!'

Lisa's eyes narrowed. 'What are you on about?'

'Your mum rang me this morning.'

'Why? What on earth for?' Stiffening, Lisa glanced with apprehension at the slightly open door.

'She found some white tablets in your underwear drawer...'

Outraged, Lisa exploded, 'You mean she's been going through my things?'

'She found them by chance – she was looking for something for Tracey.'

'Is that what all the fuss is about? They were only speed, for God's sake! I can't believe she's dragged you all the way down here just because of that.'

Rosemary's concern flared into anger. She'd tried to contain her worry travelling down on the train, but now, seeing Lisa, she was so furious she

339

could have hit her. All her carefully rehearsed tactful sentences evaporated.

'What the hell do you think you're playing at?' she hissed. 'And what do you mean, only speed?'

'It's no big deal. I've only had a few anyway.'

'God, you can be such an idiot at times!'

'And who elected you to be my judge and jury?'

'No-one. I just happen to care what happens to you.' In that moment, Rosemary realised just how much Lisa did mean to her. She was her best friend, her only friend.

'I'm not doing any harm,' Lisa said.

'We're not just talking about you! There are young kids in the house – what if they'd found the tablets? What's the matter with you – has smoking dope rotted your brain, or what?'

'Don't talk daft!' But Lisa's face had whitened, and Rosemary knew her words had hit a chord. She pressed home her advantage. 'You told me you'd never try anything else, you promised!'

'I wanted a buzz, what's wrong with that? Honestly, you talk as if I was a junkie or something.'

'Where do you get them?'

Lisa shrugged.

'Come on, is it down the pub? I've seen you talking to some right peculiar types.'

'Oh, you're such a goody two-shoes, aren't you?'

'That's not true! I've made mistakes – remember Tony? But this is so stupid, Lisa!'

'Just because I don't want to be boring, like you?' Lisa snapped.

'Yes, well, I've had to be sensible, haven't I? But

340

that doesn't mean I'm boring. You can take that back, Lisa Bennion!'

In the angry silence, Dot opened the door, and Rosemary guessed correctly that she'd been outside listening.

'Lisa, love, I just don't understand why you need to take such stuff!'

'Oh, you understand nothing! You've no time for me any more, not since Kevin was born. You've never had time for me, it was always one baby after another to be looked after!'

Rosemary watched in horror as Lisa's words caused Dot to take a step backwards.

'I had no idea you felt like this,' she said.

Seeing the pain in her eyes, Rosemary said fiercely, 'She doesn't. She's never said a word to me about it.' She turned to Lisa. 'I might not know much about drugs, but I've read that coming down from amphetamines can make you aggressive. That's all it is, Dot, it's not Lisa talking, at least not the one I used to know.'

Lisa's eyes suddenly locked with hers, and Rosemary realised that behind all the defiance there was fear too.

'Can't we talk about the whole thing calmly, before your dad gets back?' Dot pleaded.

'You've not told Dad?' Lisa's voice rose hysterically.

'He had a right to know.' Dot slumped on the sofa, her hand covering her eyes. 'I never thought one of mine would use drugs.'

'How many times do I have to tell you, it's only speed!'

'And how do you think people get hooked on

341

harder drugs?' Dot shouted. 'Do you think they just go straight on to it? No, they start off like you have, first smoking dope, then–'

'Oh, you know nothing about it!' Lisa interrupted. 'There's a lot of ignorance about drugs.'

'And you're an expert, are you?' Rosemary said. 'Or are you just repeating what your so-called friends say. Friends who have a vested interest in making a profit!'

'Yes, where do you get the money?' Dot suddenly asked.

Lisa shrugged.

'There's only one place you'd get that sort of cash. Show me your Post Office book, Lisa, and that's an order.'

Resentment in every movement, Lisa got up and flounced into the hall to fetch her bag. She thrust the passbook at her mother.

Dot opened it and checked the last entry. 'Oh,' she said.

'See, that just shows how little you know about it. Accusing me of things! Speed's no more expensive than alcohol!' She glared at her mother.

'Why, Lisa?' Dot demanded. 'Is it because you're bored, you're looking for adventure, you want to experiment? Talk to us, tell us! Can't you see we want to help?'

Lisa stood up to face them, her expression hard and defiant. 'I just believe in experiencing things.' Then she glanced at her mother and said, 'What do you think Dad will do?'

'I don't know,' Dot said in exasperation. 'I can tell you one thing – if he thinks you won't stop by yourself, he'll bring the police in.'

342

'He wouldn't...'

'Don't count on it.' Dot got up. 'We're getting nowhere. I'm going to make a cup of tea – do you want one, Rosemary?'

'Yes, please.'

For a few minutes the two girls sat in uncomfortable silence, and at that moment, Jim Bennion returned.

Hearing his key in the lock, Lisa's bravado deserted her.

He came directly into the room.

'Get your coat!' He jerked his head in the direction of the hall. Lisa got up fearfully. 'What for?'

'You'll find out!'

Tension in every line of his body, he went into the kitchen, and Rosemary heard him talk in a low voice to Dot, who followed him back into the hall.

'How long will you be?'

'Who knows!'

Through the open door, Rosemary saw him take Lisa's arm and push her out of the house. Desperate to know what was going on, she went into the kitchen, where Dot was just pouring out the tea.

'Here you are, drink it while it's hot, and then go up to bed – you look done in. I've put a mattress on the floor for you between Lisa and Tracey.'

'Where's he taken her?'

'Jim didn't go to the pub. He's been to see a mate of his, some sort of social worker.' She held up a hand, as Rosemary gasped. 'Don't worry, it's off the record. Anyway, this bloke said to take

343

her down to this sort of hostel he knows, where they look after drug-addicts. He reckons all she needs is a bit of a shock, let her see the other side.'

'She's just in with the wrong crowd,' Rosemary tried to reassure her.

'Perhaps.'

Dot looked distracted and tired, so Rosemary finished her tea and went upstairs. With the door ajar, she undressed in the dim light shining through off the landing, had a quick wash in the bathroom, and then, shivering, lay on the mattress in an effort to get some sleep.

She must have been even more tired than she thought, for when she opened her eyes, early daylight was seeping beneath the skimpy curtains. Quickly she twisted over to see whether Lisa was back. But her bed hadn't been slept in.

Full of anxiety, Rosemary hurriedly washed and dressed and went downstairs, to find Lisa drinking black coffee at the tiny kitchen table. She glanced up briefly as Rosemary went in.

'Hi. Sleep well?'

'Yes. What about you?'

'I crashed out on the sofa, didn't want to wake you and Tracy up.'

Rosemary tried to catch Dot's eye, but she was busy hustling the children off to school.

'You look terrible,' Rosemary said to Lisa, looking at her friend's face streaked with stale make-up.

'I feel it. Dad said I could take the morning off.'

Rosemary emptied cornflakes into a bowl and poured milk over them.

'So,' she asked, between mouthfuls. 'Are you going to tell me what happened?'

Lisa stared at her from dark-rimmed eyes. 'It was awful. I had no idea, honest, that drugs could have that effect on people. Oh, you read things in the papers, but it's not like seeing it for real. And some of the kids were no older than us!'

'Did you talk to any of them?'

Lisa nodded. 'Yes, we were there for ages. And I talked to some of the staff. They said it was everyone's choice whether to try drugs, but knowing of the dangers meant you made an informed choice.'

'So, what happens now?'

'It's up to me, I suppose. After all, it's my life.'

'I don't suppose you want my advice?'

'No, thanks!'

There was silence while Rosemary finished her cereal and then, obviously wanting to change the subject, Lisa said, 'I wish you'd move back. Is there any chance?'

Rosemary hesitated.

Lisa carried on, 'Still, I suppose if your mother and grandparents want you to, you'll be making your home up there.'

'Probably,' Rosemary admitted.

'I'd like to start a new life,' Lisa said wistfully. 'A new job, a proper career.'

'If you could choose, what would you do?'

'I'd have a boutique,' Lisa said. 'Sell all the up-to-the-minute fashions.'

Rosemary stared at her. 'You've never told me that.'

'Not much point, is there? It'll never happen.'

345

'I suppose you could work in one.'

'Doesn't pay enough, I've asked around. I earn more at the Department.' She grinned, her face lighting up in the impudent way Rosemary remembered so well. 'Got to have enough for my weekly fix of gear off the market!'

Rosemary laughed, and turned as Dot came bustling into the kitchen.

'That's better!' She looked approvingly at the two girls. 'Just like old times! Hadn't you better get in that bath, young lady,' she said to her daughter. 'You look like something the cat's brought in.'

'Yeah, okay.'

Rosemary waited until Lisa had disappeared before saying to Dot, 'Do you think it did the trick?'

'I think so. It shook Jim up, I can tell you. The best thing we can do now is to leave her alone. Mind you, I'll be watching her. Anyway, thanks for coming, love – Lisa always listens to you.'

Rosemary wasn't so sure but she just said, 'Any time, Mrs Bennion. I think a lot of Lisa – well, of all of you really.'

Dot glanced at her. 'You're all right, though? Your folks were pleased to see you?'

'Oh yes. They're really nice people.'

Rosemary stifled an impulse to tell Dot more. No, her news could wait. Hearing about Rosemary's prospects wasn't likely to make Lisa feel more content with her own life, and for the moment that had to be paramount.

33

Twenty-four hours later, Rosemary was back on the train to the Potteries. She sat huddled against the window, staring out at the landscape, as the now familiar scenery flashed by. Dreamily, she remembered her last journey, and how she'd furtively watched Simon from behind the covers of her book. So much had happened since then: meeting her real mother, Rose, Michael and her grandparents. Even Simon's mother, although she gave a slight grimace at the memory. Christine hadn't liked her, she was sure of it. And what about Simon? She was still angry at the offhand way he'd treated her. First standing her up, and then snubbing her like that on the phone. But Rosemary knew that deep down she desperately wanted to see him again, to have a chance to sort out their misunderstanding. Or was she fooling herself? Was she just one of many, as Christine had implied? But the memory of that last evening was too vivid, too evocative to allow such a doubt to flourish, and she resolutely dismissed it, turning her thoughts to the events of the past couple of days.

Lisa had indeed taken the morning off and, Tracey at school, the two girls had spent the hours in Lisa's bedroom experimenting with nail varnish, leafing through magazines, and listening to *Annie's Song*. 'It's just like the old days,' Lisa grinned.

Rosemary smiled, aware that only she knew how different it was. Before, the misery and grief at losing Brenda and her home, the hurtful rejection of Tony, had lain like a stone within her. Now, although the underlying sadness was there, she felt at ease with herself, full of hope and excitement about the future.

'So, tell me more about these relatives of yours,' Lisa coaxed.

And Rosemary did, although never would she reveal even to Lisa the full truth about her conception. It was enough to explain that someone had spiked the drinks at a party.

'Beth decided to have me adopted to protect her mother from the scandal,' she said. 'She's always regretted it, and they did try to find me.' While Lisa listened avidly, Rosemary told her of the attempt to trace her through newspaper advertisements.

'But didn't anyone see them?'

'Mum cancelled the papers to save money for a colour TV,' she said, repeating the reason Brenda had given. Even though Lisa was her closest friend, she couldn't bring herself to reveal the extent of Brenda's duplicity.

So by the time she left, the Bennions knew as much as she had herself until a few days ago. They knew her father was dead and that his name had been Rushton, but it wasn't an uncommon name. Its significance and the world it opened up for her – these were details she would write to them about.

Lisa had returned to work that afternoon, and Rosemary had gone with her. It had seemed strange going back into the large, draughty building, seeing everyone again. All these people had been such a large part of her life, and yet now she felt herself removed from them, almost a stranger even. Her office in reception was very much Lisa's domain, everyone was busy, and after a while, beginning to feel awkward and in the way, Rosemary made her excuses and left.

As she walked along the main road into the town, she slowly realised that this part of her life was finally over. She'd never come back to Staniforth to live, not now. Her future lay in the Potteries, where her family was, where in different circumstances, she should have grown up.

On reaching the High Street, like a homing pigeon she headed for the shop which sold fine porcelain, the same shop she used to visit as a young girl to gain inspiration for her sketches. But this time, there was only one showcase she wanted to see. The Rushton display. Rosemary stood before it, seeing again the same pieces she'd seen in the drawing-room at Linden Lodge. Only this time, there was not just one specimen vase, or jug, or cup and saucer. Now she could see and admire a complete dinner service artistically set out against fine damask linen, could look at a range of items of one particular design.

'Can I help you?'

The owner of the cultured voice looked disparagingly at Rosemary, who, conscious of her shabby appearance in this showroom of quiet elegance, said quickly, 'I was just browsing.'

'It's beautiful, isn't it? Rushton china, of course, is one of our best if most expensive ranges. We do have some more reasonable items at the back of the shop. Was there anything in particular you were looking for?'

Rosemary reddened, fighting a crazy impulse to tell this woman who she was, that her grandfather was Robert Rushton, that he owned the firm. Oh yeah, she thought, she's really going to believe me isn't she, dressed like this!

She merely said, 'Not really.'

Seeing a more promising customer enter, the assistant moved away leaving Rosemary free to stand again before the locked glass doors. And suddenly she knew that she wanted to be part of the creation of these beautiful objects, wanted to continue the involvement in her heritage. Hadn't Rose told her that she herself used to be a paintress in a pottery factory, that her grandfather Harry had worked as a packer? How many other members of her family had, in the past, spent their lives working in the production of china and earthenware? That's why I always wanted to draw vases, why I was fascinated by shapes, she realised with excitement – it's in my blood, in my genes. This is what I want to do, this is what I need to train for.

She turned and walked briskly out of the shop and into the cold fresh air, her brain whirring with plans. She'd probably have to work in the factory at first – Michael and her grandfather might think that was the best way for her to learn. And there must be some sort of qualifications needed, surely art and design, perhaps even business management.

Head down, she automatically turned into the little park where Tony had delivered his blunt, cruel rejection and, without even realising it, found herself sitting on that same seat. But Rosemary only gave Tony a fleeting thought – her mind busy analysing, thinking. Oddly, being here in Staniforth helped her to see everything in a different perspective, clearer somehow. For instance, her dream of going to university. Did she really want to spend three or four years studying for a degree, living among students? Even before Brenda's death and all it had led to, she had felt ill at ease with most people of her own age.

It was too cold, however, to sit for long in the park, and she decided to call at the presbytery, only to find that Father Kavanagh was away on a visit to Ireland.

Aimlessly, she wandered around the shops, before reluctantly being drawn once more back to the derelict site in Poplar Crescent. A passing neighbour told her there were plans to rebuild early in the New Year. For a few moments she stood there, unbidden memories bringing with them the regret that there hadn't been more joy and laughter in that house, instead of the half-understood tensions which had so inhibited her as a child.

Shoulders hunched, she left and walked back to the Bennions and while Debbie played with her Mastermind game, and Tracey struggled with her homework, she did some ironing for Dot. Later, she and Lisa went to the cinema to see *One Flew Over The Cuckoo's Nest*, and by unspoken consent, the subject of drugs wasn't mentioned again.

But now, the bubble of excitement she'd felt since Sunday, with its revelations, surfaced again as the train approached Stoke Station. The weather was still warm, and as there was only a fine drizzle, she decided to save the cost of a taxi, and began to walk to her bus stop.

Michael, leaving The North Stafford Hotel after a business lunch, saw the girl trudging along in the rain, a large suitcase in her hand, and suddenly realised it was Rosemary.

Swiftly, he pulled over the Rolls and wound down the window.

Startled, she turned and in that one fleeting moment Michael saw Beth as she'd been when he'd first met her. There was that same lift of the head, that air of pride and independence.

He opened the passenger door for her, got out of the car and put her suitcase in the boot. 'Why didn't you take a taxi?'

'I wanted to save the fare.'

Michael, noticing her already damp anorak, recalled his first sight of her walking along the pavement. Shabby but neat, was how he'd have described such an employee. But Rosemary was his niece, now part of the Rushton family. She should no longer have to penny-pinch, certainly should be able to afford decent clothes.

'Did you have a good journey?'

'Yes, fine, thank you.'

Noticing she looked pale and tired, Michael glanced at his watch. It was two-thirty. 'Have you had lunch?'

'I had a Kit-Kat on the train.'

Michael, who always travelled first class, and then only if there were restaurant facilities, frowned. 'I'm on my way home to pick up some papers – would you like to come? I'm sure Beth would be only too pleased to see you.'

Rosemary hesitated. Should she? But with her alternative almost certainly being a kitchen littered with unwashed dishes, the prospect of a breathing-space after travelling was tempting. 'Yes, I would. Thanks.'

Michael drove the rest of the way in silence, and minutes later Rosemary was going once again through the imposing front door to Beth's luxurious home.

A smiling middle-aged woman came to welcome them.

'Is Beth around, Mrs Hurst?' asked Michael.

The woman looked curiously at Rosemary, then said, 'No, Mr Rushton, you've just missed her. She's taken the boys for their dental check-up.'

'Oh, of course, I'd forgotten.' Michael swore under his breath. He could hardly change his mind now, and take the girl back to the American's place. 'Could you take Rosemary's coat, and rustle her up a sandwich or something, please?'

'Of course.' The housekeeper took the anorak with as much care as if it had been cashmere, and disappeared to the kitchen.

Michael ushered Rosemary into the huge sitting-room. 'You haven't met the children yet, have you?'

'No, I'm looking forward to it.'

Wishing she hadn't come, Rosemary sat on the edge of the sofa, and desperately tried to think of something to say.

Michael, with an inward sigh, knew that it was his fault Beth's daughter felt so uncomfortable with him. It would be in both their interests if he could get to know her as an individual, establish some sort of relationship with her.

'It was a very sudden trip to Staniforth,' he said eventually. 'Was there a problem?'

Rosemary looked at him, sitting at ease in the large armchair opposite her. She wondered whether her father had been so polished and businesslike. Michael, immaculately dressed in a dark blue pin-striped suit, seemed part of a totally different world to that she'd just left.

'It was a friend of mine,' she began reluctantly.

Michael waited.

In an effort to explain the situation, Rosemary told him how Lisa's family had taken her in when she was homeless, of the debt of gratitude she owed them.

'Lisa's my best friend. So when her mum rang and said she was worried about her, I went straight away.'

As he saw Rosemary hesitate, Michael said quickly, 'You don't have to tell me if you don't want to.'

Rosemary took a deep breath. Should she? Or

would he simply think the whole issue sordid?

'Mrs Bennion found drugs in her bedroom,' she said at last.

Michael's eyes narrowed. 'What sort of drugs?'

'Speed. I mean, I knew she smoked dope sometimes, but...' She looked at him in embarrassment, 'I've shocked you, haven't I?'

Michael didn't answer immediately, and then said, 'I'm not that easily shocked, Rosemary. When I was in my final years at university, I knew someone who got into heroin. Oh, drugs weren't widely available then, not even cannabis. But if you had the means and the contacts, there were always ways. It was a salutary lesson, believe me.'

Rosemary looked at him with new eyes, thinking how much more approachable he seemed. 'Lisa thinks we're overreacting.'

'I'm sure she does, but I don't agree.' Michael paused. 'You can tell me to mind my own business if you like, but do you also smoke cannabis?'

Rosemary hastily reassured him. 'I think I'd be too scared of not being in control.'

'Spoken like Rose's granddaughter. She insists on only one drink at any time, even a sherry.' He smiled, relieved. 'So, what was the result of your visit?'

'Her dad took her to a hostel where they deal with drug-addicts, and it scared her stiff. She wouldn't commit herself, but I think she's bright enough to make the right decision. She's a really nice girl, it's just that she's got in with the wrong company. She's bored with her job as well.'

'A dangerous combination. What does she do?'

'She's a receptionist, but what she really wants to do is to own a boutique. Fat chance, though.'

'Into fashion, is she?'

Rosemary nodded. 'She just seems to have the knack of putting things together. She's much more trendy than I am.'

At that moment, Mrs Hurst brought in a tray with tea and sandwiches, and Michael excused himself to go to his study. After collecting the papers he needed, he remembered he ought to let his secretary know he'd been delayed, and rang the office. Then he sat before his mahogany, leather-topped desk, deep in thought.

Rosemary's story of how the Bennions had helped her had touched Michael deeply. To be homeless at eighteen, destitute and without money or family – that was a shocking thing. Yet, she'd never sought her new-found relatives' sympathy, given them a hard-luck story as so many girls would have done, particularly on seeing their obvious wealth. She'd simply given them the bare facts, being more interested in finding out the truth about her parentage than anything else. Beth had seen her integrity from the beginning. Absently Michael drummed his fingers on the desk as he reflected yet again on the events of the past few weeks. A few minutes later, deciding Rosemary must have finished her snack by now, he returned to the sitting-room.

'It looks as though Beth has gone on somewhere else,' he said, glancing at his watch.

Rosemary immediately stood up. 'Yes, I'd better go.'

Michael went into the hall, where Mrs Hurst

appeared with a now dry anorak.

'Thanks.' Rosemary slipped it on. 'The chicken sandwiches were lovely.'

They went out to the car.

'Does she live in?' Rosemary asked as they went out to the car.

'No, comes in every day. Except Sunday – Beth put her foot down about that when we were first married.'

A few minutes later Michael dropped her off and after a rapturous greeting from Homer, Rosemary unpacked, and then tackled the cluttered kitchen. Judging by the pile of dishes waiting to be washed, and the takeaway cartons in the pedal bin, her presence had not only been missed, but resented.

Later, searching the store cupboard, she took out a tin of minced beef, a packet of Smash, and a tin of mixed vegetables. Not exactly a feast, but at least it would be a hot meal.

Then, hearing the front door open, she muttered under her breath, 'God, I hope she doesn't go on at me.'

But Sally Ann did go on, and she began the minute she came in.

'So,' she drawled, 'the wanderer returns.'

'Yes, I'm sorry I had to rush off.'

'So am I, kid. It was not convenient, not convenient at all.'

'I said I was sorry. A friend needed some help.'

Sally Ann frowned and took off her hat and scarf. The girl was great in many ways, but she was becoming a little tired of all the minor mysteries. She was worried too. She knew no more about Rosemary than she had when she first arrived weeks ago. Who were these so-called relatives, for instance? The girl disappeared for hours at a time, was vague about where she'd been, who she'd been with. Her only normal behaviour had been to go out with that young doctor, but even then there had been some sort of problem when he phoned. Her memory was fuzzy about the details, for let's face it she'd been plastered. That was the same day Rosemary had gone off in a Rolls Royce. And this was a girl who hadn't a dollar to her name! But it was the reference book she'd noticed out of line on the bookshelves that perturbed her. The section marked had had the heading 'Drug Abuse'. Sally Ann had put two and two together. Fancy cars and drug-dealers often went together in her experience, and boy had she had some! Her last campus had been rife with problems – she could do without them in her own home.

'Yes, well, if this job isn't your first priority, I happen to know someone who'd jump at the chance,' she said tersely. It was true – only the other day a student who wanted to flunk her course had asked whether she knew of a live-in job somewhere for a few months.

Affronted, Rosemary stared at her. She'd worked damned hard as this woman's Girl Friday, and all she'd done in return was mess things up for her with Simon. But then the thought came quickly that this could be her way out. A little premature perhaps, but at least this way the suggestion that they terminate their agreement had come from Sally Ann.

'If you really have got someone who can take over from me, then maybe that would be better...'

Now it was Sally Ann's turn to stare in surprise. She'd only meant her suggestion to act as a warning, tighten things up a bit. 'You mean you want to leave?'

'I can't guarantee how long I can be here,' Rosemary said awkwardly, not wanting to go into details at this stage.

'I see.' Yet again, no reason, no explanation. Her instinct was right, the kid had got something to hide. 'I'll check with the other girl tomorrow,' she said abruptly. 'Let you know then.'

She was true to her word, for the following afternoon Rosemary had a phone call from the student. She said her name was Helen and asked if Rosemary would give her the low-down on Sally Ann as an employer.

The words were uttered in a broad Birmingham accent.

'It's a good job,' Rosemary reassured her. 'She expects you to earn your money, but I've had no problems. I'm only leaving because of complications in my personal life.'

'I could do with a few of those,' Helen grumbled. 'Mine's like a desert at the moment.'

Rosemary laughed. 'I take it you're interested then.'

'Sure am. I want to get off this lousy course, but fancy staying around for a while. When can you move out?'

Rosemary floundered. Panic rising, she realised she hadn't expected things to move so fast. Okay, she'd anticipated leaving her job. Robert had been adamant about that. But no suggestion had been made as to where she would live.

'I'll talk to Sally Ann about it,' she said at last.

When she did, a week's notice was suggested, beginning that weekend, and with some misgivings, Rosemary agreed.

34

It was early the following morning that Simon, hastily swallowing a mouthful of toast, answered the phone to hear his mother's voice.

'Simon?'

'You're early, is anything wrong?'

'No, I just wanted to catch you before you left for the hospital.' There was a pause. 'How would you feel about my coming up to stay for a bit? To be honest, I'm feeling a bit down at the moment.'

'Come whenever you like, Mum. So long as you know I'll be busy most of the time.'

'I'll still see more of you,' Christine said. 'Anyway, I could make it a bit of a holiday, get to know the area.'

'Look, it's fine, but I'm in a tearing hurry. Give me a bell when you've decided and I'll try to meet you at the station.'

He put down the receiver and drank his coffee thoughtfully. Not that he minded his mum coming to stay – well for a short time anyway. But his new post was proving very exacting and, knowing his mother, she'd want to chat brightly each evening, would expect him to be sociable, when most of the time when he came off duty he just wanted to crash out. Although he had to admit that his hours of leisure the past few nights had been spent propping up the bar at the local pub. Brooding into his beer, his father would have called it.

Almost against his will, he crossed to the window searching the recreation ground for a girl walking a sable and white collie. But all he could see was a German Shepherd loping behind a youth trudging against an apparently bitter wind.

Simon turned away, put his mug on the draining-board, and shrugged into his sheepskin coat. It was ridiculous the way he couldn't get Rosemary out of his mind. It had only been a couple of dates – looking back he could hardly believe he'd read so much into their brief relationship. And misjudged her character, for if there was one thing he couldn't stand, it was a liar. He'd always been the same, even as a child, probably because his father had instilled into him a passionate respect for truth. There was no reason of course why Rosemary should have spent that Sunday with him – she was perfectly free to see someone else if she wanted to. But she'd chosen to lie, and that he found hard to forgive. The anger and sense of betrayal he'd felt that night had both astonished and appalled him. He was calmer now, of course, but was still unsure whether he wanted to give Rosemary a chance to explain.

Glancing at his watch, he picked up his bag. On his list this morning, there was an especially complicated operative procedure, and all thoughts of Rosemary were banished as he drove the short distance to the Infirmary.

Rosemary did walk Homer on the recreation ground, but, as she glanced up at Simon's window, it was blank. Glad to get out of the chill wind, she went back to the house and spent the rest of the day catching up on her chores. But as she worked, the menial jobs freed her mind to think, plan, reason. By late afternoon, she knew what her first step must be.

'Beth?'

'Rosemary! Michael told me you were back. We must fix up for you to come and meet the boys. And I have something I want to talk to you about.'

'Me too.'

'Oh, right. What about this evening?'

'I can't. I'm working.' Looking at the folder of notes waiting to be typed, Rosemary knew she could do no other. 'I could make some time tomorrow?' She mentally resigned herself to working on Saturday instead.

There was a pause, and she could hear Beth turning a page of her diary.

'I've been invited to attend a Works Council Meeting in the morning, on behalf of a children's charity I'm involved with, but–'

'Could I come?' the words came out in a rush.

'What? To the meeting?' Beth sounded surprised.

'No, of course not – to the factory. That's what I wanted to ask you. I'd really like to see it.'

362

Beth, taken unawares, was unsure how to reply. Such a visit had, of course, been anticipated, and Robert was already steeling himself to conduct his newly-found granddaughter around his domain. But would this be the best way – impulsive, informal?

'Of course you would,' she said. 'Look, leave it with me and I'll get back to you.'

Thoughtfully, Beth put down the phone. Ten minutes later, she rang Michael.

His reaction was guarded. 'This needs careful planning, Beth. It's important how we do this, introduce her to the workforce.'

'I know. But think about it, Michael. If Robert gives her the grand tour, how is he going to explain who she is? Can you imagine the reaction when he says, "This is my granddaughter, Rosemary?" Everyone will be trying to work out where she's come from, whose child she is. And all the time Rosemary will be standing there, the centre of attention, until someone blurts out the question. And how do you think Robert will handle that?'

'So, what are you suggesting?'

'Let her come in with me. She can wait with you in your office while I'm at the meeting – it should only take an hour. You can give her some of the brochures to look at.'

'And then?'

'I'll introduce her to Ivy.'

There was a pause, then Michael began to chuckle. 'You devious devil! So when...'

'Yes. When Robert does show her round,

another time, word will have spread like lightning. No awkward explanations needed.'

'Beth, you're a genius!'

'Let's hope Robert agrees.'

'I'll see him now about it, and come back to you.'

Half an hour later, he rang.

'What did he say?'

'Blustered a bit at first, but eventually saw the sense of it. I think he's anxious you don't steal his thunder.'

'I won't,' Beth promised and, dialling Rosemary's number, arranged to pick her up the following morning at ten o'clock.

Next, she phoned Rose to bring her up to date.

'Oh, Beth, it's not going to be easy for you. Are you sure you're up to this?' Her voice was troubled, full of anxiety.

'I haven't much choice, have I? Don't worry, Mum, I come from tough stock.'

'I know. And you've another obstacle to face. Gordon and Val are coming over next weekend.'

'Oh, right. Well, we may as well get it all over with.'

Rose was silent for a minute. It was going to be difficult for her too. Her son would be hurt and resentful – so would Val.

'I'm only sorry Granny Platt never knew,' said Beth.

Again Rose was quiet. Her mother had died the previous year, and every day she grieved for her. She'd been a rock for them all, and as a child Beth had adored her.

'Are you still there?'

Beth's tone was impatient, and Rose said quickly, 'Yes, I was just thinking.'

'You'd better sit down!'

Rose smiled at the old joke. 'It's just that she did know, Beth.'

There was a silence.

'You mean you told her? About what happened, about Rosemary?'

'Yes, I did. It was when I knew she was dying. You were away in Milan, and I just felt she had the right to know she had a great-granddaughter.'

Again there was a silence.

'What did she say?'

'Just that her heart went out to you.' Rose's voice wavered as she went on to say, 'I still don't understand why you didn't tell us.'

'Let's not go into all that again, Mum,' Beth pleaded.

'I'm sorry. Well, I wish you the best of luck for tomorrow – I'll be thinking of you.'

Rose put down the receiver and turned to put her coat on. It was time to go for her weekly shampoo and set, and the stylist didn't like to be kept waiting.

As she walked down the steep narrow street leading to the shops, her heart was heavy. For someone of Beth's sensitivity, the confession she'd have to make would take tremendous courage. But Rose knew her daughter would find it, and it was with quiet pride that she opened the door with its pink ruched blind, to enter the warmth of the small hairdressing salon.

The following day, Rosemary sensed at once that Beth was on edge and, as they drove out of Newcastle, wondered whether she'd done the wrong thing in asking to see the Rushton factory.

'Do you mind?' she asked diffidently. 'My coming with you, I mean?'

'Not at all. In fact, your suggestion gave me an idea.' Beth proceeded to tell Rosemary of the plan, adding, 'Ivy's been with us for years. She's a bit of a rough diamond, but very popular. I've always got on really well with her.'

Rosemary watched out of the window as Beth drove along the unfamiliar route.

'Arnold Bennett came from the Potteries, didn't he?'

'Yes, several of his books are based here. Have you read any of them?'

Rosemary confessed that she hadn't.

'I'll lend you *Anna of the Five Towns*. They made a film too of *The Card*, with Alec Guinness. If you haven't seen it, it does portray the Potteries during that period very well.'

Soon she was turning into the entrance of a building not unlike the ones Rosemary had seen lining the main roads, when she'd travelled on the bus through Fenton and Longton to Minsden. Old, slightly forbidding, not at all like the photographs she'd seen of the much larger prestigious Wedgwood factory. The car passed with a clang over a weighbridge and then they were through the archway, where Beth waved at a man in a small office near the entrance. She drew up and parked before a flight of wooden steps.

'That was Dave, the lodgeman,' she said. 'I'm sure Robert will introduce you when you come next time.' She glanced at Rosemary, seeing her expression as she looked up at the small windows. 'Not quite what you expected, is it?'

Rosemary coloured. 'I've only ever seen photos of Wedgwood's.'

'You're thinking of their model factory out at Barlaston. Most of the potbanks, as we call them, are like this, built in the eighteenth and early nineteenth centuries. They're unique, full of character, you'll see.'

Rosemary followed her up the steps, and into a long corridor lined with offices.

Beth turned halfway down into a small passage which had two steps up to two imposing doors of polished oak with brass plates proclaiming the names Mr RE Rushton, Chairman, and Mr MJ Rushton, Managing Director.

Beth tapped on Michael's door and ushered Rosemary in. Rosemary looked round with interest. The office wasn't unduly large, but it was furnished richly, with a green deep pile carpet, capacious mahogany desk and leather chair. Michael was working on some papers. He got up, and kissed Beth on the cheek. Then, more hesitantly, he did the same to Rosemary.

'Welcome to Rushton's,' he said.

'I've explained to Rosemary that she'll see very little this first time. Can I leave her in here with some reading matter, Michael, as the meeting's due to start in five minutes?'

'Yes, of course. I've put some brochures out for you, Rosemary.' He indicated a small armchair with a coffee table next to it. 'I'll walk down with you, Beth.'

As the door closed, Rosemary walked over to the window and peered out. Below was a large yard and on the opposite side she could see a raised covered area with packing cases being loaded on to a lorry. As she watched, a man in brown overalls came out, and stood looking up at the overcast sky. He nodded with a grin to a man in white overalls, who was passing by balancing a long plank on his shoulder. On the plank was a row of clay teapots, and Rosemary was fascinated by the way he moved, swiftly, confidently. Behind her she heard the door open and turned to see Michael enter.

'He's taking them to be dried and then fired,' he told her as he joined her at the window. 'And you see the Packing Shed? At one time, your grandfather worked in one of those as a packer. Not here, at another factory in Longton.'

They watched for a few moments, then Michael said, 'I'll ask Pauline to arrange for some tea for you. She hasn't been with us long, which is fortunate, otherwise I'd have felt obliged to tell her who you are. Still, no doubt her curiosity will be satisfied before the day's over.'

'News travels fast here, then.' Rosemary smiled, although inwardly she was quaking with nerves.

'Factories are all the same, hotbeds for gossip.'

After that, his forehead creasing, he bent his head to a sheet of figures, and Rosemary remained silent, looking through promotional brochures for the firm. Pauline, trim and efficient

368

in a navy suit, brought in a tray with tea and biscuits, darted a speculative glance at Rosemary and quietly left the room. Gradually, her nervousness increasing, Rosemary saw the hands on her watch creep to the appointed time.

'My father has called in the senior staff,' Michael eventually said. 'He's acquainting them with the news, before it becomes common knowledge.'

Almost on cue, Beth returned, and with a forced smile said, 'Right, it's lambs to the slaughter!'

'I'll get Pauline to take you down,' Michael said, explaining, 'Health, Safety and Security regulations, Rosemary. No-one's allowed to go on the factory floor unaccompanied, unless they're employed here. Not even Beth.'

Michael wished them good luck, then mentally stiffening his spine, went to support his father.

Rosemary and Beth followed the secretary back along the corridor and out again into the cold, slightly damp air. They walked through the yard and then, towards the end, with some trepidation, Beth pushed open green painted double doors. The room they entered was large with a high ceiling and huge windows. Several women wearing white overalls and hats were sitting at a long trestle table, either side of a conveyor belt, their hands moving busily, efficiently. Rosemary watched, admiring their dexterity as using small knives they removed excess clay from the edges of cup handles and feet.

'This is called fettling,' Beth explained as they stood to one side, 'Then after this process, the ware goes into a dryer and then to be fired.'

One or two of the women looked up and murmured, 'Morning, Mrs Rushton.'

'Good morning,' Beth smiled, and glancing along the line saw that Ivy's place was empty. However, her space on the bench was filled with unfinished work, and at that moment Beth saw her returning. She touched Rosemary's arm in reassurance.

'Perfect,' she said softly. 'Would you excuse us, Pauline?'

With some apprehension, she walked over to meet Ivy, stopping some distance from the other workers, and Rosemary followed slowly, looking with interest at the heavily-built woman in her fifties, whose face split in a grin as she saw them approach.

'Howdo, Beth, come slummin, ave yer?' she said, with a casual glance at the girl with her. For a split second Beth held her breath, then as she'd expected, Ivy's gaze swivelled back, and blatantly her eyes raked over Rosemary's features, puzzlement creasing her brow.

'Well, well,' she said at last. 'And who's this then?'

Beth managed to keep her voice even.

'This is my daughter, Ivy.'

Ivy took a step backwards, her round face creasing in perplexity.

'Yer daughter?'

'Yes. Her name's Rosemary.'

'By 'eck, you've kept that quiet. Where's she bin 'til now?'

'I had her adopted when she was born.'

'Well, I'm blowed! You're a dark horse and no mistake.' Ivy looked again at Rosemary, her eyes alight with curiosity.

'Well, she ain't Mr Michael's, we all know as you two can't have kids. But there's a look of the Rushtons there, or I'm a Dutchman. If I didn't know better I'd say she favours young Mr James...' She caught sight of Beth's mortified face, and let out a low whistle.

'Eeh, yer never! Not both brothers! By gum Beth, that's a bit much even for me to take in!'

Beth stood motionless, waves of shame and embarrassment sweeping over her. She and Ivy had always had an unspoken but mutual respect, and with bitterness she realised she would now lose this woman's good opinion, and she minded terribly. Yet this was only the beginning, and Beth knew she'd need all her inner strength to face what lay ahead. Rosemary glanced at her, seeing the colour rise in her cheeks, and stood helplessly at her side, feeling like a prize exhibit.

'But what did you have her adopted for? T'wasn't as though the bosses couldn't afford to put their 'and in their pocket.'

'They never knew, neither did James.' Beth struggled to find the right words. 'I didn't even know his surname. It was just a short fling, two teenagers, you know what it's like...' she finished awkwardly.

'Not me,' Ivy said sharply. 'I might have a rough tongue, but my dad would've killed me if I'd come home up the spout. And I'm surprised at you, Beth, a Catholic an' all.' She frowned at Rosemary, who reddened at her scrutiny.

'How come you've turned up now, then?'

Rosemary floundered. She'd never met anyone quite like this forthright, outspoken woman. Talk about telling the truth and shaming the devil. Now she understood what Brenda had meant.

'My adoptive mother died, and I managed to search out my real family,' she explained.

'I bet that put the cat among the pigeons, eh Beth! I'd have liked to be a fly on the wall for that one!' She guffawed, a deep throaty chuckle, causing Pauline and some of the other women to look up curiously.

But Rosemary said defensively, 'They already knew about me, they'd been trying to find me for years.'

Ivy looked shrewdly at Beth.

'Is that right?'

'Absolutely,' Beth said firmly. 'Rosemary's existence was no secret, not once I'd met Michael.'

Ivy stared at her,

'So it's all roses, then?'

'We're absolutely delighted, and I'm very proud of her,' Beth said, smiling at Rosemary.

But Ivy was no fool.

'I suppose you've brought her to see me, 'cos I've got a big gob,' she said abruptly.

'No, Ivy. I wanted to introduce Rosemary to you, in the knowledge that you're the straightest person I know. I don't want a lot of false rumours sweeping the factory. I want people to know what the real situation is. Mr Rushton will be bringing Rosemary around himself in a few days.'

'Showin' off his granddaughter, eh?'

'That's the idea. Also, Rosemary's very

372

interested in seeing how pottery is made.'

'Well, any time I can help. And don't worry, luv, I'll see the right story gets round.'

'Thanks, Ivy.'

On an impulse, Rosemary held out her hand, 'Nice to have met you, Ivy.'

'And you, lass.'

They watched her return and resume working, and seeing heads already turning inquisitively in her direction, Beth touched Rosemary's arm indicating that they should leave.

'Thank God that's over!' she muttered. 'Now let's get out of here.'

35

Sylvia was on the phone within minutes of Beth arriving home.

'How did it go, was it too awful?'

'It wasn't the most uplifting experience of my life,' Beth said grimly. 'I don't think Rosemary enjoyed it much either.'

'Robert wants to take her in one day next week. What do you think?'

'Yes, the sooner the better.'

'I don't mean to be insensitive,' Sylvia said, 'but I do think it's important that Rosemary dresses the part. I know these young people like to dress casually, but...'

Beth suppressed a sarcastic retort. There were still times when she wondered what world the

Rushtons lived in. Did Sylvia really think that Rosemary's meagre wardrobe was because of her youth? But of course, cushioned from birth from the harsher realities of life, Sylvia had never known what it was to economise.

Instead, she said, 'To be honest, Sylvia, I don't think any of us realised just how poor Rosemary is. Do you know, she was actually homeless at one time, or would have been if someone hadn't taken her in. Even now, I don't suppose she earns very much and she'll be giving that up shortly.'

There was a pause before Sylvia said, 'I find it very painful to think of my own granddaughter being in such straits.'

'How do you think I feel?'

'Well, we can only try to make it up to her. So, are you going to take her shopping, or shall I?'

'I've been dying to,' Beth admitted, 'but in the early stages I didn't want her to think I was trying to buy her affection.'

'Why don't we divide it?' Sylvia suggested. 'You're nearer her age, so you'd be better helping her to choose some decent clothes. But I do believe in good classic accessories. Let me help her with those, Beth, it would give me so much pleasure.'

'Of course you must. Tell me which days you're free, and I'll get things organised.'

The first thing Rosemary did when she got back to the house was to make herself a coffee. That and to pinch one of Sally Ann's store of chocolate digestives. She kept them in a tin at the back of the larder, and it had always amused

Rosemary that she rarely offered her one.

She cupped her hands around the mug, thinking about her first impressions of the potbank. Of course she'd only seen a small part of it so far, but even now the smell lingered with her. Clay, that was it. When she'd commented on it to Beth, she'd laughed, and said, 'Wait until you go into the decorating shops. The smell of turpentine on Mum's clothes when she came home from work is one of my most enduring childhood memories. What with that, and Dad having to shake the straw out of his overalls before he came in, I could never forget where I was born.'

But now Rosemary's quandary was how to broach the subject of where she should live. Also, once she'd left her job, what would she do for money? Oh, she had her minute savings, but they wouldn't last long. Uncomfortably, she knew she'd been impulsive, foolish even, to give up her live-in job so quickly.

She was also confused about whether to ring Simon. Suppose he rebuffed her again? Yet already she was missing him dreadfully. Oh, she knew it was illogical, after all they'd only seen each other twice, but there had been something so special between them, she knew there had. No, she determined, I'm not going to let someone else spoil things, and jumping up went into the hall and dialled his number.

Nervously, she waited while the telephone rang, and rang.

There was no reply, and deflated, she put down the receiver, and went to make herself beans on

375

toast. There was a pile of ironing to do, the kitchen floor to wash, notes to type, the afternoon stretched boringly ahead. She couldn't help a wry smile. High drama this morning, the kitchen sink this afternoon.

'And I suppose you'll want a walk,' she said crossly to Homer, who simply ignored her ill humour and wagged his tail, hoping for a titbit. She relented and gave him a dog biscuit, suddenly aware of how much she'd miss him.

Rosemary worked through the day on Saturday to make up the time she'd lost, a fact not unnoticed by Sally Ann, who was already beginning to regret her untimely outburst. On reflection, her notes were always intelligently transcribed and typed, the house was neat, and although not the most imaginative cook, the girl coped reasonably well. This kid Helen seemed okay, but students were notoriously unreliable. What you should have done, she told herself, was to be more nosy. Then you might have got a few answers.

Deciding that now she had nothing to lose, she said casually, 'That was some car that collected you last week.'

I'm surprised you can remember, the state you were in, Rosemary thought bitterly, then recalled that Sally Ann hadn't been drinking at that stage.

'Yes,' she said shortly.

'Someone you've just met?'

Rosemary, brought up by Brenda to guard her privacy, was defensive.

'Fairly recently, yes.' Unsure why she was being so evasive, for some reason Rosemary found it

376

difficult to lower her guard. But there was no reason now to be secretive, and she was just about to explain what had been happening over the past few weeks, when the phone rang. She immediately tensed, hoping, praying it would be Simon.

But it was Helen, and Sally Ann came back into the room, looking distracted.

'Helen wants final confirmation that the job's hers before she burns her bridges.' Still undecided, Sally Ann looked again at Rosemary. Did she want to try and persuade her to stay? But then, still irritated by her refusal to elaborate on a simple question, she said, 'That okay with you?'

'Fine.' Rosemary turned away, the moment for confidences having passed, and carried on typing.

The following morning, she once again went to Mass at eleven o'clock. Possibly the following Sunday she would be able to attend the family service and join Beth in her pew, as that afternoon she was going to The Beeches for tea. At last she would meet her little brothers, for that was how she thought of them. Two little boys, adopted just as she was. Two more mothers forced by circumstances to give up their children, and Rosemary wondered how much Beth and Michael knew about them. Would their children seek out their natural parents just as she had? From what she read in the papers, the Adoption Laws were being changed to give children that right.

For Beth, it was a momentous day. First, she'd taken their au pair, Maria, to one side and told her as simply as she could about Rosemary.

'A love child,' was Maria's reaction, her eyes lighting up at the thought of a great romance. 'It will be how you say, exciting for you, Mrs Rushton!'

'Yes,' Beth smiled, 'but not a word to the boys, mind. Not until after they've met her.'

There was Mrs Hurst too. She would have to be told. Beth was dreading that. The housekeeper had been with them from the early days of their marriage, and they had always had a relaxed and friendly relationship. Beth was only too aware however of Mrs Hurst's strict Baptist views.

She and Michael had spent considerable time discussing their strategy for telling the boys. Beth thought it important that they should do it together.

'If they see we're relaxed and happy about it all, they'll take it in their stride,' she said hopefully, although her eyes betrayed her anxiety.

Michael tried to ease her fears. 'I think you're worrying too much. Remember they're very young. The really awkward questions will come later, and then we'll just tell them the truth.'

'What? You mean...'

'No, of course not. Maybe when they're adults, yes.'

Beth tried to envisage a time when she'd want her sons to know that their mother had been the victim of rape, and shuddered.

'You don't ever have to tell them, if you don't want to,' Michael pointed out. 'You're worrying about something way off in the future. Let's just take one step at a time.'

As they'd eventually agreed, Beth waited until after lunch, and then said casually, 'We've got a visitor coming for tea.'

Six-year-old Andrew was busy with his Lego. 'Who?'

'Someone very, very special. Her name's Rosemary, and you'll never guess who she is!' Now she had Ben's attention too. 'She's your big sister.'

Andrew frowned. 'We haven't got a sister.'

'Yes, you have,' Michael said, as Ben clambered on to his knee.

'It's just that she's been living somewhere else.'

'Why? Didn't she want to live with us?' Andrew stopped building his digger, and looked up at them both.

'She didn't know where our house was,' said Beth. 'When she was a really tiny baby, I couldn't look after her, so she was adopted by some very kind people.'

'Like you adopted me and Ben?'

'Adopted means being chosen,' chipped in Ben.

'Yes, that's right.' Michael stroked his son's fair hair, and smiled down at him.

'Why couldn't you look after her?' Andrew's brow was creased with anxiety. 'Does that mean you won't be able to look after us?'

'Oh no, darling, that could never happen. We'll always take care of you, and Ben. You see, Rosemary's a big girl, almost a lady now. All this happened a very long time ago, before I met Daddy.'

'Oh.' This appeared to satisfy Andrew, who had implicit faith in Michael's abilities, and he turned away to become once again absorbed in his game.

Ben however, had been thinking. 'Will she bring us a present?'

Beth glanced quickly at Michael, who gave a slight shake of his head in amusement. 'You'll have to wait and see,' she said vaguely.

However, she needn't have worried, for when she went to pick up Rosemary, it was to see two small packages in her hand.

'They're only colouring books and felt-tips, I'm afraid,' she said. 'I only thought about it on the way home from church, so I had to find something in the newsagents.'

'They'll be fine,' Beth reassured her. 'When they're this age, it's just having a present that's important, and they get through felt-tips like nobody's business. They're always leaving the tops off and then wonder why they won't work!'

'I feel a bit nervous,' Rosemary confessed. 'Suppose they don't like me?'

Beth smiled and reaching over touched her hand briefly. 'Of course they'll like you.'

But Rosemary remained quiet as they drove the short distance to Beth's home.

A few minutes later, she entered the hall to see two small, but very curious faces. Michael stood behind them, a hand on each child's shoulder.

'Andrew, Ben, this is Rosemary,' Beth said gently.

Rosemary smiled. 'Hello.'

There was a moment's uncertainty, then

380

Rosemary held out the two presents.

Ben, stocky with a cheeky grin, was the first to move forward and took his eagerly, tearing at the paper.

'What do you say?' prompted Michael.

'Thank you, Rosemary.'

Andrew, dark and slightly built, took his present from her slowly, saying, 'Thank you very much.'

Rosemary smiled at them both.

'I hope you like colouring and drawing. I used to love it. I still do.'

Andrew looked at her with interest. 'Would you do some drawing with me?'

'Yes, of course, but I warn you I can't draw horses!'

Andrew grinned, showing a gap in his front teeth. 'Neither can I.'

'Mummy,' Ben cajoled, 'can we have a piece of cake now?'

Beth laughed, explaining, 'We made a chocolate cake to welcome you, and I said they couldn't have any until you arrived.'

'How did you guess that's my favourite?'

Over the next couple of hours, Rosemary drew pictures, judged works of art, gave advice on colouring, heard Andrew read, and generally enjoyed herself. Unused to children of this age, she was amazed at the way they could be collapsing with laughter one minute, and arguing fiercely the next.

Michael and Beth relaxed in the sitting-room reading the Sunday papers, and enjoying the peace.

'Perhaps there is some benefit in them having an older sister, after all,' Michael admitted.

'I'm hoping she'll bring another dimension into our lives,' Beth said. 'I know both Sylvia and I are looking forward to playing the Fairy God-mother!'

'I'll bet!' Michael laughed. 'Have you mentioned it to her yet?'

'No, I'm just trying to find the right moment.'

That moment came after the children went to bed.

Beth and Rosemary were in the kitchen, tidying up the clutter, and chatting.

'You've met Mrs Hurst, so there's just Maria now. She's our au pair, and also the daughter of our manager in Milan.'

Seeing Rosemary's surprise, Beth said, 'Oh, didn't you know we had an outlet over there? James used to run it, and that's how he met Giovanna. Her father's in ceramics and has a tile factory in the area. A very successful one too – they do the most gorgeous designs.'

'I've never been abroad,' Rosemary admitted.

'No, sweetheart, you've missed out on a lot of things.' The endearment slipped out automatically, and Beth hardly noticed, but to Rosemary it marked a subtle change in their relationship. They were drawing closer, were more relaxed with each other, and she turned her head away to hide the sudden moisture in her eyes.

Unaware that her unguarded word had touched her daughter so much, Beth was concentrating on her next words.

'We've been talking, Michael and I, about your circumstances. We think it's time you received an allowance. You're part of the Rushton family now, and there's no reason you should have to be so self-sufficient, not at your age. So, when you can, I want to take you to our bank and open an account for you. Then, a decent monthly amount will be paid in for you to use as you wish.'

For a moment Rosemary was stunned. Used to being dependent on her own resources, the thought of money she hadn't earned being put at her disposal was beyond her wildest dreams. Whatever the amount, it would give her additional security, and overwhelmed with relief and gratitude she said, 'Thank you. I don't know quite what to say.'

'You don't need to say anything,' Beth reassured her. 'But Sylvia and I do have a request to make.'

'What's that?' Rosemary wondered what was coming.

'Would you let us take you shopping? I've always envied women who can float around department stores, buying their daughters clothes. Sylvia believes in having good accessories in a wardrobe. She helped me a lot when I first met Michael, enjoyed doing it too. She says sons were never the same, somehow.'

Rosemary grinned, imagining Sylvia trailing Michael around a fashion store.

'It's really kind of you,' she said, not without embarrassment. 'I know I need some new clothes, but...'

'Money's been a bit tight.' Beth finished the sentence for her. 'I know how that feels, I've been there myself. By the way, have you decided when you're leaving your job?'

Rosemary told her how the opportunity had arisen for her to leave without letting Sally Ann down, and added, 'The only problem is that I've got to quickly find somewhere else to live.'

'You must come here,' Beth said immediately. 'I'll show you the spare bedrooms and you can choose which one you like best. We could even redecorate to your own taste.'

Rosemary was speechless. Oh, she'd hoped of course that Beth would offer, but to be welcomed without reservation, as though it was the natural course of action, made her feel that at last she truly belonged. It made her feel warm and secure, and she smiled, a smile which made Beth smile back, and in that moment there passed between them an unspoken acknowledgement of the growing bond between them. For only the second time, Rosemary impulsively gave Beth a hug. Beth's tendency to cry easily came to the fore and there were tears in both their eyes as they drew apart.

'Is that settled then?' said Beth.

Rosemary took her time before answering. Illogically, although she'd wanted the offer made, she was going to refuse. During previous nights, in the quiet hours before sleep, she'd thought deeply about how she should react if Beth asked her to live at The Beeches. And always the same instinctive answer came. It wouldn't be fair on Michael. Although her first unfavourable impression of him was fading, Rosemary could still remember the constraint in his eyes, his stiffness and reserve on that first Sunday at the church. He and Beth were happy with their little boys, had created their own family lifestyle. Her own presence, as a constant reminder of the painful past, would diminish that.

Aware that Beth was waiting for an answer, she said, 'I'm not sure, Beth. Quite honestly, I don't think it would be fair on Michael.' There, she'd said it.

'Michael would agree with me,' Beth defended.

'Yes, I'm sure he would, and it's very kind of both of you. It's not that I don't want to, but I honestly think it would be better if I actually lived somewhere else.'

Inwardly, Beth was guiltily relieved. Much as she'd love to have her daughter under her roof, she knew Rosemary was right.

'Had you anywhere in mind? I'm sure Robert and Sylvia would be only too pleased...'

Rosemary had thought of that too. Thought of what life would be like in that huge house, with a live-in housekeeper, daily cleaner and gardener. Somehow, there too, she couldn't see herself fitting in.

Seeing her hesitation, Beth said, 'Is it that you'd prefer your own place?'

'No, not at all.' It might be the dream of most young girls, but for Rosemary, the prospect held no attraction. She longed to feel secure, to be part of a family, and the memory lingered of a small cosy house, fragrant with the aroma of home cooking.

She knew what she wanted, knew what she needed, but still she found it difficult to make that request. Then she mustered the courage to say, 'Do you think Rose would have me?'

36

The following morning, Beth drove to Minsden.

'You mean she wants to come and live with me?'

'That's what she says. No pressure though, Mum. She was quite hesitant about suggesting it.'

Rose sat back in her armchair. Who'd have thought it? With those two great houses to choose between, her granddaughter preferred to come and live here, in Elm Grove.

'You did offer?' she looked at Beth sharply.

'Yes, of course I did. She said she didn't think it would be fair on Michael.'

'Did she now. Well, that shows she's got a mature head on her shoulders. She's right, of course.'

'Yes, I know.'

'And Linden Lodge?'

'I broached it, and that was when she asked me whether I thought you would have her.'

'No problem, is there? I mean with Robert and Sylvia. We all know what Robert's like...'

'No, I'm sure there isn't. She seemed to get on well with both of them. To be honest, Mum, I just think she'd feel more comfortable here – it's more the sort of background she's been used to.'

'Ordinary, you mean?' Rose said it with a smile.

'If you like. I also asked whether she'd like a place of her own, and she was very emphatic that she wouldn't.'

Beth, giving her mother time to think about it, went into the kitchen to make coffee. There was no doubt in her mind what the outcome would be, but she wanted Rose to be sure. Waiting for the kettle to boil, she looked round at the fitted modern units, remembering how it had been in her childhood. There had been a downstairs bathroom attached then, the space long since incorporated into the present kitchen. She and Gordon used to roller-skate from it across the red quarry floor and, aware now of the short distance, she marvelled that they could ever have made a game out of it. Thinking of her brother, she was only too aware that it was this weekend he and Val were coming with their two children.

'Have you decided?' she asked her mother when she took in their drinks.

'There's nothing to decide. Of course she must come here,' Rose said indignantly. 'She can have your old room. It's all in order – I only had it papered last year.'

'You're sure, Mum? I mean, it will mean more work for you.'

'She seems a practical girl, I'm sure she'll help.'

'Well, don't forget you can always have June more often if you need to.'

Rose said evasively, 'If I need to, I will. Let's wait and see.'

Beth hid a smile. It had taken her ages to persuade Rose to have some assistance with her housework. In the end, she'd won her over by stressing how much it would help the young widowed mother who lived next door to have some extra income. Rose, with only her state pension, would never have considered it, but Beth insisted on shouldering many of her expenses.

'You don't think either Michael or I want to live in luxury, while you have to count every penny,' she'd argued when her mother, fiercely independent, had initially objected. 'Anyway, it's my money to do what I want with, and if I want to make sure you're comfortable, then why shouldn't I?'

In the end she'd had her way, and the semi-detached house was maintained to the highest standards. That was one reason Rose thought one or two envious neighbours would be glad to hear a whiff of scandal. Not her old friends, of course, but some people could be so small-minded.

Beth was thinking about Gordon and Val's visit.

'It is Saturday that they're coming?'

'Yes. Why, which day was Rosemary going to move in?'

'Saturday.'

They stared at each other, then Beth said, 'It's not a problem. I'll pick her up with her stuff and she can come to us on the Saturday and stay overnight. That way, she'll already be at The Beeches when you all come for lunch on Sunday.

I take it they're staying with Val's mum?'

'Yes, it's her turn this time.'

Beth got up to go.

'Are you sure, Mum, that you want to tell them by yourself? I can do it, or if you like I can come and give you moral support.'

'No, thank you, love. I'd rather deal with it myself.'

'Well, good luck.' Beth leant to kiss her cheek, and left.

Alone, Rose sat thinking about this unexpected development. It would certainly change the solitary life she'd created for herself. She had her own routines now, had become set in her ways. But then she gave herself a mental shake. It'll do you good, Rose Sherwin, she thought, a bit of young company, brighten you up a bit. And she had to admit that the long evenings, particularly in the winter, could seem very lonely at times. Oh, there was always the telly, and her library book, but strangely enough, it was when watching a comedy programme that she felt it most. She was self-conscious laughing aloud in an empty room. That was the worst thing about being on your own, there was no-one to share the everyday happenings with. And eating alone. Now, she would not only have someone to cook for, but she'd be able to make a fuss of this new granddaughter, try to make up for all those lost years. So, she must make plans. A shopping list first – and she went to her larder, wondering what young girls liked to eat these days.

Rosemary felt a little overwhelmed by the speed

389

of events. How she was going to find time for three outings during the week, she just didn't know. Beth wanted to take her shopping tomorrow, Sylvia on Wednesday, and now they were proposing she should have an official tour of the factory with Robert on Friday. She could just imagine Sally Ann's reaction if she asked for all that time off. It was one thing to sneak a couple of hours, but these were major events. If she told her employer of her good fortune she might be more understanding, yet Rosemary felt uncomfortable with the idea. It was strange really. She'd wanted to find out the truth so much that it dominated her life. Yet now she'd found it, she was oddly reluctant to tell anyone. I haven't even told Lisa yet, she thought, and she ought to be the first to know. And Father Kavanagh, she should be writing to him. Perhaps it was because she'd had to be secretive for so long, it was becoming part of her nature. Rosemary fervently hoped that wasn't true, and made a firm resolve to broach the subject with Sally Ann when she came home.

But she wasn't given a chance, for the American came in like a whirlwind.

Harassed and breathless, she flung over her shoulder, 'I've a plane to catch!' Without removing her coat, she hurried up the staircase.

Rosemary could hear drawers being slammed and footsteps scurrying overhead, as she hurriedly finished cooking their meal. Twenty minutes later, Sally Ann reappeared, suitcase and flight bag in her hands.

'Sorry, I haven't got time to eat!' She squashed

a purple hat on top of her head and said, 'Have you seen my green scarf?'

'Yes, it's airing on the boiler.' Rosemary fetched it and asked, 'Where are you going?'

'Conference in the States. I'm standing in for a professor who's had a heart attack. Sorry, kid, I won't be back until Sunday. Settle Helen in for me, will you? Leave me an address and I'll post on anything I owe you.'

She swung round as she reached the front door, and paused. 'Good luck, honey, and thanks a lot.'

'Thank you, too.'

For a moment they hovered in awkward silence then quickly gave each other a token hug.

A moment later, she was gone, and as Rosemary closed the front door, she could see a car waiting to take her on the long journey to the airport. Slowly, she went back into the kitchen to eat her meal, bemused at the way all her problems were being solved. Sally Ann hadn't even left a pile of notes to be typed. That meant as long as she kept the laundry up to date and left the house clean, her time was her own until Saturday. Then, her new life would really begin.

What she was going to do about her future, however, lay in the balance. Still unsure of what she should do, Rosemary had decided to postpone her decision until after she'd seen more of the factory on Friday. Robert had stressed that, because of the academic year, time was crucial, but she wanted to discuss it with Beth first. The knowledge that at last there was someone in her life whom she could turn to, someone she respected and trusted, meant a lot to Rosemary. It was so important that she made the right choice – it would be stupid not to seek advice.

Not all your problems have been solved though, she mused. What about Simon? Despite all that was happening in her life, he was constantly in her thoughts. Twice that evening she rang, each time her nerves jangling as she waited for him to answer. But again, there was no reply. Frustrated, Rosemary muttered, 'I'll write to him.'

She ran upstairs only to look dubiously at the cheap lined shorthand notebook she used to exchange letters with Lisa. She hesitated. Deciding Sally Ann wouldn't miss a couple of pages of decent stationery and a single envelope, she went and looked on her desk. Yes! An expensive-looking writing case. From inside, she extracted two sheets of paper, then looked down at them with dismay. She might have known! They were purple. Good quality vellum, but still purple. Should she wait until tomorrow and then buy some Basildon Bond in white or pale blue? But she felt a compulsion to write the letter, to try to get Simon to understand. She was growing impatient to see him, was anxious to put things right. Oh, she might have completely misread the situation, she'd had such limited experience in these things, but she really had thought there was something special between them.

Deciding purple it had to be, she settled down to write.

The following morning, Christine stood as her son often did, drinking her coffee at the window overlooking the recreation ground. She had a slight headache, probably from too much wine the previous night. She'd treated them at a local restaurant, and had been very pleasantly surprised both at the quality of the food, and the size of the extensive wine list.

'Just to celebrate the beginning of my stay,' she'd said, pouring herself a third glass. Why was it that she couldn't drink as much as she used to? She'd known the time she could get through nearly a bottle without any ill effects.

'You're getting older, Mum,' Simon had explained, most unkindly she thought.

Christine hated the thought of getting old. She did her best to hold back the years, having her hair tinted and fashionably cut, looking after her skin, always varnishing her nails, firmly believing that if she thought of herself as, well, in her prime, that was how she'd look. Secretly, she'd like to marry again, but no man had appeared so far who could meet her exacting standards.

Her attention was suddenly caught by a collie racing after a ball, and she was reminded of that film, what was it? Oh yes, *Lassie Come Home*, starring a very young Elizabeth Taylor. Then her eyes narrowed. Surely the girl with it was Rosemary? She strained to see her face, and then drew back to one side so that she wouldn't be seen.

She'd mentioned Rosemary last night, over dessert.

'How's Rosemary?' she'd said casually, trying to

ascertain how the romance was developing.

But Simon had been terse. 'I've no idea.'

Taking the hint, Christine hadn't pursued the subject. But as she sipped her brandy, she'd wondered whether she'd wasted her time coming up here. It was good to see Simon, of course, but she'd sacrificed the Golf Club Annual Dinner to make the trip, not to mention her weekly bridge party. The whole point of it had been to sabotage, if possible, the relationship between Simon and this unsuitable young girl. Now it looked as though it had fallen at the first fence. That surprised her, for she'd had a few misgivings this time about interfering. She wasn't a complete monster, for heaven's sake, and the obvious delight the young couple had shown in each other's company had been charming to see. But Christine still clung to her conviction that, as Simon's mother, in fact his only parent, it was her duty to shield him from anything or anyone who could be a detriment to his career. Why, only the other day one of her friends had offered to introduce him to the daughter of an eminent Harley Street surgeon. The girl had been at boarding-school with her daughter, and had an impeccable background. Now, that would be an excellent match. The only problem was how to get Simon to meet her. She'd give a party, Christine decided. Perhaps for Christmas, or the New Year. She was sure her friend would co-operate on the timing.

Now, Christine could see Rosemary approach again, obviously on her way home after the walk. With the dog now safely on its lead, Rosemary was taking something out of her pocket – an envelope. Suddenly, Christine knew she was coming here, to the flat, and moved swiftly away from the window, straining her ears to listen for the flap of the letter-box. There it was. She'd left a letter or card for Simon! After waiting several minutes, Christine opened the door to the flat and went down the stairs.

The postman had obviously been earlier, for in the hall there was a heavy oak carved chest which acted as a hall table. On it were a couple of letters addressed to Simon, presumably picked up and put there by the downstairs tenant when she left for work.

She'd been right! On the doormat lay a bright purple envelope. Purple! What person of any breeding would use bright purple stationery? Her instincts had definitely been right about that girl.

She picked up the envelope and sniffed it. At least it wasn't perfumed. Obviously a letter though, not a card. Christine paused in thought. There had obviously been some sort of argument or misunderstanding, and this letter was a plea from Rosemary. Now why would she write when there was the phone sitting upstairs? It could only be because Simon refused to listen to her. Christine knew her son: he was like his father – stubborn and high-principled. Not a comfortable combination to live with, and many times in the past she'd had to ease a difficult situation with half-truths.

But this letter could change everything, interfere with her plans.

Christine's gaze fell on the oak chest. Suppose someone put a coat on there, the woman who came in to clean for instance? It would be easy for a letter to be dislodged. Slowly, inch by inch, she experimented, edging the purple envelope across the polished surface. It slid easily. Should she? Then, before she could change her mind, it was gone, sliding down behind the settle to wedge near the bottom. Christine leaned to peer down the narrow dim aperture. It was hardly visible. She stood back, surveying the heavy piece of furniture. Unless the cleaner moved it on a regular basis, which she would doubt, then Rosemary's letter could lie there, unseen, for months or even longer.

With a feeling of quiet satisfaction, she went back upstairs to the flat. Perhaps she'd stay for the rest of the week, just in case. But already her brain was buzzing with plans. First of all she must fix on a suitable date for her party; the two main guests of course to be Simon and Caroline. Did she feel any qualms about what she'd just done? She had to admit to a slight feeling of discomfort, but Christine had always had a convenient conscience. She believed in the old adage that the end justified the means, and surely it wasn't a crime to want the best for your only son?

37

It was with a sense of relief that Rosemary walked away from the flat. She'd now done all she could to heal the rift between herself and Simon. In her letter, she'd told him everything, detailing her discovery about being adopted, her search for her mother, and about the new life and opportunities now before her. She'd explained to him why she'd had to lie, how at that time she'd been unsure of the Rushton family's plans.

'I didn't feel I could betray their confidence,' she'd written, *'not even to you. Yet only twenty-four hours later I could have told you everything and I was so looking forward to coming round. I don't know exactly what Sally Ann said to you, but she was halfway through a bottle of whisky when I got back.'*

After much indecision, she'd simply ended the letter,

'I've missed you, and would love to see you again, Rosemary.'

So now, she thought as she went back to the house, the next move is up to him.

Beth was busy planning the shopping expedition. Rosemary had told her she had the day off, so that meant they could take their time. She left Maria instructions about the children, saying she hoped to be back early in the afternoon, possibly bringing Rosemary with her.

The young Italian girl, who had been out the previous Sunday, began to smile. 'I would like to meet her, Mrs Rushton. The boys are so happy and tell me much about their new sister.'

'She's about the same age as you,' Beth smiled. 'And well done, Maria, your English is improving every day. You like your classes?'

'Oh yes, Mrs Rushton. I am very happy.'

Maria had been a distinct success, and Beth hoped she'd stay with them for at least a year. An intelligent, kind-hearted girl, it suddenly occurred to her that she and Rosemary might become friends. Both virtual strangers to the district, it would be an ideal arrangement. Then Beth remembered that Rosemary did know someone here in the Potteries. Hadn't she gone down to Chalfont St Giles with a young man? She must remember to ask her about him.

At ten o'clock, she set off to drive the relatively short distance to pick up her daughter. This would be a new experience – well, for her anyway, for presumably Rosemary would have gone shopping with Brenda in the past.

But Brenda had never liked shopping. She'd bought nearly all her own clothes, Rosemary's too when she was small, from a catalogue, gaining great satisfaction from the commission she earned. But Rosemary loved wandering around the shops. She liked to handle things, stroke fabrics, hold objects in her hands. So now, it was with growing impatience that she waited for Beth's car to turn the corner.

Beth had decided to take Rosemary to Hanley,

the main shopping centre of Stoke-on-Trent. There were not only large department stores, but also several smaller boutiques.

'I thought we'd start with Lewis's,' she suggested, 'then go to Huntbach's and have a spot of lunch.'

But when they were actually on the fashion floor of the large department store, Rosemary found herself in a quandary. When Beth had said she wanted to buy her some clothes, what exactly had she meant? She could certainly do with some new jeans, and a sweater. As for that anorak, she was beginning to loathe even the sight of it, so a new coat would be really useful. But she didn't want to seem greedy.

Beth, guessing what was in her mind, said, 'I wouldn't mind having a look around myself. Why don't you wander off, and see if anything takes your eye?'

Tentatively, Rosemary began to search among the racks of clothing. Once or twice she removed a sweater and held it up, then glimpsing the price, hurriedly put it back. She could get three for that price off the market! Then spotting a polo neck in a heavenly shade of blue, she held it against her and went to look in a mirror. She'd never felt anything so soft, so warm.

Beth, obliquely watching, noticed the longing on Rosemary's face, saw her once again check the price-tag and put the sweater back. Then she moved on, pausing at rails of more reasonable clothes. Beth found it fascinating to see which clothes attracted her daughter, to watch the expressions of delight flitting across her face. But the really satisfying emotion was that at last she could do something for her. So many years she'd missed, not a single toy had she ever bought, not a single treat had she given. But she could do this, and in a way it was history repeating itself. For her own introduction into the Rushton family had been a similar one. Oh, she'd been better dressed than Rosemary – after all, she'd been working for a number of years. But she'd still had to budget carefully, helping Rose with household expenses. However, it was stressed to her that to be a Rushton meant dressing to a certain standard.

'People judge you by your clothes,' Sylvia had explained. 'I know it's snobbish and it's wrong. But it's a fact of life. As Michael's wife, you are in a way representing the success of the company. Never stint on your appearance, my dear.'

Sylvia's support, often despite Robert's antagonism, had been a crucial factor in Beth's acceptance by the social circle in which they moved. At first, Beth's socialist principles, instilled and honed by her father, led her to despise what she saw as a selfish middle-class culture, but gradually over the years her views had broadened. She was not the only one who gave freely of her time to raise money for charities, and she had learned to respect people for what they were, irrespective of whether they'd had a privileged background.

After a while, deciding the time had come to give Rosemary some encouragement, she went to join her.

'Are you looking for anything in particular?' she

said, and then laughed. 'I sound like one of the assistants!'

Rosemary grinned. 'I could do with some new jeans and knitwear. Is that okay?'

'More than okay. Choose whatever you like.'

Half an hour later, Rosemary had chosen her jeans, and at Beth's insistence, bought two pairs. Then she chose a colourful striped top, and a pretty embroidered shirt.

'Well, we've made a start,' Beth said, and then looked at Rosemary's thin anorak. 'What about a new winter coat?'

Rosemary's eyes lit up, and she followed Beth to the outerwear section. Pausing by a range of leather coats she glanced shyly at Beth, only to see her nod in agreement. Ten minutes later, she was standing before a long mirror hardly able to believe the reflection she saw was actually hers. Sleek and supple, the black coat felt wonderful, it looked wonderful, it was wonderful.

'What do you think?'

Beth smiled at her shining eyes. 'I think it's fabulous. We'll take it.'

Rosemary stood aside as Beth paid for the clothes, her feelings a strange mixture of pleasure and embarrassment.

'How about some clothes just for fun?' Beth said. 'I know what it's like having to wear practical things all the time.' She led the way to a different department.

'What about these?' She held up a pair of purple velvet flares, then laughed as she saw Rosemary pull a face. 'I was only joking!' She smiled in approval as Rosemary selected a pair in silver grey. 'Yes, I like those. Now, what about–'

'No, Beth!' Rosemary caught her arm. 'You've bought me enough.'

Beth saw the discomfort in her eyes, and mentally swore at herself.

She was overwhelming the girl. Take it slowly, she told herself, there'll be other times. But I'll definitely get her that blue sweater later as a surprise.

From Lewis's, they went to the exclusive Huntbach's store, and had a relaxing lunch in the restaurant.

Afterwards, despite her misgivings, Beth tried to persuade Rosemary that she needed a new outfit for her tour of the factory.

'I can wear my jeans and the leather coat,' she protested. 'You've spent enough, Beth.'

'You'll be too hot,' Beth pointed out. 'In any case,' she said briskly, 'I've had my orders from Robert. He places great store on such things.'

'Doesn't want to feel ashamed of me, you mean,' Rosemary said bitterly.

'Oh, Rosemary, don't feel like that,' Beth said with distress.

'I'm sorry. It's just that I've been independent for so long that I find all of this a bit difficult. It's not that I'm ungrateful, but...'

'I know,' Beth said. 'I always think it's easier to give than to receive. But we only want to help you. You've done a marvellous job of supporting yourself, and the last thing I want to do is take away your independence, but...'

'The Rushton reputation is at stake!'

'You're learning,' Beth grinned, and they both

laughed. The moment's tension eased, they went in search of a smart suit.

It wasn't until late afternoon that they returned to The Beeches, where Rosemary began to help Beth unload the boot.

'Leave most of them here until you move in with Mum,' Beth suggested, then turned as Mrs Hurst came out to help, her expression disapproving.

'I think you've already met Rosemary,' Beth said.

The housekeeper, who had been profoundly shocked by Beth's revelation, visibly softened as she looked at mother and daughter. Surrounded by glossy carrier bags, their happiness and ease with each other was like a ray of sunlight.

'Yes, I have. It's nice to see you again,' she said somewhat reluctantly.

'We'd love some tea, Mrs H,' Beth said.

'Aye, and there's warm scones, if you fancy a bite.'

'That would be lovely,' Rosemary said. 'Do you need any help?'

'Bless you, no. You go and take the weight off your feet – shopping can be hard work.'

But Beth could tell she appreciated the offer, and gave a sigh of relief. She'd thaw out eventually.

It was in an ecstatic mood that Rosemary walked Homer that evening. The recreation ground was empty, the evening dark and uninviting, but she hardly noticed. It had been such a wonderful day, not only because of all the fantastic clothes

403

Beth had bought for her, but also because they'd had such fun. There wasn't anyone, not even Lisa, she could have enjoyed shopping with so much.

Glancing up at Simon's flat, she could see the light shining in the window, and knowing that by now he would have read her letter, she hurried Homer, anxious to get back, not to miss the phone call she was confident would come.

But Simon didn't ring, and by the time Rosemary went to bed at eleven o'clock, her high spirits had plummeted. Why is it, she thought despairingly, that every time I have a smashing day something has to take the edge off it? It was just the same after that afternoon at Linden Lodge. Was it that he needed time to think? You're just too impatient, she tried to convince herself. He's bound to ring soon.

The following day, Sylvia, warned by Beth that Rosemary was a bit sensitive on the issue, took her granddaughter to Henry White's in Newcastle. Rosemary had been in the department store before, of course, had spent many an hour there on Saturday afternoons, but she'd never been able to afford to buy anything.

First of all, they went to the shoe department.

'What would you like to wear with your new coat?' Sylvia asked gently.

But Rosemary had already seen them. Long and black, with a tight fit and narrow heel, the boots were perfect.

'And how about a pair of court shoes to wear with your new suit?'

Rosemary nodded. She had no choice – there was certainly nothing suitable in her existing wardrobe.

Her choice of classic black patent had Sylvia smiling with approval, and after spending time in the accessories department, a leather bag, silk scarf and leather gloves were bought so unobtrusively that Rosemary felt no embarrassment at all.

But as Sylvia related to Robert later, 'There are so many things that child needs. Only today could I see how little she has. Only sleepers in her ears, Robert, and we must definitely buy her a decent wristwatch.'

'Get her one for Christmas,' he suggested.

So that was another shopping trip that left Rosemary's senses reeling. I'll always remember these last two days, she thought, no matter what happens. In all her daydreaming and wishful thinking while living in the sordid bed-sit, and even now she could hardly remember her months there without an inward shudder, she'd never expected it to end like this. I'm so lucky, she told herself, so very lucky.

But, again, although she waited anxiously, there was no telephone call from Simon.

The next day she cleaned the house, caught up with the ironing, and prepared for what she privately thought as her 'state visit' to the factory. Now that the time was approaching, she was beginning to feel both apprehensive and full of anticipation.

The evening was spent watching TV, a rare luxury as she normally worked on Sally Ann's typing, and listening for the phone. But once again it was to no avail. Tomorrow, she thought as she went to sleep, surely he'll ring tomorrow.

At ten-thirty the following morning, Rosemary waited, proudly holding her black leather clutch bag. Yet she felt slightly self-conscious in her new, ultra-smart clothes. With the leather coat loosely on her shoulders, she gazed in the mirror above the hall table. Hair freshly washed and subtly made up, her complexion shone with youth and health. And adrenalin, she thought. You're thrilled to bits to be dressed like this, and it shows.

And then, the ultimate fantasy of any teenager: the car to pick her up arrived, and at the wheel was a uniformed chauffeur. Rosemary swept out of the front door, feeling like royalty.

In a way, that was how the day progressed. Robert, with one swift approving glance at her plum cashmere suit and cream silk polo, had wasted no time. As soon as she arrived at his office, he'd passed her coat to his secretary and, after introducing her, ushered her out into the corridor. From there they went down the steps into the yard.

'First, I want you to meet Dave, the lodgeman,' Robert told her. 'Then when you visit the factory again, he'll know who you are, and will wave you through.'

Dave, seeing them coming, limped out of his cubbyhole to greet them.

'Morning, Mr Rushton, sir,' he said, standing before them as though on a parade ground.

'Good morning, Dave. This is my granddaughter, Rosemary.'

Shyly, Rosemary put out her hand, to have it grasped in a rough work-worn one.

'Nice to meet you, Miss.'

'And you, Dave.'

After that, the visit began in earnest and they made their way through the various departments or 'shops' as they were called. As they entered each one, the atmosphere subtly changed. Oh, there were deferential nods to Robert – it was obvious there was no informality in his relationship with his workers – but there were many furtive looks at Rosemary. She was introduced to the supervisor or foreman in each department who, with Robert watching closely, took Rosemary along the benches, explaining each person's role. At first, as a worker looked up, Rosemary would just smile, but gradually, gaining confidence, she began to ask questions, to admire a particular pattern or skill.

Gradually, Robert began to relax. Sylvia and Beth had done an excellent job; the girl looked every inch a Rushton. Oh, there were a few sly looks and nudges, he'd expected that, but they'd all had nearly a week to chew over the scandal. Now, having satisfied their curiosity, he was hoping they would find something else to talk about.

Rosemary, on the other hand, was finding the whole process one of utter fascination. And when she entered the decorating shops, she just didn't want to leave. It was with a sense of wonder that she saw how the skill of the enamellers, the free-hand paintresses, and the lithographers transformed the pottery into works of art. And then there were the gilders, with their fast-turning wheels and fine brushes dipped in gold.

These, she was told by the supervisor, were considered the elite of the workforce.

'They work with burnished gold, you see,' said Gladys, who was apparently due to retire the following month.

'My grandmother was a gilder,' Rosemary said with a quick smile.

Robert, observing the appreciative glances of his workers as Rosemary showed genuine interest and admiration for their expertise, almost swelled with pride. Over lunch too, taken in the boardroom, where Rosemary was introduced to the senior management, he was obviously in an elated mood.

Michael, leaving his father with the other directors, took over the reins and later accompanied Rosemary to the general offices. Here she really did feel awkward, seeing all the typists and clerks lifting their heads from their desks as she and Michael entered. She could identify with the girls and with their envious glances at her expensive clothes. It was only months since she'd sat at a similar desk, with an Imperial typewriter before her. In this environment, she felt more inhibited, and it was with a sense of relief that they returned to Robert's office for a final cup of tea.

'Well, what do you think of Rushton's?' demanded Robert.

Rosemary looked at them both, and answered straight from her heart. 'I love it.'

Robert beamed, while Michael crossed his long legs and looked at her appraisingly.

'In what way?' Michael asked.

Rosemary spread her hands. 'Just all of it. The smell, particularly the turps in the decorating shops. I know now what Beth meant about that.' She smiled. 'But the whole atmosphere is so ... oh, I don't know, I felt part of history somehow. And you're creating such beautiful things for people's homes. It just seems so worthwhile and satisfying.'

'Have you given any more thought to your future?' asked Michael.

Robert, his face suffused with enthusiasm, began, 'I think—'

Michael held up a hand. 'Perhaps we should hear Rosemary's views first, Father.'

Robert glared at him, but subsided.

Rosemary looked at them both. 'I'd really like to talk to Beth about it.'

'You couldn't choose anyone better to advise you,' Michael agreed, 'but make it as soon as you can – time is of the essence with this.'

With another look to silence his father, Michael rang for his secretary. 'Have you arranged for Frank to collect Rosemary?'

'Yes, he's already waiting downstairs.'

'Thank you for showing me round,' Rosemary said to her grandfather.

'I haven't enjoyed anything so much for years,' he said gruffly, getting up to say goodbye.

They both stood for a moment, then Rosemary moved forward and kissed him on the cheek.

'See you soon,' she said. 'I not only want Beth's

advice, I'd like yours too.'

'And you shall have it, my dear, and gladly.'

Robert watched her go with a feeling of pride that surpassed any emotion he'd felt since the day he'd lost his son. James, he thought, she's got your charm. I only hope she has a better future.

38

At the same time that Rosemary was touring the potbank, Simon was trying to tell a patient's wife as gently as possible that her husband's cancer was terminal. A few minutes later, as he left the office, he heard his name called, and turning saw a nervous young probationer approach.

'Could you ring this number, please?' She handed him a slip of paper, and, looking down at it, Simon quickened his step to return along the corridor. What did the top consultant in his previous hospital want that was urgent enough to disrupt a ward round?

His question was soon answered. It wasn't the consultant, but Laura, his wife, who without any preamble said, 'Richard's dead – he died last night.'

Simon was stunned. Richard had been a mentor to him – not only that but, despite the difference in their ages, a friend. Simon had regularly dined at his home, and one of his main regrets in taking his current post had been that he would miss Richard and Laura.

'Oh Laura... I'm so sorry... What...?'

'He had a massive heart attack on the golf course.'

'But he always looked after himself, had annual checks!'

'I know.'

The grief in her voice was heartbreaking, and he could hear her struggle against tears.

'Is there anything I can do, Laura? Anything at all?'

'The funeral's on Tuesday. You couldn't come down before, could you? I know it's a lot to ask, but...' Her voice faded.

Simon said quickly, 'Of course I'll come, just as soon as I can arrange cover. I'll ring and let you know, and Laura...'

'Yes?'

'I really am so sorry.'

Simon replaced the receiver and, profoundly shocked by the news, went to finish his ward round.

Richard had been a brilliant doctor, had contributed so much to the field of healthcare. He was only in his late forties – it was a tragic waste that his life should be so cruelly cut short.

The couple had been childless and as far as he knew Laura had no close relatives. To offer support was the least he could do for his friend's widow, and he determined to drive down that same night if possible.

In the event it did prove possible, but left him little free time for anything else. Leaving Christine still at the flat, although she was talking of returning home after the weekend, Simon set off for London, or more specifically, Hampstead. It was as he drove that his thoughts turned to Rosemary. Over the last few days, he'd begun to wonder if perhaps he'd been too hasty, too quick to judge. Her voice on the phone had sounded genuinely concerned, anxious even. Once his initial anger had simmered down, he'd tried to analyse the situation. Was his reaction partly because his pride had been hurt? Uncomfortably, he knew this was true, and yet there was still the fact that she'd lied to him. That was indisputable.

He braked suddenly, cursing the ineptitude of the driver of a large lorry in front, and then, after overtaking, let his thoughts return to Rosemary. Over the past week, he'd found himself hoping she'd ring again, had half-decided to meet her, to give her the chance to explain she'd pleaded for. But she hadn't rung, and after his brush-off the last time, he supposed he was expecting too much.

I'll ring her, he decided at last. When I get back after the funeral. And with his customary ability to put his life into compartments, proceeded to concentrate on his journey and the distressing days ahead.

Rosemary, her belongings all packed, opened the door on Saturday morning to greet her replacement.

Helen, wearing jeans and a baggy tee-shirt, under a shabby Afghan coat, grinned broadly at her.

'Hi! You must be Rosemary!' she said in her

broad Birmingham accent.

'Yes. Come in, Helen.'

The girl dumped her bags in the hall, and looked around curiously. 'So this is where the Prof lives.'

Rosemary led the way into the sitting-room. 'The house isn't hers, she's on an exchange from America.'

'Still, it suits her.'

Rosemary showed her around the house, explaining Sally Ann's routines and preferences. Before they went into the kitchen, she teased, 'He's savage, I warn you.'

'I heard him barking when I arrived. Hey, you're not serious, are you?'

With a smile, Rosemary flung open the door, and Homer leapt out of his basket, his tail wagging furiously.

It was with relief that Rosemary saw Helen's face light up as she fondled the dog's silky ears. She'd grown very fond of the collie, and wouldn't have been happy leaving him with someone who didn't like animals.

'I'll make some coffee – then you can ask me any questions you like.'

By midday, Rosemary was ready to leave. She left a short note on Sally Ann's desk, with Rose's address and phone number, handed her door keys over to Helen and prepared to be picked up. Beth had said about one o'clock.

But ten minutes later, a car was drawing up outside. It was Michael in the Rolls. With one embarrassed look at Helen's open mouth,

413

Rosemary picked up her bags waiting in the hall, and said, 'I didn't expect anyone just yet. So, it's hello and goodbye, Helen. Good luck.'

'And you.'

It was only when she was in the car that Rosemary remembered she'd meant to leave Beth's number in case Simon rang over the weekend. Oh, forget it, she thought grimly, he's not worth it. He's hardly the most sensitive person, if he can just ignore my letter like that. Think of it as another rejection, history repeating itself. But tears stung her eyes as she gazed resolutely out of the window. She'd been so sure that Simon would understand.

'So,' Beth said that evening, after the children were tucked up in bed, 'Michael says you'd like to talk to me about your future.'

'Yes. It's just that I feel so mixed up.'

Rosemary told her how she'd always wanted to go to university, had felt she'd been cheated of her opportunity after Keith Latham had disappeared to Australia.

'I thought I'd never have the chance,' she explained. 'Yet now that I have, I'm not sure whether it's what I want after all.'

Beth offered Rosemary a box of chocolates, and settled back in her armchair.

'I wanted to go to university too,' she said, 'but then my dad died, Gordon went away on National Service, and I needed to earn a wage. That's how I came to work at Rushton's.'

'What did you do?'

'I was a Management Assistant in Marketing,

414

which meant I could study part-time at the North Staffs Technical College – well, it's a Polytechnic now.'

'So you actually worked on the potbank while you were studying?'

'Yes, that's right.' Beth looked quizzically at her. 'Is that what you've been wondering?'

'Yes. I'd like to do something on the design front. Would that be possible? To study Design and Ceramics, yet work at Rushton's at the same time?'

'I should think so – the company would certainly sponsor you on a degree course.' Beth frowned. 'Are you sure about this, Rosemary? I do think going to university isn't an experience you should give up lightly. You don't have to decide immediately, you know. Either way, you're going to need qualifications. Why don't you take it one step at a time?'

'How do you mean?'

'Well, Robert's champing at the bit to enrol you at a crammer so that you'll get your A levels more quickly. And I think you should take a course at the College of Art in Burslem. Then, during the holidays you could work at the factory, and see how you like it. That way you'd have something solid to base your decision on.'

Rosemary sat in silence, digesting Beth's advice. It was true – she'd been trying to plan too far ahead.

'Mum always used to say I wanted to cross my bridges before I came to them...' Her voice trailed off in some embarrassment.

'You mustn't feel you can't talk about her,' Beth

said quickly. 'I know Brenda will always be "Mum" to you, that's why I'm happy for you to call me Beth.' She looked at Rosemary for a moment and continued, 'I suppose you find it difficult, knowing what to call all of us?'

Rosemary nodded.

'I'll have a word with everyone and see what they come up with,' Beth promised, annoyed with herself for not having thought of it before.

Beth found it almost impossible to sleep that night. Coupled with the pleasure she felt at having her daughter sleep under her roof, was apprehension about the coming day. Deceit did not come easily to her, despite the past, and yet she was going to have to lie again, or at least only tell a half-truth. It would be Val, she knew, who would be the most difficult to convince. Friends since childhood, they'd been as close in their teens as any two girls could be.

The following morning, she was busy preparing lunch when the doorbell rang. Surprised to find her hands trembling, she removed her apron and went to open the door.

Gordon and Val stood with stony faces behind Rose and, wordlessly, Beth moved aside as they all came into the hall.

Beth's older brother, his shoulders stiff with anger, said tight-lipped, 'You should have told me, right at the beginning.'

'I'm sorry, Gordon. I did what I thought was right at the time.'

Beth leant to kiss his cheek, but his reaction was cool, and with a sigh she turned to Val.

416

The two women, total opposites in physical appearance, yet as close as sisters, faced each other in the hall.

'I just don't understand!' Val said, and by her perfunctory hug Beth sensed trouble ahead.

She said quietly, 'We can talk about it later, but for now I'd like you to come and meet Rosemary. Where are the children?'

Val explained that because the two little boys had colds, they'd stayed behind with her mother. Beth took their coats, hung them in the cloakroom and led the way into the sitting-room.

The children rushed to greet their granny, while Rosemary got up nervously to face a stocky man with light brown hair. She knew he was a sergeant in the Staffordshire Regiment, and by his bearing could well imagine him in uniform.

'Rosemary,' Beth said, 'this is your Uncle Gordon.'

Gordon, obviously ill at ease, held out his hand to shake hers. 'Rosemary.'

'And this is Val,' Beth said.

Val, in a brown trouser suit, looked both attractive and capable. But her composure was obviously shaken as she looked at the girl standing before her.

'Sorry, I didn't expect you to look quite so much like...' her voice trailed off, and she muttered, 'Hello.'

Michael poured gin and tonics for Beth and Val, handed a glass of sherry to Rose, then said, 'Beer for you, Gordon? You look as if you could use one – and what about you, Rosemary?'

'Could I have a gin and tonic, please?'

Seeing Rose's disapproving expression, Michael hid a grin. Rose might have converted to Catholicism when she got married, but she'd always be a Methodist at heart.

He followed Beth into the kitchen.

'I hope you made Val's a double,' hissed Beth. 'Did you see her face?'

'Don't worry about it, she'll get used to the idea, and so will Gordon.'

Beth glared at him as he took the beers back. That was just typical of a man. Say something and it happens, while she knew very well Val would corner her after lunch.

And she did. Ostensibly it was to help with the clearing up, but Val leant against the work surface and folded her arms. 'I don't understand why you had to be so deceitful, Beth. It's just not in your nature. We used to do everything together! Why didn't you say you had a boyfriend?'

Beth shrugged, not trusting herself to speak – in any case she could only lie, and she wanted to do as little of that as possible.

'And I don't know how you managed to hide the fact you were pregnant.'

'School uniform and sloppy Joes. And I didn't show much, not until the end.' Beth turned away, and began to run hot water into the sink. 'She's a lovely girl, isn't she?'

'Don't change the subject. And yes, she is. So you were already serious with Michael when you found out James was his brother?'

'Yes.'

'Glory, it's like the plot of a film!' Val's eyes widened as she tried to imagine the bombshell in

418

the genteel Rushton family. 'What I want to know is, if you told Michael when you got married, why not us? Why were we the only ones kept in the dark?'

'Perhaps I was too ashamed.' Beth kept her back to her sister-in-law, hating the whole conversation, hating not being free to simply turn and tell Val the truth.

'Is that why you didn't tell me in the first place, all those years ago, when you found out you were going to have a baby? I thought we had more going for us than that, Beth!'

Beth stared down at the soapy water. She'd been so determined to protect Rose that she hadn't dared to take the risk. Now, her dilemma was similar, only this time it was friendship versus maternal protection. She valued her relationship with Val so much, and yet how could she let Rosemary be exposed to anyone else knowing she was the product of rape? That was in addition to her promise to Robert and Sylvia. It's all a question of loyalties, she thought in despair. Oh, why does life have to be so difficult!

She turned round. 'Can't you just leave it, Val. Please! Have you never made a mistake – done anything you wouldn't want your mother to know, for instance?'

Val stared at her, then gave a sheepish grin. 'Okay, I take your point.'

'Be pleased for me, Val,' Beth pleaded. 'I can't tell you what it means to me to have found her.'

'Of course I'm happy about that. But I'm hurt Beth, and so is Gordon. We feel you didn't trust us.'

Beth looked at her in misery, the words cutting into her. But what could she say except to apologise again?

'I really am so sorry,' she said quietly.

There was a moment's silence, as they gazed at each other, then Val relented. 'Okay, I won't push it. But no more secrets – promise?'

'I promise,' Beth said, relief flooding her that this first obstacle was partly over. Her brother was a different matter, and knowing his temperament, Beth was fully aware that she'd have to give him time.

Back in the sitting-room, Gordon was deep in conversation with Michael.

'How's business then? I see another potbank has gone into receivership!'

Michael nodded, taking a sip of his brandy.

'Yes. The smaller ones are finding it extremely difficult. There's not much security for any of us at the moment. Amalgamation seems to be the norm these days rather than the exception.'

'But surely Rushton's isn't in any danger?'

Michael, his brow creasing in a worried frown, reluctantly admitted the possibility. 'We can't afford to be complacent. I keep trying to convince my father that times are changing. The younger generation no longer want expensive dinner services as wedding presents. It's all electrical goods these days. Anything to save labour. And when dishwashers become as popular here as they are in the States, and they will, then demand for fine decorated china is bound to fall. It's a worrying time for all of us.'

He turned as Beth came back into the room.

She gave him a reassuring smile, and she and Val went to find the others. They found them in the playroom, Rose sitting in an armchair, Rosemary cross-legged before a clockwork train set. Andrew and Ben were squabbling over who was to have the engine.

'It's all right, Rose, we've called a truce,' Val said.

Rose, whose face had worn an anxious expression all day, visibly relaxed.

'You know, Beth,' Val said, tilting her head to one side as she surveyed Rosemary, 'I think she's better looking than you were at that age.'

'Thanks a lot,' Beth laughed, and Rose gave a sigh of relief to see them joking together.

But she knew that Gordon would take longer to forgive her. She'd seen it in his eyes that morning. There should be no secrets between mother and son, not when they involved the family. But it hadn't been her secret to impart, so what alternative had she had?

39

Simon stayed with the recently widowed Laura until the day after the funeral, and then in sombre mood drove back to Newcastle. To his surprise, Christine was still at the flat, having decided to stay on for a while.

'I thought perhaps you'd like a bit of company,'

she said. 'I know how close you were to Richard.'

Simon appreciated the gesture, although he would have preferred some solitude. Sobered by the suddenness of Richard's death, and the devastating effect it had on Laura, he needed time to come to terms with the tragedy.

It was another week before he rang Rosemary. She was obviously not going to ring him, so if he wanted to see her again, then his must be the first move.

He chose his time while Christine, who had at last decided to return home, was packing.

A girl's unfamiliar voice answered. 'Rosemary? She's left. She left last Saturday.'

Stunned, Simon repeated the word. 'Left? What do you mean, she's left?'

The girl obviously thought he was simple. 'Left her job. I'm doing it now.'

'But why? I mean she seemed quite happy there.'

'I dunno. Said she had personal problems.'

'Did she leave a phone number or address?'

'Not so far as I know. Some guy in a Rolls picked her up.'

Simon slammed down the receiver and swore under his breath. That was twice! What the hell was going on here? Why did she ring him in the first place if she was involved with someone else?

Just then Christine came into the room. 'I think I might leave a few things here ... is anything wrong, Simon? You look a bit bemused.'

'I feel it! I've just rung Rosemary and been told not only has she left her job, but she didn't leave a contact number!'

Not that Simon had expected her to leave a number just for him. Why should she? He knew he'd snubbed her that time she'd phoned. But surely nobody moved on without leaving some means of contacting them? Yet another mystery, he thought bitterly. He knew it was irrational to be so incensed, and as for this guy in the Rolls ... but that snippet of information he kept to himself.

'Really, how strange.' Christine turned away to hide the gleam of satisfaction in her eyes. She resisted the temptation to criticise Rosemary – she didn't need to, events were playing into her hands. It had been subtlety that paid off in the past, had concealed her machinations from her son. And now the way really was clear for her plans.

But Christine wouldn't have returned to Chalfont St Giles with such a light heart if she'd known that her son hadn't dismissed the matter so easily. It took a couple of days, but the vague feeling of uneasiness at the back of his mind wouldn't go away. Why would Rosemary give up the job she liked so quickly, and even more puzzling, why wouldn't she leave a forwarding address? The memory of Rosemary's voice when she'd rung to try and explain, how she'd sounded both anxious and yet happy, confused him. The more he thought about it, the more it didn't add up. Conversely, now he'd decided to get in touch again, he felt affronted that she'd made it so difficult. Reluctant to give in so easily, he decided to speak to the American professor herself.

So on his first free evening, Simon walked round to Balmoral and rang the bell. As he waited, his collar turned up against the cold, he could hear Homer barking from the back of the house, and then the door opened and the most odd-looking woman he'd ever seen stood there. He was still staring at the miscellany of colour facing him – wild red hair, a slash of crimson lipstick, orange and green checks – when she spoke.

'Hi.'

'Er, hi. My name's Simon Oldham, Dr Oldham. I'm a friend of Rosemary – she used to work for you?'

'Sure she did. How can I help?' Sally Ann blew out a cloud of smoke and looked at him warily.

'I wondered if she'd left a forwarding address or a telephone number?'

Sally Ann hesitated. It just wasn't the done thing to give out personal details, even if she did remember Rosemary seeing this guy. And surely if she had wanted to keep in touch, she'd have told him herself.

She remained standing in the doorway, then the memory of a young couple kissing beneath the streetlight persuaded her, and she said brusquely, 'Wait a minute.'

A few seconds later, she came back with a scrap of paper. 'I won't give you her address, but here's her number.'

Ten minutes later, Simon was back in the flat. Chilled after his walk in the frosty air, he poured himself a whisky and, taking a quick swallow, went to the phone.

Rosemary answered, and as soon as he heard

her voice, he knew he couldn't wait to see her again. She was silent as he apologised for taking so long to ring.

'I wondered,' he said hesitantly, 'whether you were doing anything on Saturday night?'

There was a pause, then Rosemary said in a breathless voice, 'No, actually I'm not.'

'So ... would you like to go out for a drink?'

'Yes, of course, that would be fine.'

Simon wrote down the address she gave him and, after replacing the receiver, returned to his whisky, deep in thought.

Slightly stunned that Simon had at last rung, it was only after she put down the phone that Rosemary allowed her feelings full rein. Joy and excitement bubbled within her – surely the fact that he wanted them to meet must mean everything was going to be all right. She'd ask Rose where they should go. She only knew one pub in Minsden, and she couldn't see Simon fitting in there!

Rose looked up from her knitting. 'I take it that was a young man,' she smiled.

'It was Simon.'

Rose was immediately all attention. Simon was the young doctor Rosemary had been to Chalfont St Giles with. But she'd understood from Beth that they weren't seeing each other any more.

'Oh,' she said. 'Is that good news or bad news?'

'Good, I think.'

Rose looked at her shining eyes, and smiled to herself.

'He wants to take me out for a drink. Is there anywhere suitable round here?'

Rose thought. 'There's a nice country pub out at Moddershall. That's not too far.'

'Oh, right. He's picking me up on Saturday.' With that, Rosemary sank back in her chair, closed her eyes and indulged in a delicious daydream of what might happen when she saw Simon again.

She had settled easily into living at Elm Grove. Sleeping in Beth's old bedroom, which had been modernised with fitted wardrobes and carpeted in a soft shade of blue, she felt that at last she had somewhere to call home.

True to his word, Robert had arranged for her to attend a private tutorial college, and she'd already begun classes. She was also due to go for an interview at the College of Art in Burslem, the following week.

She travelled by bus, which was time-consuming, but she didn't mind as it was a good way of getting to know the area.

On her return, Rose or "Gran" as she now called her, always had a home-cooked meal waiting. She was keen to introduce Rosemary to traditional local dishes, so there was lobby, a sort of stew cooked on the hob made from the remains of Sunday's joint. Full of root vegetables, celery and potatoes, it was eaten with a spoon from a basin. There was meat and potato pie and, Rosemary's favourite, Staffordshire oatcakes. Looking like a pancake, they were eaten hot. Grilled with cheese bubbling on top, rolled around crisp bacon, or simply on the side of a cooked breakfast, she loved every mouthful.

As for Rose, providing her granddaughter with a secure, loving home had become her vocation. Oh, she was realistic, she knew that Rosemary wouldn't be content to live with her forever. A year or maybe even two, and then wider horizons would beckon.

But now, glancing at Rosemary's rapt face, Rose suddenly felt a pang of nostalgia for her own youth. Left with two small children when war broke out, followed by widowhood at a relatively early age, her carefree days had been short. Her daughter too, she knew now, had been forced to face the darker side of life when only in her teens. And unfortunately Rosemary had already experienced hardship. Still, now that her granddaughter had the chance to enjoy her young years, Rose was determined to do everything in her power to help.

Rosemary was already wrestling with the eternal problem of what to wear. In the end she decided to wear her new jeans and embroidered shirt. What with her black boots and leather coat, she could hardly wait to see Simon's face when he saw her. Having good clothes to wear had been a revelation. They not only felt wonderful, but she felt so much more confident in them.

Over the next couple of days, Rosemary's emotions swung from one extreme to another. Excited at the prospect of seeing Simon again, she was also nervous. He'd reacted so coldly that time she'd rung him, which had made her realise that she didn't know him as well as she'd thought. Neither had she forgiven him for blatantly ignoring her letter.

Simon too, had his own anxieties as he drove on Saturday night from Newcastle to Minsden. There wasn't much traffic at seven-thirty and he was able to glance at the many pottery firms lining the main road as he travelled through Stoke, Fenton, and Longton. Christine had visited the Wedgwood factory out at Barlaston, bringing home proudly some china she'd purchased at the shop there, but so far he hadn't found time for much sight-seeing. It was a mistake, he realised, not to try to familiarise himself with the area – after all, he expected to be here for a very long time. He liked his work at the hospital, and could see opportunities for further advancement. He liked the Potteries people too: they were warm-hearted, genuine, with no pretensions. He grinned as he remembered one patient, an elderly man who smoked sixty cigarettes a day.

'Ar anna givin' up now,' he'd declared. 'What would I do with meself? Nay, young man, I'll tak me chances same as I did in the Great War.'

Simon had watched him go, admiring his spirit, his strength. He reminded him of his late grandfather, himself an old soldier.

But now he was indicating left and turning up the road which led to Elm Grove. He drew up outside number two to see the curtains twitch, and a moment later she was walking down the side path toward him.

She looked absolutely fantastic. There was just no other word for it. He'd thought her lovely before, but tonight, in those clothes, she was beautiful. Eagerly, he opened the passenger door, and Rosemary swung her long legs into the car.

'Hi,' she said. 'You found it okay then?'

'Yes, no problem. Where are we going?'

'Well, first, drive along to the end of the Grove and turn round, then I'll give you directions.'

It was a route along a sparsely populated area at first, and then they were driving along a dark country road. They spoke little, an awkward silence between them, and Simon was glad when they saw on the far side of a millpond the lights of the pub. It was warm and inviting, and they managed to get a quiet table in a corner.

'Gin and tonic?' he asked.

Rosemary nodded, and began to look around as he went to the bar. Her gaze, however, soon fell, and the colour in her cheeks rose as she realised she was becoming the centre of attention. Simon, returning with the drinks, frowned as he saw the glances of male appreciation and wondered whether Rosemary was aware of the picture she made with the soft shaded light shining on her dark hair.

He placed the drinks on the beer mats and sat opposite.

'Haven't they ever seen a beautiful girl before?' he muttered.

'Perhaps they thought I was on my own.'

'Well, you're not!'

His tone was sharp, and Rosemary, to her amusement, realised he was jealous.

'So,' he said. 'What's been happening with you? Leaving your job, I mean.'

'How did you get my phone number?' Rosemary countered. She had questions of her own.

'From that professor you worked for. God, she's a strange-looking woman! Is she colour blind or something?'

Rosemary laughed. 'I'm not sure. But in a strange way, you get used to it – in fact, I can't imagine her any different.'

He caught her gaze and for a moment held it, and then reaching over covered her hand with his own.

'I've missed you,' he said softly.

'Me too.' She hesitated and then said, 'Why did you take so long to ring?'

Simon explained about the funeral, and then admitted wryly, 'I'm really making excuses. It's a fault of mine, I'm afraid, holding on to anger. And I was angry you know, that Sunday, after I'd rung whatshername...'

'Sally Ann.'

'Yes. Well, when she said you weren't working for her at all that day and had cleared off with someone else, you can imagine how I felt.'

'She was drunk,' Rosemary said. 'She'd been on a bender, as she called it. Otherwise, I don't suppose she'd have said what she did.'

Simon's fingers, which had been slowly stroking her hand, became still.

'It was true though?' he asked quietly.

'Yes, but I explained–'

'No, you didn't. I, with my stiff-necked pride, didn't give you a chance to.'

'I did,' she protested. 'I told you in my letter!'

Simon shook his head. 'I didn't get any letter.'

'But you must have done. I pushed it through your door.' Rosemary could only stare at him in bewilderment.

'When was this?'

She thought back and then told him.

Simon shook his head again. 'Are you sure it was the right door?'

She glared at him.

He held up his hands in mock protection. 'Okay, okay, I apologise. But honestly, Rosemary, I never got a letter.'

She took another sip of her drink, her eyes puzzled. 'So that's why you didn't contact me straight away. And there I was thinking all sorts of awful things about you.'

Simon looked at her. 'Was that why your voice sounded so cool on the phone?'

She nodded.

'And you haven't got some other guy waiting in the wings, the one with a Rolls?'

Simon's voice was deceptively light, but as the question hung in the air, Rosemary smiled to herself.

'There is someone, yes,' she paused for a moment, continuing, 'his name's Michael,' she paused again, and then seeing the look on Simon's face couldn't tease him any longer. 'He's my stepfather,' she finished.

He sat back in his chair. 'You devil, you had me going there for a moment!'

'I know,' she laughed.

Simon looked at her and this time her eyes met his, open and frank, and he knew just why he'd been unable to get her out of his mind.

'I didn't know you had any family here,' he said, relief flooding through him.

'Whose house do you think that is? Where I'm living now?'

'I don't know.'

'My grandmother's. If you didn't get my letter, Simon, then I'd better tell you what was in it.'

Simon listened while Rosemary explained to him about her search for her natural mother, her promise of secrecy which had meant she'd had to lie to him, and how she'd left her job so that she could begin to study.

'I need to get some qualifications so I can do a degree course,' she said.

'You mean go to university?' His spirits fell – that meant she'd probably move miles away.

'Possibly.'

Simon looked at her, thinking of all she'd told him.

'Were you happy?' he said suddenly. 'With the people who adopted you?'

'It's a long story,' Rosemary said slowly. 'I'd rather leave it to another time, if that's all right with you. That is, of course,' she glanced archly at him, 'if you think there will be another time.'

'Are you flirting with me, Rosemary er ... what is your real name?'

'Legally, I suppose it's Latham like that of my adoptive parents,' she said slowly, 'although my mother's name is Sherwin.' She hesitated, then added, 'My father's name was Rushton.'

Rosemary watched his expression intently. Did he recognise the name Rushton? Did it mean anything to him? She'd deliberately been economical

432

with the truth, hadn't wanted to even hint at the china connection. To her shame, the memory of Tony's greed was still with her, lingering like a canker in her subconscious. But Simon showed no reaction.

'Rosemary Whatever-you-choose-to-call-your-self,' he said sternly. 'I'll have you know I don't take kindly to flirtatious females.'

'Perhaps I'll flirt with someone else, then?' She looked at the bar. 'Him, for instance.'

Simon looked over his shoulder to see a fair-haired young man in a pink shirt and matching kipper tie, staring at their table.

'That chinless wonder,' he said. 'Don't you dare!'

Rosemary laughed across at him.

'I'm hoping there'll be lots of other times,' Simon said, 'but how do you feel?'

'Buy me another drink, and I'll tell you.'

With a grin he went off to the bar and she leaned back in contentment, unable to take her eyes off him. At first in the car, she'd felt tense, her resentment still lingering, but now it felt as though they'd never been apart. But how odd about that letter! It had even been in a bright purple envelope, hardly something one could miss!

Later, when Simon drew up outside the house, Rosemary glanced up at the windows. The lights were still on downstairs, and she hesitated, not knowing whether Rose was still up, or whether she would have simply left the lights on for her. Should she ask Simon to come in?

But he made her decision for her.

'I won't come in,' he said. 'It's a bit late for your grandmother. So,' he gently turned her face towards him and kissed her, a long deep kiss. 'Shall I come and pick you up tomorrow?'

'Mmn,' she said, wanting him to kiss her again. 'How about three?'

'What's wrong with the morning? We could spend the day together.'

'Well...' she lifted her head and looked at him.

'Don't tell me you're working,' he warned with a grin.

'No. But I've got to go to Mass in the morning, and Gran has bought a big joint for Sunday lunch.' She hesitated, and then said, 'Why don't you come, have some good home cooking, instead of opening a tin?'

'How do you know I'll be opening a tin,' he protested.

'I've seen inside your kitchen cupboards!'

'Oh, come here!'

This time there were several kisses, and eventually, he drew away and muttered, 'Not the most romantic place, is it? I'm getting a crick in my back.'

She laughed, an easy laugh, warm and confident. That was how Simon made her feel, beautiful and special. But there was still within her a doubt, a sense of unease. Why did she have this reservation, this compulsion to be secretive?

'I'll say goodnight then,' she said, and opening the door got out of the car. Leaning down she whispered, 'One o'clock, and don't be late.'

With a last wave, Simon drove away, and switching on his radio found himself singing along with Rod Stewart's gravelly voice as he extolled the virtues of *Sailing*. Great song, he thought, I bet it will become a classic. Then, in a supremely happy mood, his thoughts went back to Rosemary's explanation in the pub. Strange about that letter – he'd better have a good search for it when he got back to the flat. And he certainly didn't relish the thought of her going away to university. Even the suggestion was a reminder of the difference in their ages. But it was just as he reached Newcastle that he remembered a couple of other things that had been niggling at the back of his mind. Why had Rosemary's new family been so insistent on secrecy? He could understand her sudden appearance in their lives causing turmoil, at least at first, but for her to promise not to tell *anyone* did seem to be taking it a bit far. The other surprise was to find out she was a Catholic.

40

Rose, to her granddaughter's amusement, became quite fussed at the prospect of Simon's visit.

'No, you go to church on your own,' Rose insisted. 'I'll go to the evening Mass.'

'But why?'

Rose shook her head, knowing Rosemary wouldn't understand. 'It'll just give me a bit more time.'

But when she was on her own, the burst of

activity in the small semi-detached house would have astounded both Rosemary and Simon. Cushions were plumped up, newspapers tidied, surfaces flicked over with a duster. The best tablecloth had to be brought out of its drawer and ironed, and silver-plated cutlery which she rarely took out of its canteen, checked for tarnishing. Tutting at the lack of fresh flowers, Rose put a bottle of Blue Nun in the fridge, polished three of her best crystal glasses, and when her table was set to advantage, basted the leg of lamb and prepared her vegetables.

'Eeh, Harry,' she said, 'a doctor, coming here for his dinner, can you imagine?' As a child she'd thought doctors were almost akin to gods, and certainly her own parents had been in con-siderable awe of them. Now, here was her own granddaughter with one as a boyfriend. What with Beth marrying Michael, and Gordon's wife a teacher, her family was certainly going up in the world.

Simon charmed her from the very first moment. She liked the look of him, as she told Beth later that afternoon. And then, when he picked up the little Royal Marine Artillery hat and told her that his grandfather had one exactly the same, it seemed like an omen.

'Does Simon know who she is?' Beth asked.

'I don't know, I never thought about that aspect.'

But Beth had, and so had Sylvia. They'd already talked about the danger of fortune hunters where Rosemary was concerned.

'I don't think she's quite realised that she's

something of an heiress,' Beth worried. 'And she's very young.'

'We'll just have to keep a close eye on her,' Sylvia had advised. 'Encourage her to move in the right circles.'

But Beth knew that times had changed. Rosemary would find her own level, make her own friends, as she had done with this young doctor. She'd ask Robert to quietly check him out, she decided. He had several influential contacts at the Infirmary.

'I wouldn't be surprised,' Rose was saying, 'if this doesn't come to something.'

'She's only nineteen, Mum.'

'Wait until you see them together, you'll see what I mean.'

What Beth didn't know was that Rosemary had her own reservations where Simon was concerned. Not how she felt about him – these past few hours had shown her that – but, even though he hadn't asked if she was one of *the* Rushtons when she told him her family name, she was still cautious. For although she could hardly think of Tony without a shudder at her lucky escape, his avarice had shaken her confidence. That was why, even in her letter to Simon, she hadn't revealed everything.

After lunch, and despite Rose's protests, dealing with the washing-up, Simon and Rosemary departed to spend the rest of the day together. As the car sped towards Newcastle, there was no doubt in either of their minds how they would spend the afternoon. Rosemary gazed out of the window, the adrenalin racing in her veins, her eyes drawn again and again to Simon's capable hands on the wheel, his long thigh so close to her own. She just knew they would be in each other's arms the minute the door to the flat closed.

Simon had no doubts. He couldn't wait to be alone with the girl at his side, but knew too that he'd have to keep a rein on his feelings. Simon had never had any difficulty attracting girls, but although he'd enjoyed his liaisons, never before had he thought of them as other than brief interludes. His studies and career had always taken priority. But now, with Rosemary, even though their time together had been limited, his whole outlook had changed. He'd thought about this deeply the previous night. What he felt for her was not only sexual attraction – there was a caring, a protectiveness there. He knew he was falling in love with her, and it was a scary prospect in a way. He had neither expected nor sought this complication in his life. Not yet, not until he got his consultancy. This had always been his goal, to be single-minded, concentrate on his medical advancement, and only then allow himself the luxury of marriage and a family. He'd seen too many junior doctors weighed down with responsibilities early in their career. But now, for once in his life, his head wasn't ruling his heart. God, how he wanted this girl! But didn't Catholics still hold out-dated ideas about sex before marriage? And even if that hadn't been the case, he must remember that Rosemary was so much younger than him.

But later that afternoon, they were both shaken by the intensity of their feelings, and Simon muttered, 'I think we'd better cool it, before this gets out of hand.'

Rosemary pushed back her dishevelled hair, and began to button up her blouse. She felt a bit shy, embarrassed even, but almost as though he sensed her thoughts, Simon lifted her chin and kissed her gently.

'I think you're a witch.'

She just leaned over and brushed his lips with hers. 'If I am, then you're a wizard.'

'You know what we're doing, don't you,' he smiled.

'What?'

'Talking nonsense, just as people in love always do.'

She looked up at him. 'Is that what we are?'

'I think so. How about you?'

Rosemary nodded, deliriously happy.

'Come on,' he pulled her to her feet. 'It's your lucky day, you're about to sample my cooking.' At her raised eyebrows, he confessed, 'Tea and toast. I don't know why, after that huge lunch, but I'm absolutely ravenous.'

'It's passion,' she teased. 'I read it somewhere – it's supposed to give you an appetite.'

'It certainly does that,' he grinned, 'but not necessarily just for food. Mind you, we could always forget the toast.'

Rosemary gazed at him, the temptation strong. After all, this was 1975 and, despite what her Catholic upbringing taught, she could hardly expect Simon to abide by it. But then the

439

sensible side of her nature surfaced. She wasn't even on the Pill, and surely one illegitimate child in the family was more than enough.

'I think I'd better put the kettle on,' she said reluctantly.

Simon began to put bread in the toaster, while Rosemary reached for a couple of mugs.

'I was wondering,' he said, 'why your family were so secretive about you, so much so that you didn't feel you could tell even me. Okay, they might not want their friends and neighbours to know, not until they were ready, but it does seem a bit over the top.'

Rosemary began to panic. Why did he have to ask her now, when she was feeling so happy, so at ease with him? Blindly, she tried to think of an answer, not even sure why she was evading telling him the truth. She only knew she felt an instinctive emotional recoil in the pit of her stomach.

'I think they were trying to protect the family's good name,' she said at last.

I suppose she means because they're Catholic, Simon thought. Wryly, he wondered what his mother's reaction would be when she found out. Christine was staunch C of E, considering the established church the only one socially acceptable.

Rosemary, however, was feeling miserable. What was wrong with her? Why couldn't she just tell him the truth? Only a few days ago she'd written to Lisa and to Father Kavanagh, telling them everything. Damn you, Tony, she thought bitterly. This is all your fault!

But Simon didn't seem to notice anything

amiss, and the rest of the evening was spent curled up on the sofa, talking and watching *Upstairs Downstairs*.

As the time drew near for Rosemary to go, he once again drew her into his arms, but this time he was careful to keep things light. The flame between them was too quickly ignited for more than tender kisses.

'When can I see you again?' he murmured, his fingers stroking her dark, silky hair.

'Whenever you're not on duty,' she smiled up at him, her eyes gazing into his so soft, so happy, that he could only kiss her yet again.

'I'll ring you,' he promised, 'as soon as I see what the week holds.'

She stood up and went to get her coat. 'By the way, I forgot to ask, did you have a look round for my letter?'

'I've searched everywhere. I even asked the woman downstairs, but she hadn't seen it.'

Rosemary frowned. It was really weird – she just didn't understand how it could have got lost.

'I'll ask Mum,' Simon added. 'Next time I ring.'

'Your mum?' She turned suddenly.

'Yes, she was staying here at the time.'

Rosemary stared at him. So, Christine had been here. But surely she wouldn't ... or would she? She remembered those sweetly uttered words, 'Simon always has a pretty girl in tow', which had almost spoilt that day in Chalfont St Giles. Now why exactly had she said that? Only if she'd wanted to put Rosemary off in some way. Was she just one of those possessive mothers? But then, she remembered Christine's first swift

441

glance, sweeping over her shabby sandals and cheap dress. Not exactly what you'd expect in the girlfriend of an up-and-coming young doctor. I know she doesn't think I'm good enough for him, she thought suddenly. But could she blame Christine for that? After all, what did she have to offer?

'Penny for them, my most beautiful girl in the world,' Simon suddenly said, pushing back the hair from her forehead.

'Do you really think I am?'

'Don't you know?' He looked down at her, and she saw in his eyes a reflection of the love shining in her own. 'I don't want to take you home,' he said, between more tender kisses, 'but I think I better had, and right now.'

'Spoilsport,' she murmured with a grin and, putting on her coat, led the way out of the flat.

On the stairs, she paused for a moment, trying to imagine her bright purple envelope lying on the doormat. No-one could have missed that, for heaven's sake!

'What normally happens when the post comes?' she asked, twisting round to face him.

'Whoever picks it up puts the other person's post on there,' he indicated the carved oak chest.

'I wonder...' Rosemary moved swiftly over to the chest and peered down the back. But the bulb in the overhead light was a low wattage, and all she could see was shadow and darkness.

'I suppose it could have slipped down the back,' she said doubtfully.

'I'll have a look in the morning.' Simon opened the front door, and they hurried to the car, shivering in the damp November air.

Rose was still up and making Horlicks when Rosemary arrived back.

'I don't need to ask if you've enjoyed yourself,' she said drily. 'It's written all over your face.'

Rosemary crimsoned and then, seeing the twinkle in her gran's eyes, said, 'You did like him, didn't you?'

'Yes, I did. Very much.'

It wasn't until Rosemary went to bed that she thought again about Christine. Somehow, knowing she'd been at the flat when she delivered the letter, cast a whole new light on the incident.

41

Christine was delighted to hear Simon's voice when she picked up the phone.

'I'm glad you've called. I'm having a party just before Christmas – can you give me a date when you'll be free?'

'I'll check it out and let you know. Mum, when you were staying here, you didn't see a letter from Rosemary, did you? She says she pushed it through the door.'

The question, coming as it did so unexpectedly, caused Christine to flounder.

'A letter?' she repeated weakly.

'Yes. In a purple envelope.'

She closed her eyes and said slowly, 'No,

Simon, I didn't. I thought you weren't seeing Rosemary any more?'

'Oh, you're way behind the times.'

His voice sounded happy, confident, with a warmth in it that was unmistakable.

Suddenly, Christine felt an emotion completely alien to her. Impotence, that was it. She'd always been able to manipulate situations. Now she felt helpless, living as far away as she did.

'Odd though, isn't it?' Simon was continuing. 'About the letter, I mean.'

Christine wasn't the daughter of a man whose overriding interest had been military history for nothing. Attack is the best form of defence, had been his favourite saying, and she said quickly, 'Well, the post usually gets put on the oak chest in the hall, doesn't it?'

'Yes, that's right.'

'So, have a look down the back, see if it's fallen down there!'

'I already have, well, a quick look anyway. I'll have to go, Mum. Speak to you later.'

Christine went back into the drawing-room. Thank God she hadn't gone any further with the party arrangements – it was pointless if he was going to bring that girl with him. Angrily, she lit a cigarette, and inhaled deeply. Was she overreacting? Simon had only known the girl a couple of months and here she was regarding her as a threat. But there had been girlfriends before, and she'd recognised them for what they were, temporary distractions. But every instinct told her that this relationship was different. She'd seen it immediately that day he'd brought

Rosemary to the house. Yet Simon had sounded so happy that she felt a stab of compunction at interfering at all. But that didn't stop her from going to the telephone.

It was Wednesday before Rosemary saw Simon again. But before then she had a phone call from Lisa.

'I can't believe it!' she screeched, so excited that Rosemary had to hold the phone away from her ear.

'You got my letter then?' she grinned.

'I told you, didn't I, you'd end up being the daughter of a Duke or something!'

'Not quite that, Lisa.'

'Near enough. Hey, how about my coming up for a visit? What about this weekend, do you think your gran would put me up?'

Rosemary thought quickly. There was Gordon's old room, that had a single bed in it.

'I'm sure she would, hang on a minute.' She put her hand over the mouthpiece and checked with Rose, who looked up from her knitting and nodded.

'She says that's fine.'

'Okay, tell me how to get there.'

The only downside of Lisa's visit was that Rosemary knew she wouldn't be able to spend time alone with Simon.

However, when he picked her up that evening, he told her his mother had asked him to go down to Chalfont St Giles that weekend.

'I've told her I can't get down until Sunday,' he said. 'I'm on duty. Apparently she's feeling nervous – they've had a couple of burglaries in the district.'

'But what can you do?'

'She's got some bloke from a security firm coming, and wants me to be there. Values my advice, apparently,' he grinned at her. 'I thought it would make a nice day out for us. He should only be there about an hour.'

Rosemary turned to him. 'Simon, I can't. Lisa's coming for the weekend! She rang just before I came out.'

'Oh, damn! That means I won't see you all weekend!'

'I know. It's not fair,' she said dejectedly.

'I suppose it just can't be helped. Now I think I can park up here.' He turned into a side street and began to manoeuvre into a space.

'I've only ever had one Chinese meal,' she told him, as he locked the car door and they walked hand in hand to the restaurant, 'and that was a takeaway.'

As they pushed through a bamboo curtain, she looked curiously around the dimly lit interior, admiring the silk screen prints of lotus blossoms and Chinese lanterns. As they followed the smiling waiter to a table set with a pink tablecloth and chopsticks, she felt a warm glow of anticipation. This would be the first romantic meal they'd shared together.

After Rosemary had spent delightfully agonising moments choosing what to eat, and they'd ordered, Simon smiled at her and said, 'Close your eyes. Go on, close them!'

Mystified, Rosemary obeyed.

'Right,' he instructed. 'Now open them.'

She stared with incredulity at the purple envelope lying on the table.

'Where did you find it?'

'Well, I told you I was going to ring Mum, and she said exactly the same as you. Suggested I looked behind the oak chest. I did have a quick look down the back after I left you, but this time I moved the damn thing.'

'And that's where...?'

'It had slipped underneath. You couldn't see it just looking down the back. Mind you, it was a devil to shift. You wouldn't believe how heavy it is. In fact, Miss Moore came out to see what all the racket was.' He leaned back in his chair, smiling triumphantly.

Rosemary frowned. 'How do you think it got there?'

'Search me. Mum thinks that perhaps when the cleaner came, she flung something on top, a duster or her cardigan or something, and then when she picked it up the envelope slid and fell down the back.'

'What day does she come?' said Rosemary curiously.

'It varies. She does the downstairs flat on Fridays, but tries to fit mine in with my duty rota. Can't have her vacuuming while I'm trying to sleep!'

I've no means of checking then, Rosemary thought. I can hardly quiz him about it, or he'll guess what I've been thinking. Not, she told herself, that you have any concrete evidence.

When the selection of small bowls of steaming

food arrived, she looked dubiously at the chopsticks. 'You're not expecting me to use those?'

'It's easy,' Simon said. 'Look, let me show you.' With expertise, he transferred some chop suey into his mouth.

Rosemary tried to copy him, but after several abortive attempts, giggled saying, 'I'll be here all night at this rate.'

Simon poured her some wine. 'Have some Mateus,' he said. 'That should help. Go on, try again, it'll come in useful when you next go to China.'

Oh, sure, thought Rosemary, although she was hoping to go to Milan after Christmas. Beth had explained that Michael was trying to fix up a business meeting with Giovanna's father.

'We'd like you to come with us,' she'd said.

'Does he know about me?' Rosemary asked.

'Yes, we've written to him. I'm hoping he'll ask to meet you while we're there, but that will have to be his choice.'

Rosemary thought of the photograph in James's bedroom, of the lovely dark, laughing girl. 'I shall understand if he doesn't want to,' she said quietly.

At one o'clock on Saturday afternoon, Lisa arrived at Elm Grove.

Rosemary had just nipped to the shop for an extra loaf, but Rose heard the taxi draw up and was already opening the front door as Lisa was about to ring the bell.

For those first few moments, Rose, as she told

Beth later, simply 'stood there like somebody gormless'.

What she was looking at, Lisa explained later, was her punk rocker look. And with typical fervour, she'd embraced the whole concept. Not only was her face a startling pasty white, and her eyes and lips outlined in black, but her short hair was spiked and dyed a lurid green. With a cheeky grin, she sat drinking tea in the conventional little sitting-room, looking like an exotic bird who'd suddenly strayed far from home.

Rosemary was fascinated. 'I'll say one thing for you, Lisa Bennion! You've got some nerve. What did your mum say?'

'Oh, had hysterics. I'm the first one in Staniforth. But she's come round, and the kids think I'm really cool.'

'Gran's tongue-tied, aren't you?' Rosemary teased.

'Well...' It was true, Rose was lost for words.

'It's okay, Mrs Sherwin, I know I look a bit threatening, but that's the fashion. And I'm only a mild case, I haven't got any safety pins in my eyebrows or nose!'

Rose shuddered visibly, and they laughed.

After lunch, Rosemary showed Lisa around Minsden.

'It won't take long,' she said, 'but at least you'll see where I live.'

'What's the plan for the weekend, then?' Lisa said, revelling in the effect her appearance was having on passers-by.

Rosemary broke the news that she wouldn't be able to meet Simon after all.

Lisa declared herself to be devastated.

'You need my opinion,' she declared. 'I mean, look at last time.'

'He's nothing like Tony,' Rosemary defended.

'Oh, yeah! Well, let's hope not. I suppose he knows you've got prospects?'

'Actually, he doesn't. I'm not completely unfanciable, I'll have you know.'

'Who told you that?' Lisa grinned. 'You'll have to tell him, though.'

'I know, and I will when I'm ready,' Rosemary said shortly. She looked away, not wanting even to think about it. When she was with Simon she had no doubts about his feelings, but then at night she would lie awake, remembering Tony's scathing words, agonising over whether Simon was truly ignorant of her influential connections. It's becoming an obsession, she realised suddenly. Not like me at all, I just don't understand it.

Lisa darted a speculative glance at her and, seeing her set face, changed the subject.

'So, am I to be kept as a skeleton in the cupboard, or can I meet Beth?'

Rosemary laughed. 'Of course you can. We're all invited for Sunday lunch tomorrow.'

'And what about tonight?'

'The Crystal, in Newcastle,' Rosemary said promptly. 'The local nightspot. I've been dying to go, but never had anyone to go with.'

'Right,' Lisa grinned. 'They won't know what's hit 'em.'

After being suitably impressed by Rosemary's black leather coat, Lisa showed off her own outfit. Wearing a skimpy leopardskin top over a torn miniskirt, and pink plastic boots, her appearance made Rose caution, 'Now do be careful not to provoke any trouble, you two. Don't walk along any dark streets either, even if the police have got the Black Panther. He's not the only criminal out there. Now, have you got enough money for a taxi home?'

'You know I have, Gran.' Rosemary gave her a hug. 'And I promise we won't do anything you wouldn't do.'

'Oh, go on with you!'

Rose watched them both go, enjoying their high spirits, and then settled down with a bag of chocolate caramels, and her Catherine Cookson library book. She'd forgotten that Rosemary didn't have to watch her pennies any more, not now she was receiving such a generous allowance. Beth and Michael had wanted to bear the cost, but Robert had intervened.

'Rose has given her a home,' he said. 'It's only right that Sylvia and I should make a contribution.'

The two girls had a fabulous time. It was ages since Rosemary had been out like this among people of her own age. Lisa was outrageous, flirting shamelessly, and they drank Bacardi and cokes and discoed until the early hours.

'You do me good, Lisa,' Rosemary gasped, leaning back in the taxi, exhausted.

'Yeah, stop you being such a sobersides.'

'We make a good team, don't we?'

'Sure do,' Lisa grinned, 'and although you've been careful not to ask, the answer's no. I've never touched the stuff.'

'I knew you'd keep your promise.'

Rose had been so anxious about Lisa's visit to The Beeches that she'd phoned to warn Beth the night before but, to her surprise, everything went well. Andrew and Ben were fascinated by Lisa's green hair.

Little Ben, after a period of stunned silence, asked in a piercing voice, 'Is she a Martian?'

Beth quickly shushed him, but it had broken the ice, and after initially being overawed by her surroundings, Lisa's natural chirpy humour came to the fore.

Later, after Beth returned from driving them back to Minsden, Michael said, 'What did you think of her?'

'Apart from that weird punk look, you mean? I thought she was great, though the complete opposite of what I expected.'

'Yes, odd, isn't it?' Michael looked at her thoughtfully. 'You remember what you were saying the other day, about doing something to repay the Bennions' kindness?'

'Yes, but I think we need to be careful not to offend them.'

'I agree with you, and offering money or even an expensive present might seem a bit patronising. But how about if we help their daughter, in the same way they've helped ours?'

But for a moment Beth didn't answer. All she could think of were Michael's words 'our daughter'. Did he realise the significance of what he'd just said? What it meant to her?

Then, seeing he was waiting, she said, 'What

are you suggesting?'

'Well, apparently Lisa is bored with her job and frustrated because she sees no chance of a fashion career.'

'Yes, that's right...' Beth leaned forward eagerly – she was beginning to see where the conversation was leading.

'And she's right on the ball with that punk look,' Michael continued, 'I saw some of it when I was in London last week. Can't you just see her with a market stall selling the latest fashion fads?'

Beth grinned. 'Yes, I can, she's certainly got the right personality. But I thought Lisa's dream was to have her own boutique? That's what Rosemary said.'

'Naturally. But she's got to start somewhere.' He leaned forward. 'What I suggest is that we offer to give her a start. Enough capital to get her going. Then, if after a year or so she proves she's got what it takes, we can look at it again. But not a gift this time, a proper business arrangement, perhaps offering a loan at advantageous terms. What do you think?'

Beth had no qualms. 'I think it's a brilliant idea. It certainly solves the problem of how to repay our debt to her parents. But, Michael?'

'Yes?'

'Would you mind if I used my own money? It might help me to feel a bit less guilty that someone else had to take on my responsibilities.'

'Even better,' he grinned.

'But I shall let Rosemary know it was your idea,' she insisted.

'Fine,' he shrugged and, hearing the boys calling, went upstairs to read them a bedtime story.

Rose was watching *Stars on Sunday* when Beth rang, and after saying that Lisa had caught her train all right, she passed the phone over to Rosemary.

Rosemary listened intently for a few moments, and then with a huge smile said, 'Thank him for me, will you, Beth, and you too. I'll write to her tonight. Yes, I think she'll be thrilled to bits.'

After passing the good news on to Rose, she leaned back in her chair feeling supremely content. Then, idly, she wondered what Simon's weekend had been like.

42

Simon's visit began well enough. He always enjoyed coming home, sleeping in his old room, being pampered by his mother. For a short while anyway. And his presence had definitely been a bonus when a burglar alarm had been agreed upon. While Christine might have been influenced by the representative's sales patter, Simon had cut through the waffle, with the result that a much cheaper but perfectly satisfactory system was to be installed.

'I told you it would only take about an hour,' she said.

Simon yawned. 'Yes, but why on earth did you make the appointment so early?'

'Because we've got guests for lunch.'

'Oh, no! Who, for heaven's sake?' The last thing he wanted to do was to spend his day off listening to his mother's gossipy friends.

Christine chose her words carefully. 'Jane Meadows has her god-daughter staying for the weekend, and when I said you were coming down, she angled for a lunch invitation. Said she couldn't think how else to entertain her.'

'Oh, lord! How old is she?'

'In her mid-twenties, I think.' Christine got up, wanting to keep the conversation brief and casual. 'I'll make a start in the kitchen – you relax and read the papers, darling.'

Simon picked up the *Sunday Telegraph*, wondering what Rosemary was doing. Perhaps he'd give her a ring. Then he remembered she'd be at Mass and with a sigh turned to the sports pages. He'd begun to follow the progress of Stoke City Football Club who, under the inspiring management of Tony Waddington, were developing into one of the leading clubs in the country.

When the guests arrived, he got up reluctantly, and prepared to be polite and slightly bored. But to his surprise, not only was Caroline attractive, but he found her a witty and articulate companion.

'This is a lifesaver,' she whispered, as he handed her a gin and tonic.

He grinned. 'As bad as that, eh? So, where do you normally live?' He offered her a dish of peanuts, before taking a few himself.

'London. I've just qualified in psychiatry.' She smiled at him, her light blue eyes warm and intelligent.

'Really. You know that's a field that fascinates me. I suppose Jane told you I'm a Surgical Registrar?'

'Yes. You're a bit young for a post like that, aren't you?'

'I know. But I'd done some research into lung cancer and I think that swung it for me.'

They went on to talk shop, and coming into the drawing-room, seeing them engrossed, Christine thought what a perfect couple they made, Simon's dark good looks complementing Caroline's fairness. Jane's news that Caroline was visiting couldn't have come at a more opportune time. She smiled to herself complacently. A small luncheon was much more conducive than a noisy party. Fate was playing right into her hands.

But over lunch, Simon began to feel uneasy. There was an expectancy in the air, and when Jane made a point of saying, 'Did you know that Caroline's father has a practice in Harley Street, Simon?' he began to have an inkling of what was afoot.

When Jane helped to take dishes out to the kitchen, he turned to Caroline and muttered, 'Is it me, or do I get the impression we're being set up?'

Caroline gave a conspiratorial smile, and whispered, 'Probably, but I don't mind, do you?'

Simon tried to evade a direct answer, cursing his mother for putting him in such an awkward situation. Caroline was making it obvious she

456

found him attractive, and her next words only confirmed it.

'Do you like jazz?'

'Love it,' he answered, relieved to get on neutral ground.

'I've got tickets for Ronnie Scott's Jazz Club in a couple of weeks.'

Before he could answer, Christine and Jane brought in the puddings.

Caroline muttered quickly, 'I'll give you a ring, but let's keep it to ourselves.'

'Summer pudding or lemon meringue?' Christine smiled at them both, noting with satisfaction the brightness in Caroline's eyes. It was all going very well, very well indeed.

But once the guests had departed, Simon immediately cornered her.

'What the hell's going on?' he demanded.

'What do you mean?' Her expression carefully blank, Christine moved towards the kitchen.

'Don't walk away,' he said angrily. 'You've been trying to manipulate things, haven't you? Hoping to fix me up with Caroline. No, don't bother denying it.' He brushed aside Christine's attempt to speak. 'What I don't understand,' he said bitterly, 'is why? You know damn well I'm seeing Rosemary.'

'Maybe, but it can't be serious, surely?'

'And why not?'

Christine's patience finally snapped. 'Grow up, Simon! She's twelve years younger than you for a start. And we know hardly anything of her background, apart from the fact that you've now told me she's a...'

'Bastard? Go on, say the word,' Simon said through gritted teeth. 'God, you sound like something out of the Middle Ages. It doesn't mean anything these days.'

'Well, that's where you're mistaken,' Christine said coldly. 'Maybe not to your generation, but it certainly does to mine. And you'd do well to remember that's where the influence is.'

'You're a snob, do you know that?'

'Perhaps I am. But at least I live in the real world, not an idealised one.'

Simon took a step backwards. 'All right then, spell it out to me. Come on, tell me of your master plan for my future. I mean, don't bother to consult me, I'm not entitled to a private life!'

'Now you're being childish.' Christine turned and went into the drawing-room.

She needed a cigarette and only after she'd lit up and blew out a spiral of smoke did she answer him.

'Right, I'll tell you. You're too like your father in some ways, Simon. You allow yourself the luxury of ideals. Though I'll admit you're more ambitious. But you need contacts in this life – sheer ability isn't enough. You need to marry someone like Caroline.' She leaned forward, her face alight with enthusiasm. 'She's attractive, educated, well connected, the perfect wife for a consultant. Her father could help you get a practice in Harley Street, or even a top research post – you know how you want to specialise in cancer!'

'I see,' Simon said icily. 'So you want me to prostitute myself in order to advance my career, is that it?'

'Of course not!' Christine was shocked. 'That's an awful thing to say. I only wanted you to have the opportunity of meeting the right person.'

'Meaning that Rosemary isn't?' he flung at her.

Christine ignored the remark. 'Didn't you like Caroline?'

'Of course I did. Actually, she wants me to go and see Ronnie Scott with her.'

Despite being shaken by the intensity of her son's anger, Christine felt a sudden flutter of excitement. Simon would find it almost impossible to turn down such a chance – he'd been a jazz fan for years. But as he glared at her, she realised that she had to be careful. The last thing she wanted was for her ambition for him to ruin their relationship.

'All right, I'm sorry, I'd only got your best interests at heart,' she muttered, and began to clear the table. The best thing she could do was to give him some space, let him cool down a bit. And if he saw Caroline again, anything could happen.

'Well, back off in future,' he said grimly, 'I'll sort my own life out.'

Crossing over to the TV, he switched it on for the sports programme, thinking that for once he'd be glad to leave Chalfont St Giles and get back to his normal routine.

Rosemary, somewhat to her dismay, was finding that her romance with Simon couldn't be conducted in isolation. Over the next few weeks, they saw each other at every opportunity, a fact not unnoticed by Beth and Michael.

'It's time we met him,' Michael said one evening.

'Yes, I know. I've put out a few feelers, but I get the impression she's not keen,' Beth said with a worried frown.

'But your mum approves of him, so he can't be a skinhead,' Michael grinned. 'You must be imagining it. Invite them for dinner – she can hardly refuse that.'

So Beth did, and as Rosemary put down the telephone, her face troubled, Rose said, 'What's up, love, you look as though you've all the burdens of the world on your shoulders.'

Rosemary tried to smile.

Rose said gently, 'Would you like to talk about it? Sometimes two heads can be better than one, and you know it won't go any further.'

Rosemary looked at her grandmother's lined face, at the wisdom in her concerned eyes, and sighed. 'It's a long story.'

'I've got all the time in the world,' Rose smiled. She put down her knitting, folded her hands, and waited.

Haltingly, Rosemary began to talk, telling Rose about taking in Tony as a lodger, how he'd wanted to marry her, how she'd thought she was in love.

'Looking back, I know now that it was just infatuation,' she confessed. 'But I'd led such a sheltered life, I hadn't even been out with a boy before then.'

Painfully, she described the fire, Brenda's funeral, and Tony's cruel jilting of her immediately afterwards.

'He said some dreadful things. I know now that he'd simply seen me as a form of security,' she said bitterly. 'A house already furnished, and a mother-in-law in poor health with substantial life insurance. Of course, as you know, Mum didn't keep up the premiums. There was no life insurance, no house or contents insurance either.'

Rose's lips tightened. She would never say anything against Brenda, but it was beyond her comprehension how anyone could be so lacking in responsibility. Hearing this sorry tale tore at her heart. A young lass like that, left in such straits, and as for this Tony, horsewhipping would be too good for him.

Rosemary looked at her and added, 'So you see, the only two men in my life both let me down. My father left without even saying goodbye, or leaving an address, and as for Tony...' She shrugged. 'How can I trust my own judgement? I was so wrong about him.'

Rose remained quiet for a while, and then said, 'But what had Beth's phone call to do with all this?'

'She's invited Simon and me to dinner.'

Rose frowned. 'What's wrong with that, love?'

'Nothing,' Rosemary said lamely. 'It's just that,' she paused, not knowing quite how to put it, 'I haven't told Simon, I mean that I'm a member of *the* Rushton family.'

Seeing the surprise on her grandmother's face, Rosemary struggled to explain, 'It was just that I wanted to be sure – you know, about how he felt about me.'

Rose said slowly, 'Let me get this straight. Are you trying to tell me that you're afraid of history repeating itself? That you're worried that Simon, to put it bluntly, could be after your money, or at least the prospect of it?'

'Not when I'm with him,' Rosemary admitted, shamefaced.

'You know, all men aren't rotters, love. I couldn't have asked for a better husband than my Harry. What's happened is that Tony's destroyed your self-confidence. You're a lovely-looking girl, you must know that. If you weren't going out with Simon, the young men would be buzzing round in droves.' Rose frowned, then decided some plain speaking was needed. 'Look, you were already seeing Simon by the time you found out, weren't you?'

Rosemary nodded.

'There you are, then. You've allowed all this self-doubt to build up in your mind, and get out of perspective. It's understandable, after your bad experience, but you've got to overcome it. Or are you going to go through life never trusting anyone?'

'No, of course not.'

'Then talk to Simon just as you've talked to me. And you must remember that he's a doctor, not some youth with an eye to the main chance. Truth is always best, love. He'll understand in the circumstances, and if he doesn't, then you'll have discovered a part of his character you didn't know about. And that's better sooner than later.' Rose looked earnestly at her, feeling relieved when she saw Rosemary give a slight smile.

'You're right,' admitted Rosemary. 'I've been a bit stupid, haven't I?'

'Of course not.' Just young and unsure of yourself, Rose thought with affection. 'Come on,' she added, 'let's have a cup of tea, and you can put extra sugar in mine. After giving all this advice, I need it.'

Rosemary leaned over and kissed her on the cheek, before going into the kitchen. As she waited for the kettle to boil, she thought yet again how lucky she was to have a family to turn to for advice and support. Nevertheless, she was still apprehensive of Simon's reaction. He'd been so angry when she'd lied to him that time, they'd almost split up. Would he see suppressing the truth in the same light? And how would he feel, knowing she'd felt unable to trust him?

43

The following evening, Rosemary walked carefully down the frosty side path to where Simon's car was waiting with the engine running.

'It's really slippy,' she said as she got into the passenger seat.

'Never mind, it's nice and warm in the flat.' He leaned over and kissed her. 'Mmm, you smell wonderful.'

'Miss Dior,' she said. 'A present from my grandparents.'

Simon frowned as he waited to turn out of the

road. 'I thought your grandfather was dead.'

'He is.' She paused, then said, 'This is my other grandfather.'

'Oh.' Simon was quiet for a few moments, and then as the car sped toward Longton, said, 'You know, that's the first time you've mentioned the other members of your family ever since you told me were adopted.'

Out of the corner of his eye he saw her colour heighten, and knew his growing suspicion had been right. There was something she was hiding, something she was unwilling for him to know. Fleetingly he remembered his mother's warning about Rosemary's background. Surely it couldn't be that there was a criminal element there? Certainly, she seemed reluctant for him to meet anyone other than Rose. Yet he'd seen family photographs at the house, had even once or twice been on the point of asking about them.

As Rosemary didn't answer, Simon left it there, puzzled as to why she was so evasive. He decided to broach the subject again later. He didn't like the feeling that there were secrets between them.

Rosemary found her nervousness increasing with every mile. They'd planned to spend the evening listening to music, and she was hoping that after a couple of glasses of wine she'd feel more relaxed. It was essential that she chose the right words, made sure that he understood she meant no criticism of him. But once she was curled up in her usual position on the sofa, she found herself impatient to begin. She waited until Simon had chosen a Three Degrees record, then picked up her glass of wine, and looked over to where he was sprawling in the armchair opposite.

'I haven't told you very much about my life in Staniforth, have I?'

Simon grinned. 'Oh, I get it, you're going to tell me about all these other men in your life!'

'Only one,' she said quietly.

He was instantly alert. It had been clear to him from the beginning that Rosemary hadn't had a lot of sexual experience, and he hadn't quizzed her about previous boyfriends. Neither had she asked him about his past.

'His name was Tony,' she said at last, and told him everything, right from the beginning. The need to take in a lodger, the fire, how on finding she was destitute Tony had dumped her, and how he'd eventually gone to prison.

'It wasn't that he had any great expectations,' she said. 'We only lived in a small semi, and that was shabby, but I suppose to someone brought up in a children's home, I must have seemed a good catch. But,' she added bitterly, 'as he made perfectly clear, I hadn't got enough to offer any man, not without an added carrot so to speak.'

The hurt was still there in her voice and, as Simon listened, appalled by what he was hearing, he longed to go over and hold her close, to comfort and reassure her. But sensing that the best way he could help was to let her talk, he remained where he was, simply taking slow sips of his wine.

Rosemary also drank some more, the wine steadying her nerves, and began once again.

'The problem is, Simon,' she said so quietly he had to lean forward to hear, 'that I now find it difficult to trust, to believe that someone truly loves me for myself. I know it's stupid, but...'

'No, it isn't, not after such a bad experience.' He couldn't help asking, 'Did you love him?'

She shook her head. 'I thought I did, but it was just infatuation, I realise that now. Though he could be very charming when he wanted to be.'

'His type usually can,' Simon said. He looked at the girl he loved so much, at the slump in her shoulders, the anxiety still in her eyes, and felt mystified. What was worrying her so much? 'Darling, you're beautiful, you're desirable and marvellous company. And I love you very, very much.'

She looked up and smiled into his eyes. 'I know you do, and I love you, Simon. And I do trust you, honestly, I don't ever want you to think I don't. As I said, it's just that I've been very stupid.' She picked up her glass and drained it.

Simon said gently, 'Why on earth should I think you don't trust me? It's hardly as if I could be after your money. Not,' he smiled, 'unless you count that leather coat you're so proud of.'

Rosemary looked directly at him, apprehension in her eyes, and suddenly with a flash of insight he recalled the Rolls Royce. He'd assumed her stepfather was a chauffeur or something.

'Are you trying,' he said slowly, 'to tell me that...'

She nodded. 'Have you heard of Rushton China?'

'Of course, we've got some at home,' he stared

466

at her. 'You don't mean...'

She nodded again. 'I told you that my father was dead. Well, he was James Rushton, and my mother married his elder brother, Michael. My grandfather had been trying to trace me for years. I'm the last Rushton, you see, because Michael can't have children.'

Now Simon was astounded. His mind was racing, trying to sort out the implications of what she was saying.

'You're not angry, are you?' she said fearfully. 'That I didn't trust you enough to tell you from the beginning?'

Simon thought for a moment. Was he? He certainly didn't relish the thought that his integrity could be in doubt, but then he tried to put himself in Rosemary's position. She was so young, and after a bad experience like that, who could blame her for being confused? The stricken look in her eyes went straight to his heart, and he went over and took her in his arms.

'Of course I'm not angry. I love you, don't you understand that? Perhaps it's just as well that I didn't know before, because now you'll never have any doubts, will you? I thought you were as poor as a church mouse, if you really want to know.'

'I was when you first met me,' she confessed.

'You haven't got any more secrets, have you? I mean, you're not the niece of the Aga Khan or anything?'

She laughed. 'No, I promise.'

'Thank goodness for that, I don't think I could cope with any more shocks.' He refilled their glasses and got up to turn the record over.

'Well, now that's out of the way, how about making room for me over there?'

Later, after he'd taken Rosemary home, Simon thought more deeply about her revelation. He knew the Rushton name not only because of the pottery, but because there was a ward at the Infirmary endowed by the family. They were undoubtedly people of influence, and as the word sprung to mind, so did the image of his mother, with her disdainful criticism of Rosemary. That had rankled, even more than her attempts at manipulating his life. And since she'd so blatantly revealed her hostility, he couldn't help wondering whether she'd had a hand in the disappearance of Rosemary's letter. A grim smile played around his mouth. Well, she certainly had a shock coming, one that she well deserved, and he didn't plan to make it easy for her.

To his surprise, early the following week, Christine rang to say she was coming up for a couple of days.

'I thought I'd do my Christmas shopping up there,' she said, 'and I can see you at the same time.'

In reality, she wanted to have another opportunity to meet Rosemary. Livid at finding that Simon had turned down Caroline's invitation to the Jazz Club, she knew that this time she would have to tread very warily. All the money they'd spent on private education in the hope it would bring him useful contacts, she thought bitterly, and what does he do? Finds himself a girl from nowhere, young and uneducated, from who knows what stock, and without a penny to her name.

Simon put down the phone and smiled to himself. Perfect. Perhaps after this, his mother would learn her lesson. Christine's social aspirations had always irritated him, but for her to disparage Rosemary because of them – that he couldn't accept.

'Of course she must join us,' Beth said the following day, when Rosemary explained about Christine's visit. 'We'll see you on Thursday then. I can't tell you how much we're looking forward to meeting Simon.'

But when Christine arrived and heard of the invitation, her feelings were more ambivalent. Surely for her to meet Rosemary's family would tend to stress that the relationship was serious, a possibility she refused to accept. But when she demurred, Simon was insistent.

'Oh, all right,' she said crossly. 'You'd better tell me something about them. I know Beth's her natural mother, but what do you know about her husband. For instance, what does he do?'

Simon paused, then said, 'Works on a potbank, I think.'

Christine's lips tightened, then she probed, 'Did he know Beth had an illegitimate child when he married her?'

'So far as I know. Actually, he's the elder brother of the father.'

'What?' Christine was genuinely shocked. 'That's almost incestuous! Was her father still alive at the time?'

469

'I suppose he must have been. Anyway, that's all in the past, Mum – it's none of our business.'

Christine closed her eyes in exasperation. This just got worse. 'Are there any more skeletons in the cupboard I should know about?'

'Not unless you count the fact that she's a Roman Catholic.'

At the expression on his mother's face, Simon's mouth twitched in amusement. Rosemary's religion made not the slightest difference to him. Accustomed as he was to dealing with terminal illness, he'd long found that a belief in God and an afterlife contributed greatly to a patient's positive attitude. What did it matter which form it took? It was often just an accident of birth anyway. But he was well aware that Christine, although she would strenuously deny the fact, held some very bigoted views.

By now Christine had decided that nothing would prevent her from going to meet these people. Perhaps when they realised that Rosemary was out of her depth with someone of Simon's background, they too would realise it was a totally unsuitable match.

Thursday was one of those days when the sky was never light, and it was in inky darkness that Simon drove to Minsden to pick up Rosemary. Christine sat beside him, and although her makeup was, as always, immaculate, she hadn't bothered unduly with her clothes, considering this was not a social occasion when dress would matter.

When Simon drew up in Elm Grove, she

peered with disdain out of the window, at the small house, at the narrow, unprepossessing street. All exactly as she'd expected. But when Rosemary came down the path, she immediately noticed the change in her appearance and demeanour, and as she slid on to the back seat, her nostrils picked up the scent of Miss Dior. She could only assume that Simon was spending all his salary on this girl, and her tone was distinctly chilly as she said, 'How are you, Rosemary?'

'Fine, thank you. I'm so glad you could join us.'

Simon switched on the radio and little more was said until they reached Newcastle, when Rosemary leaned forward to give him directions.

When they swept into the drive of The Beeches, its size accentuated by security lighting, Christine's shocked intake of breath was audible. There had to be some sort of mistake! But as the car drew to a standstill, Beth stood framed in the doorway waiting to greet them, and one glance at her simply cut black dress told Christine that her own skirt and sweater were completely inappropriate. Furious and embarrassed, she shot a look of sheer frustration at Simon. How could he put her in such a position? Why on earth hadn't he warned her?

Then as Rosemary got out of the car to kiss her mother, Christine saw clearly how the expensive clothes enhanced her natural poise and beauty, and felt what was almost hysteria sweep over her.

Simon got out of the car to open her passenger door, and she hissed, 'I thought you told me he worked on a potbank.'

Simon gave a tight smile. 'He does, he just

471

happens to own it. Ever heard of Rushton China?'

She stared at him in shocked disbelief, as he added, 'Rosemary's a Rushton. Is that connection impressive enough for you?'

Christine flinched, then, subdued and uncomfortable, followed Simon to what promised to be one of the most challenging social evenings of her life.

44

A little over a year later, the drawing-room at Linden Lodge was crowded with people, the huge glittering Christmas tree in the bay window dominating the scene. Rosemary stood by the fireplace, momentarily alone. Her fingers caressed the ice-cold flute of champagne in her hand, and she took another small sip, waiting for the minutes to tick by.

Robert was watching her. Seated as he was in a large armchair, a forbidden cigar in his hand, and unable to move freely around the room, his only pleasure these days was to observe. He turned to Sylvia, standing by him, and murmured, 'Just look at her, she's a Rushton from her head to her toes. She's a real credit to us.'

'Isn't she just?' Sylvia's eyes rested affectionately on her granddaughter. She was staying with them overnight, sleeping in James's room. Sylvia had wanted to refurnish it, to assign it for her exclusive use, but Rosemary had dissuaded her.

'It's all I have of my father,' she explained. 'All his childhood trophies, his photographs. Please don't change it.'

To hear Rosemary refer to James so naturally had touched Sylvia deeply, and the room remained as it was, each of them gaining comfort from it in their own way.

Rose, standing next to them, heard Robert's words and smiled to herself. It was typical of the man that he should dismiss the Sherwin genes. She too looked over at the fireplace. Rosemary's youth and beauty shone in the sumptuously furnished room, and her assurance and poise drew many eyes. You've come a long way in a short time, granddaughter of mine, Rose thought with pride, and took a tiny sip of the one glass of sherry she allowed herself. Her glance fell on Michael, who was talking to a tall, grey-haired man who Rose recognised as chairman of the local Chamber of Commerce, and she sighed. The past year hadn't been an easy one for her son-in-law.

Michael, in sole charge of Rushton's since his father's slight stroke earlier that year, was fighting to retain the old established potbank's independence.

'What we need,' he was saying, 'is for Prince Charles to find himself a bride. Preferably someone who catches the public imagination and boosts the popularity of the Royal Family. I honestly think that's our only hope. I give it five years and if we haven't had a Royal Wedding by

473

then, with its resultant boost in exports, I can't see us surviving a takeover bid.'

Beth, weaving her way towards Rose with a plate of food, saw the two men in deep discussion, and guessed the topic of their conversation. It was a worrying time for the whole pottery industry, and many of the smaller family firms hadn't survived the current downturn in trade. Fortunately, Michael had managed to secure from Giovanna's father an injection of capital to finance a third fire studio, enabling them to hand-paint Italian glazed tiles for the domestic market, and also to retain their skilled decorators. Not that she needed to worry about their personal finances. The Rushtons had always been a family who invested wisely, but she knew that Michael felt a huge responsibility for his workforce, many of whom had been with the company all their working lives. But tonight, she thought, is not the time to think about business – tonight is for fun, for happiness.

And on a personal level she was not only happy, but deeply content, complete in a way she'd never thought possible. Andrew and Ben adored Rosemary, who was now a fully accepted member of their family. As for Beth herself, her relationship with Rosemary was a unique one, part mother, part elder sister, and they had become good friends. I'm truly blessed, she thought, and smiled at Rose as she handed her the plate.

'Good party, isn't it?' she said.

'Sylvia seems to do it all so effortlessly,' Rose replied, trying to choose between a vol-au-vent

474

and a turkey sandwich.

'Well, she does have plenty of help,' Beth smiled, 'but I know what you mean.'

'What do you think Rosemary's future will hold?' Rose said, her eyes resting on her grand-daughter.

'I don't know. But she's got your determination, Mum, so I think she'll make a success of whatever she decides to do. She's very popular at the works, you know – people like the fact that she's willing to learn, and hasn't got, as Ivy informs me, any "airs and graces".'

Rosemary, however, wasn't thinking of her career. Her thoughts were with Simon. Even here, among the family which meant so much to her, she missed him. Glancing again at her watch, she knew that time was running out, and then suddenly the door was opening and in a few quick strides he was by her side. At that very moment, from the radio came the sound of Big Ben.

'Ssh! quiet everyone,' someone shouted, and then they were counting 'twelve, eleven, ten, nine,' the voices rising in excitement until on the stroke of twelve, their cheers rang out and people turned to hug and embrace in celebration.

Among the deafening noise, Simon looked down at Rosemary's upturned face.

'Happy New Year, my darling,' he said.

'Happy New Year,' she laughed. 'I thought you weren't going to make it!'

Their kiss was short-lived as revellers separated them, but they both knew that the following day they would be together at Simon's flat.

They'd been lovers for several months now, although they remained discreet, Rosemary ever conscious of her family's good name.

Christine, on her first visit to Linden Lodge, was on the opposite side of the room, hemmed in by people she hardly knew. As she watched Simon weave his way through the crowd, she felt a pang, knowing she had lost something precious in their relationship. Her foolish and, as she now realised, arrogant rejection of Rosemary in those early days had not yet been forgiven. Only she knew about the letter and even now, she shuddered to think how she'd tried to sabotage such a perfect match.

Simon, after kissing his mother, was kept busy refusing drinks, explaining that he was still on call. He looked over towards Rosemary, thinking how lovely she looked in her blue cocktail dress. Their love for each other had deepened into confidence that one day they would marry. But they had made no plans. Rosemary was young, eager to achieve her ambitions, and they wanted to enjoy the freedom and romance of this past year a little longer.

And then as they both heard strains of the music everyone had been waiting for, their eyes met across the room, and hurriedly they sought each other, as people began to link hands. Simon found a space next to Rose, and as she held both their hands, voices began to rise in unison to the nostalgic words of 'Auld Lang Syne', and the full circle of family and friends surged to meet in the middle. Coming face to face with a smiling Beth, Rosemary, her face alight with happiness, smiled back. Who knew what 1977 would hold, stretching before her full of love and promise? But whatever happened in her life now, she had a family, and that was the most precious gift of all.

The publishers hope that this book has given you enjoyable reading. Large Print Books are especially designed to be as easy to see and hold as possible. If you wish a complete list of our books please ask at your local library or write directly to:

Magna Large Print Books
Magna House, Long Preston,
Skipton, North Yorkshire.
BD23 4ND

This Large Print Book for the partially sighted, who cannot read normal print, is published under the auspices of

THE ULVERSCROFT FOUNDATION